Kern climbed back ~~t~~ ... ss
wash through him t ... is
head. He shook awa ... g
friend to one side, wis ... 's
presence.

The violet afterglare of power swam in front of his eyes, and he knew that he'd done it again. Embraced that which he had nay use to be touching at all. Or even knowing.

Kern felt the danger swimming up from the back of his mind before Daol ever reacted. His friend had half turned back to the rock wall. Then, suddenly, Daol's sword swept up and he moved for Kern's side.

"Behind!" was all he had time to shout.

Too late, Kern spun around in a ready crouch. A touch slow and low, his blade came up into a guard position. Hardly at strength to meet the raider leader, Kern slipped past Ossian, who lay stretched out over the ground, unconscious or dead. The Vanir's war sword swung a backhand slash for Kern's throat . . .

*Don't miss the first adventures
in the Legends of Kern . . .*

BLOOD OF WOLVES

and

CIMMERIAN RAGE

Millions of readers have enjoyed Robert E. Howard's stories about Conan. Twelve thousand years ago, after the sinking of Atlantis, there was an age undreamed of when shining kingdoms lay spread across the world. This was an age of magic, wars, and adventure, but above all this was an age of heroes! The Age of Conan series features the tales of other legendary heroes in Hyboria.

AGE OF
CONAN™
HYBORIAN ADVENTURES

LEGENDS OF KERN
Volume III

SONGS OF VICTORY

Loren L. Coleman

THE BERKLEY PUBLISHING GROUP
Published by the Penguin Group
Penguin Group (USA) Inc.
375 Hudson Street, New York, New York 10014, USA
Penguin Group (Canada), 90 Eglinton Avenue East, Suite 700, Toronto, Ontario M4P 2Y3, Canada
(a division of Pearson Penguin Canada Inc.)
Penguin Books Ltd., 80 Strand, London WC2R 0RL, England
Penguin Group Ireland, 25 St. Stephen's Green, Dublin 2, Ireland (a division of Penguin Books Ltd.)
Penguin Group (Australia), 250 Camberwell Road, Camberwell, Victoria 3124, Australia
(a division of Pearson Australia Group Pty. Ltd.)
Penguin Books India Pvt. Ltd., 11 Community Centre, Panchsheel Park, New Delhi—110 017, India
Penguin Group (NZ), Cnr. Airborne and Rosedale Roads, Albany, Auckland 1310, New Zealand
(a division of Pearson New Zealand Ltd.)
Penguin Books (South Africa) (Pty.) Ltd., 24 Sturdee Avenue, Rosebank, Johannesburg 2196,
South Africa

Penguin Books Ltd., Registered Offices: 80 Strand, London WC2R 0RL, England

This is a work of fiction. Names, characters, places, and incidents either are the product of the
author's imagination or are used fictitiously, and any resemblance to actual persons, living or dead,
business establishments, events, or locales is entirely coincidental. The publisher does not have any
control over and does not assume any responsibility for author or third-party websites or their
content.

SONGS OF VICTORY

An Ace Book / published by arrangement with Conan Properties International, LLC.

PRINTING HISTORY
Ace mass market edition / August 2005

ISBN: 0-441-01310-4

ACE
Ace Books are published by The Berkley Publishing Group,
a division of Penguin Group (USA) Inc.,
375 Hudson Street, New York, New York 10014.
ACE and the "A" design are trademarks belonging to Penguin Group (USA) Inc.

This book is dedicated to
my latest editor,
Ginjer Buchanan
with gratitude and warm wishes

Acknowledgments

Songs of Victory was a treat because I finally got to bring to a close the story I opened with *Blood of Wolves*. Kern's outcasts traveled far and fought hard to get there. Just as a large team of people traveled a rocky and adventurous road with me in the creation of this book. I'd like to thank the following people for being a part of that journey:

Everyone at Conan Properties International: Theodore Bergquist, Fredrik Malmberg, Jeff Conner, and Matt Forbeck. Also Ginjer Buchanan at Ace, for her tireless work and efforts on my behalf. This book could not have happened without your patience and support.

Don Maass, who represented me during this time. Dean Wesley Smith and Kristine Kathryn Rusch for their friendship and help (and, occasionally, a kick). And Randall Bills, who took more than his share of annoying phone calls on this one.

As always, my family. Talon, Conner, and Alexia, my own barbarian horde. Heather, my wife and my partner, who kept reading and kept me writing even in the hardest moments. And the animals who made appearances, sort of: Grimnir's "great cats" Chaos, Ranger, and Rumor, and our "wanna-be wolf" Loki.

Thank you.

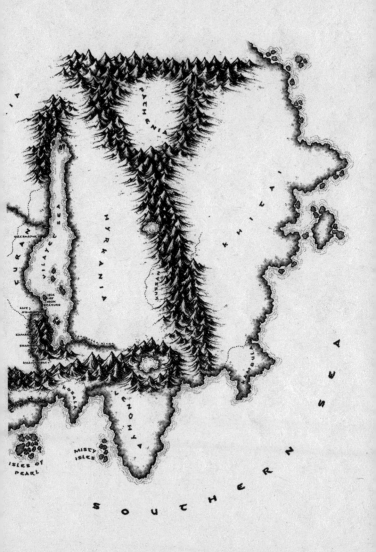

1

MORNING ARRIVED WITH a pregnant stillness hushing Murrogh Forest. Birdsong, and the lowing of cattle that should already have been set out on their early-morning graze, were replaced by the long, slow scraping sound of stone against metal. A dry rasp—honing along one edge of a broadsword, tapering off with a fast, harsh file. Then again. Drawing out each moment with the same rough whisper.

Schhh-nhik.

Kern Wolf-Eye tightened one hand over the hilt of his short sword, still sheathed at his side, and stepped out from behind the short fence of saplings he'd braced up by a single pole. Overhead, gray clouds pulled a thick blanket across the sky, reducing dawn's light to gloom and shadows. He eyed the overcast warily. Not heavy enough yet for a serious rain, he gauged. Another day of gray spring showers.

His long, frost blond hair, plastered down by an earlier drizzle, hung in tangled, twisted braids against the side of his head. He wore a chain-mail vest of tarnished rings, bracers, and a silver armlet on each of his bare arms.

Gooseflesh stood out on both arms as well, and the hairs on the back of his neck prickled. Neither of which had anything to do with the wet or the cold.

Standing on one of the narrow paths that crossed the slopes below Gorram Village, Kern looked out over the forest. What he could see of it. A thick, low-lying fog tangled its way among pine and thick birch and drooping cedars, hiding the lower trails. The fog moved as if alive, roiling through thick branches. Breathing. Pushing up against the lower slopes as if rallying its strength for the short, sharp climb. The covering blanket piled up only a stone's toss below the village's first rock wall, behind which crouched a half dozen armed men with swords already standing naked in their hands. Ready. Waiting.

Soon, he knew. There was something out there. A scent, like cold steel, and the metallic taste of blood burning at the back of his throat.

Schhh-nhik.

A few sharp glances shot his way. Warriors he didn't recognize, for the most part, hunkered down behind boulders or small piles of rock, or another of the wooden fences hastily built and propped up to shield a man. Or woman. Who waited, same as he did, for what would come. Clansfolk who were shorter than the average Cimmerian. Stockier. With brown eyes and strong, square jaws.

Eastern folk.

Only one of Kern's "wolves" crouched nearby. Aodh. Kneeling at the base of a small rock wall, sitting back on his calves. Lean and muscular from a hard winter's running and fighting. A veteran warrior of better than forty summers, only the salt-and-pepper hair he kept tightly shorn and the extra gray sneaking into a thick, drooping moustache told his age.

Broadsword laid out flat across his lap, Aodh held a whetstone clutched in his right hand. He drew the stone down the length of his blade, stropping the edge with long, even pulls, blue eyes never once leaving his work.

Schhh-nhik.

Kern ignored a nearby hiss of annoyance from one of Gorram's warriors, just as he left Aodh to his own deliberate preparations. The calm and the quiet before battle got at everyone, sooner or later. He trusted each man and woman to see after themselves.

The village was, after all, as readied as they could make it in the short time they'd had. Rock walls repaired. Brush that might have offered an easy handhold on the way up the hillside cleared. Kern's warriors had cut saplings by the hundreds, thinning the local forest, sharpening their tops to make rough-hewn spears that were anchored into the hillside, the sharpened points angled back down the slope, thrusting into the face of any attacker who might try to climb for the village.

Two dozen huts. A slaughter pit. A couple of lean-tos. Gorram Village was about as small as they came, though the chieftain of Clan Murrogh had promised it to be wealthy in cattle and strong arms. Kern hadn't believed it, coming upon the hillside village the day before. No room for oat crops. Poor grazing land. But the Gorram had surprised him, turning out forty well-armed warriors and (later) showing him nearly two dozen cattle penned back inside a cleft in the hill. The lands of eastern Cimmeria were constantly showing Kern a new face.

Such as the one that suddenly popped above another rock wall, nearly at Kern's left shoulder.

The boy wore a sleeveless jerkin and a simple brown kilt. Curly locks of honey-brown hair framed a round face still pudgy with youth. A dark smear of dirt covered one side of the lad's nose and half of one cheek as well. Gangly arms, Kern saw, and slender hands not yet built for a sword. Twelve summers, if a day.

Biting back a curse, Kern shoved his half-drawn blade back into its sheath. He rubbed a hand over his face, feeling fresh stubble scratch against his palm.

"Bad idea, boy, sneaking up on a man." He gave the child an angry glare, satisfied when the lad jumped back as if bitten.

"Truth," the boy whispered, his voice raw and full of wonder. "You do have the wolf eyes. The other boys, they said it was all made up."

So much for satisfaction.

Kern felt something inside him darken, like a door closing on a windowless room, and a warm thrill of anger he quickly smothered under a cold, dark blanket. It was always there, the rage—the *power*—lurking in the back of his mind. It tempted him at every turn, if he'd only look inward and embrace it.

And naturally the boy had hit upon the core of Kern's troubled past. One merely had to glance in his direction. The Gorram might not all fit the usual look of the Cimmerian, a people who ran toward hair dark like coal and blue eyes the color of a summer sky, but in comparison to Kern they were Crom's nearest kin. Kern's frost blond hair and waxy skin would have pegged him as an outsider no matter what. But his golden eyes, sharing a wolf's feral gaze, were what everyone remembered, and so many feared.

Just a boy, he reminded himself. "Why aren't you locked in a room?"

"Climbed out the window. Wanted to see for meself."

"Now you have. So get back to your hut."

The boy raised himself over the wall on those skinny arms. "Gonna make me?"

A touch of defiance that Kern remembered well. He'd had it, certainly, growing up in Gaud. Maybe a bit stronger than most, as an outsider even within his own clan. It wasn't a completely unhappy memory. And a bit better than most, these days.

So rather than argue, or make trouble among the Gorram by chasing the boy back up the hill, Kern shrugged. He started to turn away, paused, and pulled a long dagger from the scabbard tied into his wide, leather belt. He tossed the blade to the sandy-haired youth.

"Going to be outside, be armed."

The boy stared at the dagger, then at Kern. "Father forbids me to fight yet."

Kern did not bother pointing out that the lad's father had likely forbidden him from peeking a nose out of the hut and turned his attention back to the shroud of fog as a dark flash tickled at the back of his mind. "If our enemy makes it this far, what your father forbids won't matter so much, boy."

The youth weighed the dagger in an open palm. "Mayhap they won't come." He sounded disappointed.

But Kern knew better. The short hairs on the back of his neck stood up, bristling.

"They are already here," he said, then ducked back behind the nearby wooden fence as an arrow slashed up from the fog, shattering against the rock wall just below the boy's face.

"Raiders!"

Several voices raised the call of alarm, all shouting at once. More arrows whistled out of the morning's cover. Dark shadows down inside the fog resolved into men who moved, loosed a new flight, and scrambled forward again while reaching for another shaft.

A second arrow struck the wooden fence Kern Wolf-Eye hid behind. It shook the rickety shield with a hammer-like blow, the tip forcing its way through a thin crack between two saplings. Then a third and a fourth shaft slashed by to shatter against the rock wall as the lad's eyes went wide with fear and excitement.

"Get your fool head down!" Kern grabbed up a stone and chucked it at the boy's head. It clipped an ear and finally convinced the youth that he'd be better off hiding *behind* the rock wall.

Nearby, Aodh crabbed out from behind his pile of stones, then rolled back into cover as a new flight buried itself in the ground where he'd lain. He flashed Kern a handful of fingers. Two, three . . . four times.

Twenty. Twenty raiders would never have been enough to take Gorram Village, even before Kern's warriors arrived to help them prepare for any siege. Twenty raiders might have caused trouble. Killed a few men. Stolen some cattle if they'd kept surprise on their side. Against the entire village, armed and prepared, they had no chance. They simply did not realize it yet.

Kern's "men of the wolves" planned to show them their folly. Any moment now.

He guessed fairly close. Slipping out from behind his small fence, Kern snatched up his shield, which lay in the mud nearby, and readied himself. Glancing around one of the shield's edges, he saw that the first few shadows had nearly reached the lowest rock wall.

Vanir!

So easy to tell, with their fire-red hair and the helms they decorated with the horns of different beasts. They charged up out of the fog, ignoring the switchback cattle paths. Warriors with blades and shields readied scrambled up the mud-slick slopes, while archers with their heavy war bows covered from behind. They yelled full-throated battle cries, and Kern heard more than one maddened voice spitting out a curse of "Ymir-egh." Cursed of Ymir.

These raiders had come for *him*. Sparks of anger

jumped behind Kern's eyes, stinging at the forefront of his mind.

Soon.

Somewhere, still lost under the cover of the fog, a horn bellowed out their war call with a long, mournful blast. Driving the Vanir forward. Kern needed no such instrument. His men knew their task. Had honed it to a skill in their several months of living, fighting, and bleeding together on battlefields ranging from Conall Valley through the Broken Leg Lands and over the eastern passes of the Black Mountains.

Almost . . . now!

Like rock scorpions striking from ambush, four men, hunkered down behind cover one level below Kern, suddenly rose with bows. They fired down at the charging Vanir, slamming arrows into their upraised shields, slowing the charge. Then a second volley after the first.

One arrow slipped past and buried a broadleaf head into a raider's shoulder. It spun the man around, unbalancing him on the treacherous footing. He slipped, fell, and rolled back down the hillside until he slammed against an outcropping of boulders.

His shout of pain was cut short as his head cracked against a sharp edge of stone.

Despite the late-held volleys, two of the flame-haired northerners managed to get a hand on the lowest wall, straining to pull themselves up. One reeled away with a shriek of pain as a sword flashed out from behind that wall to come hacking down across his wrist, severing his hand.

As blood pumped out in hot splashes from the waving stump, Desagrena rose from hiding. Kern recognized her lithe form and quick movements, even from behind. She skewered her broadsword through the man's chest once . . . twice . . . and he fell back, already dead before he hit the ground.

The second raider fared little better. Managing to roll over the rock wall, gaining temporary ground on the path it had sheltered, she found herself staring up at one of the largest Cimmerians she'd likely ever see.

Reave had the strength and size of a black bear, and with his coarse, brushy beard was not too far different in appearance. He wielded a Cimmerian greatsword, an impressive length of edged steel, which he slashed overhead to cleave down through the raider's shoulder and chest. Left her bloodied and broken on the trail.

Three attackers down already. Kern still had four warriors crouched behind that lower wall who had yet to show themselves. He could have held the lower slope easily. Fought off the attack, trading time for more Vanir lives, inflicting a measure of pain against the invaders for the bloodshed and rape they had visited on Cimmeria. The bloodlust building up within him called for it. Called for their pain, their deaths. Their damnation! But the defense of Gorram was not about slaughter, however much he thirsted for it.

It was proving to the local chieftain that Kern's strategy was sound, at all levels.

An arrow hammered against the bronze facing of Kern's shield, glanced away, and buried itself in the narrow cattle path next to him. Snarling, Kern came close to drawing sword and leaping down the hillside on the assault right then.

"Nay," he whispered. It was not to be. Not yet.

"Back, back, back," he yelled down the hillside. Then watched from around the lip of his shield as Reave and Desagrena held the rock wall while the other four warriors broke cover and charged upslope. Ossian led the retreat, his shaved head easy to spot. Garret Blackpatch and Mogh. Gard Foehammer, who wavered, ready to fling himself back along the trail should Reave or Desa show any hesitation or sign of trouble.

There was none. Arrows stormed over the Vanir as Daol and Hydallan led one savage volley after another from the next level up. "Nock," Daol called out, his voice so calm and steadying. Encouraging the others to greater speed. But it was his father who waited that extra second, making certain that Brig Tall-Wood and Ehmish were also set before yelling, "Loose!"

Four more ashwood shafts slashed down. Another shout of pain, and a raider stumbled to his knees with a gray shaft sticking into the meaty part of his thigh.

It gave Reave and Desagrena time enough to scramble after the others, ducking low beneath the Vanir's return volleys.

Desa also kept her shield between herself and the raiders, and a good thing she did as two more heavy shafts slammed into it with enough force to stick through the thin, metal facing. Reave was less fortunate, and howled as an arrow buried itself into his backside. Kern jumped up, ready to lead a charge to his friend's defense, but Reave reached back to snap the shaft off, leaving the head buried in his rump. For now.

Painful, it would be. But hardly life-threatening.

Let them come, he reminded himself. That was the plan. Let the raiders come to Kern and his wolves.

They did. Taking the first level on the slope with a victorious roar. Eight warriors gained the rock wall and quickly raised shields to ward off the arrows hammering down at them, creating a large bulwark, behind which more raiders came. Four more warriors. Then the archers, some of them throwing aside their own bows for the grip of naked steel in their hands.

Then their leader, who finally broke out from beneath the fog's cover.

Kern had known without ever seeing him that he would be a Vanir warrior. Nay frost-haired servant of Grimnir. Not today. Not one of the Ymirish who had turned Kern's life upside down this last winter when he'd learned he shared blood with the strange northerners. Worse, when others learned it as well.

This man had the rawboned look of a Vanir. A thick beard with golden rings braided into the coarse, flame-red hair, and a steel cap with long, steer's horns mounted on it. He wore a boiled-leather cuirass, banded with strips of metal, and a mailed skirt of thick bronze scales. He carried a war sword in one hand, a tall shield in the other, and strode up the hill as easily as Kern might walk along a dry, forest path. A Vanir war horn hung off his wide belt, bouncing against one muscular thigh.

Arrows struck at him immediately, hammering into his shield, some piercing the metal facing with enough force to stick into the wooden back. With vicious swipes, the Vanir war leader scraped his sword down the shield's face, cutting the arrows away. When he did so, he opened his entire body up, as if daring one of the archers to put a shaft in his chest.

None did. Few even came close.

Kern had let the Vanir come this far. This far, but no farther, he promised, watching as the enemy warriors readied themselves and lost only one more of their number to the Cimmerian archers. Then they quite simply *threw* themselves up the next slope with reckless abandon and a berserker's yell at their lips.

Feet churned into the muddy slope. Swords reversed, stabbing down into the earth to be used as climbing poles; shields were thrust ahead to buy themselves a measure of grace. They swarmed forward faster than any would have thought, clawing and digging their way up the slope to get at the defenders. Their enemy.

Bows were cast aside now as Vanir fought for purchase on the second wall, one final level below Kern, and swords rasped free of their sheaths as all fell to defending the village slopes. Ten of Kern's best, holding back half again their own number. They fought side by side, back to back when necessary. Swords rose and fell, stabbed and parried and slashed back in answer.

Blood splattered on the ground, and the cries of wounded men and women shattered what little resolve Kern had managed to guard.

Drawing his own sword free, he stormed along the upper path, searching for a break in the sharpened stakes where he could easily slide down amid the fighting. Aodh was on his feet as well, though by agreement none of the nearby Gorram left their places of concealment. Their place was to protect the third and final level, and the village, which squatted on the slopes above them. That had been the agreement, and the wager, that Kern Wolf-Eye had made.

A wager he might be in danger of losing, now, as more of the Vanir clawed for purchase and gained the lower slope. Two sword-bearing warriors rushed forward and pinned Daol back against a rocky cleft, the younger man getting his own broadsword around in time to deflect a killing thrust aimed at his chest.

The second Vanir came overhead with a chopping slash, and Daol ducked aside barely in time. The blade struck sparks from the stone a finger's breadth from Daol's eye. Again, and Daol ducked in the other direction, avoiding death.

"Nay!"

Kern's yell was a full-throated roar of anger and strength. Gathering himself, he strode forward to the edge of the path and leaped out over the overhang of sharpened poles. Sword raised and shield held out to one side, he fell the length of a man, his feet stomping down on the shoulders of one of the raiders threatening his warrior, his friend.

He felt bones shift and break. Felt himself collapsing in a rough heap atop the raider, feet kicked out from beneath him. He landed hard on his shoulder, his side, against the raiders shield with the boss slicing along his arm and punching hard against his chain-mail vest.

His head struck the side of the rocky cleft against which Daol had been pinned. Violet sparks and sheets of pain washed over his vision, clouding his mind.

He retained just enough sense to hold on to his sword. A good thing, as the raider standing above him hacked down at him, ringing his heavy blade against Kern's feeble guard and ignoring Daol in the sudden confusion.

A lethal mistake. Daol jumped forward to put three feet of steel through the raider's back, shoving the blade well through the Vanir's gut, then holding him up long enough for his dying scream to fade along with his strength. Blood rained and spattered over the ground, into Kern's face and hair. Then Daol kicked him free, sending the corpse in a headlong tumble back over the rock wall and downslope.

Another body followed after it as Gard Foehammer rammed his pike through a raider's chest. Then another, missing his head.

Kern climbed back to unsteady feet, feeling a weakness wash through him that had little to do with hitting his head. He shook away Daol's hand, shoving his lifelong friend to one side, wishing no touch, no sense of another's presence.

The violet afterglow of power swam in front of his eyes, and he knew that he'd done it again. Embraced that which he had nay use to be touching at all. Or even knowing. Or . . .

Kern felt the danger swimming up from the back of his mind before Daol ever reacted. His friend had half turned back to the rock wall. Then, suddenly, Daol's sword swept up and he moved for Kern's side no matter what the other man might say or do.

"Behind!" was all he had time to shout.

Too late, Kern spun around in a ready crouch. A touch slow and low, his blade came up into a guard position. Hardly at strength to meet the raider leader, he slipped past Ossian, who lay stretched out over the ground, unconscious or dead. The Vanir's war sword swung in a backhand slash for Kern's throat.

And then it happened. Time began to slow as a rage of power and strength flooded Kern's muscles, his mind. A hammering call, which was more than his own heartbeat, rang in his ears. He felt the darkness swell within him and was drawn to it even as its foul nature repulsed him, driving away everything he had ever known to be right in the world. Such an easy task, to step out of the way and let the darkness destroy this man who threatened him. Simple enough, if he would embrace the call.

He would not. He stoppered the flow of power, as he had many times these last few weeks. Choked it back without a care to what might happen. What would certainly happen. What *nearly* happened.

Amidst a small avalanche of rock and sharpened poles and a slide of mud, a jumble of gangly arms and unsteady legs and the flash of a dagger pounced in from the hillside to bury a good length of steel into the Vanir's side. Not enough to kill—hardly enough to throw him off his stride—but causing him to shorten his powerful blow, swinging the sword in too high, allowing Kern to drop out from beneath the deadly blade.

Falling to his knees, shield slamming into the ground as he caught himself, Kern stabbed into the man's stomach, ramming the entire length of his short sword in to the blood-slick hilt.

Hot gore gushed out over his hand, and Kern's grip

slipped away from his sword as the raider pitched himself to one side. The Vanir leader slammed up against the muddy bank with his war sword raised overhead and his free hand clenched around the sword buried in his gut.

Pinning himself in place, as the Gorram youth bounced up with the speed and agility only young boys know. Shrieking a high-pitched cry, somewhere between a scream and a man's bellow, the lad rammed Kern's dagger into the chest of the hulking brute again, and again.

Half a hundred voices roared overhead in a thunderous ovation. Seeing the Vanir leader fall, and to a mere slip of a boy, the Gorram clansfolk broke cover and shook fists and weapons at the blanketed sky, letting their anger and celebration roll down off the mountainside. The cry was echoed poorly by the Vanir, as word of their leader's death quickly swept the path.

In singles and pairs, men and women of the north broke away from the fight. Leaping from the cattle trail, sliding-tumbling-falling back down to the lower path and then over the rock wall for another headlong pitch toward the forest floor and safety.

Or so they assumed.

Kern rose quickly to grab hold of the youth's hand, stopping the boy as he drew back to stab at the Vanir yet again. The youngster's breath came in hitching gasps, almost crying, as he stared up into the face of the man he'd helped kill, then into Kern's golden eyes. Tears streaked through the grime on the lad's face, but this time he did not flinch back. He stared in open defiance.

Kern shook his head, mute. Then, stepping to the edge of the trail to stare down the slope, he brought two fingers to his mouth and whistled. Three long, shrill blasts.

Like those of trapdoor spiders, five holes suddenly opened up in the ground on the lower slope. One had been disguised by thorny brush tied to a rough plank. Two others with deadwood logs simple (and light) enough to roll back. Nahud'r and Valerus had capped their hiding places with their own shields, layering them with a piece of sod to fool the Vanir into thinking they walked over real ground.

Five spiderholes opened and out came a tangle of arms and swords, cutting and stabbing at the fleeing Vanir, seeking final blood. Old Finn cut two men down as they attempted to slide by him, hamstringing one and ramming his broadsword into the chest of another.

Valerus was less fortunate in his timing. He forced his shield over just in time to catch a booted foot in his face as a raider slipped and slid right into the hole with him.

There was a tangle of limbs and weapons as the two wrestled within the pit. Then Valerus stood back up and tossed a jaunty wave at the hillside.

Kern waited alongside the Gorram youth, watching. He counted six men and one woman who actually escaped to the roiling fog cover lying along the ground below. Seven left out of twenty-plus attackers. With a quick count of his own men—including Ossian, who was sitting up with Desagrena's help, holding a red-soaked batch of wool to the side of his head—it looked as if Kern's people would all live to fight another day.

And another.

This was their life now. And it would most likely be their deaths.

"Your men. They fight like more than their number," the boy said, stepping up next to Kern. He still held the gore-streaked dagger, blood dripping off the point of the blade. His breathing was calmer now, with only a small, hitching sob left to it.

"They do," Kern agreed. He checked up the slope, saw nearly the entire population of Gorram Village standing on the upper trails, crouched on the paths, and waiting in front of huts. Their moment of celebration having passed, now they watched the final moments of death playing out below.

"I think more than you have noticed."

With the rage of battle and the luring call of power fading back, he turned his mind once again toward his purpose here. Not a bad showing at all, in fact.

"Here." The boy held up Kern's dagger. "You'll be wanting this back, then."

Kern shook his head. "Keep it." He glanced over at the body of the Vanir's fallen leader, still propped up against the muddy hillside. "You earned it, by Crom."

That and more. Twelve summers, and a man now that he'd made his first kill.

"You won't tell anyone?" the boy asked. He wiped a filthy hand across his tear-streaked face. Now it merely looked muddy. Stronger. "You won't tell that I . . ."

Cried? Kern knew the heavy burden about to be laid across this boy's—this young man's—shoulders. Too soon. And hardly fair. But necessary, perhaps, if Cimmeria was going to survive.

"I won't tell," Kern promised, then nodded the newly made man back along the path where other warriors of Gorram waited for him. "I won't," he whispered, more for himself then.

"I've gotten very good at keeping secrets."

2

BY NOONTIME, THE sun's warming rays had broken through thin patches in the cloud cover, pushing the ground fog back among the forest's darker shadows. It could not completely wring the chill from the air, not when patchy rain continued to fall whether or not the sun shone, but it helped.

Life returned to normal, or close to it, almost as fast as it had been shaken up by the arrival of Kern's small band. Cattle were looked after, let down the hillside to graze along a few running streams. Always kept under guard against Vanir or raids by other clans. The villagers of Gorram also tended patchy gardens, or sought food from the forest. Children were put to work collecting stones and repairing the damaged walls. Kept close. Older youths were sent after firewood and fresh water.

Many sang as they worked; slow, haunting tales of loss, and victory. An eastern tradition.

For their part, with the battle over, Kern's warriors set

about quickly and efficiently on their own cleanup and salvage. Their campsite quickly grew at the base of the hillside slopes. Several warriors pitched tents—a few made
from felt, others from heavy, musty-smelling canvas. Most
simply threw bedrolls onto a patch of ground, claiming it
for later, and set themselves to their next tasks. Men were
sent to collect firewood. Some cooked. A few tended the
wounded and still others set about collecting the Vanir
dead, dragging them off the hillside, and spiking a few
heads up on poles as a warning to all enemies. Clothing
was searched for good cloth. Pieces of armor and the best
of the abandoned weapons were collected. Those were all
duties they'd learned in their months together, fighting
their way across half of Cimmeria and back again. They all
knew their roles. No one shirked or complained.

And no one asked questions when Kern stumbled
through those first few hours, getting his strength back,
though Daol looked as if he'd like to.

Avoiding Daol's questioning glances, Kern busied himself with the wounded until finally his longtime friend
gathered Ehmish and they took themselves off hunting in
the nearby forest. Even then, he spent the next half hour
boiling cloths for fresh bandages and pinching together
some of the deeper cuts while Desagrena sewed them shut.

He knew it could have been far worse. Garret Blackpatch had added a new cut along the right side of his face,
the fresh wound twisting in amid old scar tissue where
Grimnir's snowcat had slashed at him, clawing out his right
eye. Wallach Graybeard pulled a blood-soaked clot of wool
out of the leather cuff that capped the stub of his left wrist
and packed it full again with fresh batting.

They had worried most over Ossian, of course. But as it
turned out, he had only a ringing headache and a gash
along the left side of his head where the Vanir leader had
nearly split the Cimmerian's head open with the edge of a

shield. The entire side of his head was already bruising up nicely, covered in splotches of black and wicked-looking purple.

"You won't want to be shaving that for a week, at the least," Desa told him. There was nothing to sew up. The best anyone could do was give the Taurin warrior a clean cloth compress and a thick unguent to help clot the wound.

Ossian grunted, ran his hand back over the right side of his head kept smoothly shaven by the edge of a sharp knife. A custom his father, chieftain of Clan Taur, had followed. And, like father like son, Ossian also grew out a long goat's beard, into which the warrior had braided four silver rings taken from the many Vanir dead he'd helped kill.

"Good to be having a head at all," he finally said.

Then, with a nod of thanks to Desa and a strong clap against Kern's shoulder, he left, already calling to Mogh and Danon to get their lazy carcasses back up the hill and drag down more of the Vanir dead.

Dour-faced Mogh and quiet, competent Danon were the other two remaining Taurin, having joined the outcasts after Kern's warriors helped break a Vanir siege of Taur. He had noticed the men spending more time together since Ashul's death, the fourth of their number, and after finding Ossian's father among the ruin of Gaud. Both losses had hit Ossian hard.

Now Kern and Desa watched as the strong-willed Taurin took charge of the salvage duties. He doubted anyone worked harder under Ossian's glare, but it was good to have the man back on his feet so quickly.

"Be fine," Desa said. She pulled back her dark, oily locks and tied them in a knot at the back of her head. Desagrena had a thin face and wide, expressive eyes that showed her usual temper all too well. Just now, though, Kern swore her look held a touch of compassion that Desa would no doubt deny. And likely give him a sharp cuff for mentioning. "It's a clean wound."

Not all wounds fester on the outside, Kern did not say. He simply shrugged and nodded Desa along to their next patient. "Think he's waited long enough?"

Reave was the only man in camp who appeared to be resting, stretched out his full, impressive length on a fold of clean woolen blankets. Lying on his belly, he cradled his head in massive hands as he watched the industry around him. Always hot-blooded, Reave wore no jerkin or vest. A traveling cloak of bearskin backed by simple wool was enough for him. And the thick kilt most Cimmerians favored. He was also one of the few who had not adopted the eastern practice of protecting his legs in a wrap of thick cloth.

Kern did not bother with leggings, because nothing—ever—kept him warm. Not with his northern blood so steeped with winter ice. Reave, he refused the extra garment for a likewise simple reason. He was as stubborn a man as any Kern had ever known.

And if Desagrena looked as if she were going to enjoy the next few moments, Kern would hardly fault her. She had to live with her man's faults and put up with them more than most.

"If'n he carried a shield," she said loudly enough for Reave to hear, "he'd have avoided the trouble altogether."

Reave did not so much as glance back. "Can't carry a shield with a greatsword," he said. His deep voice rumbled out in a slow, calm thunder, speaking as if to a child.

"Mayhap it's time to give up that great, hulking piece of steel you're so fond of," she snapped back. "Got something to prove? Always need to have the largest sword?"

Now he did look back over his shoulder, a mischievous grin peeking through his brushy, black beard. "Never heard you complain about my long blade afore." And he laughed.

It wasn't often that anyone got the best of Desagrena. The viperish woman held her own on and off the battle-field. And for slow-witted Reave to set her back so easily—truly it was a good match between them.

Not that he wouldn't pay for the jest. Desa was not above revenge. Smiling to her man's laughter, she bent down and grabbed the back hem of his kilt and yanked it up rudely to expose his bare ass and the stub of arrow sticking from one side. Kern couldn't say for certain that she had twisted the woolen kilt in such a way as to catch the jagged end of the shaft. But he wouldn't wager against it either.

Reave's laughter choked off at once, and he beat one large fist against the ground. "Damn, woman."

"A mere splinter for a *big*, strong man such as yourself."

She reached down and tapped the blood-crusted shaft, testing its movement. A trickle of fresh blood oozed out of the wound, which had already begun to scab over. Reave hissed in pain.

"We're going to fire the wound closed," she told him, while Kern retrieved the dagger they had left to heat in the coals of a cooking fire. Hot metal against a wound to cauterize it was often the best remedy. Taking a piece of dry leather, she wrapped it about the broken arrow shaft with a careful grip. "Kern will do it. I might miss and singe shut the wrong opening. Then you would be shy of the hole matching the one in your head, you thick-witted slug." And she yanked the arrow free in a quick, strong pull.

Kern did not wait. While Reave was already reeling from the pulled shaft, he slapped the reddened tip of the dagger down into the wound, singeing the wound to prevent bleeding and infection. Then he jumped back, along-side Desa, clearing away from the large man while they waited to see how he handled it.

No worries. Reave's howl was part relieved laughter,

part pain. He beat his fist against the ground again, and again, fighting his way through it. Garret Blackpatch and Hydallan looked over from where they tended the cooking fires. Garret turned and gave Reave a shake of his own back end, mocking the larger man so long as he was safely down.

"Let that show ya, Kern. Women. A pain in the ass.

"Always get you in the end, they do."

KERN SLIPPED AWAY not long after, leaving Desa fussing and fuming over Reave's injury and Reave protesting all the attention, though not a man in the campsite believed him. Old Finn and Garret began to snipe at each other, loudly, pretending to be a bickering couple, which drew laughs from Reave and icy glares from Desagrena.

Daol's father, Hydallan, refereed both matches, offering blunt and often lewd advice.

Kern grabbed up a hatchet and a leather carrying strap to go off after firewood, but he paused inside Murrogh Forest to spy and to listen, and smile in that rare moment without anyone watching and no need to pretend that he wasn't an outsider, even among his warriors and friends.

Not so long ago, it seemed, there hadn't been a need to pretend. When he had believed himself a Cimmerian, by birth if nothing else. Worried, as was everyone in the small village of Gaud (and likely all the clans of Conall Valley), about the unnaturally long winter and lack of food, the threat of Vanir raids, and tales of the great northern devil, Grimnir, who marauded through Cimmeria's west and northern territories. Not as preoccupied with his odd appearance, or the cold touch of winter set deep, deep in his bones and blood, until Cul Chieftain used Kern's strangeness to isolate him and then declare the golden-eyed man an outcast.

Kern remembered the next several weeks as disjointed fragments flashing through his mind. Running south. Striking a trail in the snow—raiders, after his clan and kin!—and chasing after them. Arriving too late.

Daol, taken prisoner. And Maev, Burok Bear-slayer's daughter.

Four warriors and one youth splitting from Cul Chieftain and the clan, joining Kern in tracking the Vanir.

Rescuing their kin, he had seen for the first time another man, colored as he was. Frost-haired. Golden, wolflike eyes. And then another of these Ymirish not long after, when Kern's bedraggled pack broke the siege at Taur. It was the first time Kern had been made to wonder about others like him, and who they might be, questions that plagued Kern as he and his warriors fought their way over the Pass of Blood. Through Cimmeria's northwest lands.

Answered, or so he thought, when he pulled Grimnir after him over the edge of a cliff in the battle above Conarch. That his choice to stand against Grimnir and the northern war hosts was what counted. That he was not—

—one of them.

"Awfully hard to collect firewood with your back turned on the forest."

Kern started, as if he'd been found in something more sinister than simply catching a private moment.

Turning, he found Daol leaning against a dead birch. Five years younger than Kern and looking at his nineteenth summer, Daol had come into his full height but still had a young man's easy grace. Putting weight back on after a close brush with death, his gray eyes still had a smudge of black beneath them, though he looked hale enough despite his recent tangle with the giant spiders of the Black Mountains.

The hunter had his bow and a nocked arrow gripped easily in a one-handed carry, ready to pull and loose at an instant's beckoning. Sword sheathed at his side. Buckskin cloak thrown back off his shoulders, trailing behind him where it would not foul his arm.

"Also, a good way to get yourself killed," his longtime friend said.

Kern shoved himself back, leaving the campsite behind him as he joined Daol near the old birch. The snag had the stubs of several branches left to it, which he worked at with the hatchet. "Has nay happened yet."

"Not, some might say, for want of trying."

Truth. From the northwest territories, Kern's warriors had fought their way back across Cimmeria, traveling the lower trails this time beneath Mount Crom and back up into Conall Valley. To Gaud. Grimnir's hordes had beaten them back, however. There weren't many of their kin left except the ones who needed to be laid to rest. And after another of Kern's "wolves" died defending the ruined village there hadn't been a reason to stay any longer.

Ashul's death *still* hounded Kern, in fact. Had chased after him when he struck out over the Black Mountains for the clans of eastern Cimmeria, looking for fresh strength to rally against Grimnir. And that much, at least, they had started to find.

Mayhap.

Kern chopped a branch off the old snag. Then a second. He stacked them on the carrying strap, which wasn't anything more than a pair of wide leather belts fastened between a pair of wooden handles. He raised his hatchet, ready to attack a third branch.

Daol was still there, leaning against the other side of the tree. Still waiting.

"I thought you were hunting."

He knew better than to try and evade the confrontation. Once Daol set something in his mind, it was like trying to pull a fresh bone away from a camp dog.

"Was. Ehmish took a rabbit in midrun. At sixty paces. Crom's golden shaft, it was a shot to see."

"And?"

"Tumbled it headlong into a briar patch, which I had to fetch it out of thanks to the wager we'd made . . . only it wasn't there. Just a skid of blood and a few clumps of hair. And a great-sized print. Wolf."

Kern glanced over at mention of a wolf. Of course, Daol could mean only one. "Frostpaw?"

A nod. "You should have seen Ehmish. Madder than old Bear-slayer the time we planted a dead fish in his bed."

A sobering thought, now that their village was as dead as their former chieftain. The clan barely survived as was, with a few dozen kin and kind having also escaped here, to the eastern side of the Black Mountains. *That* had been a reunion. Coming across Cul Chieftain leading a mixed raiding party of Gaudic and local Murroghan warriors, he and Kern striking paths again in the middle of midnight attacks against a Vanir campsite. Sizing each other up, after so many months.

Cul had only shaken his head and laughed. Unbelieving. "Wolf-Eye. It had to be you."

Kern, reeling, already struggling with more than he'd ever thought to face, had not known what to say. Or do. Not then. He waited Cul out, as the others gathered around.

"You'd best come back with us," Cul had finally offered. "Pay respects to Morag Chieftain, the least. And you've kin will want to see you. Not you, so much," he'd said to Kern. Voice flat. "But the others, yea."

In a way, finding more survivors had brought Kern's warriors a measure of hope. But it couldn't last.

Once outside the clan, always outside. The Men of the Wolves would never be welcomed home fully.

"What did Ehmish do?" Kern asked. He felt shadows stirring in the recesses of his mind, that terrible purpose he'd barely reined in during the recent fighting. Memories of *that* night weren't helping.

"About what you'd expect. Waded into the briars hisself to make certain I was nay fooling him. Growled and snarled a bit. Then readied another arrow and swore he'd get the next one as well. And he might. The boy has good instincts."

It wasn't fair calling Ehmish a boy. Not anymore. Fifteen summers and not into his full growth he might be. But he'd killed, and nearly been killed, too many times. If lads with twelve summers were taking on a man's responsibility these days, Ehmish was nearly a veteran.

Still, "You left him alone?" There might be Vanir about. Kern doubted it—didn't *feel* it—but it could be.

Daol gave Kern a look. "Aodh found us. I convinced him to take Ehmish a new direction while I went on alone. They circled off to the west, away from the animal's trail sign. Good thing. Weren't gone more than a moment when Frostpaw came skulking by with a bloody muzzle. Gave me a start. You forget how big he is. I swear that Crom-cursed wolf of yours gets bolder by the day. Ever since . . ."

Ever since it crept up on their midnight assault against the Vanir, and Cul Chieftain saw it fight alongside Kern, then leap to defend him? Was that what Daol had been about to say? Cul had not been shy, telling that story.

Kern fell back to hacking at the birch. Chips flew, and the smell of old wood rose in the air.

As easy as they'd all gotten with the huge dire wolf tracking them, accepting the band of warriors as something close to its "pack," it still rankled from time to time that the animal acted more of a loyal guardian than any kind of wild beast. Kern had first come against it, alone, in the depths of the recent winter. A long, nightmarish season of unending cold, with no sign of spring's return and Vanir raiding growing worse with every passing month. Then, Cimmeria had seemed ready to freeze itself into a solid block of ice, if the clans didn't starve first or fall victim to the raiders.

The rogue wolf attacked out of desperate hunger, and fear. In its weakened state, Kern managed to get the better of it . . . and then let it go. He never could say why, except as a recent outcast himself, he'd taken pity on the animal. Since then, the wolf had trailed him over two mountain passes and across many battlefields. Eating well, no doubt, off the trail of corpses left in Kern's wake.

It was there at the battle where Grimnir and Kern went over the side of the cliff above Clan Conarch.

It followed him over the broken rock flow to Venarium, then to what was left of Gaud after the raiders gutted away everything Kern and others remembered of their home.

It chased alongside him over the Black Mountains, where Kern and Daol had been taken prisoner by Clan Galla. And, once they'd been returned to their friends, it had trailed behind them into eastern Cimmeria, where Kern had come to rally *any* strength left that could possibly stand against Grimnir's war hosts. Against Grimnir himself. Before the giant-kin terror broke the back of so many clans that there would be nothing left to stop Nordheim's hordes from pouring across the border unchecked.

"Kern?" The voice was distant, muffled, like a fist pounding against thick gates. "Kern. KERN!"

Without realizing it, Kern had attacked the birch tree with his hatchet, swinging wildly. Another of the branch stubs lay at his feet, broken away from the pale, bone-gray trunk. Now he railed against the tree itself, hacking large wood chips out of the old snag, barely flinching when splinters and chips bounced against his face.

A voice, yelling in his ear.

A hand reaching out, grabbing his shoulder.

He wheeled, hand axe raised and readied.

Daol leaped back. Cautious. Confused. "What is wrong with you? There's been something different about you ever since that night with Cul Chieftain. Since he took us back to Clan Murrogh, and we found—"

"I know what we found in Murrogh," Kern said. He forced a calm on himself, stilling the rage that boiled so near the surface.

"And I saw that raider you landed on today." Daol's voice was calm. Nearly flat. But it carried the weight of a good slap. "You broke both of his shoulders, Kern. Nearly tore one arm away from his body. Not possible you could have done that to him from where you jumped." His gray eyes held a trace of uncertainty now. Like any Cimmerian, he trusted only what he saw with his eyes, could hold in his own hands.

As Kern had once believed.

"You tell me there was nothing more to it, and I'll believe you. By Crom, Kern, after what you did for me, after what you've led us through, I'd believe you if you said I could fly. I'd throw myself off the nearest cliff for you to prove it. You *know* that."

He did. Daol's loyalty had never once been in question no matter what the younger man believed of himself. And Kern had already been forced to ask so much of him. Of them all.

Kern bent down. He picked up the stub branches and added them to the others already set on the leather carrying strap. Then, shouldering the light load and grabbing up the hatchet, he stood to face his friend. "If you head back into camp, pass the word. We will stay for this evening, and the Gorram's songs for their newest warrior. But we break early for Murrogh, no matter what the village decides."

He pushed past Daol, leaving the hunter in the shadow

of the birch. Daol did not try to follow. He did, however, call after Kern.

"Tell me that, Kern. Tell me that there is nothing more going on."

He paused, considered for a moment, and finally shook his head. He refused to look back. "There is nothing more going on," Kern said carefully, "that you can do anything about." Then he turned for the forest to gather more wood. Alone.

There were some burdens not meant to be shared.

3

THE HORSE LODUR sat astride staggered its way down the snow-covered ridgeline, pushed forward past any hope its life could be saved. Blood caked about its flaring nostrils like blackened scabs, with a fresh trickle of bright scarlet seeping out to stain the animal's lips and mat the coarse brown hair surrounding its muzzle. Each steaming breath came in a sharp, hitching gasp, as if it might be the animal's last.

One of them, certainly, would be.

The beast's eyes no longer saw, Lodur knew. One swollen shut of infection, the other had the same dull, glazed overcast he had seen on so many dying men. The Ymirish knew death very well, in fact, though it did not take an expert to judge the horse on its final legs. Its brown hide was dry and waxy, caked in dirt and dried sweat. A hard week's ride had split all four hooves high up into the bone, and when Lodur reined in the beast leaned to one side, favoring its right foreleg, which bled from bone splinters poking out through its leathery skin.

At this point if he walked the animal over the edge of a cliff it would hardly shy away. Which was why Lodur picked out his trail with greater care, so close to his destination.

His breath frosted in the air, and not even the heavy cloak of white, northern bear or a jerkin backed by the thick, shaggy hide of a mountain ram were enough to keep gooseflesh from puckering the skin on his arms, the back of his neck. The Lacheish Taiga, he decided, were good lands. Wide and open. Still caught in winter's weakening grip this high, this far north, though infernal spring had finally settled over most of the rest of Cimmeria. A thin blanket of old snow crusted over with ice spread in a perfect white carpet down the side of this hill. It rolled right to the edge of a high country lake, with its still, blue waters so close to freezing Lodur could all but taste the ice in the air.

There were a few obvious paths around the lake's edge, churned into mud and gray slush. These all led to a wide yard which had been swept clear of snow and laid over with carefully sawn planks. Here several men, women, and youths worked: tending rafts; packing in firewood from the thin forests that surrounded the lake; dealing with the daily chores of survival.

Here, also, the first long pier had been anchored—a wide, wooden walk, stretching out far past the shallows before it branched in several directions. One in a large network of piers, it created elevated paths and platforms among several dozen stilt homes and more than a few floating huts as well. And Clan Lacheish's lodge home, of course. A two-story structure, lifted on several dozen sturdy pilings, crouched out over the deep, near-freezing waters without any need of walls or palisade.

A good, defensible position.

Not that it would help the Lacheishi. He wheeled his mount down a snowcapped trail, kicking it into a final canter as he rode hard for the village. Not that anything could help them now.

He hadn't come all this way to fail.

Two weeks! He looked upon the time as lost, if not completely wasted. Two weeks since he'd come over the Pass of Noose from Conall Valley. Since he'd hammered several tribes of Clan Galla into small splinters—that night of fire and ice and dark, leathery wings. Two weeks since he'd set his war host to hunting the mountain people through the Snowy River country. Not much less since he'd brought the core of his own war host down out of the Black Mountains. Still on *his* trail. Still after *him*.

Kern. The false one.

Cursed of Ymir.

So close. Lodur had been so close that where he crossed Kern's path the other man's footsteps echoed painfully from the ground, and the Ymirish tasted the blood they'd shared.

And that which they did not.

It was always there, that foreign taste, under the cold, pure ice that all Ymirish shared with their frost-giant god. A warm, leathery scent, not unlike that of the horse on which he rode. His grin was savage. Just another beast, Kern's mother. A Cimmerian animal who whelped Lodur's corrupted brother here, in these lands once protected by Crom. Lands once belonging to the Vanir and now, under command of the northern "frost-men," would be theirs again.

That was the promise. The power of Ymir's Call.

The snow-crusted ridge gave way to gentle slopes, then gray, sloppy trails. The horse's hooves beat against frozen ground, mixing its own blood into the slush. Riding down at the pier where two Lacheishi skinned a large stag strung up within a tripod of heavy poles and several more worked to build a large, flat-bottomed raft. Riding at them as if he'd draw free his broadsword and take their heads.

One man looked up. Then a woman. Blue-gray eyes, and dark hair shaved back from their temples, which was a Lacheishi custom. Animals, still. Cimmerian animals.

Two youths, repairing a large net they'd spread out over the ground, jumped back as he rode right across their work and reined in to a hard stop near the slaughtered elk.

There were shouts and grumbling, a few dark glares, but no real challenge. As he expected. There would be no confusing him for anyone other than what he was. Not with his dead-frost hair and fierce, golden eyes. Unlike anyone of this land. Unlike their northern neighbors, as well, with the flame-haired Vanir and golden locks of Aesir blood.

Ymirish! Blessed son of Ymir, frost-giant god of the north. One of Grimnir's faithful, who had marched for years as a great warrior, and was now a sorcerer filled with power and purpose.

They knew him. They knew his look, regardless. And if they did not yet fear him, they would. They would.

Lodur swung off the animal's back, landing heavily and leaving the reins to dangle at the side of the horse's neck. The animal sweated fiercely, its flanks heaving with exertion to pull what it could of the crisp air into damaged lungs.

"Take care of horse," he growled at the nearest Lacheishi youth, using the guttural tongue of Cimmeria.

"Take care of how?" the boy asked, staring in dismay at the wretched creature. "Looks sick."

Worse than that, Lodur knew. Dead on its feet. He withdrew his *touch*—the strength he had fed the beast over the last several days, convincing it to move just a little bit faster, a little bit harder than it otherwise would have. Took back everything he had given it in a false promise, and, always, just a little bit more.

The horse gave a last, shrill nicker. Then collapsed as if suddenly poleaxed.

Lodur glanced at the half-skinned stag. "Slaughter it," he said. Then was past the small crowd to meet his brother at the edge of the pier.

Water lapped softly against the shoreline, stirred by a stiff breeze that raised sharp, choppy waves out over the center of the wide lake. The scents of damp wood and old fish were strong. Nearly overpowering. He jumped up onto the pier, caught himself as his boot slipped on the polished worn wood, then traded long, cold stares with the man who had come out to meet him.

Torgvall was young. Twenty-one summers. Years away from hearing Ymir's Call sing in his blood, if he ever did. Like all Ymirish, he had the same hair, the same great, golden eyes. He also had a glassy burn scar against the side of his head—struck by a flaming brand some clansman had snatched from a fire, Lodur *knew*. That man had died badly.

Standing half a hand taller than Lodur, and at least two stone heavier, with the war axe he carried slung across his back, Torgvall could easily have cut a man in two. Even Lodur, if he'd dared raise a weapon to one of Grimnir's sorcerers.

Torgvall reached out, hesitant, tugged on the heavy, white bear cloak Lodur wore. "Thin blood, brother?"

Himself, he had pulled on thick boots and a bronzed cuirass common among northern warriors, and a heavy leather skirt. Nothing else against the late-year freeze, or the bone-deep chill radiating off the high country lake.

Fire danced in Lodur's eyes. He felt it spark, but reined it in. "Thick enough," he said. Stepping to one side of the wide, wooden walk he felt the water's chill reaching up at him, and fought against an urge to pull his cloak closed at his throat.

This last winter, and the return of spring, had seen many changes in Lodur's life. His Ymirish blood, once steeped so heavily in winter's ice he could walk unclothed through the worst blizzard and survive, was no longer so accommodating. Thinned, yea. Just as the power he'd come into at Venarium had eaten away at his once-brawny muscle, as well. Sapping his warrior's strength. Trading physical strength for a greater, more terrible purpose and the actual touch of true warmth.

A bargain he would not give up for anything. And one Torgvall would kill for. When his time also came.

"Tell me," Torgvall said, falling in beside him, walking half a step back out of caution, or deference. "You came over the Hoath Plateau?"

"Partly. Along the Black Mountains' eastern slopes and across one corner of the plateau. We found wounded, ran down several families in flight, all heading south. But saw more sign in the way of summoned war hosts. Warriors rallying. Villages laying in extra wood, food, and water, preparing for a hard summer."

. After such a long and difficult winter, dealing with deprivation as well as frequent Vanir raids, the Cimmerian clans should not have had such a fight left in them. Certainly the valley had fallen easily enough beneath Grimnir's mighty blade.

"Enough to see the Hoathi are strong, still. Clan Lacheish must nay be allowed to join their strength with them. Yet."

"Will nay be any problem," Torgvall promised. "Cailt Stonefist still aches for his daughter, even after five years. And with so many men dead, on either side, the Lacheishi and Murroghan will never give up this feud."

Especially with Torgvall here. Delivering warriors. Delivering supplies. Promising, if nothing else, that the Great Terror, Grimnir, had nay intention of attacking their clan.

Keeping the lake-dwelling clan stirred up, with their anger focused south. Never west.

But still Grimnir had his doubts. Which was why Lodur had been summoned away from his chase of Kern Wolf-Eye, to move his war host north, onto the edge of the Hoath Plateau, then he alone had been sent riding hard for Clan Lacheish. Into the camp of their enemy.

"There will be nay problem," Torgvall promised again, bristling when Lodur said nothing.

Still Lodur ignored the other man, paying more attention to their surroundings. Drinking in every detail. Their feet thumped heavily on the rough-hewn planks. An occasional loose board rattled in place, but for the most part the Lacheishi had built solid, and well. The first stilt homes sat just off the side of the pier, attached to the massive walk by short, solid ramps. Doors had been carved with easily recognized symbols—a crescent moon, a sword, twin trees—to tell them apart at a glance.

Then came a covered platform layered over with gray flagstone, atop which was built a stone oven and several enclosed fire pits for drying and smoking catch from the lake. Two women worked at one of the smoke pits—hanging two racks of lake perch from an overhead beam, chucking handfuls of wood chips onto glowing embers, and wrapping a woolen blanket around to make a cloth chimney to contain the heat and smoke. They ladled up water from the lake and dribbled it over the blanket, carefully soaking the material to prevent it from catching fire.

Small floating docks. Fishing rafts.

Another covered platform, under which rested shelves of coiled rope, sheets of heavy canvas, leather buckets, blades, and stacked lumber. Tools and community supplies of all kinds. Lodur paid especially close attention to such caches.

And to the people, of course. The clansfolk who

tolerated—barely, it seemed at times—two Ymirish inside their village. Many pulled back into doorways, into shadows, as the pair passed along. Braver men and women, or simply the more foolish, stood their ground, often forcing one or the other of the golden-eyed men to brush past uncomfortably close, hands on weapon hilts. The clansfolk's gray-blue eyes were cold, and cautious, and always watching—always ready!—no matter what their chieftain, this Cailt Stonefist, might have ordered.

Nay any problem? The Lacheishi were trouble waiting to happen at the wrong time.

Lodur stopped alongside the pier's edge, where he could look out over the gray waters. "I am here," he finally said, "to be certain of this."

"*He* nay trusts me?" Torgvall asked, speaking of Grimnir, the Great Terror himself. His hands clenched and unclenched, as if wishing for the haft of his battle-axe or a throat to wrap about. "Or you do not?"

"There is very little difference in that, isn't there?" Lodur gazed down past his feet, at his dull, distorted reflection wavering over the lake's surface. A swirl of water pulled his features apart, stretching them, flattening out his face until he was a grotesque parody of himself. A darkness stirred at the back of his mind, interested now. Clawing its way up from the depths where such power dwelled. Violet sparks fired painfully in his peripheral vision, and the reflection stretched, and ran, then slowly coalesced into a new image that was not his own but a face he knew nearly as well.

Grimnir!

Skin the color of rotten snow and tangled braids crusted with old, dried blood. Deep, dark eye sockets from within which golden orbs flared with the same fire he shared with the Ymirish. A snarl of cunning, of pain, and of anger—Lodur's memories: the before and after of the battle at

Clan Conarch, then the rage he had shown in Conall Valley this spring.

Lodur felt that same, savage strength stretching out over his face, and when he looked back to Torgvall, the younger, larger man started. But his hands stayed far, far away from any weapon, Lodur saw.

"Very little difference," he reminded the warrior. "Grimnir knows you. Senses us all. But here, I have his voice." He started walking again, drawing his brother after him like a dog to its master.

"And he has new orders."

4

IT SHOULD HAVE been an easy march, returning to Clan Murrogh from Gorram Village. West from the hillside community, follow the second stream for two leagues, then bear south by west for two days . . . two and a half. Keep an eye on the sun for direction. Check the mossy side of any tree if a dark overcast hid the sky.

It should have been.

Murrogh Forest, Kern had discovered in their first week over the Black Mountains, was no simple woods. An immense tangle of trees and heavy undergrowth, cut apart by wide streams, a few rivers, and many, many sheltered ponds, a man might be days running from one side to the other. Not as wide as Conall Valley, certainly, but with its own secrets and its own charms.

At times it put on a gentle face, with hidden, quiet glades full of wildflowers and open fields that ran beside cheerful, burbling brooks for as far as a league.

Often a sudden ridge would poke above the forest floor,

and one might follow the lazy, winding valley as it stretched northward, toward higher plateaus and, eventually, the distant Eiglophian Mountains.

But there was a dark heart to the Murrogh as well. Places where briar thickets suddenly choked off a path, and sunken marshland gripped at anyone attempting to pass. Where dead birch and rotted pine tilted from bogs at desperate angles, and old, diseased willows spread their shroud of slender branches over quicksand graves. A large clan might be swallowed up by the Murrogh, and one would never know.

Which was why Kern now waited in the company of Brig Tall-Wood and Gard Foehammer, the three men watching as young Ehmish rapidly climbed a tall pine to gauge their progress. Daol stood off to one side, maintaining his distance, as if insulted. Though it had been his idea to send Ehmish into the forest canopy this morning. Just to be safe. Kern had been willing to give his friend the benefit of the doubt. Only once since their arrival over the Black Mountains had Daol gotten turned around on a march, and in the hunter's defense he'd still been recovering from the spider's poison. Still a touch feverish.

That was the only explanation for his getting them lost. It just didn't happen. Usually.

Of course, Reave and Wallach Graybeard had ribbed him for days after that.

The pine was nowhere near so large as a valley watchtower tree, but high enough to give an eagle's view over the nearby forest. Ehmish hung in among the thin branches way up top, the slender trunk bending around under his weight, swaying back and forth in the breeze shaking the forest treetops, stirring along the forest floor. Branches rubbed together in a rustle of leaves and dry, creaking wood. The wind smelled of pine and cedar, soft earth, and—somewhere close—a large body of water.

And of horse.

A leather-and-sweat scent. And a kind of mustiness Kern associated with cattle as well. Valerus walked his mount over and ground-hitched the beast. Giving it a hard pat on the side of its muscular neck, he stepped over to join the trio.

His sandy-brown hair fell in tight, ringlet curls. He had strange eyes of a muddy-green color. An Aquilonian soldier—a *civilized* man—other than dark-skinned Nahud'r he was the oddest addition to Kern's warrior pack. Kern had saved the man's life on the bluffs overlooking Clan Conarch this last winter. Later, Valerus and his two cavalry companions joined Kern on the journey south, around Mount Crom and back up into the Valley.

Most Cimmerians west of the Black Mountains had little to do with horses, except for meat. Finicky beasts, hardly worth the effort to keep alive, any healthy youth could outrun them over time and often while traveling through land that would snap a horse's leg within a single morning. Or so Kern had once thought.

Spending time with the southern cavalrymen had changed his attitude. Slightly. The southerners had fought well. He could say that about them.

There had been plenty of opportunities to prove it.

And when the others finally chose to turn south, for home, Valerus opted to stay with the pack. To see more of Cimmeria and learn more of this nation where King Conan had been birthed and raised. And to keep fighting the Vanir, whom he had come to see as a true threat to all peoples south of the Eiglophian Mountains.

Everyone had their own reasons. Their own story.

"How far off?" Valerus asked. His Cimmerian was improving, but still had the sharp, guttural accent of Aquilonian speech. "Do you think?"

On the other side of Kern, Brig Tall-Wood shrugged. "I

say we've drifted south, and are closer to the lake's eastern side than the north shore."

"North," Gard argued. "Half a day, at least."

"For a spot of two throws?" Cimmerians enjoyed wagering. For honor, or for trophies. Brig was among the best—or luckiest—of men when it came to the dicing game so often played around evening campfire. Already seeking an advantage for his next game.

Gard did not hesitate. His natural instinct, Kern knew, to accept any challenge.

And no large surprise, their individual wagers. Brig would be anxious to return to Murrogh, and hoped any misstep would bring them closer to their goal. Gard, once Clan Cruaidh's protector and the right hand of Sláine Longtooth, had grown more pessimistic since his brush with blindness and abandonment by his chieftain. The poisoned welts raised on his face by Ymirish sorceries had healed over into a dozen small white scars. The white cast had all but faded from his eyes. But still, there was an emptiness to him that Kern wasn't certain anyone could fill.

Valerus looked askance at Kern, who nodded toward Daol. "Right where he says we are supposed to be."

Kern did not wager against his men. Ever.

Ehmish had started back down, dropping from one branch to the next, hands gripping at the rough, scalelike bark. At a few places, where the branches were too thin for his weight or stretched out too far from each other, he hugged the tree and shinnied down with practiced skill. No worries the young man might slip, or fall. All Cimmerians climbed from a young, young age. They scaled sheer cliff faces for war, or a contest of wagers, and, at times, just to show it could be done.

Another part of Crom's legacy. The Cimmerians' creator had blessed them with strength, and the will to stand up under any burden. Life was therefore a series of challenges to be overcome, and they would prove it to themselves if nothing else.

Ehmish hung from the final branch, dangling at least two good lengths above the ground, then let go. It was a short fall, which he absorbed in a half crouch and easy roll off to one side, coming back to his feet with ease. Seeing the young man returned, the others gathered up their own gear and readied themselves for the march while Ehmish slid his broadsword's belt over one shoulder, found his buckler and bow, and slung his bedroll as well.

Daol and Nahud'r and Wallach Graybeard joined Kern's small group just as Ehmish approached, wanting to hear firsthand.

"Half a league," the young man promised. He pointed in a south-by-west direction. "The lake is straight by. Right where Daol said."

Daol shrugged and ambled away to take a lead on the morning's run. And was brought up short when Kern asked, "But?"

He'd caught something else in Ehmish's voice, his face. Something was wrong, and it wasn't their direction.

"Smoke. Thin, like a single cooking fire, but there." There was no doubting Ehmish, who had sharp eyes and was learning the skills of tracking from Daol. And if there was a better hunter or tracker than Daol that Kern had ever seen, it was Daol's father, Hydallan.

The boy—the young man—had veteran teachers.

"Take Brig," Kern told Daol now. "Take Aodh and Ehmish. Scout our approach to the lake."

Three of the four were present, nodded, and set off together. Ehmish called Aodh in with a boisterous shout and a wave. Glad, obviously, to be included so easily. Before Kern lost sight of them, they had already stepped up into an easy run. The kind of pace any of his men could hold for a day and half a night without much need for rest.

Reave and Ossian were not far behind. Then Kern and most of the others.

Valerus dropped back, content to guard their rear, knowing his mount could have him at the forefront of any battle almost in less time than it took to call for him.

Kern's warriors worked along always with one eye on the man in front, the man behind. It was more than battle-field caution. More than Daol's getting turned around the once. It was simply the not knowing. A new land, with its secret dangers and more than a few known ones.

Not this time, however.

"Ho! Kern!"

Daol's ringing call, slipping back through the forest's natural palisade of trees, had no sense of urgency. No fear or thrill of danger. Whatever waited ahead—whoever—Kern felt certain it did not involve another Vanir war host.

He found out a few moments later, pushing his way through a small grove of young saplings to step out onto the northeastern shore of a large lake. Gray waters reflected an overcast sky, while gusting winds whipped up plenty of white chop on the lake's surface. A trio of horses had been tethered among nearby trees, able to graze on the lower branches and tall grasses at their feet. Two warriors guarded them. More men and women milled about inside the campsite spread nearby. Some with swords out and ready, most sitting back casually. Unafraid in the territory they knew and controlled.

Kern saw the spear, with its golden, cougar pelt dangling from near the head, before he saw the young stalwart standing next to Daol. Shorter than Daol, but built more like Reave, with wide, stocky shoulders and legs as thick as tree trunks. A square, strong jaw that could have been carved from granite, and the same brown eyes shared by

most clans who lived near Murrogh Forest and often took
wives from out of the Border Kingdoms.

The warrior propped the butt of his warhammer against
the ground, arms resting easily over the maul's head. "Well
met, Kern Wolf-Eye."

Better than meeting a Vanir raiding party, or one of the
marauding hosts from the upper lake country. But not by a
great deal. "Well met," Kern returned the greeting. "Jaryyd
Morag's-son."

It was the first mistake Kern had made after meeting
with the chieftain of Murrogh Forest's strongest clan.
Even Cul had warned him against involving himself. But
he had. He had. In a time when Murrogh and Lacheish
fought each other in a raging feud and the Vanir invasion
threatened all, it had seemed the height of folly for Morag
Chieftain to hold his eldest son at such a distance. Not
quite outcast, but hardly welcome inside of Clan Murrogh's walls either, with Morag instead so infatuated with
his youngest child.

That a good few dozen men and women chose to keep
the chieftain's son company on his patrols of the forest and
lakeshores, rather than remain in the safety of the clan's
stronghold, had seemed to rankle with Cul as much as the
father. Shades of Kern's return among the Gaudic funeral
procession—those several months before—causing a
smaller but no less damaging split.

Jaryyd settled Kern and a few of the new arrivals around
their small, smoldering cookfire. A couple of camp dogs
barked at Kern. One, hackles up, took an aggressive stance
and growled, deep and threatening, when Kern stepped too
close. Jaryyd kicked at the mutt, sending it fleeing for the
far side of camp.

"Smells the wolf, he does. So. Still running errands for
the Murrogh?"

There were no introductions and no time wasted in further pleasantries. Each man knew exactly what the other was about.

Kern watched his people spread out in a loose circle around him. Most pretending to relax—rest even. Every one with an eye on him and Reave, Ossian, Hydallan, and Nahud'r. Those guesting among Jaryyd's advisors.

"Returning from Gorram Village," Kern said. "You?"

"Hunting. It's good, this side of the lake. Eight trophies in the last handful of days."

Eight heads, the other warrior meant. And for him, it would not matter, Vanir or Clan Lacheish. No difference; not among his men.

Perhaps there *was* no difference. Not anymore. On more than one recent occasion, Vanir and Lacheish warriors had fought side by side. And a prisoner had bought his life back with the telling of a Ymirish advisor to Cailt Stonefist. Kern had not wanted to believe it. But then a merchant had come the day before he'd left for Gorram, straight from the Lacheish lodge hall and with the same story.

The Lacheish, it seemed, would rather seek aid from Vanir raiders than look to Cimmeria's defense. They were pointing their blades in the wrong direction!

One of Jaryyd's men produced a leather flask, taking a drink and smacking his lips loudly. Capping it, he then tossed the container to Kern, who swigged back a small mouthful of souring mead and passed it on to Ossian, who accepted the container with relish. The drink was warm, and hardly refreshing. But sharing drink was a way to show at least a basic trust.

He did not worry overmuch. Poison was hardly a Cimmerian tool, man or woman. It was a coward's battle. A "civilized" way. More than anything, it meant he was not afraid to lower his guard among Jaryyd's small force. And he wasn't. Much.

He waited while the flask was passed down the line. "It is good that you stay on your guard," he said, stepping carefully. "No one knows these woods better."

"I should hope not." Jaryyd took the flask when it came by him, sipped, and made a face as he passed it on. "Tastes like dog's water. Haven't had fresh mead in a month."

He brightened. "Some half-decent wine last night, though. A trio of your Vanir raiders all but tripped over our path yestermorn. Slogged their way out of Hanging Tree Marsh. Covered in muck and one of them infested by digger wasps. Did that one a favor, running them down. Those larvae would have eaten him from the insides out when they hatched." Jaryyd and a few of his men laughed. A rough sound, without much humor. "Good sport. I think you would have enjoyed it."

"It sport when you have ten to their one," Nahud'r said calmly, grinning one of his wide, calming smiles. The man's teeth were bright, bright, against so much dark skin. "At Gorram, we have no time for play."

One of the reasons Kern usually included Nahud'r in such meetings was for his outlook. The Shemite's way of looking at things that Kern might not have seen. Kern had discovered this about the dark-skinned man soon after rescuing him from the same Vanir slave line as Daol and Maev and the others who had been taken in winter. He'd come to rely on the man's counsel as well as his friendship in the last few months.

It also did not hurt that Nahud'r's dark skin and desert tales were certain to distract, letting Kern blend in among his adopted countrymen so much as that might be possible.

"What?" Jaryyd asked. "What is your man saying?"

Nahud'r usually shied away from talking up the exploits of Kern and the other warriors. Except in a distant method, as if telling a story that happened among other people—and often as if one of the legendary tales of Conan. In this case, he had intentionally drawn Jaryyd's attention, Kern felt certain, to limit the irritation the Murroghan were bound to feel.

"Twenty men, maybe more, came at us at Gorram." Kern shrugged. "Six or seven men made it away. Your three, they were likely from among them."

"Twenty men?" Jaryyd looked around, taking a silent count. "With what losses?"

"None."

"Nay losses?"

Kern shrugged. "It was a good battle. We held every advantage. And the Gorram honored us with song and a pledge."

That got Jaryyd's complete and full attention. "They are coming off their mountainside? The Gorram?"

Kern had let Ossian carry it, keeping it wrapped away within a blanket. Now the Taurin handed over the bundle. Kern untied the leather cord and unwrapped their token. What they'd taken from the battlefield over Conarch had been carried to most clans of northwest Cimmeria, and had finally made the trip from Mount Crom, through Conall Valley, and over the Pass of Noose to Murrogh Forest.

The bloodied, broken shaft of a Cimmerian spear.

Jaryyd might be at odds with his father, but he had some appreciation for the weight behind the token. A bloody spear, carried among the clans, was a call to war. To set aside all feuds, all petty differences, and join in the face of a common enemy.

Grimnir and his Vanir hordes were just such an enemy. But it had taken Kern's warriors nearly the entire breadth of Cimmeria before finding a chieftain willing to take on the responsibility, and clans willing to listen, and honor, that tradition.

"Such a small thing," Jaryyd said. He reached out, and Kern let him take the broken weapon up. The spearhead was blue iron, some of the best metal crafted in Cimmeria and a true rarity this far to the east. It looked rusted, coated with a dull brown that might have been Cimmerian blood, might have been the blood of their enemies. Didn't matter.

Behind the blood-encrusted head, leather thongs had been tied into place. First was a strap burned with the paw print of a forest cougar. Clan Murrogh's well-known sigil. Then the opossum's tale of Borat Village, the braided cords common to the mountain tribes who lied and fought between Murrogh and Azkel's Fortress in the Border Kingdoms, and leather ties to represent two more small clans as well.

Finally, the pale, leather strap that Gorram's chieftain had tied on the previous morning. Burned into the tag was the outline of a mountain ram's hooves. Gorram's pledge.

"Come back with us," Kern said, treading once again onto dangerous ground. "Bring your men back to Murrogh. Meet with your father."

"My father has a new family. A new son. And nay need of me underfoot." Jaryyd glanced up sharply. "Leave off, Wolf-Eye. This is not for you."

Mayhap not. In fact, he often wondered if Clan Murrogh and Morag Chieftain were for him at all. Did they share his purpose? And even if they did, without a united clan would the Murroghan ever raise their war banner? Kern thought not. "What you hold in your hand is the start of something. Or perhaps the end. If there was ever a time to see an end to your argument with Morag Chieftain, certainly this heralds it."

The other man shrugged. "One more," Jaryyd said, offering back the spear. "Only one more since last I see you. It is not so impressive, perhaps, as you would think."

Kern accepted back the bloody spear. Handed it off to Ossian, who wrapped the token once more in its woolen shroud. "One at a time," he said, agreeing in part. "That is the way alliances are forged."

"An alliance. A massive war host." Jaryyd shook his head. "If they ever see battle against these Vanir you fear so greatly, it will only be when Grimnir hisself finishes with the valley, and on the Hoath Plateau, and finally works his way into the east."

Kern shrugged uneasily, then picked himself up and brushed the dirt from his kilt. Such an outcome, he knew, was what he most feared. "You think so little of the Vanir threat because you have not seen the northerners tear apart village after village. The valley was not ready, protected too long between mountains and so many strong clans. Now most of our strength is spent, and the Vanir are here, building in number. They are."

"So say you. But the Lacheishi are the threat I know now. Not the threat that may come tomorrow. And my father, if he ever moves, will move in their direction first."

Yea, he might. And then Kern would be trapped in a bind, caught between old enmities and new loyalties. To whom could he then turn? What would Cimmeria have left but a dirge for the dead and the destroyed?

He called men to him with a glance, and gave Jaryyd one final shrug.

"If it comes to that, chieftain's son, then we have already lost."

5

T'HULE CHIEFTAIN'S RUNNER caught up with Ros-Crana and her combined war host before she quit the Broken Leg Lands and the northwest territories. Barely.

She stood at the damp-slick edge of a wide ledge, to one side of the weathered arch being crossed by a nonstop line of warriors. Flanked by two of her strongest "seconds," she looked back over the wide, deep ravine and the raging whitewater crashing through far, far below. Waiting. Feet spread wide, and flat. One hand on the hilt of her war sword, the other holding a spear with its butt end planted firmly against the ground. A gusting wind tugged at the damp strands of her dark, ragged-cut hair, whipping them to one side.

Always, always look the part of a leader. Her brother's advice. *Let them see you, ready and unafraid.*

As Clan Callaugh's war leader, she had never worried overmuch for the sake of appearances. A strong arm. A heavy blade. It was all she needed. When Narach said to kill, she killed. When he stayed her at the last moment, she obeyed. She had not questioned why he made the choices he did. Nor had she understood, then, that choosing whom to destroy and whom to spare often came down to appearance. The need to appear strong, or merciful, as benefited the clan.

And so, coming onto the ravine, with the stone arch serving as a natural bridge, she had not hesitated to cross first without the weakness of safety rope or sand.

Knowing that should she fall, the quest died with her.

Two arm lengths wide, the weathered stone was plenty wide enough. On the face of things, at least. But several thin waterfalls chattered down the opposite cliffside, feeding the raging stream below, and spray from their frothy cascades slicked the stone a dark, dangerous color. Gusting winds made it even more treacherous, whipping some of that icy spray into her eyes and setting an unsteady hand on her shoulder to give her a slight nudge now and again.

Look strong.

The advice helped. Though not so much as one other fact she would not let herself forget. Kern had come this way, into the Broken Leg Lands. And he'd crossed this arch in the icy grip of winter. She recalled his speaking of it.

Crom curse the arrogant bastard for his exploits and tales, anyway.

And again, for having the right of it.

After crossing, Ros-Crana planted herself at the bridgehead to wait for every man and woman behind her. Letting each see her, as they came astride. Letting them feel *judged*, and hoping they felt the stronger for it, worthy to be a part of her war host. Now almost two hundred strong, called and bullied from several clan villages in the northwest territories, it was a Cimmerian war host stronger than any she'd ever seen in her lifetime. And it was hers.

So long as she held the allegiance or fear of such men as the two who'd joined her on the ledge.

Dahr was chieftain and war leader of Clan Mak. A long-standing "ally" of the Callaughnan, he was the "second leader" she trusted most. Which was not much. His was a face pitted by the pox and scarred by several blades over his run of forty-odd summers. And she knew his obedience came only on the point of the knife Callaugh had forever held at Mak's throat. That his small village needed the protection of a larger clan such as hers, or T'hule Chieftain's.

Carrak was both less and more of a mystery. He was present on the direct threat Ros-Crana had leveraged over Clan Corag, promising to tear down the village palisade and put their homes to the torch if Wellem Chieftain did not heed her summons. She'd been forced to step heavily on Wellem's pride, always dangerous footing, until he'd broken, promising her a war leader and twenty strong warriors. But it was Carrak who thrust in and twisted the final dagger, stepping forward to name himself as that war leader. Taking the choice from his chieftain and certainly setting himself to challenge Wellem on a victorious return from the campaign.

He was ambitious as well as strong. And standing far too close for Ros-Crana's comfort. Too close for her pair of uneasy guards as well, whom she'd ordered too far back to do her any good should one of these *trusted* men suddenly take a mind to shove her over the ravine's long, lethal drop.

Appearances.

"Ros-Crana!"

A shout from the far side of the bridge. A stir among the warriors still waiting to cross as a man shoved his way forward from the back. He looked familiar, even from a long stone's throw distance. Thick, dark sidebeards, but his chin scraped smooth.

"Callaughnan Chieftain! I bring word from T'hule Chieftain."

Clan Conarch! She recalled the man now. Barod, his name was. From Conarch's lodge hall, and the feast thrown to honor the arrival of spring's first merchant caravan.

Where she'd insulted T'hule Chieftain, turned her back on him and stormed out on his hospitality. She had even stripped the peace bond from her weapon, throwing the leather stay into the fire at T'hule's feet. He could have called her into a Challenge Circle for that alone.

Now one of his men raced up behind her? This could not be helpful.

But she must receive him. If Callaugh hoped to stave off a feud, if there was still time for that, she would hear his words.

"You have something to say, then come across," she shouted. Crom take her if she'd scamper back over the arch as if a dog bidden by its master.

The messenger for T'hule Chieftain crowded into line, though he hesitated a moment at the bridgehead. Likely when he saw no one had bothered with so easy a safety measure as a few handfuls of sand and gravel thrown out along the weathered arch. Three steps out he wavered as a sharp gust of wind nearly blew him off the arch's back, and Ros-Crana flinched as she pictured the man's body tumbling into the rock-strewn waters below, being pulped and bloodied and broken before she heard his message.

Also as she imagined Clan Conarch's response when the messenger sent after her simply disappeared. Or was found dead downstream.

The fates were not so cruel, and Crom's gift lent the man strength enough to hold his footing and make the journey safely across. He jumped the last several strides, landing in an easy crouch, and straightened before her. "A fine challenge, that."

Ros-Crana shifted her stance only slightly, able to face the man but still keep an eye on her crossing army. Still giving them the benefit of her audience. The winds blew a few hairs across her eyes, which she ignored. A light sheen of spray splashed against her face, leaving her lips tasting of sweat and mountain ice.

"What has T'hule Chieftain to say to me?"

Barod rubbed at his smooth-shaven chin. His blue eyes were twin shards of ice, staring at her as if from a great distance. "A new Vanir threat has come down from the Eiglophians. Not a large war host, but strong enough to threaten smaller clans throughout the northwest territories."

"Good," Dahr said, though he spoke out of turn. His scarred face twisted with a grim smile. "Will give T'hule Chieftain something to occupy his time while we are away."

It would at that. Ros-Crana had left an understrength guard at Callaugh Glen, counting on their strong, palisade walls to help protect the clan's home. It would be good for T'hule to be occupied elsewhere.

She shrugged. "Kern Wolf-Eye warned us that it would be so. T'hule chose to mock his warning and his help."

"The outcast has no standing among clans and chieftains. Even if *some* talk of him as Conan, come again."

Ros-Crana laughed in the man's face as the barb failed to strike at her. There were similarities, yea, between the legends of Conan and exploits from many among Kern's band. His *Men of the Wolves*. She had even heard fireside renditions of those tales told *as* Conan stories. Properly embellished, of course. But Kern Wolf-Eye, she knew, would have been the first to admit it. He was no Conan.

"Try again, Barod, if it was your chieftain's orders to insult or anger me. Otherwise, say what it is you have come to say and leave off." She jerked her chin toward the Teeth, their snowcapped peaks towering above them. "I have a long climb ahead over the Pass of Blood."

"You are saying it is not some misplaced loyalty to the whelped one that you cross those mountains, turning your back on your own people and lands?"

She did not miss how Barod's gaze wandered, bringing the men standing beside Ros-Crana into the conversation. He spoke for their benefit as much as for hers.

"Nay. It is not."

"There are . . . rumors."

She'd wager there were. Having let Kern's warrior pack guest at Callaugh Glen for several weeks. And certainly someone with a loose tongue had seen Ros-Crana seek him out in the village's hot springs, joining Kern Wolf-Eye in the baths. For talk! Only for talk.

Though still, she recalled that one moment when she had moved toward him, moved into him, all too clear. The mineral taste of the spring's water. The steam which had soaked his pale, frost blond hair, weighting it against the side of his head. The wariness in his golden, feral eyes. And the flash of heat that had thrilled her. Briefly.

But his skin, when she'd touched his chest, had nearly burned her for as cold as it was. Not even a corpse's flesh could have remained so lifeless, immersed in the hot baths. Before she could help herself, she jerked her hand away.

"You are . . . cold," she had said. Freezing.

Kern's eyes had been two slits of golden fire. Watching her. "All my life."

Yea. She remembered that moment very clearly. The expectation that had built up, then was lost when something in her recoiled at his unnatural nature.

"Rumors be damned." Ros-Crana brushed aside the implication. "I respect Wolf-Eye's accomplishments. And feel a debt to him for the aid he gave us on the bluffs overlooking Conarch. I remember, Barod, because I was there. I watched as Grimnir's mighty host nearly crushed the best three clans had to offer. I saw Conarch burning and my brother fall beneath the swords of the Ymirish and their Vanir dogs. And *I know* we'd have lost the field that day if Kern had not dragged Grimnir over the edge of the cliff, pulling the creature with him into death."

"Only they did not die." Barod echoed his chieftain's words, said at the feast several weeks before when Ros-Crana had used the same argument. "Grimnir lives. Kern Wolf-Eye failed."

"Kern was fortunate enough to land on a small ledge, though the rocks scraped away more flesh than they left on his back, his side. And Grimnir . . ." She could not help a shiver, remembering the great man-beast who had taken the field against them that day. Giant-kin, with a thick, muscular hide the color of rotten snow and the same fierce, yellow eyes he shared with the Ymirish—and with Kern. "Grimnir's survival could not have been foreseen. We cannot hold it against Kern, when he was willing to spend his own life for ours."

"Blood debt," Dahr said. And Carrak, though silent, nodded.

The last few warriors of her host, stepping down from the nearby arch of stone, beat fists against their chests, saluting the tradition if not the man.

"There is no blood debt to an outcast *and* outsider, by Crom. The wolf-eyed man has the blood of Ymir in his veins. He admits this. Your brother knew the traditions, Ros-Crana Chieftain, and would tell you now that such a one is owed nothing."

A mistake, invoking her brother's name. Reminding her of him, of all he had been to the Callaughnan.

Narach had been a good chieftain. Perhaps even a great one, for a time of relative peace. But he had been too slow to recognize—to respond—to the dangers of the Vanir and of Grimnir. He'd known that after Kern Wolf-Eye provoked him into working with Sláine Longtooth's Cruaidhi.

He'd explained it to her, in bits and pieces, over campfires and quiet talks inside his private tent.

His words still echoed in the back of Ros-Crana's mind.

Tradition demanded we give Wolf-Eye no standing. No credence. But his actions shamed us. We appeared weak, and so we were. And so we would have remained, victims of the Vanir, had we not finally acted and also fought at his side.

"You think to use my brother's memory against me? Narach was *twice* the chieftain T'hule will ever be, and you can take my words back to him. My brother recognized the needs of honor over blind traditions. Saw that we must act. As we act now."

Dahr nodded, for no other reason than Ros-Crana expected it of him, and Carrak slapped the sheath of his broadsword. "Grimnir is also the other side of those mountains."

Barod spat to one side. "And let the Great Terror stay there. Let him fight and bleed, and be weakened. But to chase after him leaves us all the more vulnerable. These are the words of T'hule Chieftain, and they are true. The beast's host grows far stronger than you will be able to face. Any of you!"

Something lurked beneath the surface of Barod's words. Something more than a dark omen. A promise. Ros-Crana seized on it at once and turned on the Conarch warrior with a furious strength.

"What? What else did T'hule Chieftain send you to say . . . or not to say?" A flush warmed her neck, her brow. "What more does he know?"

"There is more," Barod warned. "He asks—he does nay command—that you, any of you, return to speak with him. Give him that courtesy, and he will forgive any earlier insults to Clan Conarch. If you wish to chase off after your death, then so be it."

Carrack sneered openly at the offer, but Dahr hesitated. Ros-Crana all but read his mind. The offer to shore up damaged relations. A delay, which might derail the entire quest. Mak, safe, for another season. Of all the short-sighted views!

"Weeks T'hule Chieftain has had to talk," Ros-Crana yelled, letting her fury build. "And you chase us down now, here, in the shadows of the Teeth? Looking for any excuse, or threat, to hold us back? Does your chieftain strike a bargain with Grimnir now? What does he know?"

She saw the flash of defiance behind his ice-blue eyes, threw her spear aside and reached out to grab two large handfuls of sidebeard before her seconds could stop her, or even caution her, against laying hands on the messenger of Conarch. Before she thought better of it herself, she yanked Barod forward and spun him around her, as if she might bodily hurl him from the ledge and out over the ravine's deadly drop. But she held back, barely. Shoving him right up to the edge of the drop, letting his heels hang over the edge of the damp stone and dangling him backward with only her grip on his sidebeards between safety and a long, lethal plunge.

"Speak, you little worm! Ah! Don't even try to raise your hands. And do not think to hold back from me anything that might save Cimmerian lives, or by Crom's hairy orbs I'll send you to the crows."

Pain and desperation warred briefly on Barod's face. A severe grimace. But he kept his hands down at his side, away from Ros-Crana's arms, and breathed with tight, careful huffs.

"Our warriors struck back at the raiders," he said, words rushing through clenched teeth. "Pushed into the Breaknecks." A long stretch of knife-edge ridges and broken ground. A no-man's-land stretching from the settled territory of the northwest all the way to the Eiglophian Mountains. "There, we found evidence of many, many more Vanir. Camps and slaughter pits. A few stragglers who pushed not south. But *east*. For Crom's mercy, Ros-Crana!"

She hauled him back from the edge and threw him away from her onto the safety of the nearby path. All but dared him to reach for his sword. Even a single flinch.

"East! Then the Vanir flood across the broken lands far above the Teeth! They rally to Grimnir's banner—not to come after us, but to crush any threat of the clans united!" And T'hule Chieftain would indeed sell those clansfolk to Grimnir if it kept his own carcass safe.

Barod rubbed at his cheeks, his eyes no longer so distant but wide with a mixture of fear and rage for how close he'd come to death. "We will burn Callaugh's walls to the ground, Ros-Crana. And salt the earth in which your crops grow. Conarch's vengeance will be terrible and swift, against you all, I swear by Crom!"

Dahr stood frozen, caught between the devil he knew and the devil he feared. Carrack reached for his sword, ready to draw it the moment Ros-Crana ordered this man's death. But she held him back. Held back with one upraised hand all of the snarling clansmen who stood around Barod in a loose circle, ready to tear him apart for such a threat.

"You put strong words in your chieftain's mouth, Barod. Mayhap he'll listen to you, and T'hule will accomplish this in my absence. Truth. But now you take my words back to the dog you serve. I *will* return to the northwest lands. By Crom's gift, I will. And with the men and women able to march halfway across Cimmeria and return from battle against Grimnir, you ask him how much I'll worry for turning such warriors loose against Clan Conarch."

"He does nay fear you, Ros-Crana. You or that wolf-eyed cur."

She smiled and accepted her spear back from one of the nearby guards. Held it across her body.

"Nay, I imagine he does not fear either of us," she agreed. "And neither does Grimnir."

She looked from face to face, slowly. Smiling. Showing a supreme confidence that she did not feel but was necessary for the men and women who followed her. And for the man who would take her words back to her newest enemy. Posturing, though no one else need know that save her.

"But they should, Barod. They should." She brushed past him then, leaving him standing alone at the bridgehead. "Your chieftain is fortunate that he is currently the lesser of my enemies," she called back to him.

"I go now to teach that lesson to the greater of them."

6

SWINGING AROUND THE southern end of the lake felt to Kern as if the land had buckled up under pressure. Here the lake's gray waters pushed up very close to cliff faces, part of the Black Mountains separating Cimmeria from the Border Kingdom. Here the trails often zigzagged around and through flood cuts, steep hillsides, and broken ridgelines. The land dried out—more rock and fewer muddy trails—except for some small waterfalls and an occasional stream feeding winter melt into the nearby lake.

Here the tired warriors looked forward to rest and respite. Most of them.

For his part, the closer to Clan Murrogh they came, the more distance Kern maintained from his warriors. Too many spoke of seeing family, friends again. Wondered if children looked any taller. If a sick kinsman had turned for the worse. It felt far too much like coming home.

Except that it wasn't.

Not for him.

Cul Chieftain had made that very clear, two weeks before, when he'd led Kern's pack back to the Murrogh stronghold.

"Do nay think to rest easy here, Wolf-Eye. I do this for *my* people. Nay for you or yours."

Kern was used to being an outsider. Had lived with it his entire life. Though he'd not been certain how his warriors would take to it, among their own kin. "I am here only to seek strength against Grimnir and his Ymirish."

It had seemed, for a moment, that Cul might relent. "They are an unnatural force, which spoils everything they touch, yea." He'd looked Kern square in the face. "And you are just like them."

Cul could have no real way of knowing just how close his remarks struck home. He'd not been nearby earlier that night, when terrible power had suddenly boiled up within Kern. Darkness and rage and a sudden thirst for both. So hard had it come at him, he had stifled it out of reflex. Held it off at arm's length, keeping a slippery grip on it.

And whatever Cul mayhap witnessed later—and understood—he kept that quietly to himself. For now.

But Kern had been able to think of nothing else after the battle, or on the long hike back to Murrogh. Dark power raged in him still the next morning, singing through his veins as it pushed for release, a release he refused to grant. He had known—known without thinking!—that a terrible purpose roiled within, and, if he stepped forward to embrace it, he would claim the same strengths and powers as any Ymirish sorcerer.

Wasn't enough that he bore their mark in his golden eyes, the frost blond color of his hair, his waxy, pale skin. That his northern blood had crowded aside everything he'd believed about himself—the Cimmerian heritage he'd claimed for so long from his mother's side, not knowing any better.

Winter born. That's what so many had called him before. The *blood of wolves.* No one had really known the worst of it.

That Kern was raider-get. The same blood that flowed through Grimnir's veins, and the warlord Ymirish brethren, also flowed through his. And now that blood called for its heritage. A heritage Kern neither wanted nor, it seemed, could he barely control.

"You quiet."

Nahud'r stepped up next to Kern, elbow bumping Kern's arm as the Shemite crowded alongside on the narrow trail. The path was actually one of several that snaked along a boulder-strewn hillock. Kern had veered high on the slope, giving his warriors a wide berth as they stepped up the pace, eager to return. He'd sought to be alone. And said so.

The dark-skinned Shemite wore a long woolen scarf wrapped about his head in desert fashion. Usually covering all but his eyes, he'd opened it enough to bare his entire face. Now he smiled, showing white, white teeth, and nodded farther up the slope.

Frostpaw. The dire wolf had skulked up on Kern's left, running a higher path as it scrabbled among thorny brush and rocks. Eight hands across the shoulders and easily twelve-stone weight with the return of spring's bounty, for a large animal it moved with remarkable grace, powerful muscles rippling beneath a silver-gray pelt. The dire wolf had one white paw and a dark band of fur slashing across its eyes like a mask.

Seeing that Kern has stopped on the lower trail, the animal paused, stared down with its fierce golden gaze.

"You never alone," Nahud'r said. There was no recrimination in his dark brown eyes, but perhaps a soft touch of wistfulness to the man's voice.

Kern could guess. A native of the fabled southern deserts of Shem, brought into service and educated with a merchant's family in Nemedia, the black-skinned man had traveled across more lands than Kern had even heard tell of. He read. He wrote. And he was as deadly with the scimitar he carried at his side as any man who fought with Kern.

He was also one of several slaves taken by a Vanir raiding party and rescued by Kern after he chased down the northerners to free Daol, and Maev, Burok's daughter. He'd had no home to return to, so he'd stayed with Kern. And welcome to have him.

"Mayhap not," Kern finally admitted. "Not quite so alone as some, anyway."

He started walking, leaving room for Nahud'r to remain at his side. The wolf stalked forward, pacing them. Kern glanced down the shallow slope, over the rest of his pack, who struggled and straggled along different trails. Daol and Reave and Ossian. Hydallan and Wallach Graybeard. Long shadows stretched out behind them, as the sun prepared for its final fall behind the Black Mountains.

"To them, this is as close as they have felt in months. That they are coming home. It should feel that way, shouldn't it?"

The Galla had mentioned to Kern the survivors from Gaud's ruin crossing the Black Mountains. Cul, of course, had only been a shocking first. Kohlitt, Reave's cousin and brother by marriage, had been among the prisoners rescued out of the Vanir camp. And Halei, Garret's niece. The outcasts quickly learned that several score had survived the attack on their village, the fires, and the ruthless hunt. Two of these succumbed to wounds. Another chose to be "released," his broken legs slowing the clan down and risking all. Another was lost to the mountain spiders.

Still, better than fifty men, women, and children of both Gaud and Taur had braved the mountains and come down into eastern Cimmeria, and now carved out an existence in the shadow of Clan Murrogh's stronghold.

And few, if any, were pleased to see Kern Wolf-Eye back among their dwindled numbers.

"How does it feel, Nahud'r? You nay have family here. Or kin of any kind. There is nay one person we've seen who even looks as you do. Do you get tired of the stares, the talk?"

The Shemite walked and thought for a moment. "You remember first morning we spend after freeing us?"

He did. Crisp and quiet, it had been. And with supplies stolen from the raiders, it was one of the first mornings in months when Kern had felt as if he'd had enough to eat. They all had.

"You stare at me that morning," Nahud'r said. "Watch me, like I was part of *show*." He saw Kern's puzzled face, realized he had slipped back into the Aquilonian tongue. "Like strange creature."

Kern remembered. He had watched Nahud'r perform some morning rituals. Had stared at the Shemite when he strolled out of camp to relieve himself. But the man's piss had been as golden as anyone else's.

"I remember."

"That last five days. Maybe six. Then you, you stop staring at me in such a way. All your warriors stop, after time." He glanced over. "Answer your question?"

Kern considered. Then laughed softly. "Nay. I understand that we grew comfortable with you. But still, you face every day knowing you are nay any closer to home."

Nahud'r stopped. He crouched on the path to pick up a sharp-edged rock. In the trail's hard-packed dirt, he scratched out several lines and curves, forming the rough letters he'd once taught Kern, who'd been fascinated with the thought of a man having so much time as to be able to learn to write and read. Who could devote entire days, and months, to such a pursuit.

He read them now. The first words Nahud'r had taught him. Also crouched alongside a trail those several months ago.

"A miracle happened this morning."

Nahud'r offered the stone to Kern, who took it in a strong hand. He bent down, and scraped out the rest of the sentence, sounding it out as he carved each letter into the ground.

"The sun . . . rose . . . in the . . . east."

The letters weren't perfect. Kern had not practiced them in weeks. But good enough to recognize. "Every day is a new day," Kern said, still fighting with the Shemite philosophy.

Nahud'r shrugged. "Every day a new day," he repeated, as if agreeing. He rose and brushed his hands clean.

"That," he said, "how it feels."

The Shemite had little else to say, and Kern wrestled with that small piece of desert wisdom on the rest of the quiet march. They saw a few other clansmen, some heading out in small hunting parties, others gathering wild berries from the hillside brush. There were few waves. Fewer welcomes. Quite a few stared openly, and Kern ignored them as he saw Nahud'r doing. Kept to himself, still chewing on their earlier conversation, until disturbed by shouts ahead as the first of his warriors finally cleared the trails and trotted down toward the lakeside settlement and stronghold of Clan Murrogh.

Of course, the stronghold itself was hard to ignore. At the peak of the next ridge, Kern stared over it, always with an eye toward where a weakness might be found—and fixed—before the Vanir came. Not an easy task. A large, triangular spit of land jutted into the lake where the waters crowded closest to the cliffs. Out on this rocky peninsula the Murrogh had built their magnificent lodge hall and, surrounding it, large stables and many of their homes. Then they had walled off the peninsula with rock and timbers, forming more of a long, low run than the tall palisades Kern had come across in the northwest territories.

Not quite as inspiring. Still, over the years it had apparently proven plenty strong.

Spreading out along the lakeshore was a widespread village, broken into several distinct neighborhoods, and many small camps formed by the warriors who had answered the summons of Morag Chieftain. And there, closest to the eastern approach, was the small community toward which Kern's warriors streamed. Among those huts, and homes, people moved about with ease. Peacefully. Today, at the least. Some tended crops or cattle. Others applied themselves to the never-ending need to build. More walls. More homes. It never ended.

Fortunately, for the Gaudic and Taurin refugees, there was plenty of rock that could be quarried by hand out of the nearby hills, or at times found among the rubble calved off the cliff face. And they had not settled for ramshackle hovels, but had built fair-sized homes with stone foundations and walls of woven branches and mud, and well-thatched roofs. And a long wall that stretched from cliff face all the way to the lake, protecting themselves as best they could from any attacking war host who might come at Clan Murrogh from the east.

Cul's doing. As with most clans in Conall Valley, Gaud had lived through too many peaceful years to worry overmuch about walls and fortifications. Cattle stealing and raids for new wives was part of the way of things, and walls rarely helped. But after suffering the true strength of a raider attack, that lesson was well learned.

Word passed quickly that the outcasts—the *Men of the Wolves*—had returned. There were a few shouts of recognition. Even a few calls of welcome. From atop the ridge Kern saw Reave and Desa up near the front, each of them scooping up a wild tangle of long, gangly limbs, which would be Reave's surviving niece and nephew. Kohlitt's children, Bayan and Cor.

"Good to have someone waiting," Nahud'r said. Then he turned down into the next switchback, ambling along in no particular hurry. No one waited for him here.

Kern held his place on the upper path a moment longer. Also in no hurry. Feeling a cold flush prickling at the back of his neck, as if in warning. The sensation of being watched. Almost by reflex, Kern glanced up and back, searching for the dire wolf, assuming it had crept down closer.

No sign of the wolf. Instead, Kern's gaze grabbed at a child who crouched on the upper slope near a cluster of nettle and purple foxtail. The boy had dark hair, glossy as a raven's feathers, brown eyes, and a square face he recognized at once. Mal, son of Morag Chieftain!

Four summers, Kern knew, but the boy had size and speed for a lad nearly twice his age. And a sharp mind as well, though the child hid it behind a stoic silence, which also didn't seem natural for a small boy. One who should be running in a pack of his own, tumbling over his own feet and finding trouble up in the rafters of the lodge house, or setting rafts loose from the docks that lined the nearby shore. Always so serious, so intent.

And set loose to run where no boy of four summers had a mind to be.

Kern did another quick search for the wolf, worried that

Frostpaw might not see a child and instead see prey. Part of Kern's pack the animal might be, following, protecting even, but it was still a wild beast and could run the lad down in mere heartbeats. But Frostpaw had already gone to ground, stalking carefully while so close to so many people. No doubt it would hide for the rest of the day. Perhaps sneak in toward night or run off to hunt.

But always, always to return.

"Come down from there, Mal." Kern saw no one else so far out from the village. No other boys, and no older man or woman to keep an eye on the chieftain's son. A dangerous place for him to play. "Come on, now," he said, a touch stronger.

But the boy gave Kern a curled-lip grin—nearly a snarl of his own—and leaped down the hillside at an angle away from Kern. Hit a smooth, steep shoulder and slid several lengths toward the lakeshore community below.

Glanced back once, eyes flashing a dangerous glare that rocked Kern back on his heels. A chill rushed through Kern, and in the back of his mind dark shadows played.

Nay! He'd not let the power rise again. But his control was slipping, he knew, when a scolded child nearly set him off.

Part of it, he felt certain, was that instant of surprise as the boy's eyes seemed to burn with a familiar golden fierceness. That single flash of inner fire. But Mal's eyes were brown and the boy was certainly Cimmerian, born to Morag and the Lacheish woman whom the chieftain had stolen from his rival nearly five years before.

Jumping at shadows.

Kern shook his head. He had enough troubles to worry about without borrowing more. He started down the hill as well, far behind the boy, who fled strongly for the village proper and had already passed Nahud'r as well. Bringing up the rear, just as he had the two weeks before when Cul Chieftain led them into Murrogh.

And, like now, he had both anticipated and dreaded the moment. Hanging back, letting the others approach first. Watching as Brig Tall-Wood stood talking with Cul, always one of the Gaudic chieftain's friends and strongest supporters. Seeing Reave take his sister's husband home, to hold once more his niece, his nephew, and grieve again for the loss of his sister and her youngest, whose bodies they'd found in Gaud's ruin. And Ossian, counting up the two dozen Taurin lives who had escaped a Vanir slaughter not once, but twice. Some even welcomed him warmly as the son of Liam Chieftain.

But other than those few, the greetings had been cautious, and cold. These were warriors who had abandoned their clan—and no matter the reason—once outside, always outside. It was stretching the boundaries of tradition even to welcome or treat with them. To exchange hands, and hugs, and stories shared with food around the fires that night. And Cul had not stood against them, which was a surprise. Though perhaps less so when the entire community had quieted on *her* arrival.

She was there today as well, of course. Waiting at the wall, with a nod, or a casual hand clasp, as the warriors returned. Kern had learned that quickly as well, through rumor and the talk that filtered back through Daol and Ossian. Nothing happened among this small community, even with it tucked up to the side of Murrogh's strength, without her notice and approval. Cul still led—he was chieftain, after all—but she stood closest to his side and was the foundation of his strength now. Had to be. He was a chieftain who had let his clan be nearly destroyed. She was Burok Bear-slayer's daughter, and respected no matter what her condition.

Maev.

She stood the other side of the low, stone wall, hands resting on the uneven top as she guarded the switchback gate through which everyone had passed but Kern. Her blue eyes were deep and calm, and her hair pulled back into a severe tail that hung halfway down her back. She looked pale today, and had dark smudges beneath her eyes.

"First out," she said, as Kern approached. "Last back."

"Everyone has come back," Kern said. "And with good news for Morag Chieftain. That is all that matters."

"And a dozen Vanir heads on spikes, according to young Ehmish." Her eyes had a cold, savage bite to them. "That matters as well."

One of the Gaudic clansfolk taken by Vanir and one of their Ymirish masters, Maev had more reason than most to hate the northerners. To hate *him*, in fact, though she remained civil enough. Part of their bargain, as he recalled, two nights that he could never forget, no matter the reasons that had led up to them. Her worry, not for what the clan might think, but what only *she* could know and be forced to recall every day if the worst happened. Her plan, to seek Kern out at those times. To come to him. Taking the devil she'd known over the one who had forced himself upon her.

And a wise precaution it had turned out to be, Kern decided. And could not help the touch of regret, and shame, that burned coldly within him as he came through the gate, and as Maev backed away from him, arms coming down to fold protectively over the slight bulge in her dark, woolen shift.

Her pregnancy had finally begun to show.

7

KERN WAS GIVEN the night to rest, then Morag Chieftain sent for him.

The sun was a dimmed, distant brand, still low on the horizon and working to burn off a thick, gray haze that blanketed the sky. Midday, Kern guessed, before it could free itself. And it would be welcome. A cold snap the night before had powdered the ground with a touch of ice, raising gooseflesh on most of his warriors already up and around. Breath puffed out in thin, frosted streams.

The messenger sent to fetch him along waited while Kern finished off the oat flat cake he'd already torn into several steaming shreds. A brown-eyed warrior with a Murroghan's square jaw and a scar twisting from the corner of his right eye to the clipped edge of one ear, he shifted from one foot to the other as if trapped inside the small circle of canvas tents set up for those without space—or simply not welcome—inside one of the nearby huts, ready to be away. He spoke briefly with Old Finn, then Nahud'r, waiting while Kern bounced his last two pieces in a well-callused hand to cool them.

Fresh from the cooking fire, with a few early berries mashed into the paste for sweetening, what the flat cakes mostly tasted of was the animal fat in which they'd been fried. Better had been the eggs Ehmish had found, or filched, and the warm, fresh milk Garret Blackpatch bartered from the Murroghan for a few of the best blades brought back from Gorram Village.

Finally, he dug his sword belt out of a nearby tent and strapped it on over the wide leather strap securing the top of his kilt. His chain-mail vest and a new knife to replace the dagger he'd given up in Gorram, and the bloody spear he'd already carried so far, and he was ready.

"Morag allows you to bring two men."

Daol had slipped away early with Aodh, before sun's rise, to hunt the slopes of the Black Mountains. Reave was within sight, coloring the water at the lake's nearby edge, but the large man was more comfortable with action than talk.

"Nahud'r," Kern said, and caught another flat cake tossed to him by the Shemite. He nodded his thanks, drew his knife to impale the cake before it burned his hand, and motioned for the dark-skinned man to follow.

Another glance around. "Ehmish."

"Yea, Kern?" The young man said it with such enthusiasm, Kern almost relented and let the lad come. But not when he didn't know the chieftain's mood. "Sorry. Nay. Go kick some doors. Rouse Ossian from whatever bed he's found. Have him catch up before we reach the lodge hall."

It was a short, muscle-warming run to reach the lifted gate that allowed entry onto the large spit of land thrusting out into the lake. The calm waters reflected back a clear blue sky this morning, with the sun scattering its light in a thousand sparkles spread far out as the eye could see. Kern walked around a disguised pitfall, set just beyond the gate, and chose one of the nearby paths before the Murroghan warrior could order him forward. The trio scattered a flock of chickens and chased off a bleating goat, twisting between homes and huts as they worked their way up a rocky upthrust to the magnificent lodge set atop with a commanding view of the lake and several leagues of shoreline. It would take much for the Murroghan war host to be caught off their guard.

The lodge itself was equally impressive. Easily as large as T'hule Chieftain's lodge back in Conarch, the Murrogh had used quite a bit more stone and massive, rough-hewn timbers to help support a roof not thatched but shaked with split cedar. Built long and low, to resist the winds which at times stormed across the lake, it could pack inside its sturdy walls the men of Clan Murrogh and likely those of several neighboring villages as well.

Ossian caught up with the trio just short of the lodge hall, hardly winded from his sprint but scowling with his head half-shaven and the crusted scar on the right side of his head slathered over with the stale grease he'd been using to stand up the dark, bristling hairs.

"Yea, and you couldn't give me a moment more," he said.

Kern tossed Ossian the uneaten half of flat cake he'd carried along, sheathed his knife, and tied a leather stay about the handle. "Morag Chieftain wants to talk."

Not just to the outcast leader, either. Kern counted half a dozen standard-bearing spears, each one driving into the ground outside of the Murroghan lodge hall. He recognized the antlers of nearby Galt, and Borat's opossum's tail. Small villages, but hardy, and each able to put forward at least a score of strong warriors. Kern might have counted up each of the others by name and likely numbers as well, except that he saw the next one in line—with its collection of ebony fangs dangling down on thin, white cord—and, recognizing them, suddenly shouldered his way past the messenger for the darkened lodge hall doors and through the small knot of people crowded just inside.

"Kern!"

Maev grabbed at him before he shoved past her, pulling him in at her side with a grip like steel and a sharp dig of her fingernails into his flesh. Cul glanced over from Maev's other side, where he'd been speaking with Brig Tall-Wood, then away again. Even in the dim light, falling through the door and a few narrow windows, Kern recognized from the small groups clustered around them representatives from the several gathered clans and villages. All of whom waited to be taken back through the long house, where the leader of Clan Murrogh and many of his clansmen must have been holding a private council.

"Clan Galla," Kern said, as Ossian and Nahud'r caught up. The messenger, his task accomplished, left the unruly outcasts among their own. "I saw tokens outside of the Spider's Teeth tribe. Have the Galla come down out of the hills?"

"Survivors have," Maev said. "We do not have the entire story yet. Morag Chieftain bids us wait." She released him then, obviously trusting Kern to be reminded of his place.

He did. He also noticed Maev's sudden closeness. Could smell her clean, damp hair, washed in the lake only this morning no doubt, hanging in thick tangles over both shoulders. He saw the restlessness in her eyes. Her thin, compressed lips, the pale touch on her cheeks.

Morning sick again, he guessed.

At least he could be happy that she lived, even if catching pregnant with child had been among her most undesired fears. Kern had wondered for months what might have happened to Burok Bear-slayer's daughter. Thought of her. Kept her memory close and recalled her every time he caught her scent—or believed that he did—on the blanket they'd shared.

He remembered the first moment when she'd touched him, recoiling as if burned. But she hadn't been so put off to leave. Or, more likely, she'd been desperate enough to set aside her fear. Her revulsion.

He also recalled the few moments of kindness she'd showed him when she'd had no reason to. All but challenging Cul when the Gaudic chieftain cast Kern out on Burok's funeral march.

But mostly, he remembered the words she had spoken to him on her father's deathbed. The day before Burok's passing. Kern had come from within the draped sickbed, ducking quickly under the hanging bearskins in his hurry to escape the foul, rotting odor of the black gangrene eating away at his chieftain's leg. There had been Maev, working, honing daggers, oiling them against further rust. Busywork, certainly, but work that still benefited the clan.

Setting aside the most recent blade, she had looked him to the door and waited until he was ready to pass through, back to the fresh air and the cold grip of winter.

"It should be you," she said then.

Lying on the deathbed instead of her father. Brain feverish and blood poisoned by the slow, crawling death eating away his leg.

He remembered. Clearly as if it had been yesterday.

He wished he didn't.

"Wolf-Eye!"

The summons came from the far end of the lodge, barked in a deep, strong voice with just a touch of rasp to it. A voice made to carry, to be heard through the deep clefts of the mountains or along the darkest forest paths.

Kern felt Cul's glare burn at the back of his neck as he stepped forward, drawing Nahud'r and Ossian after him as they left the others behind. They strode down the empty

central aisle, which gave way on both sides to long tables
and benches, and cold, dark fire pits. Only a few flickering
torches lighted the way. Kern had seen the room packed to
bursting with lively talk and gaming and feasting, filled with
the scents of meat sizzling over open flame and of strong
wine and mead. But that was not this day, this moment.

Now the trio approached the far end of the cold, dim
hall and a much more select gathering. Men whom Kern
recognized with their tattooed faces and chests, and their
dark hair pulled up into topknots. Others whom he did not,
right away, with braided beards, and ritualistic scars slashing up the sides of their faces. All of them were filthy from
what had to be days of hard travel and fighting. Bloodied,
he saw, and bedraggled. And for every one of them at least
two of Morag Chieftain's kinsmen stood nearby.
Twenty . . . thirty men and women all told, surrounding
their leader, clearly stamped with the looks of Clan Murrogh. Morag's strongest warriors or most sage advisors.

And his family, of course. Kern spotted Deirdre at once,
her youth only slightly spoiled since being taken as
Morag's new wife five summers back. She still shaved the
hair over her temples in Lacheish fashion, but she appeared
comfortable enough as the chieftain's wife, standing next
to her husband's chair with one hand on his shoulder. With
the other she held the hand of their young son, Mal, who
stamped and shifted about, always straining against his
mother's grip, wanting to be away.

A waste of time, and a distraction, keeping the boy
leashed down for such a meeting. Mayhap he would be
Morag's heir one day, if Jaryyd was not allowed to return.
But for now he was far too young to be included. Kern
found himself wishing that the wild boy would break his
mother's hold and dash off.

"Close enough, Wolf-Eye," Morag growled as Kern approached, barely stepping inside the large circle of men and

women. His dark, dark eyes watched every move around him with quick, furtive gestures. "You've brought it?"

If the chieftain's young son at times tweaked Kern's sensibilities, Morag positively offended them. The man had once been a powerfully built warrior with a great reputation for sword and the strength of his rule. The song sung of him most was a daring summer raid against Clan Lacheish where his men had taken ten cattle and Morag himself had taken a wife who was nearly as valuable. Daughter of Cailt Stonefist, Deirdre was a prize if for no other reason than her influence among some of the small, upcountry villages. And Morag had taken her—and held her—from the east's largest and strongest clan.

But there were other songs, and these were of the misfortunes that soon fell on Clan Murrogh. Morag himself fell ill on the journey home, taking an infection after one last skirmish deep in the Frost Swamp off the Hoath Plateau. He had lost weight, a great deal of it, and his hair had fallen out in patches. No one had given him odds for survival.

Except that he had. Regaining some of his strength, and fathering a child on Deirdre. The boy bound her to Clan Murrogh more strongly than any other custom, and though by all whispered tales her husband quickly grew tired of her, she had stood by her duty as wife and mother.

Morag was no longer possessed of the great strength of his tales. The man had sunken eyes and pale, loose skin. His hair was thin and wispy, though still dark, and his teeth were gray, rotting stumps. Nor did he pick up a sword to lead his people forward in battle. For that, he had war leaders. Most recently, Crom had delivered Cul Chieftain to Murrogh, and it seemed a good match. Cul traded his strength and cunning against the Murroghan's generosity and protection for his people.

And for that, if no other reason, Kern accepted the man.

Morag might be the choice forced upon him, but Cimmeria needed strength wherever it could be found.

Morag frowned as if sensing his thoughts, and Kern chided himself. The anger buried at the back of his mind stirred and was ruthlessly smothered. The man was known to sniff out trouble. Kern knew better than to go looking for it.

He reined himself back in, if slowly.

"You have it?" Morag asked again, this time more forceful. There was little lost from his strong voice, at least.

"Yea, Murrogh Chieftain." Kern had peace-bonded his sword and dagger, as was required, but he carried the bloody spear still wrapped in its small shroud of woolen blanket. He cradled it in one arm, as a mother might her newborn. Unwrapping the broken shaft, he gripped it by one end and held it flat out toward the other man.

Not threatening. Not in any manner.

Still, Morag recoiled slightly, as if wanting to sink into the clean rushes that were woven in a covering mat for his high-backed seat. "Gorram Village has pledged their support to me?"

"Against the Vanir," Kern said, steering the conversation with great care. "The northern raiders have raided Gorram twice. I do not believe they will be back."

The chieftain laughed. Cold, but not completely unpleasant. He reached up and scratched deeply at a bald spot within his hair. Plucked out a long strand and dropped it on the floor. "Killed them all, did your wolves?"

"Most, but not all." Kern still held out the spear, but the chieftain gave no orders for anyone to take it from him. He lowered it. "Jaryyd caught a few of the escaping men, however, and finished what we began."

At the mention of his older son Morag grew agitated. "Do not throw his name about so casually, Kern Wolf-Eye.

Especially in mine own lodge." He shifted his gaze left, and right, then settled back. "I should declare him cast out and be quit of him. Him and his cutthroats."

The casual viciousness rankled, but Kern swallowed back a sharp response. "Any sword raised in the name of Morag Chieftain strengthens all of Murrogh," he said. "And all of Cimmeria." Reminding the man of the other clans gathered without, and within.

"Yea, well, some new blades may have been found, Kern Wolf-Eye, which is why you have been summoned." He nodded to the small gathering of Galla, and those whom Kern had finally recognized as belonging to Clan Hoath. "It seems your Vanir threaten to overrun the plateau."

"Morag Chieftain," one of the Hoathi complained. This one had three scars slashing across each cheek, and white hairs grew from them amid his dark, lustrous beard. "We waste time discussing small villages and wayward sons. We have peoples, both of us"—he included the Galla in a curt nod—"being hunted down and slaughtered. Clan Hoath has been turned away by the Lacheishi, so your strength is all we have left to ask after, but I will not waste another moment in the presence of your pet *Ymirish*."

So this man, at least, knew very well of Kern's blood, and Grimnir's brood. The Hoathi spat the Ymirish name out with as much venom as he could, and his dark glare all but threatened violence.

Kern readied himself, but Morag intervened with a dark glance and darker voice. "You'll *nay* tell me what will be. Not in mine own lodge, Hogann." He waited, and the Hoathi, recognizing his weakness, settled back. "Tell him." He nodded to Kern, but his eyes never left the Hoathi. "Tell this one what you told me."

Hogann had a large, cruel mouth that drew itself out into a strained grimace. As if he'd bitten into something distasteful. "Vanir!" he said. "By the dozens and by the scores. We held them down all winter. But then, as the snow finally thinned, they massed together behind a great northern demon and smashed at us again. And again. Always driving us back. Always clipping off a piece of our strength, here or there. The plateau's edge. Horace Falls."

He snarled at Kern, as if it had been his fault. "This last month, we gave up the Field of the Chiefs."

Even though they'd certainly heard the story already, several men among Morag's advisors made large fists. A few beat against the sides of their legs, their chests. Angered beyond simple words.

For his part, Kern was also taken with a cold, speechless fury. And he expected a similar reaction among his own warriors, and those clans who waited for word back by the lodge doors. The Field of the Chiefs was a revered place among Cimmerians. By legend, the ground where Crom battled Ymir, the frost-giant god of the north, and finally threw the great beast down in defeat. If there was a greater place of power in Cimmeria, it could only be Ben Morgh and the House of Crom itself.

And the great demon of which Hogann spoke?

"Grimnir." Kern said the name in a whisper, cautious and careful. Though even mention of the giant-kin was enough to set off new, painful sparks behind his eyes.

The Hoathi nodded. "Yea. Blood of Ymir hisself. Saw him, I did, and amazed to live to tell of it. Took a spear through the throat and pulled it out as if it were nay trouble at all. Skin like corpse flesh and the face of a beast. Half again as tall as our strongest man. Surrounded by his tall warriors, and spidery sorcerers who draw down storm clouds from the sky and raise the walking dead from the ground. Dead-frost hair, all of them. And eyes like great wolves. Eyes like *yours*."

Hogann took a strong step forward, several of his men

pressing up behind him, hand on the hilt of his sword. Madness spun in his gray eyes. A blinding rage like the kind Kern had come to know so well. Certainly a threat that anyone could recognize.

Kern recoiled, dropping back into a ready crouch. He already held a freed weapon—the only person in the room to do so—and reversed the bloody spear with a quick flourish, holding it up at shoulder level with one hand clasped just behind the blue-iron head, and his other braced against the butt, ready to thrust it home through the man's heart if he so much as took one more step.

Nahud'r and Ossian jumped forward, flanking Kern, hands to the hilts of their blades and damned be the courtesies due Morag's presence. Several more Hoathi reached for blades, and there were shouts of "Treacher!" and "Ymirish!" used as curses.

Other shouts, from the front of the lodge hall.

The sound of running feet.

A boy's laugh, as Morag's son found the sudden chaos entertaining.

The first swords rasped free, and Kern's cold flesh warmed with sudden strength as he prepared to sell himself as dearly as needs be. But the blades belonged only to the kin of Morag. Murroghan men and women who jumped forward to put a fence of sharpened steel between the Hoathi and Kern's small trio. Most of the blades pointed in Kern's direction. Most of the angry glares as well.

"Kern! Nay!"

The command came from behind him, but Kern did not relax his posture. Not when Hogann and his men had yet to back down, and so much naked steel sided against him. It took all he could do not to strike the first blow. To cut and slice and call up the strength that boiled in his blood, so desperate for release that Kern felt it charging into his muscles, taking control as his arms readied for the first, violent thrust.

Then cold steel kissed the side of his neck as Cul's sword slid up from behind, tucking a sharp edge just beneath Kern's left ear.

"Back down, Wolf-Eye." Cul's voice was soft and dangerous. His wrist a simple turn from letting out Kern's life. "If someone has to die today, it will be you."

Morag Chieftain had never left his chair, though several of his best men had crowded in around him and his wife. The boy had escaped his mother's grasp at last, though, and crouched off to one side, eyes darting from Kern to Hogann to Cul, then to Kern again. He seemed merrily excited about the idea of bloodshed in the lodge hall.

An inexcusable insult, should it happen.

"Kern?" Maev stepped up to his side, slipping between him and Ossian. Her belly brushed against him, and the spark of warmth that jumped from her to him in that moment shattered Kern's concentration.

He glanced in her direction. Read the concern and not a little fear as the tension in the room continued to mount.

"Kern." She raised her hand, slowly, and put it on his arm. Gently, firmly, she pushed against his straining muscles. "Take hold of yourself."

He tried. Desperately he tried. A violet haze, like the afterimage of a lightning strike, blurred his vision. He felt the threats building around him. Morag's men. Hoathi. Cul at his back with a blade right up against Kern's throat! Only Maev's calming words helped him reason through it. Helped him fight back the flood of power. He let his arm be pushed aside and down, lowering the spear he held until it pointed harmlessly at the lodge hall's stone floor.

Then, with a violent shrug, he slapped Cul's sword from his neck and spun away. Retreating from the chieftain's council, the Hoathi and Galla, and his own people.

"Ymirish!" Hogann's call chased after him. "We are not finished yet!"

But Kern was. For now. He was quit of the council and the company of so many men he could not trust. Seeking a quiet moment to regain his temper and control.

Before he tore the entire lodge hall down to bare, broken earth.

CUL FOUND HIM, not long after, standing down by the lake's edge. Bringing Brig Tall-Wood along.

Kern felt their approach without having to look behind him. He simply *knew*. A sound . . . a *taste*. It was there, in the back of his mind. Warm and heavy and a touch burned, like flat cakes left to the fire too long.

He grabbed the sides of his head and *squeezed*, wanting simply to push the thoughts, that dark roiling power, out of his head and away from him. Far away. It wasn't natural or sane. He shouldn't "simply know" such things. Just as he *knew* Ossian and Nahud'r waited farther up the trail, in the shadow of the lodge hall. Watching over him. Waiting for him to come back of his own choice.

Cul had never been so patient.

"Quite a display," the Gaudic chieftain said.

"Pull it back," Kern whispered, still working at his control. Staring into the sun-dappled waters. "Drown it."

He felt stronger, at least. Stronger than he had in Morag's lodge. Strong enough, now, to glance back, though he never quite released his focus on the lake. He needed something large, and calming, to help smother his roiling thoughts.

Brig did stand next to Cul, though the warrior looked less comfortable now than he had several months before, in Gaud, after helping Cul claim his place as chieftain. Nothing too obvious. It was in the way he shifted from one foot to the other. The gaze, which flicked from Kern to Cul. And the tense muscles, as if he stood ready to draw his blade at any moment in service to one, or both, of them.

A beast with two masters.

He immediately felt the worse for making such a comparison. Was this how Kern repaid a man who had saved his life several times over? Actions spoke louder than empty words ever would!

But Cul, Kern had little reason to hide either his dislike or distrust of the man. "Does Morag Chieftain summon me back?" he asked, as if speaking to a simple messenger.

Cul glowered, his face darkening. "Take care, Wolf-Eye." But he did not advance on Kern. "Nay," he finally said. "Morag Chieftain speaks with the Hoathi and the Galla. He will likely forget your outburst since the man threatened you."

He swallowed against a tight knot in his throat. Pull it back! "I did nay see your blade near Hogann's neck."

"And you shouldn't. Clan Hoath is strong, and would make a better ally than your dirtscrabble pack. Isn't that what matters? Forming the strongest alliance possible to face the Vanir?"

"If we are ever set to face the Vanir," Kern said, letting a touch of rebellion color his voice. Anger peaked up again, sending a thrill coursing through him. He recalled Jaryyd's words. "Are you certain we won't push for the highland lakes?"

Cul shrugged. "With Clan Hoath as an ally, all villages from here to the Eiglophians will flock to our standard. Clan Lacheish will nay be able to stand against us then. They will accept a peace, and an alliance, or we will crush them for good."

"You are gaining Morag's obsession with Clan Lacheish. An obsessed man does not make good decisions. Cimmeria can afford one enemy now. One! And that is Grimnir. Try to remember that."

"Did you remember it, Wolf-Eye, when you nearly caused a brawl in Morag's lodge hall?"

"I've done worse among better," Kern said. Thinking of Ros-Crana. T'hule Chieftain. Sláine Longtooth. What a force those clan chieftains might have raised!

"Kern—" Brig said, taking a warning step forward, but Cul cut him off with a raised hand, just as done with caution.

"Wolves take you back for their own, Kern! What do you think to accomplish, insulting Morag Chieftain and Clan Hoath?"

"More than you did for Gaud, cutting away at our strength right when we would need it most!"

Kern had pushed past all boundaries. He knew it. And didn't care. When Cul clawed for his sword, he leaped forward as well.

To find Brig Tall-Wood standing suddenly between them. One hand clamped around Cul's wrist, keeping his chieftain and Morag's war leader from drawing blade. The other with his own blade out and ready, brandished in Kern's direction.

"Back down! By Crom, Kern, I mean it."

Kern could have swept Brig aside with ease to get at Cul. To get at *someone*. The scent of blood was thick with every breath. He tasted the warm, metallic flavor of it at the back of his throat. His need for it drove him to the edge as power raged behind his eyes, never fully banked since the confrontation in Morag's lodge hall. Like a living thing, or a force guided by another's hand, it surged and pressed and hammered at Kern for its release.

Knowing there was such a part of him he could not control, could not understand, Kern feared it. Feared it so much he had kept a stranglehold on that pressure for several weeks. And, like any dam forced by a raging torrent, his was also weakening. Letting small trickles seep past. Bending under the weight of so much strength.

Even now, though, he refused to give in. And no matter what else Brig was about, straddling the great divide between Gaud's survivors and Kern's outcasts, his actions swept aside so easily and forgotten. By the simplest laws of nature, he had served the pack well, and Kern did not, ever, forget one of his own.

Pull it back. Drown it!

Nowhere else to go with the power raging at the forefront of his mind, Kern spun away from the confrontation and *pushed* his confusion and anger out into the lake, beneath its calm, cool waters. An instinctive reaction, but leaving him feeling the better for it. Setting himself back on even footing for the first time since entering the lodge.

It gave him control enough, for now, he managed to wrestle back the beast's great strength, caging it once again in the darker shadows. Chaining it down. Never, *never* wanting to loose it again.

Somewhere, in the back of his mind, he heard the echoes of a frustrated roar.

He looked around, sweating and spent. Brig had succeeded in pushing Cul away by several paces. But the other man's dark look promised that Kern's words would not be soon forgotten.

"We are not done, Wolf-Eye."

Kern nodded. He believed it. What was between them reached too far back. To Cul's declaring him cast out from the clan. The animosity that had always welled up between the two, even as youths.

But Kern also had something new to chew on, now that his thoughts were back in order. Something Cul had asked of him without realizing how important the question truly was. What was Kern trying to accomplish here? With the raging power no long blinding him, he still could not see an answer, and it bothered Kern more than he wanted to admit.

He looked up the trail, where Nahud'r and Ossian stood, torn between rushing down to involve themselves and wait-

ing for some call, some signal. Kern sent them one. He circled a hand overhead, then pointed off in the general direction of the Gaudic community.

They rose and set off at once, together, to round up the
others; whatever Kern had in mind.

Not much, actually. Only the shadows of a new plan.
One that needed discussing among the entire pack. Kern
waited until Cul and Brig moved off, then he followed as
well.

And none of them saw the underwater rocks, nestled in
the mud near the shore, glowing a dull, dark red as they began to boil the lake water.

8

KERN GAVE HIS warriors the week to decide.

Fate allowed them three days.

That afternoon rolled in with a taste of early summer. A cloudless, bright sapphire sky and the sun, having already crossed the line between winter and summer solstice, hanging in it fairly high, smiling down with a lasting, buttery warmth. It sparkled in a thousand tiny gems out on the lake waters. Quickly dried the morning dew. Encouraged children to leave off their chores for games of chase, stripping down naked for a dive into the lake, and playing at King Conan.

Not a game most parents approved of, of course. They might tell Conan's tall tales around fires and lodge hall feasts, but just as often his name was slapped out as an insult. A lesson not meant to be followed. Conan, for all his legendary exploits, ultimately chose to abandon his clan and Cimmeria.

And once outside the clans, forever outside. A lesson Kern had learned very, very well.

But it was hard to explain such to excitable boys and more than a few girls who used large, thick branches for swords and buckets for shields. Each staked out a claim on the green slopes rising up from Murrogh, and it became a contest of who could knock the others down, claiming the highest point for themselves. There was bruising and a great deal of laughter.

Kern watched their play for a short time while taking a break on the practice grounds. Sweaty, aching, he had dipped up a large cup of water from a nearby barrel. Now, looking up, he poured the tepid water over his face and shoulders, washing away the salty taste burning on his lips. Clearing his eyes.

The children could stay at it for hours, he knew, listening to their distant calls and their curses. Watching one get clubbed against the shoulder, hard, knocked over to tumble down the grassy slope. The other boy raised his *mighty sword* overhead in victory, shouting a high-pitched battle cry; only to have one of the girls sneak up behind him and take his legs out with a quick, vicious swipe. Then he, too, made that long, desperate fall toward the bottom, clambering right back up again.

Kings rose. Kings fell. Doing one's best in battle seemed to be the important thing.

And so it was, he decided, returning to his own training.

The clan warriors did not bother so much with tricky slopes and carefree rules. Murrogh's practice grounds sat on a wide, flat area not far from the slopes, cleared of most brush and surrounded on three sides by the Gaudic settlement and two of the larger warrior encampments. Wooden targets set up against moldering straw bales provided an archery range for bow and arrow. Cleared ground, packed down hard, for grappling and tests of strength. And several Challenge Circles set down with rings of stones or simply cut into the ground by the point of a blade.

Here the men and women rallied by Clan Murrogh wrestled and fought for wagers or simply for honor. It was where they worked hard to improve their swordplay, their fighting ability. Kern had led a handful of his men to the field today, each taking his turn inside a circle, defending against one attacker after another. Reave's greatsword. Gard Foehammer's pike. Kern's nimble blade. Others trickled in as morning turned over into afternoon, until most of his warriors and many from the Gaudic community had gathered here. Daol and Brig and Aodh split away to challenge each other with bows at thirty paces, then sixty. Desagrena watched Ossian wrestle with Mogh, offering advice on handholds. Not all of them kind.

Most, however, stayed with the Challenge Circle. Demanding, and not a little dangerous with naked blades being used to batter aside shields and sword strokes. Looking for that opening, and being able to pull away just in time to prevent real injury, it took masterful control and a disciplined mind. Not just muscle and heavy steel.

Of course, that didn't explain why Reave still held his position at the center of the circle, having knocked Kern out four rounds before, then dealing just as easily with Ehmish and Gard and Danon.

Now he fought Nahud'r, the two circling each other carefully. Like most of the Cimmerians, Reave wore nothing but kilt and boots. That and the dark thatch of hair that covered his massive chest and broad back. Sweat glistened on his face, his arms.

Nahud'r had pulled on the tattered remains of his southern-style breeks this morning, the black silk pants he'd worn when captured by the Vanir. And a loose, sleeveless jerkin. He'd cast aside the scarf he often kept wrapped about his head when traveling. The polished blade of his scimitar flashed in the sun as he shifted from one stance to another, anticipating Reave's next attack.

Reave's performance had drawn a small crowd of warriors from several different clans, men and women who stood at the edge of the circle, cheering or offering advice, or simply watching and waiting. Kern recognized a few with the scarred cheeks of Hoathi. More with the hook-shaped noses common among Clan Borat and the squared jaw of Murrogh.

And there was Mal, again. Morag's young son, left to run wild over the compound as the boy saw fit. He stood between two large men, Hoathi and Murroghan, his eyes bright and alive with interest, idly plucking long strands of dark hair from his head as if keeping score in some fashion. Like the others, he watched for the first mistake. But he did not join in with a rowdy cheer or even a child's laugh, Kern noticed. The boy stood mute, ignoring the boisterous calls of men and women who stood around him.

Some offered wagers on Reave, for his size and sheer strength. A few backed the Shemite, for his exotic appearance if nothing else.

Reave's sword point hovered about the height of Nahud'r's chest. He stayed flat-footed against the ground for greater stability. Strong, Cimmerian style. When he moved in, it was with a great leap and a savage, hoarse cry.

Nahud'r took Reave's first blow against the light shield he raised overhead, ducking beneath the attack.

His scimitar flashed back once, and again, in small, biting movements that could have cut deep into Reave's legs, his stomach. But the large man was no easy target. He pulled his sword back on guard, deflecting the fast, slashing strikes.

Then it was Nahud'r moving in on a pressing attack.

There was no warning. No shift of movement or even in

the eyes that Kern saw. The dark-skinned man sprang forward with blade flashing and striking and slashing from every direction in a whirlwind of activity. He whirled around in a graceful, dancing spin, the wide flange on the end of his sword ringing again and again against Reave's heavy Cimmerian blade. Several men hooted and cheered in delight at the performance.

But Reave was not to be bested this day. He kept his greatsword on guard, deflecting one attack after another. "Sure, and you . . . are a feisty one."

The words came out in gasping breaths, but there was a smile in his voice. Slowly he shuffled about in the Challenge Circle to turn Nahud'r in close toward the ring of stones. Too late, the dark-skinned warrior realized how close he was to the boundary, and he overreached himself trying to turn back into the center of the arena and keep up his attack at the same time.

It was all the opening Reave needed.

Knocking Nahud'r's scimitar up in a high, blocking sweep, he stepped in and delivered a heavy kick into the Shemite's gut. Nahud'r folded over, and Reave came back down with his greatsword to smack the flat of the blade against the back of the other man's neck. Another head collected.

Then Reave gave the Shemite's rump a second kick, propelling him from the circle to the cheers and laughter of many in the small audience. Nahud'r stumbled over the encircling stones and fell, but rolled off his shoulder and quickly back to his feet with the catlike grace he'd become known for among Kern's pack. The dark-skinned man rubbed at his bruised stomach, grinning wide to show his white, white teeth.

He touched his chest and his forehead, then saluted Reave with a quick wave.

"Fearsome," he said. "When your front side you offer the enemy. Not the back."

It took Reave a moment to realize Nahud'r referred to the arrow he'd taken in the rump the week before, but then he laughed full and strong. "Yea. A blow to my pride, that was."

Grinning, he waved off two new challenges by Garret Blackpatch and another from Ehmish, finally surrendering the arena. So it was those two who took the circle next while Reave and Nahud'r joined Kern near the water barrel. Hydallan also sat nearby, with the wrapped bloody spear laid across his lap. And Danon, a shallow cut on his arm being wrapped by Old Finn. Earlier, Danon had let his concentration waver. It wasn't a mistake he'd soon forget. Or likely repeat.

Reave didn't bother with the ladle, but simply dunked his entire head in the barrel, then whipped back up, spraying a sheet of water from of his long hair. "Yea. A good afternoon."

Kern agreed. Though he could hardly call himself warmed by the activity. No matter the sun or the false flush of color to his normally pale skin, inside he was chilled. That touch of winter deep down in his bones, like the cold taste that blew down off the Black Mountains.

Still, his muscles had a looseness about them that felt good. And he'd counted a strong showing from nearly all his warriors this day.

Except Danon. Who hissed as Old Finn finished tying the bandage off over the wound.

"Wallach would have bitten out a piece of your hide to go along with the gash," Kern said.

Wallach Graybeard knew more about teaching sword-play and had fought in more Clan feuds than anyone else in Kern's pack. Falling into the role of weapons master for the group, even with one hand he was as canny and savage a fighter as Kern might hope to lead.

The Taurin nodded, recognizing the truth of it. "I would have deserved the bite," he agreed. "Losing my grip that way." He glanced back over one shoulder, as if worried that Wallach might be stalking up behind him even now.

He wasn't.

In fact, Wallach Graybeard was the only man whom Kern had not seen this day. Most everyone else had taken turns with the Challenge Circle, or worked with Daol on their archery. Doing a quick glance over the practice grounds, Kern even saw Valerus, the southern cavalryman, running his mount hard along the far side of the fields, racing two Murrogh riders who sat their chargers bareback. Valerus carried one of the metal-tipped lances he favored from horseback. The Cimmerians used lighter, faster spears.

As a unit the three horsemen turned, advanced, then wheeled around and raced back in the other direction. All under Valerus's lead. Not surprising. Cimmerians were no great horsemen, even on the eastern plains. While Valerus had trained most of his life to fight from horseback.

But nay Wallach.

Mayhap he was ill. Or tired. Or simply healing, Kern decided. The older man had reopened the wounds on his wrist several times, pushing too hard as they came across the Black Mountains, and even lately in the battle at Gorram Village. Better, then, that he stay at ease. Take the entire week Kern had offered them all to rest and think about the very simple question he'd put to them.

What did they hope to accomplish?

He hadn't considered the idea that fate would intervene. Though perhaps he should have, as he saw Cul Chieftain appear on the practice grounds not a dozen heartbeats after thinking the question to himself once again.

The Gaudic leader looked less happy than at their last encounter. He strode forward as if he were crushing the life out of some enemy beneath each step, grinding his anger beneath his heels. No doubt of his destination, as he made a straight line for Kern's small pack.

So focused on Cul, Kern did not think about the clansman who followed after him. Did not recognize the man at all, in fact, until they were less than twenty paces away, and by then even Reave had noticed Cul's determined approach.

"Trouble," the large man muttered. And shifted around to put his large frame between Kern and their former chieftain.

He never reached for his sword, for which Kern was grateful. But there was no doubt that Kern's warriors had all shifted into a protective semicircle. Cul saw it as well and stopped several paces short with the other clansman stepping up next to him.

"You guested with these warriors?" he asked Kern. It wasn't a casual question, but one barked out coldly. More like an accusation.

Kern recognized the second man as a tribesman of Clan Galla by his tattoos and topknot. And yea, he remembered this one particularly by the thunderbird design stretched over his face, its wingtips slashing from temple to temple in a dark, blue band across the eyes. One of the warriors who'd captured Daol and himself on the trail over the Pass of Noose. And had later saved Daol's life from the spider's poison. One of Tahg Chieftain's men.

He also remembered the man from Morag's lodge hall, standing to one side in cautious silence as Kern's men and the Hoathi nearly came to blows. That had been three days before, and very little had filtered out into the encampments about the Galla since that time. Only some little news of the Hoathi and the talk of alliance.

"I know them," Kern finally said, not quite certain of

how the nomadic tribe viewed his short stay at their camp-site. "Tahg Chieftain dealt well with me, and this one saved the life of one of my warriors."

That got Hydallan's attention, who knew immediately of whom Kern spoke. The old man came to his feet.

"Tahg Chieftain is dead," the Galla warrior said in a gravelly, damaged voice. Kern saw the scar that slashed across his throat, still angry and weeping. No doubt a hair-breadth from having taken the man's life; it was a wound not many could have survived.

"And chieftains of t'e Black Water tribe and Stonefall tribe as well. Many of our people are dead, Kern Wolf-Eye. Women. Children. T'e Vanir and t'eir devil-masters scat-tered us from snow line to t'e lower slopes, and t'en hunted us as sport."

Though his voice was certainly not up to it, the Galla warrior recited events as they had happened after Kern's departure. It was not the anger-laced recital of the Hoathi, but far more straightforward. Speaking of their battle with Vanir and two Ymirish—one who wielded a strong blade and the other who commanded the darkest winds of the mountains. Savage creatures, striking out of the night, and the fires and bloodshed. Cut off, herded, Tahg Chieftain had commanded his people to flee down into the lower valleys.

Of thirty lives who began that final journey, not ten of them were left. Though he hoped more might still make it down off the mountain.

"Could be," Old Finn said, his voice dry and leathery, but still with some strength left to it. "That was hard coun-try up there, Kern. Good places to hide."

Reave nodded. "Worse for them once they come down. Stragglers would be easy meat for Vanir raiders. Or Jaryyd's patrols, if'n he did nay know any better."

His tale finished, the man had lapsed into silence for a

moment, mustering his strength. Now, "You offered the bloody spear to Tahg Chieftain. Will you offer it again?"

He could. Hydallan carried it just now, the token never out of the hands of Kern or one of his men. But the direct request surprised Kern nonetheless. "Morag Chieftain did not offer it to you?" He looked to Cul, who gave Kern a warning shake of his head.

"Clan Hoath is the stronger ally," Cul said. "We've no time to search for stragglers." He nodded toward the tattooed clansman. "This one would not even give his own name, speaking only for his dead chieftain and their lost tribesmen."

Mountain tradition. Names were shared between those who deserved them. Usually among warriors who had tamed the mountains for their own. Warriors such as those would make for strong allies, Kern knew. One man, or ten, Cimmeria needed to muster all the strength it could if Grimnir was to be defeated.

And like a wolf with the scent of prey in its nostrils, Kern accepted the answer he'd wrestled with for three days. Now or next week, he knew, it wouldn't change. It wasn't what he hoped to accomplish. It was that he would try to accomplish *something*. No more waiting. No more delays.

"I'll go," he said. He looked to Cul, whose face darkened with an angry flush. "With or without Morag's order, Cul. Tell him that." Then turned aside to the Galla tribesman. "I can promise you one blade at the least, ready to travel by nightfall."

He reached to Hydallan, who passed him the spear's broken shaft with its blood-crusted head and the leather tags each fastened in place behind the metal tip.

The mountain warrior never hesitated. Pulling a knife from the scabbard tied into his belt, he slashed his hand.

Dark blood welled up inside his cupped palm, then he reached out to grab the spear, adding a fresh stain. "Let our blood mix with t'ose who have already stained t'is spear. Let us fight toget'er until t'e Vanir are destroyed." He stepped back. "My warriors will be ready when you call." A pause. "Tergin promises you."

Then he left, turning away from Cul Chieftain and trotting back the way he'd come.

Which left Cul standing there alone, surrounded by Kern's warriors. Not that he showed any fear or worry of being threatened in any way. His growl was low and dangerous. "You take too much upon yourself, Wolf-Eye."

"Someone must," Kern said. "I would have left for Hoath Plateau by week's end regardless. There is nothing more for me here." Though it hurt to admit it, thinking of Maev, and her condition, and what could have been if events had happened only slightly differently.

"You make that decision for all of your people?" Cul asked. "When they have only recently come home?"

"Is this home for them now, Cul? You've guested us well, which is more than we could have asked for, but there has been nay feeling that it was anything more than that. Are you now ready to accept them back? All of them?"

"Yea! Crom take you! For the clan and Morag Chieftain and Cimmeria, I'll break tradition. All of them are welcome back. Even you, Kern."

It was an admission Kern never thought to hear. A hard one for Cul to swallow. And he never would have, no doubt, if not driven against a wall by Kern and by circumstance.

And now Kern had to throw part of it back in his face.

"Tell the others," he said to Reave, to Hydallan and Finn and Danon. "Let them all know. But I travel north this night. I've already made my pledge."

"Then we go with you," Reave said at once. Finn and Danon nodded immediately.

"Your niece, your nephew, have already lost Ros," Kern reminded him. He saw the pain flash across Reave's face at the mention of his sister, the loss reflected in the man's glacial eyes. "Kohlitt, I'm certain, would welcome you back and counsel you to stay, my friend."

"You think—"

But Kern waved him to silence. "Tell them all," he said. Then turned away, not waiting around to argue. His bedroll and a leather sack of provisions would be all he'd need. And with however many of them decided to come, he would be ready and away from Murrogh's stronghold before nightfall. As he'd promised.

Even with Cul's generous offer, he could do little else, he knew.

There truly was nothing for him here.

9

EVERY MAN AND woman of Gaud and Taur—every survivor who had survived Conall Valley and made the trip over the Pass of Noose, by whatever path—waited for Kern when he returned to the community commons later that day. Some leaned out of windows, or against an open door's jamb. Many sat in small family clusters out in front of their tiny huts.

And every one of them stood when Kern walked up from the lake's shore.

Even Cul Chieftain and Maev.

Kern was honestly surprised at the quiet demonstration of respect. As much as he was to find sixteen warriors ready to travel. Some, he'd figured, would follow. Just as he'd been certain the call of kin and community would hold some of them back. But there they were, with bedrolls lying at their feet, shields slung across backs, and leather sacks of food being hastily packed.

And grim smiles of determination. On every one of them.

Cul could not be happy to see his offer so easily rejected, which was likely why he had arranged the send-off. To put the best face on it with at least a token show of his support.

Reave was first to step up as Kern entered the commons. His bearskin cloak lay back across his shoulders, traveler fashion. He covered his chest in a thick, quilted jerkin, traded from someone since the practice grounds almost certainly.

Kern shook his head. "You'll nay listen to any good sense put in front of you. What about Ros's children?"

"Bayan and Cor? Figure I'd like to be able to look them in the face on any day after the morrow." He grinned, showing strong, white teeth. A predator's smile. "Cor wanted to come, but we talked him out of it."

"How many lumps did he take?" Kern asked, knowing the family.

Reave's smile widened. "More than a few."

Daol was right behind Reave, standing with his father. "You two as well?"

Hydallan thumped his son hard on the shoulder. "Young pup here would never forget or forgive the debt owed to you. And if he did, I'd be having to kick him hard in the arse for being so thick-witted. Where you go, we go."

Desa. Ehmish. "Yea," she said, agreeing. Ehmish nodded once, curt and strong.

Gard Foehammer and Nahud'r and Valerus waited in a trio off to one side. Men with no ties to the community, but who might have made a life at Murrogh beyond running and fighting. Old Finn stomped around at the edge of the village, never comfortable among the people who once cast him aside as worthless, ready to be off.

Garret Blackpatch handed Aodh a full-loaded quiver of arrows, then picked up his bedroll and slung it over his shoulder.

Wallach Graybeard looked a mite peaked, and pale about the eyes, but never hesitated as Kern walked up. Nor Brig Tall-Wood, who stood ready to travel though his eyes came back to Cul Chieftain as often as Kern.

And Ossian, Mogh, and Danon. The three Taurin who had chosen to follow Kern over half of Cimmeria and back again. Ossian nodded for them all. "Where you go, we go," he repeated.

Too much. All of it. Kern stood there for a moment, struck nearly dumb. "Why?" he asked in a hoarse whisper.

A shrug. "Ashul." He said it like it made the most sense of anything so far.

Except that Ashul had died terribly, stretched out in the muck at Gaud. Choking inside on her own blood until Kern had taken a blade and ended her suffering. Her dying words had accused him then. Barely able to speak, she'd coughed it out.

"Wul—Wolf! Whu—whun—One! One of . . ."

One of *them*. Of the enemy. Of the marauders who had stolen away her clan, her village, and now her life.

"Ashul," Kern said. Nodding. Ossian and the others, they sought revenge for their fallen kin. Badly enough that they'd stay with Kern even in the face of her accusation.

So be it.

He checked the sky. The sun bent low toward the western horizon. There the Black Mountains reached up to smother the warmth long before true twilight set in, but that left several good hours still. Following the lakeshore, sticking to the better-known trails, a small, strong pack could make four leagues before rolling into bedrolls for an abbreviated sleep, up and running again before dawn.

"North," Kern whispered. He found Daol, and Ehmish, gathered them in with a look and nodded them to the trail.

The three Taurin nodded a few last farewells and struck

out right behind, some of their kinsmen walking alongside for a bit. Then others drifted out after them. Aodh and Old Finn. Wallach, Gard, and Nahud'r. The others, also drifting out singly and in pairs, while Kern paused for a final word with Maev.

As he passed near, Cul stepped aside to speak with Brig Tall-Wood. Or more, Kern suspected, to avoid another exchange of hot words. Maev folded her arms across her chest and stared coldly at him. "Cul can never make such an offer again. You know this."

He did. He nodded. "Was nay a good idea to make it the first time. Too much left to do. I have to go."

"And I guess I have to stay." Her blue eyes searched his, as if waiting for an answer. Some second choice for either of them.

But once decided, Kern was not about to give up the path stretching ahead of him. He'd already given Murrogh enough of his time. And Maev had the right of it; she belonged here, didn't she. Here and safe and with a future that looked past the next meal, the next battle.

Such were their lives, now.

So he nodded, then stepped past Maev. Setting off with a determined stride that carried him from the commons, the community, and, eventually, from Murrogh. Never trusting himself to look back.

Not once.

BRIG TALL-WOOD WATCHED Kern part ways with Maev. Saw the flash of mixed anger and disappointment before she was able to smother it. Wondered if Kern had said something to hurt Burok Bear-slayer's daughter, or if she had failed to say something of importance to him.

From where he stood, it could be either, or both.

Whichever it was, it had passed quickly between them.

An awkward moment in an otherwise cold relationship. But then, how could they know anything else? The news had come home with Maev, along with the others Kern had rescued and sent back to Gaud. That she had lain with him, woke up beside him, at least twice. The once, right after her rescue. Brig had not been there that night, but he'd heard the whispers. And he'd seen it himself their last night in Taur.

And here Maev fetches pregnant with Kern Wolf-Eye's child.

Or was it?

It left him wondering what might have happened, had Kern suddenly accepted Cul's declaration to break with tradition. If he'd decided to stay.

He glanced at the man standing next to him, and saw Cul Chieftain watching her as well. Wondering the same thing? Mayhap he was.

Or, mayhap not, as Cul shifted his gaze at Kern's retreating back. "Still alive, after so many weeks. So many months." Cul spoke softly. He shook his head. "I never thought you could fail me so readily."

Brig unstoppered his flask and took a deep pull of the warm, leather-flavored water. It would be a long, hard run until dark. His body needed the water, but two leagues along and he'd have to force it down as his stomach tightened. He swallowed. And again. The two men started walking, passing by Maev without a nod or a word, Brig bringing up the rear of the departing warriors.

"It never seemed to be the right time," he finally said.

"What right time?" Cul hissed. The scar on his face, carving a twisted path from his chin to the right corner of his mouth, flushed dark in warning. "I wanted Kern dead, Brig. With or without Maev coming back, that wolf-eyed creature was never to return to Gaud."

"Then mayhap you should have challenged Kern and killed him yourself."

Where was that defiance coming from? Did he wish to remain an outcast for the rest of his life as well? But it was out before Brig thought to rein himself in, and so he stood up for it as a man should. "I say there was nay a time for it. You were not there."

"Nay time? Not in weeks of travel? If *half* the stories are true—and even that I am not certain I believe—you saved Wolf-Eye's life over the Pass of Blood. And mayhap you nearly got yourself killed for others in that pack time and again."

Truth. Brig had considered it an easy task. At first. But Kern had surprised him, the outcast being thrust into leadership when his entire life all he'd ever wanted was simply to belong. Accepting that heavy mantle of responsibility, and doing well by every man and woman who chose to follow him after the Vanir. Doing well by kin, by clan, and by Cimmeria itself. Crom's mighty blade, but Wolf-Eye had been everything Brig had thought a leader should be.

Brig had been unable to turn treacher at first, always caught out in the wrong moment, the most difficult of circumstances. Then he'd been unwilling to carry out his chieftain's order, his honor at war with his duty.

And, finally, he'd *chosen* not to follow through. Thinking that they would never see Gaud or Cul Chieftain again had made that choice easier.

Finding Gaud a ruin, and so many of his kin slaughtered, had made it hard again. Part of Brig had even accepted the destruction of Gaud as Crom's punishment for failing his chieftain, though the stronger side of him knew that Crom did not care for the affairs of mortals. Cimmeria's god had done his part, making his people strong enough to challenge life and take it on their own terms.

If Brig chose to be weak, it would be for others to punish. Like Cul.

"I sent you north, Brig. It was on my command that you left. And you were the one man among them all who would have been welcomed back to Gaud."

In time to be slaughtered, or sent running, with the rest?

Cul seized Brig's arm, yanked the other man to a halt. "So why does Wolf-Eye still live?"

"He *earned* it." Brig jerked his arm free. "Every step along the way, Cul Chieftain." Almost he'd left off Cul's honorary. Almost. But Brig could not deny that Cul was still chieftain of Gaud. He glanced at the ground. "I could not take from the man that which Crom's gifts earned."

"You mean Ymir's blood. The foulness runs in Kern's veins as surely as it runs through Grimnir's black heart. Do nay forget who he is, Brig. Do nay forget who you are."

Nay. Brig could not forget anymore what he was. What Cul had made of him. An assassin without honor. Damned to winter's ice if he obeyed. Damned just as readily if he didn't.

"Listen to me," Cul told him. Pushing him along again, the two walking past the low fortifications that protected the lakeside stronghold. "We have the men we need. Morag Chieftain would have ridden out in a few days. A week at most. Now Kern leaves early, and he still carries the bloody spear used to rally so many warriors. It raises questions."

Brig would just wager that it did at that.

"Morag has told the others that the Men of the Wolves move forward on his order, as a vanguard for our war host. But Kern must not detour into the mountains or move so far north past the Frost Swamp. Keep them in the valley, Brig. Do what you must, but keep them *here* and ready to turn back when we send riders.

"And if Kern falls, by any hand, you will take command of that pack and stand ready for our orders."

"To move north," Brig said, nodding. But Cul remained silent. "For the Hoath Plateau."

Cul stopped, and nodded Brig onward. "Stand ready for our orders," he said again.

Brig watched the other man move away. Looked for the confident set of Cul's shoulders. The proud bearing he'd always looked up to in Gaud. Talbot, Brig's brother, had once pointed out that a leader—a true leader—could be seen in the way he carried himself as well as in the way he cared for his people. And Brig had noticed, since finding the Gaudic survivors, that Cul Chieftain did not look so large and fearsome anymore.

Did he pale so greatly to leaders such as Morag, or T'hule of Clan Conarch, or Sláine Longtooth? Even Ros-Crana. Great men—great leaders—whom Brig had been fortunate enough to meet.

Or had Cul always looked this small, and Brig simply had never seen it?

"Cul."

His chieftain paused, looked back.

"Why is it still so important? Grimnir's shadow falls across Cimmeria. Gaud is gone. And for some of . . . our kin"—he nodded forward, where the rest of Kern's pack had nearly reached the lakeshore woods—"this is all they have left. Why take that from them?"

Cul glanced back toward the community he had helped rebuild. Brig saw as well that Maev, Burok Bear-slayer's daughter, watched from the edge of the commons, her raven-soft hair sweeping to one side while she hugged her midsection with protective arms. "Have you stopped trusting me, Brig Tall-Wood?"

Certainly the answer did not come as easy, or as fast, as either man would have liked. "Nay, Cul Chieftain."

"Then you only need know that it is necessary. And it

shall be done as I command it." He started to turn away, but then hesitated. "Brig?"

"Yea, Cul Chieftain."

"Gaud is not gone. Not so long as I live. Do nay forget that, either."

Brig wouldn't. That was what worried him.

That he wouldn't be forgetting that at all. No matter what else it cost.

10

STORM CLOUDS PILED up over Cruaidh, smothering the sky in a greasy, black blanket as they darkened the early afternoon with a false twilight.

Thunder cracked and rolled across the heavens. It hammered at the ground hard enough to knock warriors from their feet. Drowned out the calls and cries of battle.

Sleet fell in desperate, stinging sheets.

Swiping at the long, tangled strands of hair plastered down in front of her eyes, Ros-Crana charged ahead for the valley's engorged stream, leading forward a thick line of warriors to drive a handful of Vanir swordsmen back into its frothy waters. She held her spear high overhead, the point angled down and forward like the stinging tail of a rock scorpion. To either side of her, kin and kind bellowed with anger; slashing and stabbing as they collapsed around their enemy.

Buying themselves time. Moments, only.

With more corpses clawing their way out of the Cruaidhi funeral grounds, shambling forward with the reek of disease and soured earth, her war host hung on by its fingernails, and she knew it.

The battle for Cruaidh was now in its second day, the first taken up by a series of small, widespread skirmishes as the Callaughnan-led war host fought its way down out of those deep-snow valleys still choking the Pass of Blood. The Vanir's thin presence had been unable to hold them back. Not even when a pair of mountain yeti stormed into her line with clubs the size of small trees and banshee wails unnerving her warriors did Ros-Crana do much more than pause her rapid march.

It cost her a few good men and women, but the two creatures finally fell beneath a concerted rush, and by evening time her war host had smashed its way through to Cruaidh.

Ros-Crana had never visited this side of the Teeth before, but she'd heard merchant tales of Cruaidh and had thought well enough of Sláine Longtooth to expect a fortified village very similar to Callaugh Glen. Cresting that final ridge, she'd been shocked to look out over the valley below and see that the strongest local clan was hardly more fortified than the weakest village of the northwest territories.

A broken palisade surrounded only three-fourths of the village proper. Kern had mentioned Grimnir's devastating raid against Cruaidh, how the Great Beast had brought down part of their tall timber wall. Unable to repair it quickly, they had instead built a switchback of overlapping stone walls on that side, the tallest of them hardly more than waist high.

These repairs, plus the large, raging stream that cut through the shallow valley, were hardly a challenge for the Vanir laying siege to Cruaidh. A hundred strong at least, this northern war host, led by at least one sorcerer and a pair of Ymirish warriors.

Pushed ahead of her, now desperate for time, the raiders threw themselves at these defenses with reckless abandon and were turned away only by the determined strength of the Cruaidhi defenders, who dodged out from behind their walls again and again to grapple with the raiders. Fighting back and forth among the stone walls. Throwing the northerners back at a high cost in blood and bravery.

As darkness and black weather finally drove the combatants apart, Ros-Crana had been certain by first light the Vanir would have retreated and her host could easily reinforce Sláine Longtooth's village. And when the Vanir did not retreat, she'd made her first mistake in attempting to press through from behind.

To be surprised as reinforcements boiled out from the eastern forests.

Made to pay for each stride forward, until finally her momentum ground to a halt on the valley's floor far, far short of Cruaidh's protective walls.

"A stand-off," she complained to Dahr, fighting side by side with the Makha. A counterthrust by the Vanir stopped her line from driving the raiders back into the frothing whitewater. "We can't break past. The Vanir can't turn in either direction to finish off one force."

"Won't . . . stay that way," Dahr said, grunting through clenched teeth. "The sorcerer. . . ." He ducked aside, thrusting his shield forward to turn the heavy broadsword of a Vanir berserker and reeling backward as the heavy blade smashed and cut through the target's thin metal facing.

The sorcerer. Ros-Crana fought back the chill fingers clenching inside her gut. If she tried not to think about it, if she did not look, she could almost ignore the sour odor of graveyard earth and rotting flesh that overpowered everything else. Almost.

Not long before, she had seized high ground at the northern end of the valley, throwing Carrak forward with a

full third of her fighting force to try and force a breach in
the northern line. For a moment she'd thought they had it,
watching as Carrak seized one bridge and led twoscore
warriors across, through a wide expanse of muddied earth
thinking it was nothing more than a turned field for un-
planted crops.

The wind had howled a low and miserable call then,
wailing through the valley, and the rains—falling all day in
a miserable pour—turned icy. There had been a single
flash of lightning, sheeting across the sky, and a terrible
thunderclap.

And the first arm burst up through the earth, a hand
grasping at the leg of one of Carrak's men.

A violent swipe cut the arm in two, though its hand continued to flail and grasp at the air. Then the corpse fully un-
earthed itself. Determined to rise again though swords
hacked and beat at it, shambling forward to fall against one
of the nearest clansmen, using its teeth and claws to bite, to
rend, until finally a blade took its head and sent the horror
back into death.

The mud began to boil then, like a thick, evil soup. It
caught two men like quicksand, the warriors sinking in up
to their waists.

They yelled for help, then they screamed, as below the
surface more of the risen dead attacked. An enemy they
could not see. Killing them slowly. Ros-Crana's shaman
had deserted her then, wide-eyed and fearful as he hobbled
upstream to help as he could against such a ghastly, terrible
sorcery.

More corpses lifted out of the roiling earth, covered in
muck, their own skin sloughing away to show worms and
nesting insects dug into the rotting flesh beneath. They
pushed and herded Carrak's warriors. Ran them back for
the safety of their own lines while chasing after in a slow,
shuffling walk. A few of the risen dead disappeared into

the raging whitewater, swept downstream to be beaten against sharp-edged rocks, finally clawing their way out on the far side. Most had the mental capability to at least use the bridge.

Carrak re-formed his line, using spears and swords to hold back the shambling corpses and Vanir warriors, but again, it was a matter of time. For every corpse they sent back to the grave, another clawed its way from the funeral grounds where the Ymirish sorcerer now waited, digging his hands into the foul earth.

"Sure and here's one more!" Ros-Crana yelled, swinging her spear around in an arc to club the nearby berserker over the head. It stunned the Vanir, long enough for Dahr to slip forward and push three feet of broadsword through the man's gut.

With a violent cheer, the nearest warriors surged forward as Dahr kicked the dead man from his blade. Ros-Crana led them forward, once again pushing at the small knot of Vanir defending this side of the raging stream. A dozen of her best against nine—eight now!—northern raiders.

Seven! As another Callaughnan came overhead with a greatsword, crashing it down into a skull, splitting it in two as blood and gray matter splattered against her arm, wet and warm.

Like a flash flood the tight knot swarmed forward, breaking over the Vanir in a cascade of flesh and steel. Ros-Crana kicked one man square between the legs, doubling him over and leaving him for someone else's blade.

Spear raised high, she cut another raider away from the group, chasing him into the shallows. When the man slipped on mossy rocks and went splashing down into the whitewater, she thrust forward and down, spearing him through the chest and pinning him beneath the torrent. The frothing water ran pink, then red. Then pink again as the raider's heart gave out.

She wrenched the spearhead free and let the body get swept out into the flooded current. Wading back to shore, she dug the sopping hair from her eyes again and counted her men in a practiced glance. Two of her own were down, one missing his arm with the last of his life's blood spraying out dark and glistening over the ground, but no Vanir remained standing. She had ten strong warriors, and could throw them north to reinforce Carrak's line against the risen dead, or south where a full score assaulted a bridgehead held by just as many Vanir. Another dozen rallied to a line farther downstream; but she could see from the way their middle bent, they would be retreating soon.

Across the flood, one of the risen dead ambled along the bank, passed quickly by a half dozen raiders running downstream to join the fight at the bridgehead. Ros-Crana wanted to call for archers, but knew their bowstrings were too wet now to be of any use. The day had started with that truth and gone quickly downhill from there.

Dahr stumbled forward, also dividing his glances between the walking dead and the bridge. Blood coated the side of his head. His, a Vanir raider's—nay matter. He was alive, and so many others were not. "Cold death or warm?" he asked.

Was that her only choice? How she would die? Ros-Crana used the back of her hand to wipe blood away from the corner of her mouth. Grinned. It might very well be, she decided. But Crom's gift be damned if she'd not find a more glorious end!

"Wet enough as is," she said. And growled at the heavy skies as thunder shook the earth. Icy rain stung at her face, her arms. Her traveling cloak was a sodden weight on her back. Driving her spearhead into the earth, she grabbed out her knife and slit the cloak's leather ties, letting it puddle at her feet. Slipped the knife back into its scabbard, took back up her spear.

"Can nay get much worse."

Dahr blinked water and blood from his eyes. Followed Ros-Crana's gaze. "Wet enough? To go . . . By Crom it can, Ros-Crana! You saw the beating those corpses took. Should have killed them again."

Everyone was watching her now. She held her spear across her body, breathing rapid and deep. Eyeing the distance across the flood-charged stream. Her best jump would land her right in the worst of the frothing waters. Even if she splashed out to one of the larger, wet black rocks, and took the extra help, she'd be lucky to clear the raging flood without a twisted ankle or busted arm.

"You mean to try it," Dahr said, watching her. He swiped one hand across his face, smearing the blood and muck. "By Crom, you do."

That dark rock sticking partway out of the water. A shatter of white spray one step farther out, where there had to be another stone just beneath the surface. Might work.

"They aren't ready for us to try and cross," she pointed out.

"*We* aren't ready for us to try and cross."

"Carrak!" Her first bellow was lost in a heavy peal of thunder that exploded over Cruaidh, nearly driving them all to their knees. She shouted again, as it rolled off in the distance. Saw a vague form stand back from the line, wave a sword overhead.

"Kill me that sorcerer!" she commanded him, not knowing if he heard her or not.

"Ros-Crana!" Dahr reached a hand out, but she swatted it away and sprinted for the river's edge. "Damn woman."

Spear held crosswise, knees reaching high as her legs pumped, splashing through the water, Ros-Crana worked her balance into a forward lean. Jumped up, her foot slipped dangerously on the first black rock. It was a long stride to her second foothold, and that one a guess, but she'd committed herself. Her boot kicked through the spray, came down hard on the sharp edge of second rock. Then she *leaped*! As hard and as far as she could.

Still not far enough, but close. Another length, and she'd have come down safely, if wet, in the far shallows.

Ros-Crana leaned into her jump, bending forward as she struck down with the butt end of her spear. Putting her weight behind it as the shaft plunged into the raging stream, started to get pulled beneath her but then caught behind another underwater rock. Her muscles strained against the sudden force, but she held into it, vaulted across the worst of the rapids, and fell heavily onto her side into the shallows. Rolling and splashing forward, she tumbled up onto the far shore, barking her head against a mostly round stone, and finally ended up in a clattering pile.

Dizzy. Bright points of light swimming at the edge of her vision. Ros-Crana untangled herself, pushed up onto her hands and knees. She looked back across the waters at a mad, dancing group of warriors who shouted and waved and pointed, while Dahr launched himself at the water's edge to follow in her footsteps. Or die trying.

Lots of commotion, she decided. Pressed a hand to the egg-sized knot on the side of her head. For such an awkward landing.

Which was when she smelled it. The sour earth and rotting flesh. Sitting at the back of her throat with a slick, rancid taste.

A heavy footfall, a shuffling scrape.

Right behind her!

Pitching herself forward, Ros-Crana ducked beneath the hand that brushed at the back of her head and nearly scraped her with its diseased claws. Sprawling full length beside the stream, she rolled over with her spear in both hands, flipping it end for end to point back at her feet. At the walking corpse she'd seen just a moment before, sham-

bling alongside the stream. Which loomed above. Leaning
forward. Falling at her.

With a yell she punched the spearhead into its chest. Impaling the corpse, holding it off her. It gargled, something
between a growl and a moan. Its breath was fetid and warm
and smelled of the grave.

The dead clansman flailed with its hands, still trying to
reach her but not quite able to figure out what prevented it.
Until one hand struck the spear's shaft and fastened on by
reflex. Then it *pulled*. Burying the spear point farther into
its chest, wrenching the tip out through its back as it fought
its way down the shaft, intent on its victim.

Still trying to reach her when Dahr finally waded out of
the flood, several dozen paces downstream, and sprinted to
her aid. Ros-Crana set the butt end of her spear against the
ground by her shoulder and rolled out from beneath the
corpse's grasp.

Getting out of the way as Dahr came up fast and took
the thing's head with one hard, violent cut.

"Told you it would work," she said, struggling to her
feet.

Not for everyone. Not quite so easily. One after another
her warriors came at the raging stream. The third man
across made it about the same way she did, splashing into
the shallows and quickly wading ashore. The next few
ended up caught by the frothing waters, battered against a
few rocks before they managed to pull themselves out of
the water's grasp farther down.

The next warrior slipped on the second foothold, or
missed it altogether. He went headfirst into the whitewater,
was spun about in its merciless grip, smashed into several
underwater boulders before he went under and did not
come up again.

Her only loss. One of the women was pulled from the
waters with a gashed head. A man with a broken wrist.

"Nay my sword arm," was all he said, rasping his broadsword free from its sheath.

There were cries of victory and dismay from the bridgehead, as Ros-Crana's warriors realized their chieftain had crossed the stream and the Vanir were forced to peel away several warriors in an attempt to get after her quickly. Beyond her position, between the stream and the rock walls leading in at Cruaidh's defenses, the large Vanir host had come to that realization as well. One of the mighty Ymirish warriors quickly pulled a dozen raiders to him and split away from his fellow to stage a hasty rearguard action.

"North!" Ros-Crana ordered.

Throwing her bedraggled group upstream, into the path of two more of the risen dead, she looked ahead and across the still-raging waters. There, Carrack led forward a much larger force into the teeth of a stronger resistance. But the pressure on them eased as they trampled the closest corpses, and fewer were left to take their place.

Because the sorcerer flung them into Ros-Crana's path instead.

It was a race she could nay win, she knew. Her small band struggled toward the funeral grounds, chased from behind by a small Vanir patrol while a larger force moved in from the side to pin her back against the frothing floodwaters.

Carrak, battling his way to the upper bridge. Too many Vanir holding their ground at the water's edge.

Her forces downstream might break free, with her distracting the Vanir. But they could hardly catch up in time to help.

What she did not count on was Sláine Longtooth.

A roar of challenge rose from the palisade and stone walls. The gates, reinforced against the battering they'd taken in the last two days, suddenly flew open. Like dogs unleashed, the Cruaidhi defenders rallied, surged forward, and swept aside the nearest Vanir. These raiders died quickly, hardly knowing how or why the battle had so suddenly turned against them.

Barely understanding, in fact, that the Cruaidhi chieftain had led his charge right into their strongest position. Hacking and slashing their way forward in an attempt to reach the second Ymirish warlord.

Confusion reigned on the battlefield. The Vanir, for the moment, were divided among three masters and uncertain which they should rally to first. Some fell back from well-defended positions. Others charged forward, but without strong support. The Ymirish swordsman charging down on Ros-Crana's side was suddenly leading forward not half a dozen men, while the rest fell back to prevent a rout along their entrenched positions.

The sorcerer dug frantically at the earth, as if in search of more bodies, more demonic servants to fend off the advancing Cimmerians. The freezing sleet doubled its efforts to cloak him, falling in a hard crash and cutting visibility down to less than fifty paces.

Too late. Carrak smashed aside the Vanir and stormed the upper bridge. Ros-Crana turned her small line into the advancing Vanir force, setting for their charge and jumping in two on their one.

A pike-wielding raider leaped at Ros-Crana, but she knew the reach and speed of such a weapon better than he, obviously. Ducking beneath his wild slash, she took her war sword in both hands and slashed side to side, and back again. Laying open his thigh, his chest, then back once more to draw a dark, bloody gash right across his throat.

He collapsed at her feet, spraying warm blood over her boots, the hem of her kilt, and bare legs.

The Ymirish warrior thought to take the raider's place, rushing forward. But as he did, Dahr came at him from one side and a Callaughnan woman from the other. He deflected one with his shield, the other with a sideswipe parry. Then another of her warriors jumped forward. And a fourth. And the Ymirish went down under a swarm of bodies.

The sorcerer!

Leaving Dahr to hold on his own, Ros-Crana bent to snatch up the pikeman's fallen weapon and quickly sprinted forward for the funeral grounds. Two of the risen dead converged toward her, lurching along with their shuffling gait. She avoided both, letting them trail after her. Splashing through muddy puddles, feet digging at the soft earth as she climbed a short rise, she raced up as Carrak's line spread out in a half circle, trapping the sorcerer against the ruined, boiling pits he'd made of the funeral grounds.

The man had a shrunken, furtive manner. Like a whipped dog, quickly searching for a direction to bolt and, finding no retreat, coiling in on itself with hackles raised and a growl rolling deep in its throat. A cowardly animal, suddenly turned dangerous when trapped.

Hunched over. Head bowed and hands splayed against the fouled earth. Seemingly in defeat.

Except for the oily, dark cloud that roiled up behind him, spreading out in a demonic halo. Reaching for Carrak.

"Carrak! Nay!"

But her warning was drowned once again in a crash of hard thunder.

Clan Corag had not been involved in the battle above Conarch. No one from Carrak's village had seen the powers of a Ymirish sorcerer up close. But Ros-Crana had. And she'd seen what that oily cloud of soot and evil had done to men. Driving them into blind insanity, then death.

Carrak took another step forward, intent on the trophy, not the threat.

Never the pikeman Gard Foehammer had been, still Ros-Crana knew spears and the balance of a good weapon as well as any might. With a forward jump, she levered the point of her weapon up and over. Putting her body's entire weight behind her arm as she hurled the pike forward in a short, flat arc that barely missed Carrack's shoulder before it flashed down and speared the sorcerer through the throat. Pinning him to the ground.

Just as the tendrils of oily smoke reached for Carrak, dissipating right before they wrapped about his face.

No matter whether he'd seen the danger at the end, or was reacting to his near brush with Ros-Crana's thrown pike, Carrak stumbled back quickly. Ros-Crana slowed to a walk, coming up beside him to look at the dead sorcerer.

Standing there, the two of them, as mud-stained arms broke the surface of the boiling funeral grounds one last time. Clawed hands grasped at the sorcerer's head, his chest, and his legs. Pulled him down into the earth as easily as if the boiling mud had been the thinnest of quicksand.

Then the ground firmed, stilled. And it looked as solid as it had ever been.

"A good throw, that," Carrak said. His voice was shaky. When he looked to her, his eyes had a haunted look in them. Certainly he had seen the danger there at the end. And he was thanking her for the saving.

"Yea," she said. Panting, she caught her breath. "It was."

Already the sleet had faded back to a steady, thinning rain. Warmer. A natural fall. It sizzled at the mud, washing muck and blood from the arms and faces of the warriors standing on the slight rise.

Ros-Crana looked back down the hill and saw that it was over. Dahr had already put the Ymirish warrior's head up on a spear, parading it forward as more of their men rallied to his side and the Vanir raiders chased after their one remaining master for the surrounding forests. Few men gave chase, too happy to see the invaders away.

"Save me two Vanir for questioning," she told Carrak, "if you can find any left alive among the fallen." She

started to head down, to regroup with Dahr, then approach
Sláine Longtooth. "Gather our wounded. Get them behind
the palisade walls."

"What if Longtooth bars the gate on us?" the man
asked.

A reasonable question, perhaps, given the terms under
which the Cruaidhi last parted company from the northwest clans. But Ros-Crana wasn't particularly worried.

"He would nay dare it with me," she promised. "And I
will make certain he knows it, yea." She surveyed the valley. Its litter of bodies. "After the price we paid this day,
those walls are as much ours as his."

Still, Ros-Crana knew she would be able to enjoy them
for only a short period of time. Enough to tend her
wounded. Restock her provision sacks. *Possibly* convince a
few of the Cruaidhi warriors to join her war host and ride
for the eastern lands. Chasing after the retreating Vanir.

She wondered how many of these survivors she'd see at
the next battle. Or the next.

How many would make it to Grimnir's side, in fact, before she could ride them down and send them back to
Ymir's cold soul?

11

AFTER A PROMISING start, several days of heavy rain-
fall slowed Kern's warriors and the Galla in their trek
north. Visibility measured by a number of paces. Long de-
tours where swollen streams flooded their banks, spilling
out into dozens of small, short-lived lakes, which had to be
waded, swum, or (better) hiked around.

Even away from those many streams pouring off the
Black Mountains, in several places still the ground had
softened into mire; black loam and forest compost turned
into a thick, clinging soup that smelled of earth and damp
wood and rotting leaves. It sucked hard at the leather soles
of their boots and clung to legs and arms and the trailing
hems of waterlogged cloaks. This basically left Kern feeling as if the land itself had turned against him for spurning
Morag Chieftain's hospitality.

"Regrets?" Tergin asked when he caught Kern staring
southward again.

They stood upon a rounded knoll, away from the thick

forests but still fighting thickets and heavy brush. Ahead,
Gard Foehammer disappeared around a bend in the trail.
But they could each see a decent distance behind: the warriors struggling through a gray curtain of rain, fighting the
marshy ground.

No warming fires or dry bedrolls this night. There
would be cold meat and stale flat cakes. And worry for
those they had chosen to leave behind. Again. Regrets?

"Many," Kern finally allowed. Then a wolf's howl
turned him back around, searching the tall brush to the
north and west. Close. Very close.

He shook his head. Water dripped down into his eyes.
"But nay for being here now." He gestured back along the
trail where the Galla tribesmen mixed among his own men
and woman. "One more life saved, another strong arm
added in Cimmeria's defense, would have been worth it.
We've found seven of your kin. And there may be many
more wandering the valleys. We'll find them."

Tergin had followed Kern's gesture. Certainly counting
over and again the survivors from his tribe. With the weak
and injured and the very young left behind in Murrogh,
their fate resting on the generosity of Morag Chieftain, the
Galla had put six strong warriors on the trail heading north.
Hair shaved up into topknots. Tattoos coloring their faces,
and chests, and arms. They moved fast and quiet, and kept
to themselves more often than not.

"Four more added to t'e trail," the Galla warrior said.
"T'ree sent back to Murrogh." He nodded once. "Better
t'an we knew before." His hands clenched into fists. "And
you rescued anot'er dozen Hoat'i."

Not much of a rescue. A dozen struggling men and
women and children being chased down by half again their
number in Vanir raiders. It had been butchery, not bravery,
laying a trap alongside the trail, falling on the northerners
with bow and blade. If one of the Hoathi had nay been so

eager to charge forward, breaking the line, the small, mixed host of Cimmerians would have come out the other side without the loss of even that single life.

Of course, the fallen man's kinsmen had not seen it quite the same way. They had seen too much death and destruction at the hands of Ymirish lately to trust Kern, and only a forest of sharpened steel at his back kept several of the men from attacking him outright.

And the stories they gave grudgingly, full of broken pieces and secondhand knowledge, could have been horror tales as much as anything.

Grimnir, the fire-eyed demon, the Great Terror himself, was indeed on the plateau. He and his Ymirish brethren rampaged unchecked over the western and northern edges, putting to the torch every farmstead and village they came across. Newly budding crops were torn up. The ground salted so nothing would grow again. People slaughtered like sheep.

There were also signs of a massing army unlike anything Cimmeria had ever seen rallied against it. Clan Hoath would fall soon, pulled in too many directions at once. Then nothing stood in Grimnir's way of a full invasion of the eastern lands.

Kern feared that every bit of those stories was true.

Afterward, carrying the body of their fallen man with them, the Hoathi headed south. Dark glances were still sent in Kern's direction as if he had not done enough.

And mayhap he hadn't. If he'd moved from Murrogh sooner. If he hadn't been drawn so heavily to the Gaudic community, thinking he might actually resume his life among them.

Welcome among Cimmerians . . . a wolf. A Ymirish!

One of *them*.

"Counts for somet'ing, Kern Wolf-Eye." Tergin nodded, as if sensing the other man's dark thoughts.

"Could have counted for more," Kern said.

"Mayhap." The Galla warrior walked in silence a moment, slogging through the ankle-deep muck. He tried walking to one side of the path, but it did not help. "Still and all, t'e Sp'der's Teeth tribe is in your debt."

Kern accepted the heavy words with a nod of respect. Though nay anyone had as yet named Tergin their chieftain, not within Kern's hearing or that of any of his warriors, the Galla warrior acted as one and so obviously spoke for his people as to make little difference.

Brig Tall-Wood slogged by without a glance, keeping his gaze fastened to the trail ahead, looking like a drowned lynx with his dark hair plastered flat, hanging half into his face. Then Nahud'r, his head wrapped in thick, warm wool. And staying drier than most by wrapping a piece of oilskin over a spread branch, holding it overhead in a kind of water shield. A trick he'd learned in Nemedia, he'd once told Kern.

Next followed a trio of Galla tribesmen, who traded cold, determined looks with Tergin. Then Wallach Graybeard and Desagrena. Desa wore a conical hat she'd fashioned from a wrap of thick leather, holding it closed with a small, thin dagger pinning the ends together. It covered her oily locks and half of her face when she bent forward. Still, Kern could see she looked worried. And Wallach looked pale and feverish. High splotches of color on his cheeks, peeking out from the wiry curls of his iron-gray beard. Dark smudges beneath his eyes and a thin, drawn set to his mouth. He stumbled along the trail, as if measuring the last of his reserves. And the journey was barely a week along.

"Holding up?" Kern asked his weapons master.

"Well enough, Kern. Well enough." He put a bit more strength into his step and Desa matched him, glancing back only once to give Kern a warning glare.

At Wallach's age, most warriors were dead or living off

the charity of their clans. Kern was fortunate to have such a veteran. And he respected the other man enough to give him space. The last several months had been hard on Wallach, pushing forward before his injuries had time to fully heal. Always at the fore of any heavy fighting. Not one to back down. Ever.

Kern and Tergin fell into step behind the two warriors, following the mud-slick path down a slope, twisting around some tall bellberry brush. Ahead, another howl had Galla clansmen reaching for their blades out of reflex, had Kern's people searching the rain-drenched brush for sight of Frostpaw.

It had taken the wolf three days to discover Kern had left Murrogh and to track the small band north along the edge of the Black Mountains. The night of their last campfire, a light rain just beginning to fall, the scent of cooking meat had certainly helped lead in the animal. Tergin had shown little surprise when a pair of great, golden eyes stared back from the dark. Barely any more when Daol scavenged the guts from a rabbit he'd killed that day and slung them out into the darkness.

The large animal had skulked in carefully, obviously aware of the several new scents and the Galla's aggressive body posture—every one of them leaning forward with hands on their blades. Edged forward just far enough to snap up the bloody intestines in its powerful jaws, then retreated for the night and the thick forest underbrush.

After a moment, Tergin brushed aside the incident very simply.

"We tame t'e sp'ders," he reminded his people. Referring to their method of capturing the giant mountain spiders, milking them for their poison and their strong, spun webbing.

After that, no one bothered much if Frostpaw made an appearance or called out while on a hunt.

"Half t'e year," Tergin said now. "T'ey talk about it in t'e lodge at Murrogh. Morag Chieftain and Cul and Hogann." Kern glanced over at mention of the Hoathi who had challenged him in the presence of the others. "Told many tales of you and your Men of the Wolves. And t'e great animal that tracks you."

"Did they?" Kern asked.

He wanted to know more about what might have been said in his absence. At the same time, he did not want to attach too much importance to it. Tales were just that. Tales. They rarely told the entire truth. Often exaggerated for the sake of entertainment, Kern had also heard a few of his own moments disparaged as the work of a coward, a weak leader. An enemy.

One of them.

"Cul. He nearly shoots t'e animal, when you find each ot'er?"

"Nearly," Kern admitted.

He could not keep the edge from his tone. It was not a moment he enjoyed remembering. The night when his Ymirish heritage had bloomed into full force, the dark power singing through his veins as it tempted him toward the abyss. Knowing he could reach out and snuff the life from any Vanir, or all of them. Hearing the whispers at the back of his mind, another voice in his head urging him onward, to accept, to draw down the power and take on the mantle of a sorcerer of Ymir!

Except he hadn't been able to. Not even for the lives of his people, any one of whom could have been struck down at any moment by an enemy's blade.

But to satisfy Tergin, and distract himself, he gave a sketchy retelling of that battle. The Vanir pressing forward. The timely arrival of Cul Chieftain, leading forward several Murrogh warriors to join in the attack.

"The entire fight might have turned, yea, had Cul Chieftain not been there. At the time, I thought it strangely fortunate that another clan had been on the same path. But there were the prisoners to account for. Two were from Gaud, the others from Murrogh. Cul had come for them more than for the Vanir."

Kern wiped a large hand across his face, scrubbing the water away. Long, frost blond strands lay plastered against his forehead, down against his cheeks. He raked fingers back and through his hair, scraping them away.

"I did not know who it was, then. Even when Cul and I all but ran over each other, both chasing after the Vanir war leader. The large northerner crashed through some underbrush in his flight to escape, tripping over Frostpaw." The animal was skulking about the clearing as Kern's pack fought and bled. "I remember breaking through in time to see him raise his warhammer, ready to smash it down on the wolf's skull."

And he recalled time slipping away from him again. Slowing, as the power inside him built. But rather than loose its fury, Kern had hurled his blade forward, burying a good measure of steel into the northerner's side. Saving the wolf's life.

"Frostpaw leaped in and tore the man's throat out, ripping the life from him. Cul saw all of it, of course. My thrown blade. The wolf's savage attack."

And when Frostpaw rounded on Cul, teeth bared and a dangerous growl rolling out from that muscular chest, he'd raised his war bow to put an arrow into the beast. The power had risen and shot out from Kern before he could think about it, slicing through the bow's taut string to snap it in two before Cul could get off the shot.

It had been the first and last time Kern had consciously released the dark energies storming within him.

Even with the memory of it now, he felt the power stir in the dark shadows of his mind, begin to sing in his veins. He stifled it, as he had at the lakeside, clamping down with all the distrust and abhorrence he could summon. Pushing it from him.

"Fortunately, his bowstring snapped." It sounded like a weak ending, even in his own ears. "Must have been frayed."

"Must ha'e," Tergin agreed, deadpan.

Of course, the man spoke in such a flat voice most times, Kern could not tell if he believed it or nay.

Not that it matter for the moment. Or would come up again for some time. A shout ahead warned them of something happening, and word passed quickly back for Kern to hurry forward. With Tergin one step behind, Kern splashed and slid down the muddied trail. The thinned forest pressed in close again, and Kern pushed aside several slender branches that slapped at his face. Passed several Galla and a few of his own warriors as he hurried up on the small gathering waiting at the bottom of the brushy knoll.

Reave and Gard Foehammer held back the press, but let Kern and Tergin through to stand among a smaller gathering of Daol and Ehmish, Hydallan, Aodh, and Ossian. Daol didn't say anything, but pointed ahead where the ground opened up between a pair of towering, thick cedar.

The rain, filtered by overhead branches, fell in fat, steady drops instead of a normal shower.

Kern saw several dark-charred fire pits. Smelled the latrine odor of a slit-trench that had not been filled back in afterward.

And Frostpaw, circling a body stretched out over the muddy ground.

The wolf behaved oddly, circling with its hackles up. Back end always pointed away and muzzle twisted into a dangerous snarl, as if the body presented some new danger. It stopped. Howled short and sharp, then skipped to one side and began circling in the other direction.

The man was obviously dead. No one lay so still in the misery of the muck and rain, with a beast twelve-stone weight so close by, ready to kill. Vanir. Kern saw the red hair spread out into the mud. Missing any breastplate and helm, he still wore the heavy leather skirt of a northern raider.

"Something new," Kern said, stepping into the open area. Leading Daol and Tergin and the rest forward. Frost-paw jumped back. Held his ground a moment against the intrusion, then bolted for the nearby brush.

The others spread through the camp, encircling the fallen Vanir. Hydallan pointed out areas of crushed grasses and disturbed ground. Even after the heavy rains, the signs were there for those who looked for them. "Thirty, forty men I'm a-guessing. Yestermorn."

"How can you tell that?" Ehmish asked. He sounded torn between sounding impressed and skeptical. He shivered as if cold.

But Hydallan could be patient when teaching his craft. Tracking and hunting had been his life in Gaud. He'd taught Kern some of that, and Daol just about everything he'd ever known for either.

"They had a fire, pup." He pointed out the obvious first. "Means they found wood dry enough to burn. Can do that in the wettest weather, if'n you spend the work for it. But look there, and there." He pointed out a couple of boot prints, filled with rain. "Them's deep prints, made after the ground turned soft. A day of rain or better. Full of ground-water, so at least a half day. And the grasses are wet, but they should have started springing back if it'd been longer than two days. That sets it plumb in the middle of this Crom-cursed downpour."

"Yea." Daol nodded. "And figure they broke camp in the morning. Which is just plain common sense."

It was, when explained by a couple of veterans. Ehmish

exhaled noisily and set himself to studying the camp signs, putting them to memory.

Kern, though, had caught a strange note in Daol's voice. Something not quite normal. A dark edge. "What is it?" he asked, walking up carefully on the body.

"I'm nay sure." He wrinkled his nose. Shivered. "It's like . . . like . . ."

"Sp'der," Tergin said. He stomped up to the half-naked raider, used the toe of his mud-caked boot to turn the man's head from side to side. He leaned over to sniff deep, then hawked and spat to one side. "Scent nay washed away easy."

Kern noticed deep, sunken eyes and pale skin turned slack in death; the raider's battle with sickness was still evident. Not sickness. Poison! He smelled it as well, lying under the latrine stench like a rancid oil. A vile scent he recalled from the Pass of Noose and the great spiders that had attacked Daol and Ehmish and himself.

"Bit?" Kern looked about the forest. "Down here?"

Tergin knelt in the soupy mud. Checked the man's neck, his arms. He found it on the underside of one wrist. A blackened vein, twisting up the arm. Tinges with angry red welts. "Nay. A scratch. Put sp'der poison on t'e edge of a blade, or cake it under sharpened fingernails."

"And to know how to do this?" Kern asked.

Tergin nodded. Stood. "Galla. Had to be."

Prisoners. Taken for slaves, or a few women for entertainment. Now they knew that more of the mountain tribesmen had made it down into the lower valleys. Now Kern had a stronger goal to seize on.

"But which direction did they take them?" he asked out loud.

Back over the mountain pass? North, to the Hoath Plateau? With rumors of Ymirish welcome in the lodge hall of Clan Lacheish, they could not discount the idea of an eastward push.

"North."

Ehmish. He stood at the north side of camp, rubbing at his nose. Moved back from the nearest paths with paled cheeks, breathing very shallow and fast.

"Eager pup. You canna tell that by looking at the nearest trail," Hydallan scolded. "Paths twist and turn about. Could be they needed to hike around one of them flood-lakes."

But the young man shook his head. "North," he said again. He held his cupped palm over his mouth and nose both now. Looking seriously as if he were trying not to retch. "And I'm not reading the Vanir's trail sign, Hydallan. I'm reading what was left for us by the Galla."

Everyone looked at the body. "Him?" Kern asked.

"T'e scent," Tergin said, showing an excited and dangerous gleam in his eyes. He stepped over the dead Vanir and walked bent over toward the trail Ehmish had found.

"Whoever killed that raider knew they'd likely strip and leave the body. Best sign they could leave us." Ehmish watched as Tergin found a branch, broke it off, and carried it carefully back. "The underside of that switch is caked with the foul-smelling scent. They knew which direction they were going and left us a sign."

Tergin nodded, rejoining the group. "North," he said, backing up Ehmish's judgment.

Hydallan did not apologize for his earlier scolding. But he gave the young man a clap on the shoulder. High praise. "North," he said.

Kern nodded. He stared up through the cedar's overhanging branches and into the swollen, gray skies, letting fat drops splash into his face a moment. Drawing one last deep breath during this moment of rest. They would move hard now. Running long into the night and likely through to the next day. His eyes would find whatever thin trails there were. They'd track the Vanir and wouldn't rest until they had back the lives they'd thought to steal. Or they'd die trying, he knew.

Not too far away, directly north, Frostpaw howled again. This time the long, low call of hunger. And Kern smiled, recognizing the sound of it. Wanting to echo it himself.

His wolves were on the hunt.

12

LODUR'S FUR-LINED BOOTS hammered at the Lacheishi pier. Each forceful step gave back a hollow drumming as it echoed in the dark space between smooth-worn planks and the lake's frigid waters. Like half a hundred fists beating against breastplates.

A stiff breeze tugged at the weighted hem of his bearskin cloak. It whistled coldly against one ear, and whipped his long strands of frost blond hair to the other side.

Overhead, dark clouds rolling by on the easterly winds lowered themselves in a respectful salute to his strength. His power.

The waiting, the patience he'd been required to harbor against so many dark glances and hostile talk, it had worn on Lodur. Worn him to the point that all he'd wanted to do for days now was set this village to the blade. His blade. Torgvall's blade. So long as every one of them died, and he was allowed to feast on the taste of their deaths, it would not have mattered.

But Grimnir's touch had counseled him to patience. The Great Terror himself, reaching across the Hoath Plateau, whispered into the back of the Ymirish sorcerer's mind. All in good time, he'd been promised. And now that time was rapidly approaching.

At last. After too many days delayed along this path, the time had come to *act*. To move mountains and reshape the northern lands.

The lodge hall of Clan Lacheish rested on several large pilings driven deep into the lake bed. Narrow but long. Connected to the main pier by a well-anchored ramp. It had walls of carefully sawn planks painted with the same boiled tree sap used to stain and preserve their rafts, their docks. The hall's high rooftop had been laid out on a very shallow angle, almost flat, Lodur had discovered already. The better for clan bowmen to set up atop the lodge where they would have a commanding view of any attacking force trying to storm the piers.

He'd also seen how the different piers would be so easily hacked free, to drop their long boardwalks into the freezing waters and quickly isolate any portion of the over-lake village from the rest. To prevent the spread of fire, perhaps, or also in case of attack, as unlikely as either might seem.

Of course, when you guested the enemy within your walls, such was a greater threat than one supposed.

The lower lodge hall doors stood open, and Lodur passed through them without a worry for who might wait with a naked blade in the dark shadows to either side of the door. There were guards there, he knew. Guards he'd spotted at times before, his golden eyes pulling in the light to turn the shadows into a hazy twilight gloom. Every time he approached Cailt Chieftain there was the chance they'd

take it upon themselves or at their chieftain's word to attack him. He'd not spent so many months, as had Torgvall,
to ingratiate himself with the Lacheishi. And his great
power, wrapped about him in a dark shroud, frightened so
many of them. The simple creatures. He might have dampened the fires that now burned within him to more easily
pass for a warrior, but why should he?

Certainly not for so mundane a reason as to spare the
chieftain's pride.

Lodur wanted the man to sit uneasily. Needed Cailt
Stonefist to war within himself between the benefits and li-
abilities of any alliance with the north.

Such was Grimnir's plan.

To reach the second level, Lodur had to walk down the
entire lower length. Near the far end two wooden ramps
rose from the floor on either side of the lodge, lifting
halfway up the wall, then turning inward onto a small landing from which a final ramp led into the middle of the upper floor. He strode past two guards posted at the head of
the ramp, nodded to Torgvall, who waited just ahead, then
the two of them together approached the open wall in
which the chieftain of Clan Lacheish and the strongest
leader of all the northeast clans sat in silhouette on a heavy,
carved bench that resembled a throne so much more than a
simple chair.

The open wall was so much more than a simple window. Like gates to a strong palisade, the entire wall opened
outward by two massive doors that swung on simple turning poles resting inside of metal-forged hinges. With a
sweeping view out over the lake's gray waters, enough
daylight poured in to brighten the entire second floor. Also,
to put that light into the eyes of anyone approaching Cailt
Stonefist, leaving the chieftain's face cloaked by thin shadows while he and his closest advisors were magnificently
backlit.

Cailt's bench-throne was draped in heavy furs. White wolf and golden fox, mostly. Stonefist himself wore eastern-style leggings trimmed in rabbit, a heavy, red kilt with gold stitching, and a mantle of snowy-gray ermine the furs of which were highly prized among merchants and other clans.

Nearly as large as Torgvall, Cailt Stonefist was every stone's weight a Cimmerian chieftain. Thirty-five summers at the least. His arms were bare and thick with muscle. His hands large and scarred and clenched into hammerlike fists. He had gray eyes, much like the Hoathi, and shaved his dark hair so far back from his temples that very little grew down far enough to reach his ears.

It was the chieftain's honor to speak first in any formal setting, so Lodur stood quietly, fuming, while the Cimmerian dog of a leader looked the difference between both Ymirish, then to his most respected aides. Few of them were young men. One, with a thick fall of silver-white hair and pale skin, might have passed for a Ymirish save for his size and the dark blue eyes. Cailt's shaman.

"Torgvall promises me this is important," the chieftain said finally.

Holding on to his role, here, Lodur nodded with a partial bow. "Clan Murrogh's war host has left the lakeside stronghold. Moving north." Now he truly had their attention. Several of Cailt's advisors whispered quickly to each other. Lodur had let a trace of his power seep into his voice, coloring it with dark overtones. Making the threat sound even more dangerous than Cailt would imagine it.

It worked. Stonefist was not so easily tempted into a re-action as some of his aides, but his eyes widened ever so slightly. With the shadows falling across his face, one might not have seen it without the golden eyes of a Ymirish.

"North is the Frost Swamp and its demon creatures.

And the Hoath Plateau. Neither worries me overmuch, Lodur Frostbeard."

But Lodur heard the slight tremble in the other man's voice. The pent-up rage, the shame that had festered in this proud man for five long years and had been so easy for Torgvall to exploit.

"It is Morag Chieftain, who robbed you of your honor as well as your daughter. Does Deirdre mean less to you now that she has whelped his seed?" He pretended not to see the violent start Cailt gave at mention of his daughter's name and the reminder of the child she had quickly borne Morag. It was an open sore that could still hurt if jabbed. Could kill, in fact.

"Morag is loose with a host of better than a hundred men. Does *this* worry you overmuch?

"Yea," Cailt growled. "It might. But if he has chosen to aid the Hoathi, why should I allow our feud to interfere? It did not sit well with me to refuse them, however much you counseled patience."

A light breeze whipped through the room, coming off the lake. It tasted of fish and of ice. Torgvall faced into it without so much as a shiver. Lodur saw many of the Lacheishi huddle back in their cloaks and refrained from the same only out of sheer determination. The flame that now burned at his core was all the warmth he truly needed. Ymir's own cold fire.

"Torgvall counseled you, Stonefist. I warned you. Do not come against us on the Hoath Plateau, or we will next turn the north's entire might at Lacheish."

Cailt Chieftain pounded one large hand against his thigh. "Come and be damned, winter-born! By Crom's swinging pike, we'll send you back to the wastelands whence you came!"

Anger. Scalding and meaty and rich, like sizzling venison fresh from a skewer. Lodur hardened his gaze, letting none of his pleasure show. Anger would only work against Cailt Stonefist and toward Grimnir's ultimate plans.

With the outburst freeing up many tongues, it was Cailt's advisors who rushed now to make Lodur's arguments for him. The clan's champion, Loht, wanting vengeance for the men lost in Murrogh earlier in the spring. Two of the village elders worried about what Murrogh might do if the Lacheishi war host turned to the east.

"Also, Cailt Chieftain, think about the advantage to come after." This from a gray-haired man with a thick, unruly beard and a wily look in his eyes, like a hunting fox. "Grimnir punishes the Hoathi just as he punished Conall Valley, but he will eventually return to his homelands. Yea? Let him weaken our enemies. Let him smash Morag first. Who, then, could ever stand up to our strength?"

Next to him, Torgvall stiffened. Lodur knew then that this gray-haired fox was the man his brother of the ice spent most of his time with. Sound advice, if one ignored the supposition that Grimnir would ever return to the northern wastelands.

Nay. Cimmeria was too full of warm-blooded game to leave off now. And after Grimnir's defeat of this last winter, when the false one nearly killed the Great Devil himself, Lodur knew Grimnir would never leave off. Not again.

Not ever.

Only the silver-haired shaman stood mute. Studying. Holding his counsel.

Torgvall had warned him that the old man was a danger. Truth-sensing, he'd claimed. He'd supposedly betrayed several false witnesses to Cailt over his many years of service, and to Cailt's father before him.

Though Lodur sensed no real strength in the feeble Cimmerian, he remained determined to tell no falsehoods and would be just as satisfied for the man to remain mute, and forgotten. The pretender to true power offended him. With his master's leave, the Ymirish would have unleashed his dark purpose in an instant and left the old man dying in agony.

But not before he finished his purpose.

"I am nay here to coddle you, Stonefist. To tell you what you wish to hear." Truth, Lodur knew. "I merely pass along what I know, as Torgvall swore to you we would always do. Now I leave. Whether you wish to take this opportunity to strike at your enemy is of nay importance to me. Or to the Great One. But I will do so. My host awaits me on the edge of the plateau, and whether the Murroghan turn for your gates or nay, I will strike with all the strength at my command."

The shaman leaned forward, as if trying to hear the words Lodur did *not* say. The whispered undertones. The secrets he carried in his voice. But nay. The elderly man frowned and settled back again.

Cailt Chieftain had calmed himself. And now he smiled. "Success be yours, then, Frostbeard. That I can truly wish you, for Morag is indeed my enemy. His insult will nay be forgotten, or forgiven. But I see nay any reason to aid you or oppose you, either one."

"As you see fit, Stonefist. If I thought to change your mind, if I cared for your bloodline, I'd make a greater effort. But I weary of my time here, and I see nay any reason to delay. Strength to your people. I believe they shall need it."

Lodur had never intended to leave it at that. Though he backed away, as if finished with his interview, and turned for the back of the lodge on the very edge of what Cailt might determine an insult.

About to pause for one departing blow, when the shaman interrupted.

"Bloodline," the man whispered. His voice was thready,

as if lacking the strength to speak much more than a few simple words. "Something more . . ."

His words grasped at Lodur, stopping him midstride. And though the Ymirish sorcerer felt no stirring of true power in the room, still he rallied his own strength as if readying to defend himself. He turned back, his gaze drawn to the shaman. Ready to meet any challenge with violence.

No need. The man had spoken his piece and had given Lodur the perfect opening. "Did I nay mention Deirdre?" he asked. He feigned innocence so badly, it would take no truth-sensing to know he'd withheld it on purpose.

Cailt froze into a statue of pure ice. It radiated off him, almost at the same strength Lodur might have tasted from one of his northern brethren. But there was still a hot spike of anger buried deep within his voice. "What about Deirdre?"

Lodur smiled, and not pleasantly. "Your daughter, Cailt Stonefist. She, too, has left Murrogh. She travels north with Morag Chieftain."

A fire lit behind Cailt Stonefist's eyes. Slow-burning, but—once set—it would consume all in its path. Clan Lacheish would be heading west. Lodur did not doubt it.

The right words. As Grimnir had promised him, they could move mountains.

FOR TWO DAYS, Ros-Crana had tried to find the right words.

A way around the insult with which T'hule Chieftain had struck Sláine Longtooth after the battle over Conarch. A bid of strength, to goad the older chieftain into joining her on the paths eastward.

Now, she was down to raw anger and threats.

"You bargain your honor like a southern merchant, Sláine Chieftain! If my warriors had not bled and died for you, your walls might already be burned to the ground, your people put to the blade or dragged north in chains."

Cruaidh's entire courtyard had been ringed with tall spears hung with strips of cloth dyed gray and blue. The colors of Clan Callaugh. Within that large confine, by mutual agreement, her people were welcome and safe. Outside of the staked area, nearer the cattle yards and homes of the local clansmen, Cruaidhi warriors patrolled to keep their kin and kine safe.

Many of them, as well as small pockets of Callaugh's warriors, gathered about Carrack and Dahr with hands resting in the hilts of their blades, waiting to see which chieftain would first call for blood.

Sláine Longtooth had hardly changed since last Ros-Crana saw him, with thick, gray stubble on his cheeks and a white tuft growing out from his bottom lip. With thin, salt-and-pepper hair, hard lines around his mouth, and those pale, summer-sky eyes, no one could mistake him for anyone else. One of the oldest chieftains she had ever heard of among any Cimmerian Clan, past or present, Longtooth was an unheard-of seventy summers.

And still fit to cross blades with any of her warriors. She'd seen him fight. Knew what the man had burning deep within him when he called upon it.

Now he called down the curses of Crom on her, sputtering at the outrage of comparing his honor to one of the "civilized" bandits who bartered and cheated along the trade routes from spring through autumn.

"Woman! Your brother would have stropped a dagger across that viper's tongue of yours if he hadn't feared ruining a good blade. Narach was a pup's age by my eye, but he dealt fair once Wolf-Eye shamed him out from behind his walls."

"Shamed you both, Kern did," she reminded him. "Then T'hule Chieftain behaves like the stubborn, selfish-eyed prig he's always been, and you storm off like a bawling mooncalf. Expected him to open his gates and feast you for the next year, did you?"

"Nay more than you expect it of me now!" He gestured wildly. "What I saw outside my walls was impressive, nay mistake about it. But it returns the debt we put on you by coming across the Pass of Blood this last winter, and *nay one thing more*."

"Overbearing, ancient crust of a man!"

"Wet-eared slip of a girl!" His hand fell heavily to the hilt of his broadsword and the peace-bond stay that tied it into its sheath.

Her hand came up as if ready to draw the war sword slung across her back. "Demon seed!"

"Slattern!"

Ros-Crana reared back, ready to draw blade or rake her nails across his insufferable, arrogant face, or simply to slap him and let the insult run before injury. Instead, she beat at the air with a closed fist, half yelling, half laughing.

"Crom's sharp shaft! What ever caused Kern to think you were an honorable leader?"

Sláine Chieftain held his composure for only another few heartbeats. Then it cracked with one lip twitching. That crack let a short bark of laughter slip through, which quickly blew outward as the opening of a full-chested laugh. "Yea. The wolf-eyed one spoke well of you, and your brother, as well."

A more formal meeting, two leaders who had not known each other before, and their argument could just as easily have ended with bloodshed and a feud that might last generations. Still might have, Ros-Crana realized, as the hard laughter cleansed them both. But somewhere within the threats and the insults—unpardonable during the best of times—were two strong-minded leaders who had shed and spilled blood together, and beneath it all had a healthy respect for the other and for the man who had once brought them together.

"Narach would have come himself, I believe, if he'd lived."

Longtooth sobered. Nodded. "Sorry I was when he fell at Conarch. T'hule insulted his memory as well when he ran us off, the job half done."

She nodded, then gestured to one side as Callaugh's shaman limped up with the flask she'd asked him to hold. Arguing was thirsty work. She took a drink, then offered it to Sláine Longtooth, who started a sip for the sake of courtesy, then drank deeper and with great surprise when he discovered it was no sour ale or thin mead she'd offered. Ros-Crana had brought along a good southern wine, tapped from a cask she'd bartered out of a merchant before leaving the northwest territories. Sweet and flavored. A good token for smoothing things over.

Also, she'd wanted Longtooth to think about his last comment a moment longer.

"Why not help us finish what was started?" she asked. "By your own admission, Grimnir has torn apart every small clan and village in Conall Valley. Many of these looked to Cruaidh for protection. For strength. Nay for hiding behind their walls and letting the northerners rape our lands and people."

"Don't get us started again," he warned, taking another healthy draught. Then he handed back the leather flask, with some regret and not a little sadness.

"It is because Grimnir has gutted the valley that I can nay afford such a risk. There are clans who will never rise again. My own kin will be years in recovering from our winter battles." He hesitated. "At some point, Ros-Crana, you must look to the future."

"At some point, Sláine Longtooth, you must ask if the future is worth looking toward."

His expression slackened. "That is a dangerous path to travel. I looked down it several times this winter and spring, after Alaric was killed by Grimnir's assault on Cruaidh. Children came late for me, Ros-Crana. Getting past my son's death was nay easy."

She had not forgotten the elder warrior's pain. By all accounts—and she'd heard plenty from Gard Foehammer while he recovered at her village—Alaric Chieftain's-Son had been a man whose loss was worth grieving. But she had not mentioned him first, waiting for the father to bring up his son.

Now she slid in for the kill, or to start a real feud between their clans.

"Children have not come to me at all, yet. So I can only imagine." He nodded. "But how many more sons will be lost in the coming years, as Alaric was, how many clans will fall to never rise again, if fathers do nothing now?"

She said this low, for Longtooth's ears alone. Watched as the elder man bent slightly, shouldering more than his share of pain, awarding her a murderous glare. Then bucked up right after with a strong, dangerous gleam in his eye. A look that promised they could be allies, or enemies, and that Sláine Longtooth would give either one his all. He had lived too long, believed too much in his own legend, to let much hold him low for long.

And she knew that she had him.

"You did not learn such patience, lying in wait for an exposed throat, from your brother. Narach's anger was warm." He said this not kindly, but with respect at the least. "A wolf's tactics."

"Patient hunters bring down their kill," she said. "So long as, when they strike, they do so with ferocious abandon."

"If you go setting the hunt at Grimnir, you'll need both. It is a long trail across the valley and onto the Hoath

Plateau. And the fire-eyed demon has already proven himself impossible to kill."

She recalled something one of the Aquilonians had said at her lodge hall council. Dredged it back from memory, building on what she remembered from that final battle over Conarch. "We saw it bleed," she said. "Saw the creature in pain, and raging. Which means it fears. If it bleeds, and fears for itself, then it can be killed, Sláine Longtooth. And I will be there to see it."

Longtooth hesitated, just for the space of a single heartbeat, then nodded. "And I," he whispered. Then, stronger, "Yea. Crom hates a coward. And never meant a man of Cimmeria to live so long as I have anyway."

He held out his hand. Ros-Crana reached forward to grip his wrist; and he, hers. There were some brave cheers, more than one battle cry hollered out to see the chieftains in accord, and lots of hands beat against thighs, against chests, against shields. An ovation from warriors of both clans.

"Tell me," Longtooth said after a moment, the two of them standing there, listening to their warriors' support. His hazy blue eyes were more alive than she had seen since walking through the gates of his palisade. "Tell me, bloody spear or nay, do you believe Kern Wolf-Eye ever truly believed we'd head east? Either one of us?"

Ros-Crana wanted to say that she would never bet against what Kern Wolf-Eye might do, or even expect. Certainly he'd proven his own expectation to be high, very high. But instead, she smiled with her teeth. A predator's grin.

"Let us go find out," she offered.

13

SLOWLY, SO SLOWLY one might not notice, the elevation rose as Kern's warriors and the Galla tribesmen ran north alongside the Black Mountains. Ehmish felt the change in the air; turning thinner, colder, forcing him to breathe deep and leaving a raw ache in his chest he hadn't felt since winter'd released its stranglehold on Cimmeria.

One morning there was frost on the ground again, as the morning dew iced over. By that evening, he saw his breath frosting by the sun's dying twilight.

The following morn brought a light ground fog, cold and clammy. It seemed to flow down out of the north.

"Nearing the Frost Swamp," Hydallan said. "Might be on the edge of the Hoath Plateau by nightfall." The old man limped about camp, obviously feeling the cold deep in his joints. Stretching, limbering up for the day's run.

Old Finn was the worse for it as well, Ehmish saw. Stoop-shouldered and hobbling about, barely able to lift the weight of his own broadsword and tie it across his back.

The gout in his leg reacted badly to severe changes in weather and temperature, but the tough old bird never voiced one note of complaint. Never had, that Ehmish recalled. Not when Cul Chieftain drove him from the village. Nor when Kern expected (and at times pushed) him to pull his own weight among the outcasts.

That was the way Kern Wolf-Eye worked. He never expected, or accepted, anything less than your all.

It was the way of the pack.

Camp broke apart quickly, with stale flat cakes handed out to be washed down with a few last swallows of the milk they'd carried out of Murrogh. Water, from now on, and just as well. Days old, sloshed about, the milk was starting to turn. Ehmish filched an extra cake from Valerus and dry-swallowed a few more chunks of the crusty flatbread, preferring oats and stale grease to the chalky taste sitting at the back of his throat.

Daol and Brig ambled away from camp first, striking the trail that everyone else would follow. Then a trio of Galla warriors. Hurrying now, wanting to catch up with the front-runners, Ehmish gathered up his bedroll and one of the leather sacks filled with a share of the pack's provisions. Tucking his leggings into the tops of his boots and snugging the laces tight, he felt someone move up on his left as he checked the strap on the small buckler tied to his arm. Glanced up at Wallach Graybeard.

"Ready?" he asked. Something of a reflex, wasn't it? One man encouraging another?

Except Wallach looked nay anywhere near ready. Not to Ehmish's eyes. The man's skin was pale, cheeks sunken, eyes dark, and sweat already stood out on his forehead. Always one of the group's most stalwart veterans, today he looked wasted and abused.

He tucked twists of blackened, blood-soaked cloth under the leather cuff he wore over his amputated wrist. The one with a pike's head driven through the end, giving him a blade where his hand had once been. With a grimace of pain, he tightened the cuff's belt strap back around his elbow. Then glared sharply at Ehmish.

"Mind your own, boy," he rasped.

The rebuke stung, deeper than Ehmish wanted to admit. He'd worked hard, come a long way in the last several months. He'd killed, and nearly been killed, many times.

Weapons master or nay, Wallach had no call to be talking down to him. Then again, the man was obviously feeling ill. Ehmish decided he could overlook the slight, and slipped away to find Gard Foehammer. Gard might also speak harshly to him at times, when he thought Ehmish was still acting the pup. But he was usually game for a good wager, and Ehmish could use a bit of contest this morning.

"First man to fall back?" he asked. His breath frosted in a large cloud in front of his face.

"For what stakes?" Gard looked him over, squinting. The haze in Gard's eyes had cleared as much as it was going to, leaving a slightly milky cast over dark, fathomless blue. He still had white, teardrop scars surrounding his eyes, splashing across part of his face, from the welts raised by a Ymirish sorcerer's foul magic. An attack that had blinded him for a time, though he'd refused to lie down and die as many men might have done.

"Half a ration of meat this eve?" Hedging his wager only slightly, in case he lost. Ehmish was the faster between them, but Gard had deep, deep reserves.

"Done," Gard agreed. He immediately started forward at a strong pace, ducking around Valerus and his horse, leaving Ehmish to wait for the animal before he could follow and catch up.

Planning to race the day away.

Except the morning's ground fog only grew thicker as

the day wore on. The path, twisted. Less certain. Slowing, they worked harder to follow what little trail sign was left. The trees leaned in overhead, dripping tangled curtains of feathery moss over the trail. And there were several standing ponds to work around: old, stagnant water with broken stumps sticking out, smelling of mud and water-rotted wood, a rime of ice and black scum frozen near the edges.

From behind them Kern's wolf howled, as if calling them back. Whatever was ahead, Frostpaw wanted little to do with it.

Ehmish began to believe the same thing.

By their noontime rest with its short, sketchy meal, many warriors had clumped up behind Daol and Brig and Ehmish and Gard. Not much of a race, Ehmish decided, squatting over a patch of hard, frost-dusted ground, tearing more flat cake into small, bite-sized pieces. And he had still not forgotten the hard words spoken by Wallach Graybeard. Something in them bothered the young man more than the simple insult. He watched Graybeard move off to one side with Desagrena, letting her change the bandage on his wrist and smear a thick salve over the stump. A terrible wound, refusing to heal properly.

Ehmish knew all about that. He'd nearly been killed on the trek over the northwest territories as well. Taken a Vanir blade along his side, flaying the skin back from his left breast down toward his hip. The sword had chipped into his ribs. Scoring them. Cracking a couple.

He'd missed that final battle on the bluffs overlooking Conarch, and had never totally forgiven himself for it. He'd lain under Desa's care and the attentions of Callaugh's shaman for weeks after, fighting infection, regaining his strength, which he only recently felt he'd recovered at full measure. The scar no longer pulled too badly against his left side. And he rarely dropped back on a hard run anymore. No pain—not even that barest twinge

that had plagued him through Gaud and over the Pass of
Noose.

Starting out again, he felt healthy and strong if a bit un-
nerved for now by the forest's dark canopy. By the unnatural twilight and the shifting fog that rolled in the clammy
breeze. By the sounds of insects and chirping frogs and
creatures that scurried in the brush without ever showing
themselves.

Passable ground came in short supply as the ponds
stretched out wider and longer. An unnatural place, this. It
certainly wasn't cold enough to freeze standing water, but
ice skim over the brackish water grew thicker regardless.
The hanging moss dried and turned brittle. In some places
it froze solid, with tiny icicles burrowing through the feathery leaves.

Ehmish wondered if it were the ground itself that radiated the cold, soulless feeling. He would have voted to
skirt the edges. The Vanir seemed ready to run right
through the swamp's black, frozen heart.

It began to play on his mind. At times, walking near the
front of the line, he believed he saw shadows leaping between trees ahead of them. Silent, drifting spirits. Or there
would be a quick splash of water off to one side or the
other. A rat or some other kind of swamp vermin, certainly.
Though he wondered. He wondered. He reached for his
blade several times, but always resisted in the end, marking
it down to nerves. To childhood tales told in the dark, late
at night, and which he had not yet forgotten.

Then he saw Daol, blade naked in his hand and shield
unslung, and Brig Tall-Wood with an arrow nocked and
half-pulled, and did not feel so bad for his own fears.

It wasn't what they could see, Ehmish understood. It
was what they couldn't. The fog would thicken. Dark shadows danced and drifted inside the curtain. Arms and long,
blackened blades sliced apart the curtain in glimpses, in a

haze. Dark voices whispered at the edge of his hearing. Then the gray curtain thinned, cleared, to show an empty stretch of swamp water or maybe a thin, scraggly tree with branches reaching out like arms, or a blade. Stalks of cattailed grasses rubbed together, whispering in the clammy breeze.

There were cries ahead, and around them. The distant, mournful calls of strange birds, perhaps. Perhaps.

Then Desagrena's blade rasped free from its sheath. Tergin's as well. And strong broadswords carried by two other Galla warriors.

Ehmish looked back at those who followed. Kern, sliding his shield off his shoulder, drawing his short blade. Reave, behind him, greatsword already gripped in massive hands.

Not Gard, who left his blade sheathed but held his pike in a strong, ready grip at a crosswise angle across his body. He glanced back at Ehmish, saw his hand on the hilt of his weapon, and nodded.

Sometimes, Ehmish decided, it might not be childhood tales come back to haunt him. He recalled the stories he'd heard more recently in Murrogh. The battle Morag Chieftain fought against strange creatures on his way back from raiding Clan Lacheish. Shape-shifters, some of the tales said. Dragon-spawn, another. Ehmish wasn't sure what to believe, but certainly something out there, amid the foul waters and icy fog, had the others worried.

He pulled free his broadsword. A bit heavy for him still, but a beautiful blade he'd taken in spoils after their battle on the Pass of Blood. Chased with silver, etched along the blade on both sides with the outline of a stalking snow leopard, it was a treasure as well as a tool.

Most of Kern's warriors and at least half the Galla had clumped together within direct sight. Daol still led them forward, but cautiously.

An animal screeched nearby, in fright or challenge, and everyone started.

A pair of large splashes ahead. Another behind.

Daol and Brig turned back to back. Tergin and Kern. Reave stood alone, mighty blade up and ready, but Gard crouched down near the other Galla warriors to present as small a target as possible.

Ehmish swallowed dryly, tasting the Frost Swamp's sour odor on the back of his tongue. He crouched and shuffled over next to Wallach Graybeard, who held a broadsword in one hand, held up the pike that was his left. Both points readied, Wallach peered out into the gloom.

"Someone's out there, sure enough," he whispered. "Can nay see them. But they're . . . *there*."

He stabbed his pike-hand forward, pointing to a thin veil of mist between two leaning cypress trees. Ehmish thought he saw . . . something. A dark shadow shift from hiding behind one tree to the other. Heard a distant splash of water.

"See that?" Wallach asked.

"Mayhap," Ehmish admitted.

He searched between the trees again, saw nothing. Then followed the line back to the tip of Wallach's pike. The leather cuff strapped around the stump. The belt then laid back along his bare arm to tie off around his elbow and upper arm.

The long, blackened vein snaking up the inside of Wallach's arm! And the corrupted flesh turning black at the edge of the cuff.

Ehmish's hand shot across, grabbing Wallach by the arm to pull him closer. He could smell the corruption now. Not just the smell of the swamp, but of Wallach's flesh. The older man winced, drawing a sharp breath through clenched teeth and tried yanking his arm out of Ehmish's grip. Failed.

"Leave off, Ehmish."

By Crom he would not! Forgotten just then were the shadows. The swamp's strange noises and the sudden worries of the other warriors. Ehmish saw one of his outcast brothers in pain, and in trouble, and he acted. Standing, half-dragging Wallach up with him.

"Kern!" he whispered. His voice breaking on their leader's name, coming out as a harsh croak.

But anything he might have said, any warning, was lost as Daol suddenly yelled, "Down!" and an arrow whistled out of the shifting fog.

It buried itself in the thick bole of a nearby cypress. Then a second sank into the tree, the shaft quivering with a low hum.

Then a third arrow punched in with a more meaty *thwap*, and someone yelled in pain. And kept yelling, even as the Vanir broke from hiding and splashed at them through the muck and shallow water. As more arrows sliced in to shatter against shields or stick into trees, or be lost behind them in a whistling instant.

And Ehmish, falling hard to the ground, staring at the arrow that had pinned him through the left forearm, sticking into the wooden back of his buckler, realized only then that the warrior yelling in pain . . . was him.

GARD FOEHAMMER HAD dismissed his irrational fears of the Frost Swamp right up to the moment Daol rasped his sword free and Brig Tall-Wood nocked an ashwood shaft into the hunting bow he carried. That was when he knew it was nay just him.

Truthfully, he'd felt a prickling sensation since that dawn, when the morning fog had rolled up to surround the encamped warriors. Though there had been no danger at that time, anything that limited his vision bothered him more than he cared to admit.

An aftereffect of the sorcery inflicted on him by one of Grimnir's Ymirish.

A fear he could never bury, and he would nay have to live with much longer.

Gard's eyes would never fully heal. He'd accepted that long before, grateful his vision returned at all. Those early days had been the hardest, locked away in a dark cage, abandoned by the chieftain and clan to which he'd sworn his life. No doubt Sláine Longtooth expected Gard to release himself with the edge of a dagger some night. Gard couldn't say he'd not have expected the same if a warrior under his command had fallen to the same fate.

But Ros-Crana's shaman had thought there might be hope for his eyes. So he waited. He suffered the humiliation of being led about, for a time anyway, if only to find a better method of dying than releasing his own life's blood onto the ground. And his eyes did begin to heal, eventually. Returning to him a world of dark shadows and dimmest light. Then a gray, blurred haze. Finally, color returned to the world, though never as sharp as it had once been. As if a thin haze had permanently settled into his eyes.

He could live with that, though, for a time. To find a new life, and hopefully a better death. And he had found the former. With Kern Wolf-Eye.

Grimnir, he knew, would take care of the rest.

But the fog. It pulled a second veil across his vision and made it hard even to tell one warrior from another at ten paces. At twenty, he was lost in a gray nighttime he could never explain to anyone and would wish only on his darkest enemy. It didn't help, either, that the swirling mists reminded him so much of the oily, soot-stained cloud the sorcerer had summoned, slashing at his face, its thin tendrils burning with the touch of acid.

So, yea, he'd felt the point of a dagger digging at the back of his skull that entire day. Ehmish's challenge had been unable to distract him. And the sudden tension of the others went a long way toward proving he'd been right the entire time to hate and fear the fog. But mayhap this was it for him. The end of his journey.

Then Ehmish screamed, and fell, with an arrow stuck through his left arm, pinning it to the buckled shield he wore.

Gard leaped forward as shadows darkened against the veil of frozen, white mists. Burly men and tall, wiry women, wearing the heavy leather skirts and wide-horned caps common among the Nordheim warriors, and all with savage cries at their lips. He put himself between Ehmish and the advancing raiders without a second thought. Crom damn them all to the northern wastes again! So much as he hated to admit it, Gard had grown fond of the boy, this young man who reminded him so greatly of Alaric Chieftain's-Son. Of the charge he'd failed to protect.

Nay this time! With a hoarse cry, Gard heaved his pike forward as he might a javelin, hurling it in a flat arc to take one of the advancing raiders in the chest. The northerner's feet kicked forward, and he dropped into the swamp's evil waters with a scream of pain and a great splash.

It bought him time. A few pounding heartbeats only.

Spinning his shield off his back, he set his left arm through the leather strap and locked an iron grip on the metal handle. His broadsword was in hand in an instant. And none too soon, as the raiders swept up at the mixed group of Cimmerians, blades rising and chopping and shields ready, hurtling forward with reckless strength breaking the allied band into a half dozen smaller fights.

One of his attackers had an arrow stuck into his shoulder. Courtesy of Brig Tall-Wood, if Gard had to guess. The Vanir's blade cut through the air, and Gard ducked beneath it. Stabbed out with his own sword, and felt it turn hard off the bronze-faced shield of one of his attackers.

A second raider, a woman, slashed at him with a curved saber. Her arm was light, but fast. And any one of her slashing cuts could lay him open to the bone. He thrust his shield into her face, let her beat against it.

The two drove him back several long steps, but he held them off while Wallach Graybeard helped Ehmish back to his feet. He had very few opportunities for a return swipe, but took one when he could. The raider with the arrow in his shoulder was a mite slower than he normally would be, and Gard managed to open up a long, bloody cut down the inside of his shield arm.

As blood poured over the ground, spattered against his boots, the raider would only grow more tired all the faster. He already had the drawn, desperate wildness of a hunted man with nothing left for him but to take an enemy life with him.

In fact, he also had muck spattered to the side of his face. And slopped through his long, red braids, sticking them together. Dried blood stuck to the side of his neck from an earlier wound. From that morning, or the eve before.

The woman was also coated in muck and had twigs and leaves stuck in her wild mane of hair. And a leech, which she hadn't noticed or couldn't be bothered with, attached itself to one leg, swollen to bloating.

These weren't warriors who had lain in ready wait, fresh for an ambush.

They were battered and bloodied. And likely on the run themselves.

"Fall back!" Kern shouted from somewhere nearby.

Gard recognized Wolf-Eye's voice easily enough, though he had lost Kern and several others among the tangle of trees and hanging moss and the infernal, Crom-cursed fog.

"Set a new line. Brace up!"

Gard could hear the reason for Kern's retreat. More battle calls, howling out of the fog and screen of dark trees. A second rush of Vanir warriors. And the angry, piercing cry of a hawk, which sounded very familiar and in no way belonged to this swamp.

There wasn't much he could do without abandoning Ehmish and Wallach Graybeard, however. He did try to turn the two raiders away, but they circled back on him, forcing Gard to backpedal again. Ehmish was at least on his feet now, Gard saw. With a savage yell, he broke off the arrow pinned through his arm, casting aside the feathered end. Then, retrieving his blade, he set forward with Graybeard to split the two raiders coming at Gard.

Gard ended up with the woman coming at him, as ferocious as a maddened wolverine. Spitting mad, with a wild, berserker rage in her eyes, she slashed at him again and again. Hammering her saber against Gard's shield, cutting apart the thin metal facing, she chipped away at the target's wooden backing. When he thrust at her with his broadsword, she beat it aside with a savage backslash. Then was on him again.

Shield then sword. Sword then shield.

But never worried for the two together, Gard noticed. He immediately came at her with an obvious, overhead slash, striking his broadsword at her shoulder.

Steel rang heavily against steel as she threw every bit of her weight into a clashing blow, driving his sword to one side and stepping out from under the cut. But he was already following it up, side-arming his shield into her side. Then again, shoving her back with heavy crashing blows against her arm and her bronzed breastplate.

He cut at her again, but she beat his sword aside once more.

The target had no spiked boss, but turned to one side it had a chipped and wicked edge. Gard sliced it forward this time, raking the serrated edge across her face. It tore through skin and muscle, laying open her cheek and splitting her ear.

She reeled back, tried stumbling to one side. And Gard put a good length of steel through her side, punching the tip of his broadsword right between two ribs.

Ehmish and Wallach had taken care of their man as well. Wallach had slid his pike-hand right through the man's gut, twisting it around, while Ehmish chopped deeply into his neck. They kicked the dead man away, back into the swamp, where a darker stain slowly spread out from his wounds to color the muddied waters.

A pair of gray rats did not even wait for the battlefield to calm. They broke out of some nearby brush and rushed upon the floating body, drawn by the blood's warmth and fresh scent.

Wallach leaned up against a diseased elm, covered in a yellow-tinged bark that crumbled beneath his arm. Panting, his face flushed and sweating, he let his pike-hand hang loose at his side as if the blade were too heavy to lift.

Ehmish did much the same with the arm holding his buckler, face twisted in pain as what was left of the arrow shaft continued to dig at the wound. Blood seeped out, dribbling down his wrist and palm, running twin trails along two fingers. He rested with the tip of his broadsword shoved down into the earth.

"Which . . . way?"

Kern! And the others! Gard remembered hearing the cry to fall back and set a new line. He had barely registered, then, the shadows of Reave and Tergin and Desagrena, moving away, pursued and attacked by more Vanir.

They could hear the echoes of battle still. The yells of rage, and pain. The clashing ring of sword blades beating against shields and other swords. But those sounds twisted about in the fog, and among the moss-draped cypress and

willows, until they could have come from any direction.
And seemed to.

Gard peered into what was, for him, a dense wall of
gray cotton. He did not see the tree with the arrows in it.

Did not see the path they had been standing on before
the battle began.

If he had to guess (and it was a guess) it was back along
an unfamiliar-looking direction from which the loudest
cries *seemed* to come.

A good thing, then, that Kern broke through the fog
from the completely opposite direction. Splashing through
knee-high waters as he waved a large broadsword overhead. The gray mists swirled thickly around him, but there
was no mistaking his stringy clumps of frost blond hair, or
those great, golden eyes.

"This way," he called. "Hurry!"

His voice carried poorly across the brackish waters.
Hollow and weak, as if a distant echo. But it was Kern.

Ehmish took a step forward, into the ice-rimed waters,
wading away from the trail. And Gard moved to follow.
Wallach laid a hand on the young man's arm, though, holding him back a moment.

"A moment," Wallach said, struggling down off the
path, holding Ehmish back. Gard wondered about that.
Far, far behind them Frostpaw howled, and he glanced
aside as if searching the fog. So did Wallach and so did
Ehmish.

Kern did not.

"No time," Kern yelled. His voice stronger. He rushed at
them, kicking up a spray of muck and scummy water.
Stopped. Looked behind him as if worried for who might
be chasing, the heavy broadsword held up and out in a
guard. He backed toward them, looked back and gestured
again. "Move it, boy. The two of you drag him along."

In their months of travel together, Gard had never heard

Kern speak so sharply to Ehmish. Not for any reason.
Ehmish recoiled as if slapped.

He waded after them. Two leeches clung to Kern's
lower legs. Bloated and full. Another on his arm. He'd lost
his silver armlets somewhere in the swamp, and his kilt
was caked heavily with dried mud and blood and fresh
muck. His face thin and haggard, he looked desperately
near the end of his strength.

Or maybe it was all a trick of the poor light and the veil
of fog.

"The others!" Kern called, nearly frantic now. Closer.
Only a few steps. And Gard did hear the shouts and cries,
the crash of blades, as the three of them moved forward.

Though still, they seemed to come from behind.

Wallach stumbled forward, ahead of Ehmish and Gard,
then pulled himself upright and saluted Kern with a flourish, bringing the tip of his sword up to his forehead, and
slashing it down. "A relief," he said, "to see you alive,
Wolf."

And Kern mirrored the salute. "Nay for long, if we do
not move fast."

Now it was Gard who hesitated, and Ehmish as well.
The two of them glancing at each other, and the odd way
Wallach, then Kern, had begun to act. Wolf?

But for his part, Wallach Graybeard appeared satisfied.
He dropped the point of his blade and waded forward,
passing Kern on his unguarded side. Glanced back quickly.
"Well?" Wallach asked of Gard, and Ehmish. "You two are
nay going to come?"

Kern's glance back at them, following Wallach, was
equally frustrated.

All the more so, in the next heartbeat, when Wallach
spun hard and fast. And slashed his pike-hand right across
Kern Wolf-Eye's throat.

14

IT WOULD HAVE been hard to be more prepared for an ambush and so stunned by it at the same time.

The ferocity of the assault all but bowled Kern over at first, putting him and many others on the defensive, giving ground quickly as they traded one long step after another for time. Time to regain their footing. Time to call up those warriors who had trailed the main pack.

There were shouts along the back trail. Calling forward for the wolves and the Galla to hold, and back to rally the others. No way to know if they'd be in time. Swords rose and fell, slashing and stabbing, and Kern retreated behind his shield to let that first, maddened rush burn itself out.

Except that it didn't.

One of Tergin's men stepped forward, matching his opponent with a series of clashing parries, unused or unwilling to fight within a concerted group. Vanir to either side

turned into him and ripped their blades across his ab-
domen, his chest.

Tergin nearly gave his life away then, leaping forward
to save the man, who was already dead. Daol prevented
that by tackling the Galla warrior around the chest, lifting
and driving to all but carry him toward the back of an overmatched, bowing line.

Two raiders launched themselves at Kern, but their
swords tangled and Kern punched his short blade once,
twice into the throat of one of them. Warm blood gushed,
rushing down the length of his blade and spraying across
the back of his hand before he fell back again. And again.

Another mud-spattered warrior threw himself onto
Reave's greatsword in desperation, impaling himself with
a good arm's length of steel running out his back. Reave
dropped his blade to catch the raider's arms, the flame-
haired berserker caring only to take a Cimmerian with him
into death.

The raider spit blood, wrestling with Reave back and
forth across the muddy spit of land, taking a long time to die.

Which was when the second group of Vanir swarmed
out of the fog and frozen waters, drawn to the sound of
combat. Within that second pack stormed a Ymirish warrior with rage and glee twisting his face into a horrible
mask, wielding a large broadsword and a tall, full-body
shield. A head taller than Kern, they still shared the same
golden, lupine eyes and frost blond hair. And Kern remembered this one from Gaud. The man who had attacked
Kern's warriors among the empty shell of their former village. The one whose raiders had cost the Cimmerians
dearly, mortally wounding Ashul and leaving her to die in
the mud and filth and rain.

This Ymirish wore a thin, patchy beard, though Kern recalled it as having been full and thick at Gaud. He still
commanded a great red-tailed hawk, which circled over-

head, diving behind him again and again, emitting great, piercing shrieks.

Vengeance stirred within Kern, and for the first time since smothering the call of dark power at Murrogh's lakeside, he felt the thrust and surge as the darkness nearly burst forth again. So easy. To tap into that power. He tasted it, sharp and metallic. Felt it pounding at his temples, lighting off violet sparks at the edge of his vision.

But before any thirst for personal vengeance, there was the need to keep his warriors safe. To protect. Reave still wrestled with the dying berserker. Daol and Tergin fought side by side against a large man with a warhammer gripped in meaty hands. Brig had already cast aside his bow, broken after he smashed it across the face of one raider, and was trading desperate cuts against that one *and* another.

They could not stand now. Not against such fierce recklessness and such odds.

Which was when he gave the order to fall back. Retreat, and reset their lines.

Not that it had helped, in the end. The Ymirish warrior had whipped his raiders into a frenzy, throwing away the well-ordered battle plans he had run at Gaud in favor of a swarming, all-out attack. Kern's warriors managed a short retreat, losing Gard and Ehmish and Wallach somewhere along the way, picking up a dozen warriors as Nahud'r and Ossian led forward a mixed line of Galla tribesmen and more from their own pack.

Valerus rushed up astride his horse, but without room to build up a charge, he quickly ground-hitched the beast and set himself in line with his cavalry saber. Hydallan and Aodh and Mogh drew blades and waited. Tergin's men and a few women packed in tight. And the Vanir smashed into them like a mighty hand, breaking them into two lines and driving each side away from the other.

"Again!" Kern called out. "Back again!"

Kern held his ground to the last, turning blades aside with his shield and sword, once taking a light cut against his chain-mail vest, protected by the overlapping scale of rings. But as the Vanir pressed, he turned and fled after the others. Racing back along a new trail. Then splashing across a narrow, shallow stretch of frozen water, feet smashing large prints through the ice, busting the surface into a spiderweb of cracks and several brackish puddles. He gained dry land at the foot of a narrow hillock nearly as tall as he was. Clawed his way to the top. Set himself between Ossian and Reave, Tergin and Brig, as six Vanir warriors and their Ymirish master rushed after them.

Finally, though, the frantic energy that had sustained the enemy rush, even through several wasted and unnecessary deaths, began to fade. The Vanir raiders counted the near-even numbers. Saw Kern's group had the advantage up on the small hill. There were no more reinforcements. The battle had broken into two larger fights. From the sound of it, possibly more. Each piece was lost among the trees and the great curtains of frozen moss, the icy fog that distorted the shadows and the distant echoes of combat. Until no one could be certain of their direction.

They hesitated, calling curses down upon the Cimmerians. Waiting for the Ymirish to command them.

The frost-haired warrior grinned, feral and humorless. He stalked the muddy trail on the other side of the iced-over channel, stalking that turned into frustrated pacing. The large man frowned, as if uncertain of just what to do.

Then a piercing cry ripped through the swamp as the Ymirish's hawk dived at its master again. This time, however, it came away with a talon filled with stringy, blond hair. Claw wounds along his temple bled freely, dripping along the side of his face. More bled at his neck, Kern saw, angry and red.

Anger blazed in the warrior's eyes. He swiped at the

bird with his sword, but too late, then blotted the bloody wounds with his fingers. Stared at his red-tipped fingers.

Then, reaching up again, he scratched at his scalp as if it worried him, and came away with long strands of his own hair stuck to bloody fingertips.

"What do you wait for?" the Ymirish finally asked, staring back at his warriors. He spoke Nordheimir, of which Kern knew a few words. Enough to follow. The Ymirish man's voice had a hollow echo to it, slightly apart from the language's usual nasal flatness. "Finish them!" he yelled.

More afraid of their master than worried for his health or his sanity, the Vanir waited for no other command. They threw themselves forward, swords waving overhead, shields ready.

"Hold," Kern commanded. He waited as the raiders smashed into the ice and splashed up more of the stagnant, brackish water. Counted each step as they came across. "Hold . . ."

Reave had picked up a Vanir broadsword somewhere along the way, having lost his great Cimmerian blade in the first struggle. He looked ready to leap forward. As did Tergin. Brig and Ossian. Kern waited another desperate heartbeat. And another.

"Now!"

He rushed forward, picking up speed coming down the hill with short blade held down by his side and shield levered forward to absorb the coming blow.

Tergin got off late. But Kern and the other three came off the hillock and smashed into the raiders while they were still wading out of the ice and muck and foul-smelling waters. Reave smashed in high against one man, Ossian low. That raider went down as if running into a wall. A wall studded with sharp, cold steel.

Brig ducked a wild swing and raced forward, second-guessing what Kern was about. Kern smashed his shield into the face of another raider; the target's spiked boss rammed right through the northerner's throat.

The man went over backward, and Kern stumbled atop him before catching his footing and chasing on after Brig.

The Ymirish let them come, ready behind his tall shield, heavy broadsword waving to one side. His feral grin intact, he seemed to welcome the battle. Then, at the last possible second, his eyes flared a bright, mossy green and his features clouded over, as if drawn back into shadow. Brig startled, nearly lost his blade as he stumbled to one side, his face twisted in pain and loathing.

But Kern felt something within him *repel*, refusing the image that tried to force its way into his mind. The darkness boiled up, tearing that image apart, shredding it. Until the creature standing before him showed no face at all. Nothing but a seamless blank without mouth, or nose, or wrinkles.

Nothing but a pair of wide, green glowing eyes.

Kern *knew* then that the Ymirish he'd seen at Gaud, the man he'd thought this thing to be, was dead. And this . . . this *copy* had taken the Ymirish's place. He nearly recoiled for the strangeness of it. The horror of such a thing—whatever it was—that had taken on human form. And not just any human, but one Kern recognized. One he might have thrown away everything to get at.

But now, the glamour ruined, all that was left was shield and blade and muscle. Kern ducked its wild slash, came body to body against the swamp creature and stabbed it in the leg as he shoved himself to one side.

It came at him again. He feinted, and it bit hard on the lure, sliding its shield to one side. Kern stabbed it in the chest. In the arm. Ducked another wild slash and let his shield absorb the next blow.

Lunged forward and dug another hole into the creature's gut.

There was a good reason Wallach Graybeard had taught Kern the short sword, even if it was twice as light and several hands shy the length of a good Cimmerian blade. The same reason such a sword was often used with village youths. Kern's muscles, more used to a wood axe than the feel of a blade, had needed time to develop. And, at a thrust, short blades often equaled and at times exceeded the reach of heavier blades which favored wide, sweeping slashes. Even in the hands of a novice, the short sword was still lethal.

He was no longer a novice. Kern had grown into the weapon, and its fast, strike-and-fade style of battle. His muscles were tuned for the weight, the balance. And he had grown accustomed to his shield as well, able to work with its balance. Knowing how to dodge behind it for protection.

This copy of a Ymirish warrior had the size and strength, yea. But it had no feel for the blade. No head for battle. It was nothing more than an illusion.

Not *much* more than an illusion, anyway.

Kern jumped back as the creature drew upon its desperation and, tossing the tall body shield aside, nearly skewered him on the point of the broadsword. He slipped to one side barely in time. The blade cut hard against his ribs, but not strong enough to get through the chain-mail vest. It managed to slice a few chains apart, but that was as close as it was going to get.

Kern turned, clipped the side of the broadsword with his shield hard enough to send it flying out into the broken ice, then continued his spin to come all the way back around with the short blade, digging it through the creature's throat.

Blood sprayed out in a froth, hot and steaming as it gushed across his hands and spattered the side of his face. It spilled the way a man's might, and for a moment Kern wondered if he'd been mistaken. That the rush of power through his mind had dreamed up such a terrible creature.

But nay. The red blood turned black, and foul, as it continued to flow. And the thing screamed a high-pitched, warbling cry that no human man would ever have been able to make. Especially with a cut throat.

It staggered, fell over, kicked and thrashed through its death throes.

Kern stood over it, and watched it die.

He never thought of the Vanir left behind him. That of the four who had been left, one might follow behind Brig and him as they rushed what the raiders still thought of as their Ymirish master. Grimnir's brethren. He didn't think anything of it until Brig, crouched to one side and staring, as if frozen in place, suddenly leaped forward and slashed his sword up from an underhand arc to guard Kern's back and knock away the blade that struck at him from behind.

The Vanir had no more fight left in him other than that coward's strike. He turned and fled, running away from Brig, and Kern, and the thing he had followed in a final, futile charge.

Brig nearly gave chase, but Kern put a hand out to stop him. The raider fled deeper into the swamp, and within a few dozen steps was lost in the thick, roiling fog. A glance over at the others found Tergin standing over another body. And two more shadows disappearing in different directions while Reave and Ossian paired up to chase after as well. Kern shook his head, discouraging pursuit of the Vanir.

The swamp would take care of them.

FINDING THE OTHERS and working their way south out of the swamp took the balance of the day. Wounds were tied off quickly and slathered with lard, to be cared for later. One unconscious man to pack out between Reave and Gard. One dead body carried by his kinsmen. And four Galla prisoners rescued when Gard and Ehmish followed some desperate shouts and found them tied by stout cord and slave collars to a drowning cypress.

Two men, one woman, and a young girl.

No one worried overmuch about salvaging the dead. Lucky they were to come out with near everyone they had walked in with, plus the four more. Recovering Reave's sword and most of their abandoned gear. Losing only the one Galla swordsman, and several provision sacks to scavengers and the gathering gloom.

Even being so fortunate, Kern doubted they would have escaped before middle night, if at all, had Frostpaw not kept at his occasional warning howls. The dire wolf provided a beacon of sorts, drawing them back from the Frost Swamp's grasp. Keeping at it until Kern and the others broke out of a thicket of bellberry brush and stunted basket cedar to find the animal pacing among the leavings of their noontime camp.

It stopped pacing. Stood there a moment, golden eyes aglow with twilight's last shred, staring at the returned pack. Then the wolf turned and stalked its way south, out of the clearing.

"Never come close to setting one paw inside the Frost Swamp," Kern said.

Reave nodded. "Sure, and the dumb animal had the right of it."

Something screamed in the distance. North. Back toward the swamp. Something that might have been human.

Might not.

"Dumb animal, yea?" Mogh asked. He stared back toward the swamp. "So what's our excuse, Ox-heart?" The dour Taurin threw his bedroll down and collapsed atop it, never minding the mud and muck-soaked clothes he wore.

Kern shook his head. "Nay, Mogh. We'll not bed here."

If he wanted to argue, the warrior showed no sign of it. He merely set himself to tying the bundle back up. Reave and Gard had laid aside the Galla tribesman they'd carried out. Old Finn checked him and shook his head. With the bruise darkening alongside his head, he might be out for a while to come. If he ever woke at all.

Daol shrugged. He had his bow ready now, his sword sheathed once again, but he looked as ready as ever to strike a trail wherever Kern might point. "Want to be farther away?" he asked.

"Far as we can reach before we collapse. We move back to our morning camp and watch the swamp for a day." Another scream. Could have been an animal. "See what, if anything, comes out."

No one dissented. Ehmish glanced between Gard Foehammer and Wallach, as if wanting to ask a question. Or several. Gard shook his head, and Wallach, drenched in blood and looking far more pale than he should, merely stared right through the younger man.

None of them looked to Kern. If anything, they seemed to avoid him.

Kern let them be. What they had reported, told in hushed voices to prevent the others from hearing, would have unsettled him as well. The similar creature that he *had* seen had been bad enough. Worse, that another had worn his face.

How close had it been, to make a strong enough connection? To mimic his voice so well?

Could he have been replaced? His warriors never to know the difference?

Questions for the morrow. He nodded Daol and Hydallan onto the trail. Set Ossian and Nahud'r and Valerus on his horse to follow at the back of the line. Guard their rear and ware for stragglers. No one said another word that night, but fell to with a purpose.

No one save Reave.

"Never saw anything like that," he said. He shouldered

his half of the heavy man again, lugging the body past Kern. "Whatever it was. Nay, not a thing like that at all."

And Kern, unable to help think about what he'd seen, comparing it to Ehmish's story and considering how much it reminded him of something else, stared out into the dark, dark woods.

"I have," he said.

Then he followed his large friend, sticking close on the trail with Desagrena and Tergin following right behind. And a sinking feeling worked its way down through his stomach, nesting deep in his gut.

As worried as he was to admit it, he believed that most all of them had seen something just like that. At least once before.

15

KERN WOKE LONG before dawn with the scent of frost numbing his nose, and the skin on his arms, his chest, prickled with gooseflesh. He'd slept in his kilt and fur-lined boots, wrapped loosely in a coarse woolen blanket, his felt mat doubled beneath him for insulation. Still, the ground's chill reached through to settle a winter's ache deep, deep in his joints.

Or maybe that was just his northern blood, reminding him of his difference from the others.

He sat up once, checked that two guards remained on watch at either side of the crowded encampment, and saw Nahud'r crouched at the fire pit, quietly shaving wood over a bed of dry moss, getting ready to kindle a morning fire. Then he lay back for a time, staring up into the sky as first the grayness lightened, then deepened toward a dark, sapphire blue.

Only a few clouds passed overhead, pulled into thin, wispy threads by the building winds that swept off the

Black Mountains. But despite the clear day or prevailing winds, still the same frozen mists rolled down out of the distant Frost Swamp. His breath frosted in the air above him.

There had been no more distant screams or screeches in the night, or they were too far away to hear them.

Finally, as men and women stirred around him, he kicked away his blanket and rose for the day, joining the ragged flow of warriors as they each made a short trip into the forest to relieve themselves of a morning bladder. Coming back, Kern slipped bracers around each wrist, and his armlets of beaten silver. Donned his chain-mail vest. Buckled on his wide leather belt and short sword. Then he stomped his way around the campsite, hammering the blood through his feet. Not to warm himself—never that— but at least he could take the edge off the cold, creeping numbness.

Noon, he predicted as the sun rose fully above the horizon. Light sparkled among the thin layers of fog. It would burn off by noontime.

He would be wrong, of course.

Breakfast was a quiet, isolated meal, and the morning spent tending any wounds from the night before that had gone untouched. Kern stood over Ehmish as the boy's arm was unwrapped and the wound cleaned out again. The hole went through clean, missing bone and major veins. At Ehmish's nod, Reave brought over a heated blade to slap hot metal against the open wound first on one side, then the other. He managed to hold his yell in until the second time, and even then it came out angry and strong. A good sign, always.

Afterward, Ehmish panted, staring at the glassy burns, sweat standing out on his forehead, his upper lip. He sat up, looked to Kern. "Wallach," he said as if just remembering. "Have you seen to him?"

Only Reave and Desagrena and Nahud'r were also close

enough to hear his question. Desa hissed in a sharp breath. The two men glanced uncertainly at Graybeard, last to rise and just beginning to stir on the far side of the clearing.

"Why for?" Reave asked. "Nay saw anything wrong with him."

But Ehmish looked suddenly afraid. Not for himself, though. "His wrist, Kern."

It was more in the way Ehmish said it, Kern decided later, that sent him quickly across the camp despite Desa's call to wait. He remembered the fresh blood on bandages. The recent pale, slack skin and day sweats. An illness, he'd thought. Anything else, and Wallach would naturally tell him, get himself taken care of. Wouldn't he?

Apparently not. The old veteran was still half-dressed and had yet to strap the leather cuff over his amputated wrist. Tied only in a loose bandage of boiled cloth, there was no hiding the black corruption circling his wrist like a foul bracelet, or the dark, infected veins that bulged and twisted up the inside of his arm.

Or the stench it gave off. Wet, rotting flesh. An odor that reached back in Kern's mind to dredge up memories of Burok Bear-slayer, and the slow, lingering death the Gaudic chieftain had known.

Gangrene!

Wallach pulled his arm away from Kern's grasp. But not before Kern felt the feverish heat burning in the skin. Wallach's eyes had dark smudges under them, and his face was pale and sweating.

"Leave me be, Kern. Nay anything for it."

Now they were pulling in a crowd. Galla who looked at the wound and made a warding gesture. Looks of concern—even horror—from Wallach's companions in Kern's small pack. Brig Tall-Wood hissed through clenched teeth. Old Finn stomped away, muttering to himself over and over, "Damn, damn, damn."

"You didn't say anything?" Kern knelt on one knee next to his man. The veteran who had saved his life many times and had taught him a warrior's skills. "How do you nay say a thing about this?"

"Nothing to say," Wallach groused. He lay back on his blanket. Tired, tired. "Turned black on the way to Gorram. Desa helped me treat it. We shave the corruption away every morning. But it's in my blood now. You've seen what this does. I can only hold it off for as long as I'm able."

"We could have tried another cut. Off at the elbow." A dangerous attempt, but possible. Men lived through it. "We might have saved it."

"And mayhap we wouldn't. And there I'd be, stretched out on some floor again, fighting the tremors and the infections. And nay any use to you at all."

Wallach sat up again, struggled to his feet without help. Kern rose with him. "I thought of it, back at Murrogh. You think I wouldn't? I nay wanted to go through it again, Kern, but I thought of it. And then we're talking about the northern trek, and there was nay any time."

"You might have stayed behind."

Wallach shook his head. "Where you go"—he nodded to Kern, to some of the others who stood close by—"I go."

Crom's bloody hand! What was Kern supposed to say to that?

Not much, as Wallach pushed away from him for the nearby forest. Leaving Kern standing there. Mute. Unable to fathom the depths of such a sacrifice. For the pack? For *him?*

What had he truly done to deserve the loyalty of such men and women? Led them off into danger. Bought them a half year of hardship and pains. And each of them paid for it. They paid in blood and sweat and the scars both little and great. Reave's shoulder and Ehmish's side. Garret's eye, clawed out by one of Grimnir's snow cats. Wallach's hand, taken in that same battle. Ashul's life.

Ashul. He still could not shake the memory of her death. Lying in the muck and rainwater at Gaud. Staring up at the pack, barely seeing, as she stammered out his name.

Whu . . . Wull . . . It had taken great effort for her, choking as blood filled her lungs. *Wol . . . Wolf!*

He'd leaned in close. Wishing there had been anything to do for her.

Whu-whun . . . One of . . .

One of *them.* She hadn't finished her accusation, but Kern knew. He knew. This had been her price for leaving the clan. For following an outcast. Ashul knew it. One of the Taurin who had joined him with Ossian and Mogh and Danon. A fine warrior, and a good woman who had become important to Aodh as well; until her death it had seemed that Kern's pack led a charmed existence. Some close calls, but every warrior surviving battle, after battle, after battle.

But not then. Not at Gaud.

And not here, either. Wallach was just as dead. He just refused to lie down and accept it yet.

Finn had the right of it. Sure enough. *Damn, damn, damn . . .*

With Wallach Graybeard set in his path, refusing to discuss it any longer, the morning lapsed into an awkward silence. Finally, Kern sent out patrols in different directions, no longer willing to risk approaching the Frost Swamp but wanting to search the local area as best and as fast as they could. Looking for Galla survivors. Searching out any trace of more Vanir.

He led one of them himself, running Reave and Ossian and Nahud'r far out to the east, not stopping until after midday. They found trail sign of a small group on horseback, likely coming around the eastern edge of the Frost Swamp, heading south. No way to tell if they were Cimmerian or Vanir. Lacheishi or Hoathi refugees or even a patrol by Jaryyd Morag's-son, searching for fresh hunting grounds.

They tracked the signs for another league. Kern marked the general direction, and they returned to camp.

The frozen mists had not yet thinned or burned away, despite a strong sun climbing across the southern skies. Kern held no doubts now that the unnatural fog crawled out from the Frost Swamp, and so long as they remained in close proximity, they would feel its chilling reach.

He made plans to strike camp and move it before nightfall, but waited until the rest of his patrols all checked back.

Daol and Aodh had found no new signs to the south, but where the fog thinned, vanished game had been plentiful. Three spring-fat rabbits bagged, a grouse, and a wild boar. After losing several leather sacks inside the swamp the day before, anything that added to their provisions was a bounty. Waiting, sitting around idle while a midday meal was prepared by Finn and Desa, the warriors watched and hungered as two of the hares crisped to a light brown over a bed of coals and low flames. Juices sizzled and dripped down into the fire. The scent of meat was strong.

Strong enough, it seemed, to call back in the final two patrols.

Surely by coincidence, Gard Foehammer and Ehmish raced up before the game was half-cooked, both men winded and sweating from a long, hard run. Valerus rode in a few moments later, looking properly disgusted and not a little embarrassed.

He hitched his horse to a tree outside of camp, grabbed a scrap of wool blanket, and began to rub down the sweaty beast.

Tergin's patrol, with several of his Galla kinsmen, had the far northwestern run and were the last ones back, though they still arrived in time for a shred of fresh meat and some wild shallots Desa had discovered growing near a small stream. They also led in a pair of cautious, Hoathi warriors with a lean, hungry look about them and haunted eyes that had seen a great deal of recent fighting if Kern was any judge. Both had ritual scars slashed across their cheeks. One had a fresh scar, crusted with dried blood, stretching across his forehead.

They wouldn't say much, and when they saw Kern their first instinct was to reach for blades, no matter that Tergin had warned them. The larger of the two licked his lips and rehomed his half-drawn weapon.

"You are the wolf-eyed one, then. You fought Grimnir above the Broken Leg Glen."

How that tale had made it up on the Hoath Plateau, Kern was eager to know. At the same time, remembering how much anger and resentment Hogann had shown him in Morag's lodge, he did not want to press these men too hard, too fast. "I was there," he said simply. Then nodded to Desa, who threw each man a strip of golden skin and fresh, steaming meat.

And as hunks of meat were ripped off the rabbit, tossed from hand to hand to cool, there was finally some open talk of the night before. Talk of the battle, and the strange creatures that had grafted themselves with illusions to appear as the Ymirish, and as Kern. Their guests were let alone to listen in as they desired. They nodded at the descriptions of the swamp creatures.

And they could put a name to them.

"Doppelgängers," the smaller man said.

Hydallan started. "Heard tales o' them." The tracker was well traveled, after all, having led several raiding parties over the Pass of Noose in his day. If anyone had picked up a hint of such a creature, it would be him. "Conan fought one on the slopes of the Eiglophians."

Of course he had. The Hoathi also knew that tale. And

with their plateau so close to the Frost Swamp, they knew the creatures as a very real threat.

"Use glamour and shape-shifting to steal the guise of another man. Or woman."

Tergin nodded. The little girl they'd rescued from the swamp sat on his knee, quiet and calm as she listened to her elders talk. Kern remembered her from his brief stay among the Galla encampment. A curious, brave child.

"T'e deeper canyons of t'e Black Mountains have a similar creature," he said, and she nodded. "At times, t'ey try to take t'e place of t'eir victims. Live out t'eir lives."

"Why didn't it try to kill Kern?" Desa asked. She raked fingers back through her oily hair. "Take his place?"

Kern paced around the outside of the small gathering, keeping his distance from the Hoathi. He tore slivers of warm meat from a rabbit leg, slowly, making it last. "Never got close enough. Too many people nearby." He looked from Gard to Ehmish, to Wallach Graybeard, who had finally and reluctantly joined the group, ignoring any pitying looks. "It would have copied one of you, if it could have gotten you alone. Or killed you all. Then come back to the rest of us wearing your face."

He caught Wallach's eye, and asked, "How did you know? That it was nay me you put your blade to?"

The pale man shrugged. "Did nay move like you. Or quite sound like you, though close. Close enough, mayhap, if it weren't for the sword."

Ehmish remembered, his eyes wide. "The broadsword!"

"Yea. Kern's turned a deft hand at the short blade, but he couldn't swing a broadsword so easily if he tried." A shallow, dry grin. "Sparred you enough to know how you hold a blade, I have. And when it repeated that silly flourish, answered to 'Wolf,' I knew. Yea, I knew."

And that creature died the same way as the other. A lit-

tle less blood. More of the gushing, black ichor. It
screamed and thrashed through its death throes, tearing
large chunks of its own hair out, its face running like
melted wax.

Finally, when it had stilled, the only face left to it were
unblinking, open eyes of fading green.

"So," Reave said, "we know what to call them. We
know what they do." He slowly picked his way over the
conversation in his careful manner. "Are they any more
worry to us?"

Reave looked suspiciously at the warriors closest to
him. Daol reached over and slapped him upside the head.
Both men tried on smiles of grim humor. They suited.

Kern shook his head. "The illusions aren't perfect. You
have to be willing to buy into it. I've seen nay anyone here
acting suspiciously, or showing signs of . . . cracking
around the edges." He changed what he'd been about to
say, wanting to hold back his one, worst suspicion.

Not yet ready to put the rest of them in the same danger.

"What is our plan, t'en?" Tergin asked. He set the child
down, sent her scurrying off to her mother with a swat.
"South? West, around t'e Frost Swamp, and up on t'e
Plateau for Clan Hoat'i?"

Kern had considered this the night before on their long
trek out from the Frost Swamp and throughout most of this
day as well. Learning of Wallach's injury, if anything, had
pushed him toward stronger action. By Crom, he would do
whatever possible to repay the man's trust and his sacrifice. How could he not be willing to give up just as much?
Risk all?

"We know the Hoathi are not faring well against
Grimnir." He looked at the two warriors. They sat mute.
"The Terror has smashed several war hosts now and
pushed them out from the Field of Chiefs, even." Kern
spread his hands. "To my mind, there is nay one thing

more important than setting ourselves against the northern monster." A pause. "Unless it is to be certain we kill him this time."

"The Beast can nay be killed," one of the Hoathi said, speaking up. The larger man put out a restraining hand, but his companion shrugged it away violently. He had held this pent up within him for some time, and like a boil the poison spilled out quickly when lanced.

"Saw it, we did. Grimnir came through our lines at the head of his Ymirish and Vanir. No one stood against him long. But before Cahn Chieftain fell he put a spear through the giant's chest, skewered Grimnir through the heart, then drew his sword and ripped out the Great Beast's throat. Grimnir barely slowed. He came on, and on. Tore Cahn Chieftain apart with his bare hands." Winding down, his voice got small. "That's when we ran. Marik War-leader led the retreat. Nay anything else we could do."

"And Grimnir not chases you down?" Ossian asked, skeptical. "Finishes you off?"

Now it was the larger Hoathi who shook his head. "He sent a Ymirish-led war host after us. As many Vanir running the plateau as there are, he can pick and choose. Mayhap Cahn Chieftain wounded the Beast badly." A shrug. "Mayhap rumors of a western host come through Cruaidh are true, and he turned to deal with them."

Suddenly, the entire gathering was on its feet. Excited and not a little strident.

"A western host?" Daol asked.

"Cruaidh?"

"Is it Sláine Longtooth?"

The questions hammered thick and hard at the Hoathi from all sides. Beat them back into silence before Kern regained control. But they truly could not—or would not—answer anything more. What they knew came (supposedly) from captured and questioned Vanir who had been in a large battle at or near Cruaidh. Marik War-leader sent some men running west, to discover the truth, and these two for the south, to seek further aid from Clan Murrogh. They had no chieftain, so no bloody spear had been sent. Standing by traditions most cautiously. They knew that, but little else of the final rumors being whispered among veterans, except the host was supposedly led forward by a strong woman with a sharp tongue.

Ros-Crana!

Kern wanted to believe that. But with the Hoath Plateau between them, there was little he could do nay already being done.

"If it is truth," Kern said. He waved down the shouts and questions. "*If*," he said, "then mayhap there are enough Cimmerians rallying to put Grimnir on the defensive, to drive him from our lands once and for all times." He stared them down, each one. "Mayhap to kill him."

"But how?" Desa asked. "You near sacrificed yourself the last time, and still the Terror lives. Hurt the Beast, yea. You did that. Riled him as well, I'd say."

And set the giant-kin and his hordes to marauding through Conall Valley. Wiping out villages, entire clans, in his fury. Kern caught the dark looks cast in his direction by the Hoathi, but set them aside just as easy. He already knew the consequences that hung over his head.

Knew the price he was willing to pay for them.

"I can nay tell you how it can be done," he finally said. "But alone, I do know we will fail. We *need* Murrogh." He looked into the distance. Then back at his warriors, and at the Galla and the Hoathi. The bright, normal eyes that met his golden gaze without flinching. Waiting.

"I intend to deliver them," he promised. "One way or another."

That started a new round of chaos. Discussion. And several arguments. Of the best path by which to return to

Murrogh. The best way to convince Morag of the need, the desperate need, to strike now. If Clan Murrogh's war host would even be strong enough, with or without aid from the west, and how fast the Cimmerian host might travel north and whether it would be in time to save the Hoathi.

"Listen. Listen!" Kern shouted them all down and stared them back to their places. Only Tergin and the Hoathi remained on their feet. The rest squatted, or grabbed a knee, or rested back on their haunches. Kern crouched to their level, rubbing one hand over his face, knowing the argument he'd receive.

"We do not have time for much discussion. This is best done quickly. I leave before nightfall, and no one else—no one else!—will follow." He stared back at several dark glares. Swallowed heavily. "It's six days back to Murrogh under the best circumstance. I can cut that by two, running at night. No one else can see the trails as well as I do, and I won't be able to slow for you."

As good an excuse as any. And it happened to be truth, with his golden eyes allowing him to see on the darkest nights as well as most could near the end of twilight. With a moon up, he would hardly be slowed at all. It didn't matter that it was hardly the reason he wanted no company.

"Clan Murrogh will march north. That I promise you. Stand ready for them." He noticed Brig startle. "Be ready to lead them around the swamp, up onto the plateau."

There were confused expressions, and a dark glower out of Daol and Reave, who may have heard the finality in Kern's tone. Might know him well enough to raise an objection, a question, and ruin his plan entirely. But Brig spoke up first, and after that, no one had time to even think to question Kern. They would all be too shocked.

"Morag isn't six days back, Kern." Brig stood, drawing all attention to him. "He's two." The man swallowed hard, but his stare was without any hesitation. "He left Murrogh four days back if they held to plan."

Silence reigned. And suspicion. Kern ignored the others, keeping his place and his gaze leveled on Brig Tall-Wood. "What plan?" he asked.

"The one Cul Chieftain warned me of the day we left. Morag would rally every man and woman he could, leaving a token force to defend Murrogh, and follow us north. We were never to go past the Frost Swamp, and not up into the mountains, and stand ready to turn back as vanguard to the army."

Kern could think of only one way Brig might have been able to ensure that. And then he knew—he *knew*—the secret Brig had carried with him since arriving that morning with Hydallan and Garret. Cul's order. Of course, he'd had suspicions before. But nothing he could act upon.

Yet here was Brig, offering up proof at last. Kern stared evenly at him. Cocked his head to one side in an unspoken question. Brig nodded.

Kern could hardly imagine the private war Brig must have waged with himself every step along the way. How he could have held off for so long. How many times had Kern handed Brig a perfect chance . . . to kill him?

How many times had the man instead saved Kern's life?

"By Crom and Cimmeria, Brig. Is there anything else?"

The warrior hesitated, considered, then nodded once. "Nothing absolute," he promised. And Kern believed him. "But I do not believe Morag has any intention of setting foot on the plateau."

Lacheish! Kern stood now, feeling the need to draw his sword and rail at the skies. Instead, he paced hard along the edge of the gathered warriors.

Of course Morag would take the opportunity to strike at his strongest rival for dominance in the east. It was what Jaryyd had warned—and what Kern had feared—from the start. And no matter what he vowed among the other chieftains, or to the warriors under his command, it would take the slightest provocation only to turn their rage away from where it belonged.

And why would Morag care?

"Trail sign!" Nahud'r shifted. He turned to the others, and explained what Kern's patrol had found on their eastern run. "Could be . . . word . . . flank! Flanking patrol for Lacheishi war host. If right, Morag wants Cailt Stonefist come after him."

Crom's treacherous blade! Morag would not be the only one to want this. More and more, things made sense now. Ymirish advisors in the lodge hall of Clan Lacheish? What would serve Grimnir's purpose better than to hold back one of the east's strongest clans, then set them against their feuding cousins. Put both war hosts in the same area, at near the same time, and Cimmerian tempers would do half of Grimnir's work for him.

Which put Cailt Stonefist south of the swamp! Closer to Morag and the Murrogh war host than Kern!

Moving quickly, Kern left the gathering and collected his bedroll, checking to be certain he had the bloody spear and only the most basic provisions. Flask of water. Some dried oat cakes and a few small twists of dried beef. The others stood, milled about, waiting for his order. But Kern saw only one chance. He had to race ahead as hard as possible, then run through the night. So many hours lost! The only way he saw through the other side, before Cailt and Morag came to blows, was to swallow his pride and take advantage of a particular resource.

"Valerus!" Kern called over to the Aquilonian. The cavalryman elbowed his way forward, stood stiffly as he often had before Strom, the Aquilonian officer who had left Valerus in Kern's keeping. "Valerus. I need your horse."

To his credit, the southern soldier hesitated only an instant. "You have it," he said. And ran to saddle and fetch the beast. It took a moment, but he was done nearly as fast as Kern, who was handing out quick orders to Daol and Ossian and, yea, Brig as well.

Kern did not remember the animal being quite so large. Or so busy. Stamping one foot, then another. Always shifting. Head shaking about and a tail whisking back and forth, back and forth. It smelled of leather and sweat and nervousness.

Or mayhap that last was Kern.

"You mount on the left," Valerus said, dragging Kern to the proper side. He steadied the horse's head while Kern climbed awkwardly into the saddle. The horse seemed to sense its rider's trouble, Kern's hesitant nature, and it stamped impatiently. Valerus soothed it with steady, strong pats.

"Use the reins sparingly. She'll take her head on long stretches, and you can guide her with your legs once you get moving. Hold yourself off the leather on a canter, or she'll slam your backbone up through your skull in short order. Bend low over her neck if she starts to get out of control. Slap the reins aside her neck if you need to—"

"Never mind all the talk." Kern shook his head. "Give me your most basic lesson."

Valerus pursed his lips. His green eyes were alarmed. But he simply pointed at the horse's head. "Point that end the direction you wish to ride."

"Good." Kern looked down. It seemed a long way to the ground. Quite the fall. "How hard can it be pushed?" he asked.

Valerus grimaced. "Hard as you need, as long as she'll last. But you'll kill her if you push too hard for too long."

Kern reached down, clapped the man on the shoulder. "I'll nay kill her. I'll push as hard as I can for the night, and when she tires, I'm off at a run. We can hope she makes it back here." He saw the flicker of doubt. "If one man dies between Murrogh and Lacheish, it will be too late. If I had an extra day, I'd make better time afoot."

It was no brag. Time and again the Cimmerians had proven that, over distance, they were as fast or faster than a horse, which needed rest far more often. A running man rested by slowing to a jog. Kern could keep up such a pace for several days, and had.

More of his warriors crowded around, nervous to see Kern on horseback. Or perhaps it was seeing him ride off alone.

Brig stepped forward. "You really think you can do this alone, Wolf-Eye?"

"I can do what I can," Kern said, avoiding the question. "Enough to stop a fight.

"And, hopefully, start a war."

16

BY THE TIME Kern and Frostpaw skirted Cailt Stonefist's war host and were finally located by a pair of Morag's scouts, he recalled little of the hard, bone-jarring ride that had started this race and was already a full day and an extra night behind him.

Sweat. He remembered that part.

Bruised muscles and blisters inside his thighs. Those were hard to forget.

And the warm, musty smell of horse, which stuck with him long after he'd slapped the beast's rump to send it galloping back the way they'd come. The following day he even threw himself down while crossing a creek in hopes of washing away the stench.

He'd ended up smelling of wet horse the rest of that day and the next night as well.

At some point (and he could no longer say for certain when, though it was after he'd abandoned that four-legged demon Valerus called a horse), he'd found Frostpaw. Or, more to the point, the dire wolf found him, tracking Kern across the hard, frost-dusted land below the plateau. He must have sensed the wolf much earlier. Caught a glimpse out of the corner of one eye, or heard one of its low, mournful howls, then forgotten. Or his mind had, for a time, simply retreated. Slept, while his body worked and pushed and ran.

Because one moment, he was running down a forest trail, alone.

The next, a silver-gray shadow with powerful shoulders and a mouth that had torn the throats out of other men ran next to him.

So close, Kern felt the light fall of its padded feet on the trail. Heard the panting and all but smelled the carrion reek of Frostpaw's warm breath.

And it neither surprised nor alarmed him.

So they ran. Man and wolf. Two evenings without sleep. A day without rest, or much in the way of food or water. Kern's muscles burned down to the bone, and his chest felt as if he'd swallowed live coals. His skin had flushed an almost natural pink, though he still shivered with cold. Always, always the cold. And he stank something fierce.

Amazing, it was, that Cailt's camp dogs did not sniff him out. Or the picket riders they avoided by laying into some nettle. Or Cailt himself.

They didn't. Kern and the wolf slipped past them all in the dark, listening to their songs of prowess and preparation. Some warriors sang while they sharpened their blades. Others, while matching up in tests of strength— arm wrestling or lifting—or simply sitting around one of the many beds of orange coals, which Kern took great care in counting before stumbling onward, taking a blind stab at where he would find the Murrogh war host.

Not so difficult, actually. He simply drew a straight line along the last half day of Cailt Stonefist's march, starting at the turn they'd made to swing away from the lower plains and toward the Black Mountains. The Lacheishi scouts, at least, had earned their keep. When Kern cleared a forest grove and dogged over one last rise, saw the dark spread of tents and bedrolls staining a moonlit meadow, he reminded himself to thank them later.

He looked back. Frostpaw hunched down low to the ground, just this side of the crest. Great, golden eyes aglow in the sliver of moonlight. Making no move to pace Kern, or follow him down toward so many men and women with their blades and arrows and fire.

"Far enough?" he asked, his voice weak. Kern felt numb. Beyond any need to gasp for breath. His body had stopped demanding sense of him the day before. "All right."

But he did dig into his oilskin pouch for the last slivers of beef he'd brought with him. Stuck one between his teeth and lower lip, sucking the juices out to clear the dry, pasty taste out of his mouth. Swallowing carefully at first, letting his stomach loosen, get used to the thought of food again.

He tossed the other piece to the wolf, which jumped as if startled and bared teeth at Kern. Growling, it crept forward slowly and snapped up the small treat. And Kern had no doubt the animal, for all its strange companionship, was ready to bite the hand that fed it.

"I get that a lot these days," he said, feeling light-headed enough that talking to a wolf seemed a perfectly reasonable idea.

Then he left the animal there, climbing down off the ridge. Waving overhead as a pair of guards with bows and ready arrows stepped out of the lower brush line, ready to shoot. He had seen them easily from the crest of the ridge, with his eyes drawing in the moonlight and bathing the predawn countryside in a soft twilight glow. But there was still no safe way to approach nervous men in the night.

"Gaud," he called down at them, knowing that few outside of Murrogh would know much about the resettled valleymen. "Is Cul Chieftain about?"

He was. About six hours into sleep, rolled into a blanket and camped under a lean-to he'd pitched with a felt mat and two good stakes. Other Gaudic men and women slept nearby, stirred when the guards escorted Kern down and called for Cul to rouse. Kohlitt, Reave's sister's man. Several of Ossian's kin that he recognized.

If Kern had his preferences, he'd nay be rousing the man who'd wanted him dead. But with battle only a half day away, at best, no one but a trusted kinsman or one of the war leaders would be able to get Kern access to Morag Chieftain. And he needed that. The sooner, the better.

"Wolf-Eye."

Cul's voice was sharp, for being roused from a deep sleep. There was no disguising the antagonism. Or the resignation. Crawling from his half tent, he was a shadowy outline against the lightening eastern sky.

Kern recalled one of Brig's favorite greetings, and threw it back at his former chieftain now. Nodding. "Still alive, Cul Chieftain."

"So it would seem. Your pack with you? Come back for the fight after all?" He folded arms across a large, bare chest. "Cailt Stonefist comes at us with his best warriors. Grimnir, and the Hoathi, will have to wait. Morag has a feud to settle."

"I've come alone, with a hope to end this feud before our fighting serves Grimnir's ends. You've been manipulated, Cul. You do not even see it."

"I've been manipulated? You think old Stonefist has a thumb on me, yea?"

Kern stepped forward, pitching his voice for Cul alone. There were too many ears awake, now. Listening to them argue. "Why would two leaders *want* such a war when

Vanir are ripping the guts out of Cimmeria?" He asked it as if the answer should be obvious. "Unless someone whispered poison in their ears, what stops them from joining forces, at least now?"

Cul laughed. "I think Morag has forgotten to send Cailt the bloody spear."

Kern did not. "That is my plan. I've brought it back to do just that."

"You'll not!"

"After first light, with Morag's blessing. What harm to try? That is tradition, yea? That feuds are set aside. Why would he not allow it?"

Cul stepped closer. His hands opened and clenched, and opened and clenched. He looked ready to throttle the life out of someone. Kern, likely. "He'll not allow it for many reasons. Nay the least of which is that Cailt's war host is here, and we've the strength to crush him. Stonefist has come at his own peril. Morag'd not offer him a reprieve."

"And what kind of leader does that make *him?* Hardly better than Grimnir."

"You'll not want to say that in his presence," Cul warned.

But Kern had come quite some distance to do just that. And more. "Get me in to see him, Cul Chieftain. And see."

He'd counted on Cul's desire to see him disgraced. See him dead. Morag was prideful and paranoid. Kern handed Cul the opportunity to have away with him without any further loss of honor.

Honor that had always meant so much to Cul.

"Give up your blade," Cul ordered.

Kern did so, releasing it sheath and all and tossing it to Cul. Then he untied his flask, after one more drink for strength. He pulled the wrapped spear from the center of his bedroll and dropped the last of his gear to the ground at his feet. He cradled the spear in the crook of his arm. Nodded Cul forward.

"All right. Follow, then."

It was a short march from Cul's chosen spot to the center of the camp where the tent of Morag Chieftain had been set up. A large framework of tied sticks, draped with a heavy, canvas covering, it was large enough for a dozen men to sleep in. A pair of torches set up on tall stands guttered in the soft, nighttime breeze, casting a flickering orange light over the open yard in front.

Cul had Kern wait, stepped in, and spoke with the inside guard. There were words and a low argument. Then Cul returned, and soon an armed sentry was dispatched on the run to wake more of Morag's advisors.

Cul shook his head. "Your life will answer for this, Wolf-Eye. I'll take it myself."

"You be challenging me openly, then? Or set someone else's hand to it again?"

He had the decency to look abashed at the open secret between them. Exhaled noisily. "Tall-Wood," he said. "You killed him?" Kern stood mute. "Nay. He made his choice, then. I wouldn't have thought him one to turn on me."

"Why?" Kern asked. He stood patiently, arms loose, no threat to Cul. In truth, he was on the last of his strength after the hard, fast run. He had only enough left for his duty, and the conversation. "What reason did you ever have to put a knife at my back?"

"Because a new chieftain can nay brook a challenge to his authority," Cul said in a savage whisper. "You were a knife at *my* back every moment you lived, winter-born. But to act in the open would have undermined me as badly. You *weakened* me with Reave and Daol and Hydallan—all important men of Gaud. And with Burok Bear-slayer. And with Maev."

The anger poured out of Cul in a hot rush. No guard on his tongue. And why not? Kern was already dead, wasn't he? But, "Maev? She had nay use for me, Cul. Except for her contempt."

"Her fear, you mean. She did nay understand you. But she valued what you did for her father. What nay other man could have done, packing him back through that blizzard, nay matter he was already a dead man when you did it."

"She wished me dead. She even said . . . that it should have been me—"

"—challenging for chieftain instead of that ox-headed lout, Reave, who you and Daol encouraged to stand against me."

Kern's mind reeled at the idea that Maev had thought him a successor to her father. Or, at least, that she had thought him a real challenge to Cul. Nay matter that entering the Challenge Circle would have turned most every man in the village against him . . . unless they'd also been too afraid of his strangeness.

"I did nay want it. I would have stood for you, after your victory."

"Too late," Cul said. "It's always been too late for you, Wolf-Eye."

Mayhap that was so. Especially when the runner returned with Hogann and two Murroghan veterans whom Kern had often seen in Morag's lodge hall. And then Kohlitt also hurried up, with Maev.

Kern had expected a larger audience, actually. Though Maev was a surprise that nearly unraveled his nerve. Wrapped in a thick, shaggy fur of mountain ram combed full and dyed a snow-white, her long, raven-slick hair pulled back in a severe tail. The slight bulge showed at her midriff.

Halfway along her pregnancy, and she traveled with the Murrogh host?

"What are you about?" she asked at once. "Kohlitt over-heard something about—"

Kern held up a hand to forestall her. Knowing that if he entered any argument with her, now, after what Cul had said of her, after the tiring run he'd come through to make it here on time, he'd lose.

"Nay now, Maev. If you ever trusted me once to do the right thing, give me peace for the moment."

The simple request was enough to stop her cold. Her eyes cast back a dim glow from the torchlight. She raised a hand as if to reach out to him, hesitated. Let it fall back to her side. But she remained quiet. She was willing to go that far for him, at least.

Then the guard reappeared and gestured. Kohlitt was not allowed inside, though he tried to follow. No one tried to stop Maev, who crowded between Kern and Cul at the back of the tent and held herself as tall and sturdy as anyone else. Oil lamps burned in two corners, throwing steady light through-out the small space, washing a buttery light over Morag, who shifted from one foot to the other, standing between his two men. And Hogann, glowering darkly off to one side. As far from Kern as he could likely get in the small space available.

A good thing.

Also, the tent's large room was cut in two by a sheer stretch of fabric, pinned to the canopy and hanging down to shield the chieftain's sleeping quarters. And a shadow moved the other side. Kern assumed it was Deirdre of Lacheish.

Of course Morag had brought his trophy. How else to assure Cailt Stonefist's appearance?

"Cul says you have words for me, Wolf-Eye. Words I'll nay like." Morag's hair, thin and patchy, was more di-sheveled than ever. As if the man had not slept well this night, if ever. The bare spots on his scalp were puckered and glassy from long-healed scars.

"He says you will present Cailt Stonefist with the bloody spear. That you've brought it back."

Kern nodded at the bundle in the crook of his arm. Slowly, as if following through a formal ritual, Kern reached up and peeled open the wrapping of thick blanket. Dropped it at his feet. He held the spear now, in both hands. As an offering.

"Yea, I've brought it back. Though I nay longer believe you worthy of it." The Murroghan warriors to either side of their chieftain glowered, hands on their swords. But the blades remained in the sheaths, per Morag's paranoia. "Rather offer to Cailt Stonefist, is truth."

"You'll give it to me," Morag said, nearly shouting. His dark, deep voice rang with a near-frantic echo. Then, calmer. "It's mine. All this. This moment. This life." His smile was savage and cruel. "You'll give me that bloody spear, and I may only strip the hide off your back before I send you and your wolves fleeing for the mountains from which you came."

"You'd find that difficult, Morag." Kern deliberately left off his honors. Just as he deliberately left the spear stretched out at the limits of his reach. Dangling it before the chieftain, whose eyes did not leave it. "I've been to the Frost Swamp. And I know you for what you are."

A gamble, to challenge Morag so openly, in the presence of his supposed kinsmen. To insult him again, and again. A true chieftain would have ordered Kern killed. Or sent out to die in a hastily erected arena. A warrior chieftain would do the job himself for any of the slights Kern had thrown at Morag's feet.

But if Kern were right, the man had no honor to protect.

Only greed. And malevolence.

And a dark, desperate secret to protect.

"I said to give it over!" Morag yelled. Which was when he shoved forward, one hand reaching out to grab the spear as if he could easily wrest it from Kern's strong, two-handed grip.

Too late, Cul saw it. As did Hogann, Kern thought. Both men reached for swords. The two Murroghan reacted out of reflex, one turning to grapple with the Hoathi. The other, to block Cul.

Maev, too, moved now. Turning toward Kern as she finally read in his actions what he'd intended all along. "Nay!"

All too late. Kern twisted the bloody spear and *pulled*, locking Morag's arm out straight. Then leveraged it to drag the other man forward. Yanking them body against body. Wrenching the spear free of Morag's bony hand. Reversing it.

And Morag saw it, too. The lesson none of them remembered from Kern's last interview in Clan Murrogh's lodge hall. None of them but Kern.

That the broken, bloody spear was, itself, a weapon.

A weapon Kern drove forward with the last of his flagging strength.

Right through the chest of Morag of Murrogh.

17

WITH THE CLOUDS piling up thick and black and heavy
with moisture, blocking out the sky and sun, dawn crept up
as a general lightening of the dark, finally settling on a
heavy, downtrodden gray. Freezing rain fell in halfhearted
drops—promising a wet, terrible day—and short echoes of
thunder rumbled in the distance like the slow, heavy footfalls of Ymir himself.

Lodur approved.

He paused on the side of a hill, his broadsword already
in hand, though he had no intention of using it. Surrounded
by men and women with thick furs wrapped around their
wide shoulders and metal breastplates polished to a gleam-
ing shine, heavy leather skirts banded with strips of metal
or studded with spikes. He smiled thin and hard, encouraging those few who dared look him in the eye. Pushing them
by will alone for the top of the ridge, the end of their hard
march, and the prize that waited for them on the other side.

The fruits of his treason. Sweet nectar of the north. Such a difference a single season could make.

At first he had detested the arrival of spring. Though it was late coming to some parts of Cimmeria, the signs were there as birds returned and game stirred, and the sun climbed in the southern sky. Unwelcome heralds. He saw these as nothing but a reminder of their failure. A waning of Grimnir's power that had come after the First One's fall from the bluffs overlooking Clan Conarch.

In the northwest territories, in the valley, with Ymir's lasting winter choking life from the clans, the Ymirish had walked as gods for a time. Unstoppable forces, or so they'd thought. Lodur's own fall from grace came at the hand of his false brother, Kern; the one of thin blood, who smelled of corrupted ice and Cimmerian beast. And he might have remained low had not Ymir's Call lifted him back up among the ruins of Venarium. Blessing him with a deep warmth he had never felt his entire life as that cold, frozen spark within him suddenly flared to life, and his own power was born during a night of darkness, and screams, and blood.

It came strong to him, Ymir's touch. Strong enough for Grimnir to summon him back, to allow Lodur to earn his redemption for past failures.

Which was how Lodur knew now that it was not fate but their God's hand that placed him on an eastern path, in place to support Grimnir's final plans. Letting him taste the blood of Kern's fallen warrior at Gaud. Carrying with him the smell of the funeral pyre and visiting a similar fate on the mountain tribes that had dared to stand in his way.

And even though Kern had slipped from Lodur's reach, for now, the sorcerer felt his false brother's presence many times. Knew when Kern had touched on his own flickering power in the defense of Gorram Village. When Kern had burned powerful bright at Murrogh's lakeside stronghold, and Grimnir's will bore down on him to accept, to cross over, to honor his blood.

Knew Kern's victory in the Frost Swamp.

Knew this morning when he killed Morag Chieftain, and had laughed for his brother's despair and pain.

"Kern." Lodur's whisper was cold, calm. "You should have accepted Grimnir's hand and Ymir's blessing, when you had the chance."

Now it was too late. Too late for all.

Lodur looked up into the sky, drawing down the winds, the clouds, the rain. A breath of winter's lingering touch wrapped about him, the winds whipping at his frost blond hair, tugging the hem of his cloak, shrieking in his ears. He pulled in a piece of the zephyr, binding to it a part of himself—that which warmed him from within. Breathing dark life into it.

"Torgvall . . ." he called, whispering to his warrior brethren traveling within Cailt's war host. A simple summons. And one the other Ymirish expected.

All was in place. Cailt Stonefist and Murrogh's war host. Kern Wolf-Eye. And his own warriors, of course. Spreading out across the back side of the ridge, hunkered down with blades standing naked in their hands, waiting for his final order. For his display of true power.

Now!

Ready, he tugged at the thin tendril of power leashed at the back of his mind. The connection he'd made over the Pass of Noose, bonding to his whim one of the darkest, strongest creatures of the Black Mountains. There was resistance. There was the feel of frigid wind rushing against leathery wings. And a shrieking call that raked talons against Lodur's nerves.

Obey! He fed a measure of his rage to the creature, letting it feel the pain for its refusal. Felt its own anger and hatred build, the wildness within it that wanted to reach through their link and rend him apart with talon and tooth. To kill him. Yea, it would, if he gave it the chance.

But until then, it feared as well. And fear, like anger and pain, could be used to control. He tugged harder and felt the shift of weight, the quick turn and the rush of wind as it dived out from the clouds. Lodur, staring ahead at the snow-frosted ridge, felt the shadow passing up from behind him, then over him, rushing by with the beat of leathery wings and a shriek of rage.

Then the wyvern was past, flashing by the ridge to fall upon the first of its victims.

Lodur smiled. Then raised his sword overhead and waved it forward, sending the Vanir on their charge. Up, over the ridge. Never to be denied their own bloodlust. Lodur climbed after them, but then stood upon the ridgeline to look down on the formerly peaceful village of Lacheish.

"Summoned my war host," he whispered, remembering Cailt's shaman. "Marched it at my enemy, I have." And if Cailt had expected to find Lodur's warriors on the southwestern trail, ready to help him defeat Murrogh, that was all the worse for him.

It was perfect, for the northerners. Especially with Cailt Stonefist poised to smash Murrogh's war host. Or, mayhap Murrogh would stand the stronger even without their chieftain. That did not matter so much to Grimnir's plans, or Lodur's orders, so long as either happened. And it would. It must! Lodur saw no other path left open to fate.

Crom had long abandoned Cimmeria.

And Ymir walked these lands once again.

KERN DRIFTED THROUGH a dark, cold void. Blacker than any night he'd seen, with no moon and no stars. A metallic taste in his mouth, which might be (his) blood, but no sensation of pain or comfort. Not even the feel of ground beneath his feet or against his body.

Only the cold.

That frozen spark buried deep within him, which he'd lived with his entire life.

He was at the same time trapped in that experience of drifting, yet apart from it as well, looking down on his own body as it floated against (or through) the seamless dark. There was no concept of the passage of time, though every so often, after an indeterminate length, the entire void flashed—for an instant—with color, and a touch of sound. Like sheet lightning. And broken thunderclaps. He began to expect them, and cling to those interruptions as a drowning man might a rope that was thrown to him. In this shadowed, frozen place, they were the only flashes of life to be found.

Flashes of his life, as it turned out.

The violent eruption of color came at (he believed) shorter intervals and for greater and greater durations. First there was the long, dark void. Then the world erupted around him, instantly returned in bright color and loud sound. But still, he was not fully a part of it. It was as if he existed in three places. Inside the scene, acting out his role in it. Floating, drifting, across the world; or, drowning in it, as if the world were now deep lake that had swallowed his body. And again, the spectator, watching his drowning body submerge into the (streams of) memory.

The first memory he recognized was of the Challenge Circle, where Reave had faced Cul's supporters and lost. It still wasn't much more than a quick flash. Just enough to latch on to, and hold after it was gone.

Then that cold run south, after Cul cast him out. Feet kicking through the snow. Legs pumping and his breath coming in ragged, frosting clouds.

And the wolf, racing next to him, pacing him the entire time (or had that come later?).

The scenes changed. Blended. None of them happening exactly the way he remembered. He watched as Ehmish lay bleeding on the ground, with a battle-axe caved into the boy's side. Not the way that had happened, certainly. Or when he'd met Ros-Crana in the hot spring baths, he knew that Jaryyd should not have been there, standing guard over them. He had not met Jaryyd yet.

Faster they came. Fragments blurring together in a mix of old and new. And through them all Kern watched himself make his mistakes or celebrate a few hollow triumphs over and over. Soon, it was as if he ran back through the last several months of his life, pursued by Vanir, and a Ymirish sorcerer, and Grimnir. Grimnir!

Yea, the Great Beast was there. The golden-eyed Terror. Stalking Kern, even when the giant-kin could not have been there. Watching, and raging when Kern turned from one path to the next and so narrowly escaped death each time. Then, after a time, studying him with some measure of respect. His cracked lips and crooked teeth splitting into a bestial grin. A deep, cunning look haunting his golden eyes. To think of Grimnir as a simple beast was a mistake. The giant-kin had intelligence and cunning, and a physical strength that transcended mortal ken.

And he heard Grimnir's roar of approval as Kern shouldered aside Brig Tall-Wood and Cul Chieftain and Maev, bursting into Morag's tent with a savage snarl curling his lip as he used the bloody spear to stab Morag again and again and again.

Nay. Not the way it had happened.

That memory was too recent, too strong. Kern seized it and twisted it back into place. Relived that quick, brutal strike as he shoved the spearhead through Morag's chest.

Twisted it inside, digging for the man's heart. Felt that first jet of hot blood splash across his hands. A few warm drops spattered his face as well, burning on his lips. Tasting of . . . blood. Fresh, human blood.

Had he been wrong?

They pulled him off their chieftain, the two Murroghan warriors. One tackled him high. The other doubled his hands together into a great fist and hammered it into the side of his head. Kern stumbled back, collapsed. Was buried beneath the one warrior and the sentry who'd run inside, and Kohlitt right after. And Maev, as well, throwing herself at them, screaming for everyone to stop, cease, to hold!

Blows hammered at him, but Kern shrugged them aside with the last of his strength. Captivated by Morag's final moments, the chieftain staggering back into Hogann, who held him upright while bright red blood continued to pour down his chest.

Cul leaped forward, grabbing the spear as if he might pull it free and save Morag's life. Too late for that.

The sheer fabric that had shielded the sleeping area inside the tent was ripped back. And Deirdre was there as well. Watching as her husband bled to death.

Watching as (finally!) the red blood darkened, turned black and foul, and Morag's face melted. Like wax held too close to a flame, it softened and fell in on itself. It ran with bloody streaks as parts of Morag's skin simply sloughed away. And the chieftain jumped out of Hogann's grasp, thrashing about violently as it screeched with a high-pitched keening Kern recalled from the Frost Swamp. And Hogann knew as well, the horror giving way to recognition, then disgust.

Which was when one of Morag's warriors kicked Kern aside the head, and darkness came crashing back down for an instant.

An eyeblink.

Thunder cracked through the heavens as the world shifted. And now Kern clung to the side of a sheer cliff. The ground falling away far, far below. The edge, outlined against gray skies, still far out of reach above. Muscles straining as his fingers dug for small cracks and holds above his head. His toes lifting against small outcroppings not much larger than a fist.

Face pressed against the cold, black granite, he looked to one side and saw ten . . . twenty warriors all on the same climb. Scaling up this cliff for the edge of the Hoath Plateau. He knew where they were. Just as he knew the woman who clung nearby on the cliff facing, struggling upward with her sword and spear lashed across her back.

Ros-Crana.

If it were truly her. If Kern was someone here. She led her warriors on a difficult climb that no Ymirish would think to patrol. She'd make it onto the plateau.

And, likely, she would die there.

Kern clenched his eyes shut, shoving aside the thought, the vision.

Opened them with his hands no longer straining against rock, fighting the pull of gravity, but with leather reins wrapped around them. Again. Racing over frozen ground. But not the same. Nay. Not here.

He sat on the horse much easier this time. He (. . . Torgvall . . .) leaned forward, rocking easily with the gait of the stolen animal. He rode with a gray patch of sky on his right, the coming of dawn. Riding north. Eager, glad, to be away.

Cailt's war host was finished. Stonefist himself might die, and that would be best for all. Ymir's justice, after suffering the chieftain's poor graces for far, far too long.

But it was not to be as easy as he thought. When three shadows rose up ahead, standing atop a grassy knoll, he pulled the reins to turn away from them. Away from the bows being stretched overhead.

He heard the *twang* of release. Caught his breath. Then exhaled again as he raced away, and the arrows missed.

Except for one, which struck downward like a bolt of lightning, catching the horse right in the side of the neck. Burying itself up to the feathers. And the horse screamed, diving forward in a violent, stumbling roll that pitched him from the saddle. Sailing him through the air. Sailing . . . sailing—

—out over the lake. He watched, standing on the ridge, as the wyvern spread its leathery wings to catch at the air, banked sharply, and dived again at the over-lake community.

"Good. Good," he yelled. And laughed into the building storm, his voice carried away on the violent winds that continued to sweep his hair and his white bearskin cloak straight out to one side.

The village burned in several places. A few of the homes set on stilts. A covered platform. Men fought along the piers, and on the shore still, though the Vanir had gained the upper hand there, finishing off the thin line of defenders.

Someone had chopped free several piers in the network, isolating parts of the village from the fire, from the attack. So, it would not be a complete loss. But enough. Enough.

The wyvern shrieked as arrows slashed through the thin membrane stretched over its wings. Another caught it aside the neck. But then it stooped hard, dropping beneath the next flight, and flashed across the top of the two-story lodge hall. Taloned claws slashed downward, and snatched up two more archers from the thinning pack. Carrying them up higher and higher.

Yea. It would be enough. Now was the time to return to his master. Grimnir waited, watching through his eyes, and was pleased. Was stirring. Was clawing his way forward, out of the dark depths that boiled with power and dark purpose in (Lodur's) mind. Eyes of savage, golden fire, and a face twisted in rage. Rage and . . . fear?

But the Beast's voice was terrible and laced with power of its own. And it screamed inside Lodur's mind, shaking him from his feet. Hurling him backward to land hard on the frozen, unyielding ground.

"KERN!"

Darkness crashed over him. Pain throbbed across most of his body. And in his ears, the shout still echoed.

"Kern. Kern?"

He opened his eyes. One of them had swollen partly closed, but he could see well enough. See Maev, kneeling beside him. Still draped in her white fur of mountain ram. Kohlitt and Cul Chieftain standing over her. Their expressions running the gamut of concern, and confusion, and anger.

No longer in the chieftain's tent, he'd been carried outside and stretched out over the hard, cold ground without benefit of blanket or mat. But he lived! Not sure why, at that, but it was a start to realize he was awake and whole and . . .

"Not . . . dead," he said, voice a thin croak.

"Nay," Maev assured him. Her smile was thin. Forced. There was a measure of relief in them now that he'd spoken, but only just. She shook her head.

"Not yet," she said.

18

THE BODY OF the creature pretending to be Morag Chieftain was buried just after dawn. Still wearing Morag's clothing, soaked as it was with its black, pungent blood, it was dumped into a shallow grave, covered over with dirt topped with several large stones to prevent the camp dogs from digging up the foul remains.

Someone stuck the bloody spear into the ground, as a marker.

There were no songs for the dead. No chants of Morag's victories, or any valiant final stand that should naturally have accompanied the fall of such a long-ruling chieftain. No words were said. No honors rendered. The Murroghan worked quickly, quietly, and with a grim frown of distaste drawing at their faces.

Watching it, still under guard, Kern understood better than most how difficult this had to be. The lack of ceremony. Eastern clans used song the same way valleymen and western clans passed their histories and the names of great leaders along by lodge hall tales. The entrance flap to Morag's tent should have been stained with the blood of mourning. His body given a tall funeral pyre, or sewn into a shroud for the long, hard trip to the Field of the Chiefs where he could be interred with other great chieftains of Cimmeria.

But Morag had obviously died years before. Within the Frost Swamp, Kern guessed. Though some argued it might have happened on the trail home, or in the years after. Even recently, after leaving Murrogh.

The arguments made little sense. But then it had to be hard to accept that the switch had been made so long ago, and a doppelgänger had not only taken over for another, but it had been a chieftain's life. A chieftain's family and duties to the clan.

And what must it be like for his wife, Kern wondered, who had shared her bed with the man, the creature. Deirdre made one appearance at the gravesite, just as the final stones were set in place. She no longer looked so self-assured. So polished. A touch of gray speckled the hair just above her shaved temples, and Kern doubted anyone could say for certain whether it had been there the day before. Cul accompanied her, but maintained a distance of respect. Everyone did. At this point, no one was certain what her position among clan and kin would be.

She walked up with strength in her spine, though. Kern admired that. As did many of the warriors who saw, no doubt. She stepped up to the cairn, staring. Then spat. Rejecting the thing that had masqueraded as her husband.

And might even have fathered a child on her.

Then she did something no man or woman could have expected. She leaned down to wrench the broken spear from the earth and stomped over to shove it back into Kern's hands.

Power flickered in the back of his mind. Primal and unchained. Living darkness, still not laid to rest following his attack on Morag and the strange dreams that followed. Now it lit violet sparks at the edge of his vision, prickled the skin on the back of his neck, as if the bloody spear— the token of alliances—created some kind of threat to him.

The guards to either side of Kern stiffened, seeing a weapon back in his hands. But there was nay anyone about to gainsay Deirdre. Not at this moment.

Maev stepped forward then, leading Deirdre away. And with the necessities concluded, Cul dismissed Kern's guards. Though he did draw and hold easy his war sword, the blue-iron weapon Kern's warriors had returned to Cul after recovering it from Vanir raiders. Kern stared at the blade. If Cul recalled and appreciated the irony, he did not let it bother his voice. Calm and strong.

"I should kill you. Many inside this camp would breathe easier for it."

Kern tensed, but not because he feared the threat. His reaction was involuntary, as the power flared with a sharp stab of pain. Tamping it down, smothering it beneath a false aura of calm, he forced himself to shrug. Stretched his head to one side to bare his neck for Cul.

"Need an easier target?" he asked.

The way he felt now, run out and beaten, it might be a mercy.

"Crom take you, Wolf-Eye! Do you realize what you've done? I must meet with the other war leaders now. The Gorram. The Borat and the Galt. There is nay idea of who speaks for the war host. Mayhap it will break apart, and with Cailt Stonefist bearing down on us. Best to be behind the stronghold walls at Murrogh."

It would. If they could make it. "Cailt will run half of your force down before you could make it. It's too many days, Cul."

"Yea. We know that. But will the others worry for the

war host, or their own lives now? There are nay many men could hold a host like this together. Who can be seen to carry that"—he nodded at the broken, stained weapon in Kern's hands—"even before. I can lead Murrogh's warriors, but they would not have me as chieftain." What had to be a hard admission. "I've sent runners south, searching for Jaryyd Morag's-son. But we do not have days to wait. We've hours, at best, to plan."

"Nay," Kern said. "There is nay plan to salvage this, Cul. Not when you must deal with Cailt now. Not with Ros-Crana loose on the plateau. If we have a chance, any chance, there is one course you can take. If you have the stones for it."

"I'll consider anything just now, Wolf-Eye. Even your dark advice. So let us have it."

Kern swallowed dryly, thinking about what he'd seen coming out of the darkness. What he'd *thought* to spy from Grimnir's plans. The Great Terror's single fear.

But even if he had not seen all he believed, and it were nothing more than a pain-induced hallucination, he saw nay other way out of their current circumstance. Not without a terrible loss to all of Cimmeria. So he said it straight out.

"You'll have to surrender."

THEY CAME JUST before noon, Cailt's army. Breaking from the forest to the east. Swarming along the edge of hills to the north. Twoscore. Then three. Soon, four. Some astride horses, bareback. Most afoot. They raised blades and spears overhead, calling down with savage yells, then beat those swords and shafts against their shields over and over again in an ongoing rhythm, creating a pounding, harsh, artificial thunder.

The same thunderous claps that had broken through the darkness in Kern's dreams.

"There," Hogann said, pointing. He stood on the far side of Cul from Kern, at the end of the line that included war leaders from the other small villages around Murrogh. As far away from "the Wolf-Eye" as he could get and remain part of the group. Circumstance had forced the Hoathi to make a temporary peace with Kern, but Crom take him if he'd make it easy.

Kern followed the man's directions. At a small gathering of saddled horsemen up on the ridge. Five clansmen. One held a shield up on a tall pole, the target painted with small totems from all the villages that had contributed warriors. Another raised the bearing spear of Clan Lacheish's totem, dangling a ram's great curling horn from the crossbar.

Nay method to tell at such distance which of the other three would be Cailt Stonefist himself. Still, Kern could well imagine the confused and suspicious expressions passing back and forth among the chieftain and his nearest companions as they gazed out over the spreading meadow. Mayhap their scouts had reported something of this nature. But who would have believed it?

Murrogh's war host was nay ready for any battle Cailt would be expecting. Bedrolls and provisions bundled up into carrying packs. Swords in their sheaths. Chargers standing next to their mounts, and every warrior set in one of two column-lines, as if ready to begin the day's run.

Which they were.

Cul stepped forward, leading a small procession of him and Kern, the other war leaders, and Deirdre, Cailt's daughter, escorted by Maev. Kern had tried to convince Maev to remain behind. She'd had none of it, though.

"Better be certain about this, Wolf-Eye."

The flares of dark power. The trembles of pain and deep cold wracking his body. Kern could only be certain that his control was, finally, beginning to give way.

"We'll be the first to know," was all he said.

Cailt's war host was not so large as Murrogh's, which might have been one reason for his caution. Or, mayhap the sight of ten clansmen marching forward on his line was enough to get his interest. Whatever the reason, he held his position.

And certainly, once he recognized Deirdre in their midst, he was not about to attack. Instead, he spurred forward, followed by his four closest advisors. Riding down the hill to meet with the Murrogh contingent. Close enough now to recognize the chieftain by the mantle he wore—snowy-gray ermine, worn thick over his shoulders in a rich display—and the strong, easy way he sat his horse.

It was an unequal meeting from both sides. Five men on horseback, towering above twice their number afoot. No one with weapons bared, not counting Cailt's bearing spear or the broken shaft of the bloody spear that Kern cradled in the crook of one arm.

Cul brought his group to a halt while still several dozen paces shy of the bottom of the hill. Waited while Cailt Stonefist came down to meet them. Then, when the chieftain reined in, he stepped aside to allow Deirdre to join him.

"Think to taunt me with the child you stole?" Cailt asked. His voice was strong, and even. He stood up from his saddle, searching. He frowned. "Where is Morag?"

"Morag Chieftain is killed," Deirdre said. Her voice still had sorrow in it, but it was strong. Cul and Maev had decided that she should deliver the news to her father. But hold back some of the details. "Dead. Your feud is over."

That caused a moment's quiet, then some whispered discussion among the five. Kern counted the two obvious warriors, each bearing one of the standards. Another man, as large as his chieftain, with a rawboned face and a murderous stare. War leader or champion? And an elder

Lacheishi kinsman with long silver-white hair and pale, pale skin. Kern nearly thought him a Ymirish.

Finally, Cailt spoke again. "My feud is with the Murrogh as well as their chieftain. But I'll take you home now. Come, Deirdre. There is no reason for you to stay any longer."

Here was where Morag's woman could destroy them. If she left now, if she denounced the Murrogh and punished them for what nay anyone could have known these last five years, they were done for.

But she knew her own duties as well. "I have a son, father. Your grandson." Did Cailt see her shiver, wondering if she had birthed an heir, or a monster? "I stay because it is the thing I should do."

"And I am here to end this feud because it is the thing I should do," Cailt said. "And should have done years before." Still, he had to be counting the men and women lined up on the field. Weighing Murrogh's greater numbers against Clan Lacheish's reputation for battle.

Then his gaze swept the near line and stopped on Kern. Blood roared in Kern's ears.

"Have your own Ymirish advisor as well, yea? Hope that one shows greater courage than the creature who tried to run off on us this morn."

Torgvall! Kern had seen him during the darkness and his dreamlike visions, escaping by horseback. Was it an indication that the rest of his visions had been real as well?

Cul stepped forward. "Kern Wolf-Eye does not advise," he said. "He acts." Another admission that likely twisted a dagger in Cul's guts. "He acts against Grimnir and the northerner's invasion of our lands."

The elder man with the silver-white hair leaned in to whisper. Shook his head. Kern wished he knew what the man offered, as Cailt listened closely, then clucked his mount forward, leading his fist of horsemen right up to Cul's line.

He dismounted, along with the elder man, and ground-hitched his horse as he stepped within a sword's reach of Cul Chieftain and the others. This was no man afraid for his own life, not even against twice his own number. He stood as tall or taller than any warrior in line, with powerful shoulders and thick arms and fists like great hammers. On one side he wore a vambrace, protecting his elbow and forearm and easily used for a guard instead of the shield he'd slung over his back. Under the ermine mantle he wore a breastplate of blue-iron steel chased with silver. His kilt was closer to a northern skirt, leather backed by thick wool.

Cailt shaved his temples in a thick bar that nearly passed around the back of his head. His eyes were a dark gray very similar to Hogann's. Not a great surprise. The Lacheishi often raided for wives on the plateau.

"You," Cailt addressed Kern. "You fight Grimnir and the rest of his Ymirish?"

"Yea," Kern answered. Not trusting himself to say more just that moment. "I do."

The kinsman with silver-white hair nodded. Cailt's shaman, certainly. "He speaks truth."

"I was told that all the north belongs to Grimnir's brethren. And all Ymirish belong to Grimnir."

Kern might be many things. Including of northern blood. But one of Grimnir's many blades to hold at Cimmeria's throat he was not. "You have been lied to, Cailt Stonefist." He paused, then decided to take a chance. "Grimnir uses your feud with Murrogh to divide Cimmeria, to hold us at a distance while he destroys the Hoathi and the last of the plateau clans. Then the Great Beast will come for you."

Cailt hesitated. Glanced to his shaman, who stared fixedly at Kern with deep, deep blue eyes. He rubbed a large hand against the side of his face. "You claim to know much of Grimnir's plans for a man who says he opposes the Great Terror."

"I've chased this enemy across half of Cimmeria," Kern said. "Across the Teeth and back again. Through Venarium and round the base of Mount Crom and over the Pass of Noose I've come. From Murrogh's forests to the Frost Swamp. Yea, I know Grimnir and his Ymirish. And I know they've already struck the first blow against Clan Lacheish in your absence. Your village burns, Cailt Chieftain."

It all came in a flood, once he let loose the dam. And this last was a gamble. Kern couldn't say for certain the village he saw under attack was Lacheish, though it matched the descriptions he'd heard from travelers' tales. The risk, however, seemed worth taking if it shoved Cailt back on the defensive.

Cailt spun around on his shaman, and the elder kinsman hedged. "He believes this" was all he could tell his chieftain. "Mostly. He doubts, yea, but he does not deceive."

"A trick," the large man on horseback called out. His hand slapped at the broadsword strapped to his side. "To make us worry, Stonefist." He spat to one side, rejecting the Murrogh lies. "Grimnir's plans! It was Torgvall who counseled we hold back."

"And Torgvall who ran off on us this morn, nay forget that, Loht." Cailt did not look to his man, but his tone was biting. "Yea, he counseled us patience," he admitted. "But how do you lead a swine?"

Deirdre recognized the adage. "You push him away from where you wish him to go," she said.

Cailt considered it for a full moment, letting the tensions draw out. Then he glanced back to Loht. "Bring them," was all he ordered. There must have been little doubt to whom he meant, as the warrior wheeled his horse about and kicked it into a gallop, heading back up the hillside. The chieftain of Clan Lacheish faced his daughter, Cul, and Kern.

"Convince me," he said. "Tell me all there is to know."

Kern held back very little. Something more than the shaman's truth-sensing warned him not to deceive this man. And with everything he knew of Grimnir and Lodur and the rest of the Ymirish, he painted a fairly complete picture of the desolation and death being visited upon Cimmeria.

It took some time, especially when he reached his retelling of what he saw of Lacheish, and the destruction brought to it. Cailt asked many questions. The shaman hung on Kern's every answer, as if ready to denounce him on the spot and, so, make it all untrue.

By the time it was over, the shaman stood on weak legs, shaking, sweating. "It must be true," the elderly man said, looking as frail as his years suggested. "By Crom, let it be not."

Cailt held himself rock-still for most of the telling. At times he paced. The small group slowly bent in around him, though he never once worried for it or ordered them back. It was as if the others simply were drawn in against their will. Kern felt the pull as well. The strength this man radiated. No wonder he had held his feud for so many years. Kern doubted there were few things this man would do half-heartedly.

Cailt glanced down at the weapon held in Kern's hands. "And this you have carried to every chieftain?"

"This is the bloody spear I brought from the bluffs above Conarch. It has tokens from every eastern tribe assembled, including, now, Clan Murrogh. And it is yours, Cailt Stonefist, if you lead us north against Grimnir." He glanced at Cul, at Hogann and the others. "They will recognize no one else to lead them."

And with that, the tale was ended. Cailt traded stares with every man. He showed no sign of being impressed with the story or Kern's offer on behalf of the war leaders. He kept his own counsel well. He waited, until Loht could be seen working his way down the hillside with a dozen armed warriors.

And four prisoners with hands bound before them.

New pain spiked through Kern's temples, and at first he had eyes only for the lead captive. A tall Ymirish with the build of a warrior to rival Cailt Chieftain, or, among Kern's pack, perhaps only Reave. The man's golden eyes blazed with hatred. A dark, purple bruise covered half his face, and his arm was bound in a splint.

He saw and recognized Kern as well. And maybe something in Kern's eyes, as sparks leaped and danced between them. Kern tasted deep, raw ice. And steel. Recognizing a piece of himself in the other man. Their shared blood.

Distracting, at the least. It wasn't until the Lacheishi group was near the bottom of the hill that Kern realized that the other men behind the Ymirish were easily recognized as well. For an entirely different reason.

"Daol! Aodh!" He saw the two men look up. Move apart. The man behind them was just as familiar. "Brig!"

Three shadows, rising up on the hillside. All with bows. They had been inside his vision as well.

Men of the Wolves.

"Your warriors?" Cailt asked. Kern nodded, momentarily struck dumb. "They described you to me this morn. I accepted what they told me as lies and barely listened." The chieftain nodded once, curt but strong. "As it turns out, they kept their honor. I do nay often make mistakes, Kern Wolf-Eye. But if these warriors are yours, you may have them."

He nodded, and the three were released. Loht swung

down from his horse and used a sharp dagger to cut the leather stays bound around their wrists. As simple as that.

"And the Ymirish?" Kern asked.

Cailt's smile had little to do with humor. "He was one of *mine*." Another glance, and the tall Ymirish was wrestled over to stand before the Lacheishi chieftain. "Is what this one told me truth?" he asked. "Did Lodur betray me?"

"Stonefist Chieftain." He showed no fear. His voice was strong and steady, and he sneered at Kern. "As I said. I rode north to find his war host."

The shaman leaned in. Hesitated. His blue eyes stared hard into the face of the frost-bearded warrior. Shook his head.

"Did Lodur betray me?" Cailt asked again. Pushing for a direct answer.

The Ymirish started to answer, then looked to the shaman and hesitated. Kern leaned in, also waiting, willing Torgvall to answer. Warmth flushed over Kern's scalp, and Torgvall startled. Then,

"Never to my knowledge," he said carefully.

"Lies," the shaman whispered.

"Lodur burns my village?" Cailt's calm was glacial, never once raising his voice. Barely a whisper of emotion on his face. He might be discussing the spring's hunt or trade with a merchant. "You knew this?"

Sparks jumped in Kern's vision, pressure surged against his temples, splitting his head.

"Nay!"

"Lies," the shaman said. More certain this time.

Cailt Stonefist looked to his champion, Loht. The large man appeared completely undone. Clearly, he had once believed Torgvall. But no longer. His face darkened in a threatening storm. His grip on the hilt of his sword was strong enough to whiten the knuckles.

Kern stepped forward, power raging, singing in his blood again and begging to be released. The other Ymirish, though larger, shrank back as if burned. Kern pressed. "You were to keep us at each other. Until Grimnir finished with the Hoathi and turned against Lacheish. Weren't you?" He all but shouted this last.

"Nay!" Now Torgvall sounded desperate, all the calm and strength fled from his voice. "Cailt Stonefist, I have served you well. Grimnir has nay interest in your clan or your people or—"

"Lies, lies, and more lies!" The shaman turned and stormed away, clearly unable to stand in the face of such treachery any longer.

"Where were you to find Lodur?" Cailt asked, his voice nearing a whisper.

His treachery unveiled, his confidence shaken in the presence of the shaman, and Kern, Torgvall let his anger burst free. "I would not know!" he yelled at Cailt. "If I did, chieftain of sheep, I would tell you to watch you rush to your own death. You head there regardless. Lodur knows you come now. As does Grimnir. He sees through our eyes, every one of us!"

Cailt moved so quickly, with such grace and power, Kern barely saw it coming, and would have expected it from Loht. The Lacheishi chieftain was standing there one moment, immobile and steady in the face of such rage. And in the next he had drawn his broadsword and slashed, once, quickly and violently across the Ymirish's shoulders. Striking his head off so cleanly, so smoothly, that it rolled for a moment in the fountain of blood, and Cailt's sword was back in its sheath before the head ever hit the ground.

"Think Grimnir saw that?" Cailt asked. *Now* he let his voice fill with rage.

Moving to his horse, he vaulted into the seat and reined

up right next to Cul Chieftain and Kern. He looked down at each man in turn. Finally, he nodded.

"I must see to my kin and clan, but my war host moves north for the plateau." Kern shifted, ready to renew their offer, but Cailt cut him off with a glance. "You've carried the bloody spear this far, Kern Wolf-Eye. You carry it farther. Carry it to the end and drive it through Grimnir's black heart, if you are able. I will be there to see it. That I swear."

He looked to the rest of them. The southern clans. His daughter. Clearly, he was not finished with this matter of honor. But he knew where his priorities as chieftain outweighed those as a man.

"You offered me the bloody spear as a token of peace. That is nay what it should ever be. I do not release our feud, men of Murrogh. Not now. But I set it aside in the face of a greater enemy. You go as you will. But I give you my oath. Any man I meet on the plateau, *he* is my ally."

With that, Cailt reined his horse around and drove it hard up the hillside, calling to his men to rally. Rally at their campsite. Rally for Lacheish, and Cimmeria!

The blood pounded in Kern's ears, as loud as any of Grimnir's challenging roars. He reeled with the tempting thrill of power, and the pain of holding it in check, brought the fingers of one hand up to his temple, pressing hard as if he might hold back the surge. And he smiled through the pain.

Grimnir had made mistakes before. He'd make them again. But, Kern believed, one of the very worst the northern war chieftain had ever made was to make Cailt Stone-fist his enemy.

Finally, the man whom Kern had searched for across half of Cimmeria.

The one who might unite the clans.

19

MUSCLES BURNING AND the sting of sweat in the corners of her eyes, Ros-Crana dug in on the slope with all fours, scrabbling crosswise from one loose-packed trail to the other. A dry fall of dislodged stones rattled and bounced their way downhill. As if the Vanir did not already know right where they were, shouts chased after them from around the bend. Half a dozen. A dozen. She couldn't say for certain. There hadn't been time to count heads with arrows smashing into the rocks around her head.

"Keep moving," she said, gasping for breath. Her voice cracked, and she dry-swallowed. "Come on. Come on."

A small, stunted clump of heather grew out of the hillside. She grabbed for it, to pull herself up another few lengths. It ripped out of the soft earth and left her sliding backward, dislodging another fall of rock and dirt.

Carrack, just behind and beneath her, cursed as several of the sharp-edged rocks bounced off his shoulder and one side of his head.

"Careful!"

She spared him a furious glance. "Stay back from me if it worries you," she snapped.

An arrow whistled in, digging into the slope right at Carrak's feet. They both glanced back, saw the lone archer far back on the trail, just this side of the bend. Reaching for another shaft. Yelling in his native, nasal language for the others to hurry. He had them.

Carrack redoubled his efforts to climb after her, ignoring the cascade of stone and earth that struck at his face and chest. "Not likely, by Crom."

Clawing their way uphill and over, uphill and over, both fought for every handhold, every desperate ledge. Where the trail suddenly gave out from an earlier slide, neither warrior hesitated. They threw themselves across, digging in for a new purchase and climbing, scrabbling for the upper edge.

She reached it first, hauling herself over the edge, rolling to one side and reaching back down for Carrak. He caught her hand, and she heaved back. Yanking him forward and up.

Nearly clearing the slope before the arrow caught him in the meaty part of the leg.

Two more arrows slashed overhead as they both crabbed clear of the drop-off. Ros-Crana risked one glance back. Saw five . . . six . . . eight Vanir and still more spread along their back trail. Fighting the slope, same as they had, in order to catch them.

"Never knew the Hoath Plateau . . . could be so amusing," Carrak said, fighting to keep his breath even. He checked the groove slashed through his thigh. A shallow, bloody trench, dug by the arrow's glancing blow. "Have to come here again . . . someday."

Ros-Crana fought for her breath as well. "Have to survive this trip first."

She untied the flask from her hip, poured a quick splash of warm, leather-tasting water into her mouth, then threw the container to Carrak. Risked another glance.

"Not much more," she said.

He shook his head. Passed back the flask. "Good to go."

This part of the run they had it easy. Downhill, most of the way. Around a sharp bend, then another. They heard the first Vanir gain the edge behind them. On a small rise they glanced back, saw him already on the run after them. Forty . . . maybe fifty strides. She'd forgot to count. The next man just now throwing an arm over the ridge.

The dry wash was just ahead. A wide arroyo carved by spring flooding, just now it was dry and littered with the usual castoffs. Branches. Small trees. Round, waterworn rocks. They raced up to the edge and jumped down, landing in crouches a full length below. The bank here had been undercut, creating a small lip above them.

Above, on the trail, they heard footfalls. One set.

She grabbed Carrak by the shoulder, pulled him back with her into the shadow of the overhang. Both warriors drew their blades. And waited.

Not for long. The Vanir did not bother to hold up for his companions. Did not check before he leaped. He landed right in front of them, war bow gripped in one hand, arrow in the other, still fighting to nock the shaft.

Carrak hamstrung him across the back of the legs. Ros-Crana waited until he'd flopped over and opened his belly like a gutted boar, spilling his intestines over the rocky ground. Her new war sword handled light in her hand, as if it weighed half as much as her old blade. A true pleasure to put to use.

They left the raider, screaming and dying, behind them.

"Slow them down just a bit."

Not too much. The Vanir would not bother wasting time on a dead man. A mercy blade through the heart was the best that one could hope for. But they did pull together, not wanting to repeat the archer's mistake of getting too far out in front alone. By the time they were climbing out the far end of the wash, Ros-Crana looked back and saw that at least ten raiders had grouped up to come as a pack.

And then slowed. Shouts of warning raised, then died on their lips.

Stumbling to a stop with wild glances left and right as a dozen, a score, *twoscore* warriors suddenly swept up on either side of the arroyo. Bows and spears held at the ready. Boxing the raiders in with no hope to fight their way free.

One Vanir reached an arrow out of his barkskin quiver. And died the next instant, pinned to the ground with half a dozen arrows. As did the man who threw himself at the side of the shallow trench, thinking to get at one of the enemy with his blade.

No one else tried.

Ros-Crana left Carrack at the end of the wash, leading a small group of Coragin warriors who waited to plug the gap should the raiders try to run for it. She walked calmly back down the upper edge of the arroyo, behind her line of warriors, watching the Cruaidhi across the way enjoy their part in this little trap.

Sláine Longtooth waited on a ledge directly above the trapped men. Studying the haunted, shamed looks on their faces.

Enjoying every moment of it.

"Good to see you again," he said. "Thought maybe the dogs had you this time a-sure."

"This rabbit still knows a trick or two."

"Never would have believed it. And that's twice we've led them into a similar trap, thank Crom."

"Thank Kern," Ros-Crana told him. It was Wolf-Eye's tale of a similar trap his wolves had set in the Breaknecks that had inspired her. And the Hoath Plateau was full of blind draws, good twisted trails, and shallow washes such as this one to lead a merry chase.

She looked down into the soulless eyes of her former predators, now her prey. Selected one at random. He looked to have no more or no less intelligence than the others. And asking for their leader was a waste of time and trouble.

"That one," she said. Then turned away from the wash.

The singing of bowstrings and the screams of dying men chased after her. Strong in her ears, even after they finished questioning the one survivor and then put him down as well. Still echoing as they hiked back to the Field of Chiefs.

The Field of Chiefs was a place of power to all Cimmerians, where the most powerful chieftains met at times, and where more than once a long-standing feud had been settled by a fight to the death. It had to be nearly as important to the Vanir. Here marked one of the final battles—some legends said *the* final battle—between Ymir and Crom.

Set at the southern feet of the magnificent Eiglophian Mountains, it was a cleared field of beaten earth with rune-carved stones set in a strange pattern. Dozens of small "eyetooth" bluestones framed the basic outline: vaguely star-shaped, with two of the six spines sticking out farther than the others. Then, twisted off center in the star, was a circle of sandstone megaliths. Hewn out of rock very common to the nearby Eiglophians, the megaliths were each as tall as a man, massive slabs that would have required the strength of half a hundred men to move.

But they were still not the great mystery.

That would be the Standing Stone, set off center within the megalithic circle. A massive, stark, black shaft of rock. Smooth from the polish of mighty hands, or over centuries of weathering, no one could say. No one knew the type of rock it was, or how it came to be standing on the Hoath

Plateau, or even the why of it. One legend claimed it was a missile in that long-ago war between Ymir and Crom. Another, that it was the anvil rock for the forge of Crom.

Ros-Crana had seen it once before. She'd had no answers then or now. All she knew was that the Field of Chiefs defied explanation.

And that Grimnir had been at it.

"What do you think he planned?" Sláine Longtooth asked, walking up behind her, joining Ros-Crana among the strangely carved megaliths, in the shadow of the Standing Stone itself. His voice wasn't a whisper, but it was softer than he normally spoke.

"Crom?" she asked, looking at the standing column of black rock.

A snort of laughter. But again, a soft one. "Grimnir."

There had never been any real doubt, not in her mind, that Grimnir had taken to the Hoath Plateau. All signs pointed east from Cruaidh, and if she ever did wonder, the violent destruction of several farmsteads and a few small villages along the way always reaffirmed that the Beast, the Great Terror, had been through ahead of them.

And patrols were strong, ready to summon a host to defend the plateau's more obvious access points. Scaling the cliffs above Spider Lake had given hers and Longtooth's war host a chance to prepare, and fight on their terms. Or so they had believed then.

They quickly learned the Vanir were not ready to take on such a large force loose in their midst. Discovering this not long after Hult Village, where their combined host of one hundred strong had surrounded and slaughtered and taken the heads of a Vanir patrol numbering only twenty-five, including a Ymirish warrior. It was the only real opposition they found as they moved hard and fast for the Field of Chiefs, everything else being scattered campsites and a few lone scouts.

Ros-Crana had wasted an entire day, in fact, scouring the land around the Field of Chiefs. Certain Grimnir would be waiting, preparing, and ready to defend this landmark.

Now, walking around the Standing Stone, she wondered. "Something," she said.

Grimnir had not made the Field of Chiefs his camp. Had not hammered at the megaliths in his usual style of wanton destruction. Instead, he'd built a sturdy wooden tower to rise up next to the Standing Stone, lashing stripped alderwood tree trunks together with strong leather cords that were wet, stretched, so when they dried—and shrank—the structure would not shift easily. All to raise a narrow platform, barely large enough to stand upon, almost even with the top of the shaft.

She had climbed up there, once. Found nothing more sinister than some burned leather stays, a loose timber in the platform, and an abandoned war sword forgotten atop the Standing Stone. A blue-iron blade with a fine edge and good balance, she'd kept that for herself.

She saw no reason to climb up again. Even that first time, she had not felt right about challenging the height of the Standing Stone.

"He treated the Field with something like respect after taking it away from the Hoathi and their allies." Her voice came slow and measured. Thinking aloud. "This was different. He did not come here to destroy. There was a plan."

"The Vanir," Longtooth said. "He knew nothing. Was not even part of the host Grimnir brought here to do this work." He kicked the base of the wooden tower. All that time and effort to trap a couple of men for interrogation, wasted.

She nodded. "Still. This was important to him. But either he completed his work here, or mayhap something interrupted it." One hand resting on the hilt of her new blade, she raised the other to rub the prickling flesh on the back of her neck. Then turned in a slow circle, as if some new sign would show itself among the strange carvings or from the Standing Stone.

"I think he didn't finish," she said. "I can nay say why I feel that, but I do."

And she could almost hear the echo of Grimnir's angry roar. Felt a touch of his sudden rage and the peril of his distraction.

Saw the charge of power that had shimmered in the air over the Field of Chiefs, cracking the sky in a harsh clap of thunder. It shook the ground. One Ymirish sorcerer keeled over as the darkness took him forever. All their work, lost, with nay time to begin again.

And there was Grimnir, picking himself up off the ground where the discharge of sorcerous power had thrown him down roughly. Staring south and east, and knowing where the distraction had come from.

Roaring a single name at the heavens . . .

She swooned. Stumbled. If Sláine Longtooth had not been there to catch her, support her arm, she'd have lain out over the ground in the same place where Grimnir himself had fallen.

"Easy, woman. Easy."

He tried to sit her down, back to the cold stone of one of the large megaliths, but Ros-Crana shook her head. Staggering under the weight that had struck at her just now, working off the deep, deep cold settled into her joints, her muscles, she forced herself to keep on her feet until they had cleared the eyetooth stones. Then she sagged to the ground as Dahr and Carrack and several Cruaidhi warriors jogged up to see what was the matter.

Ros-Crana recovered her strength quickly. She climbed to her feet, ignoring the offered hands, the concerned frowns and the sidelong glances.

"Get the host together," she ordered Dahr and Carrack.

"We move, running the night and all of the morrow." The two men hesitated for barely a heartbeat. "Now!"

Both fled to carry out her command. Longtooth nodded his own men after them. Leaving just the two chieftains, once again. "What?" he asked.

"Whatever Grimnir planned, the work was interrupted and lost. It killed one of his sorcerers. Don't ask me how I know, Sláine Longtooth." She shivered, recalling the ripple of power tearing through the air above the Field of Chiefs. "Just be thankful that it is so."

"How did it happen? What interrupted it?"

"Not what. Who." She shook herself. Threw off the last of the chill that had settled in deep, deep. "Only one man could make Grimnir *that* insane with rage." The name she had heard bellowed at the skies.

Kern.

"He's still alive," she said, staring south and east across the plateau.

"And Grimnir is moving directly for him."

20

IN HIS LIFE, Kern had never thought to see a Grand War Host.

It assembled on the plateau's eastern steppes, north and west of the Frost Swamp but still east of the final peaks of the Black Mountains, just after first light, while morning dew was still fresh on the tall, sharp-edged grass of the sward and an easy, dry breeze promised a good day's weather. Murrogh's strong force had arrived the day before, bringing the warriors and still bearing tokens from half a dozen villages. Gorram. Galt and Borat. And at this dawn came the war host of Clan Lacheish, eighty men strong and representing the best warriors of the north-plains clans.

This many men and women he had not seen gathered in one place since the last battle against Grimnir, on the bluff above Clan Conarch. Everywhere Kern looked, there was activity. Weapons inspected for rust, for nicks, being stropped against hand-sized hunks of black whetstone. Water carried in leather buckets from the nearby creek, always careful to dip above any man or woman coloring the stream. Bedrolls being tied up for travel. Horses fed.

And where men and women gathered, there were contests. Feats of strength. A few blows exchanged to settle honor debts or simply for the entertainment. Dicing, yea. Kern saw one man lose a fine dagger with a ruby the size of his thumbnail set in the pommel. Another ring, sketched out where the tall grasses had been beaten back or pulled from the earth, the bones running hot, cost two women a friendly grope.

Kern wondered, at the end, how many kin were going to find themselves picked up and carried off to a rival clan.

But by far the largest exchange was not in gambled treasures or honor, but trade. Two good knives for a leather vest studded across the shoulders with blue-iron spikes. Golden rings for silver armlets, much like the ones Kern wore. And tales and songs. Those were high stock among the easterners. The story of Cailt Stonefist's challenge to become chieftain was worth at least as much as the song for Deirdre's capture, as told from the Murrogh side. And one could always throw in a legendary exploit of Conan to sweeten the deal.

His battle against the wizard-king of Golamira.

Conan's brief marriage to the black pirate queen.

The warrior's victory at Gorram Village, where Conan fought through an entire morning, slowly retreating up the mountainside and leaving a trail of dead bodies at every step . . .

Kern hurried on, tall grasses whipping at his legs.

Not everything was so easy, however. There were bloody fights as well as bruising ones, and one killing that Kern heard tell of, though the other man involved was cast out from Lacheish for violating Cailt Stonefist's pledge of alliance. There were also a great many hostile stares and dark mutterings wherever Kern went. Hands reaching for blades, or balling into heavy fists. People knew who he was. Some even accepted him with a simple nod or a word passed. Most, though, had lost kin and kind to the Vanir raiders and their Ymirish masters.

Not much for Kern to do about such feelings. He always passed on quickly, never staying in one place long enough to be challenged. Or, for those looking for him specifically, easily found. He moved from group to gathering, listening in, and watching. Counting the number of times he saw fine leathers traded for wine, and mead. Or extra swords, a spare shield, some heavy furs . . . for food.

This last was the problem that concerned Kern most. The Murroghan host—more specifically, Morag—had not planned actually to set foot so far north. And Cailt Stonefist had sent back many of his supplies (and a few dozen warriors) to bolster the survivors at Lacheish.

Cailt had dismissed Kern's concerns when he brought them up the night before, the chieftain arriving on horseback far ahead of his main force. "Tomorrow we hunt, and we feast," the leader promised.

Though Kern had seen very little in the way of active game bounding across the steppes, Cailt had sounded very certain. And Hogann, who knew these lands as well as any clansman could, had nodded.

"Something to witness," Deirdre promised the doubters among the group. Mainly warriors who had come up from the thick, well-stocked forestland surrounding Murrogh.

So far, nay anyone had found a reason to doubt Cailt Stonefist. So none questioned it further.

"Kern!"

His name brought a few heads turning and silence from several nearby knots of warriors. The dark power surged, feeling out for any threat, any challenge. Since that morning, after Morag's doppelgänger's death, it had never quit him. Never allowed him to smother the call completely, banishing it as he had once before. It was one of the reasons he avoided the others.

One of many reasons.

But it was only Ehmish this time. The boy trotted up with a wary expression, suddenly aware of the uncomfortable silence that surrounded them. Kern pulled him along with a glance, working their way across the encampment.

He said nothing. Let Ehmish keep up or fall back as he wanted. Waiting for the other to speak first.

"Kern, Jaryyd has arrived. And his men with him. They look for Cailt."

That could be trouble. Had anyone told Jaryyd how Morag had been a creature of the Frost Swamp? Or had they merely told him that Morag was dead, and Murrogh's war host pledged to Cailt Stonefist of Lacheish?

He nodded. "Find Daol. Find Aodh and Brig." Jaryyd had always seemed to get on well with the hunters. And those three had also been close to hand when the feud was set aside.

"Nay anyone knows where Brig took himself off to," Ehmish complained.

"Ossian, then! And rouse the others."

"Why for?"

"When I know, you'll know. Off with you!"

With a glare, Ehmish turned and ran for the western edge of the large encampment, where most of Kern's warriors had set up their own small community. As usual, preferring their own company.

Used to it, by this time.

Kern had not meant to be quite so hard on Ehmish, but ever since his return the questions had come faster and with sharper points to them. His warriors wondering what had happened and why Kern had not told them his plans ahead of time, and what chance did they really have of finding Ros-Crana, creating a lasting alliance with the Lacheishi, and routing Grimnir's hordes.

For the first, he was not of a mind to speak of it. The latter . . . as he'd said, when he knew, they'd know.

Just now, he knew he had to find Cailt Stonefist and Jaryyd Morag's-son.

THAT MORNING BRIG Tall-Wood had hitched up his leggings, grabbed his bedroll and blade, and decided to take some time in a walk around the war host's encampment.

At the fire pit, Ossian used a charred stick to scatter the last of the morning coals. He'd piled a few last flat cakes on a rock at its edge, and when Brig stomped by, the Taurin stabbed one off the top with his dagger and offered it. Brig hesitated, waited. And then, teeth clenched hard enough his jaw hurt, took the oatmeal cake from the blade and traded it for a nod.

No one else bothered him. And by the time he'd lost himself in the bustle of the breaking camp, he'd already lost his taste for food.

He could nay take it much more, he decided. The heavy silences that followed him around. Followed them all around, really. But then there were those long pauses when he spoke with the others, that little shrug when they made up their minds to talk with him, and the way they then acted as if nothing had ever happened.

As if it did not matter that he might have, at most any moment, challenged Kern. Or, by simply not pulling his own weight among the warriors, let the Wolf-Eye die under a Vanir blade. Or under a mammoth's feet. Or in the clutches of the snow serpent on the Pass of Blood.

When Kern rode off on Valerus's horse below the Frost Swamp, Brig had expected to be challenged right there.

Kern had seen the truth about him, and certainly others had as well. But Kern's only comment among his preparations was to pull the other man aside, and whisper, "Still alive, Brig Tall-Wood."

Despite Brig's best efforts? Or acknowledging his ultimate choices?

Unable to answer it for himself, Brig could only follow his gut. There had been a note of finality in Kern's comment, and Brig couldn't say it did nay bother him. So he'd gathered his bedroll and a fresh flask of water and set out after Kern not a moment after their leader had ridden away.

"What do you think you're about?" Daol had asked him then, seeing Brig's preparations.

Now? Was that the accusation Daol did not put on the end of his question?

"You think he'll nay need help?" Brig asked in return.

There had been the first long pause, and to be fair the only one he'd gotten from Daol. Then the other man gave that little nod Brig had come to know so well these last days and quickly stripped his own kit down to the basics. Bedroll and blade. Light food and plenty of water.

It had been a long, hard run.

And now, with it over and Kern returned to them, the Men of the Wolves waited. Milled about, as if uncertain of their direction, their purpose. Among such a large gathering of clans and kin, it was easy, too easy, to lose their sense of purpose. Brig wasn't certain how much longer they could wait.

Not that he expected to find answers among the different groups who diced and bartered and traded songs for stories, blades for food. A diversion was what he'd sought. But the games of chance and tests of strength held no appeal for him this day, and Kern had heard—and helped build—enough legends of mighty Conan to have his fill of stories as well.

Nay many of them believed anymore that their own adventure would end with anywhere so neat an ending as the
Cimmerian legend always managed.

So he wandered. He ate the scorched oat cake slowly
because his body needed the energy. Chewed absently.
Struck a trail through the swordgrass not already trampled
by others and was thankful for his leggings as the sharp-
edged grass slapped at him with every stride.

That was when he spotted a familiar face, lugging deadwood branches of pine and hemlock. Topknot. A spider-
shaped tattoo on his shoulder. Clan Galla. Brig knew him
for one of the men who had chased north with Kern's
wolves, looking for their kinsmen. And there was another,
also with his arms piled high of evergreen branches,
though his looked still to be fresh, green wood.

And another.

If diversion was what Brig sought instead of answers,
he had found it. Bending his path through the tall sward, he
followed after them to the outskirts of the encampment
where Tergin and a small party of others worked to uproot
grass over a wide clearing near one of the small creeks.
They grubbed on hands and knees, getting down below the
sharp blades to grab up the grass stalks and rip out handfuls at a time.

The Galla saw Brig's arrival, and many traded nods of
greeting with him. No pause. No hedging. If for nay other
reason, Brig decided to stay. Even help as the mountain
tribesmen built a good-sized fire in the center of their
clearing, and began to pile it high with tinder-dry branches
to create a blazing bonfire that might have warmed dozens
of men at night but seemed a wasted effort and a danger
among the grass sward during the day.

A few men stood nearby with leather buckets already
full of water. And others were wringing out a large blanket
they had doused in the creek. Precautions, in case a stray

spark set the grass afire? But the grasses were too wet, and Tergin had planned well; there was too great a distance between fire and sward.

"Planning for a large cooking fire?" Brig asked, breaking the silence. He knew the Galla could go for the entire day without talk. And often did. If he wanted to know, he needed to ask.

Tergin watched as his warriors added more branches. The flames danced higher than his head, and the crackling roar of dry tinder being consumed brought a small circle of onlookers to surround the Galla. Standing closer to the flames than most, Tergin let the heat work against his face, his bared chest and arms. Soon, sweat glistened against his skin. And Brig's.

"Cailt Stonefist needs more warriors," he finally said. As if this answered Brig's question.

"And a fire will help this?"

"Yea."

Brig had seen stranger things, he decided. And watched as the green stick branches were hauled over to be thrown atop the crackling blaze. Then armloads of the wet grasses he'd watched the Galla tear from the ground. More branches.

"They'll smother it."

"Yea," Tergin said again.

And they did. Burying the flames until thick, acrid green smoke roiled out of the fire. Their audience backed away, eyes tearing. The Galla crowded in closer, and Brig with them, squinting into the stinging smoke. Feeling the green scent burn up into their nostrils, scratch at the back of their throats.

Then Tergin called for the blanket.

Brig remembered then Kern's tale of being taken to the Galla campsite. That Tahg Chieftain had claimed to know how many Vanir pursued them up into the Pass of Noose by the smoke from their campfires. As Brig or Daol or Hydallan might read trail sign, knowing the size of a herd by counting prints, or broken twigs, or the width of a trampled bramble, so the mountain clansmen often looked to the skies.

Now Brig stared west, where the Black Mountains rose to snow-dusted peaks, and wondered.

The large, dampened blanket was spread between four men, Tergin among them. At a rush they threw it over the blaze, bringing it down and holding it until they might have smothered the fire themselves, but really they waited just long enough to build up the heat deep inside and contain the smoke.

Then, they stripped back one side to let a heavy cloud roil out and up.

Covered the fire again, holding it for a silent count. At Tergin's call they stripped the other side, and again a thick cloud of smoke pushed for the clear sky.

Again, and again. When the blanket began to dry, warriors splashed water from their leather buckets over it. The sky overhead filled with a drift of artificial clouds. Small ones. Long, large ones. Brig saw nay pattern to it, but trusted Tergin knew his craft. And after a time the work was rewarded when one of the Galla stopped and pointed.

Far up on the slopes of the Black Mountains, a long column of smoke rose in a dark, waving banner.

Then another.

There was a great deal of pointing and excited talk among the crowd as well. Some pushing. Some arguments. More than a few suspicious glares thrown at the sweating, struggling Galla. To some, Brig knew, it might seem like sorcery. And the clansmen knew enough to want no part in what they did not understand.

He debated stepping back to explain it, but the idea was interrupted when a blaring horn sounded from the center of

camp. Nothing like a Vanir war horn, Brig knew, counting
four short blasts. Looking toward the center of camp, he
saw several tall banners being waved. One black. One red.

The hunt was about to begin.

And just in time. The crowd dispersed, black looks
traded for cheer and expectation of a good day and a large
feast at its end. Most of them, anyway. There were still a
few distrustful glares spent on the Galla, who continued to
work their fire so long as it poured out thick, green smoke.

"They aren't certain what this is," Brig said, as if apologizing for the other flatlanders. The horn sounded again.
Again with four summoning blasts.

Tergin shrugged in Galla fashion, tipping his head to
one side, then back. "They can ask," he said. A glance at
Brig as he, too, moved away. "You did."

So he had. And, Brig realized, at times the solution was
just that simple. Isolation and silence could be overcome,
after all.

He considered this, stepping back into the bustle of the
encampment, getting caught up in the new activity but not
completely losing himself in it. Not this time. That, he'd
already tried. He'd gone looking for diversion.

He might have found the beginning of an answer.

NOT TOO DIFFICULT, Kern discovered, to find Jaryyd
and Cailt.

The leaders had gathered near the center of the large encampment, where the many different bearing spears had
been stuck into the ground in one long line. No one totem
was raised significantly higher than the others. None stood
forward of the rest. Kern saw the ram's horn of Lacheish
between the spider's teeth of Galla and the wolf's pelt of
Clan Laeda, a Lacheish ally. It was a careful, well-thought
gesture, Kern decided.

The wolf pelt itself did give him a heartbeat's pause.

Though not so much as seeing Jaryyd Morag's-son stepping in to slug Cailt Stonefist hard in the mouth.

Now Kern ran forward, hand on the hilt of his short sword and mouth suddenly dry as baked wool. Waiting for blades to be pulled and the slaughter to begin. Knowing that at any moment the call would be raised and the battle between Murrogh and Lacheish, avoided the other day, would spill across the encampment here and now.

Except that it didn't. There was a cheer from among Jaryyd's warriors, and not much else. Then Cailt waded back in, and his huge fist came around hard and fast to smash against the side of Jaryyd's head.

Jaryyd never tried to duck the blow. Kern saw the explosion of pain cross Jaryyd's face. And Morag's son stumbled to his hands and knees. Cailt stood above him, surprised, likely, that the younger man was still conscious. He held down a hand and helped Jaryyd back to his feet.

"Well struck," Jaryyd said. Shaking his head. His left eye was swelling shut, and a large bruise already spread across the side of his face.

Cailt Stonefist smiled through a split lip. Spat blood to one side. "The hunt is mine," he said. And laughed.

Now it was the Lacheishi who cheered. One man with shaven temples retrieved a red banner, another held overhead a black. The cloth flags were long and tapered. The poles extra tall, to be seen from a greater distance across the sward.

Cailt picked up the curling ram's horn, held it to his lips, winced, and passed it to Loht, the Lacheishi champion, who blew four strident blasts. The campsite buzz of conversations increased, and the men and women hurried now to finish their stories, to collect winnings or close a barter, and to grab up their gear in preparation for the day's hunt.

Jaryyd waited next to Cailt, both men eyeing each other as if they'd like another exchange of blows. Each gave Kern a measuring stare, seeing the frost-haired man trot up with his frown of concern.

"Nay worries, Kern Wolf-Eye." Cailt spat blood aside again. His teeth were stained red when he grinned. "A matter of honor only."

Jaryyd was not so casual. Setting his thick-muscled legs in a wide stance. Hands on his hips. Looking Kern in the eyes, holding that golden gaze (something not many men did overlong) he held his peace a moment. Mayhap remembering that Kern had guested at his camp, and vice versa, and each had always paid the other respect even if he hadn't been made welcome.

Finally, he said in a careful tone, "Some say you killed my father."

Pressure built at Kern's temples, at the back of his head, with the implied threat. Kern smothered it, waiting. "I killed the creature who pretended at your father's face."

"That is another story I hear," Jaryyd admitted. Though he didn't sound as if he quite believed it. Yet. "We are not through, you and I. But first we will see who Grimnir's war host spares. That, at least, you spoke truth. The Vanir were a greater threat than any of us believed."

"At times it is hard to know what to believe, Jaryyd Morag's-son."

"Or whom to trust." He turned away then, and Kern did notice Hogann and several Hoathi join Jaryyd's men. He looked back only once. "After," he promised.

Fair enough. Kern also did not miss the suspicious looks sent his way by other men who followed Jaryyd. Certainly they would remember Kern's involvement in trying to heal the breach between father and son. Some of them had to wonder if this were Kern's solution, to bring all of Murrogh's strength back under one man. The tale of the doppelgänger was, Kern admitted, a far-fetched story if one had not been there to see, to hear.

The Hoathi knew, of course, and believed. But what would they *say* about it so far as Kern was concerned?

Four more blasts from the horn, and now the entire camp came alive as the bearers of the red and black banners separated on a run to head out east and west from the bearing spears. Kern waited, knowing he should return to his own warriors, but wanting to observe, and catch a further word with the Lacheishi chieftain.

"This hunt will supply us with enough food for the next few days?" he asked.

Cailt traded glances with his champion, then his daughter, who had joined the small gathering. It was Deirdre who answered. "This hunt will provide food enough for weeks, should we need it." A downcast glance. "Though we do nay expect Grimnir to give us such time."

Nay. The Great Terror would not be far. And it was time to warn Cailt Stonefist. "Grimnir may know already where we are," he promised. "And come at us sooner than we think."

"Because he sees through your eyes?" the leader asked. Saw Kern's start of surprise. "Torgvall admitted the same, did he not?" As calm as he might be discussing the day's hunt, Cailt talked of Kern's possible—if unknowing—aid to Cimmeria's enemy. He shrugged, as if he had not yet made up his mind. "Our other choice, of course, is the same courtesy we showed Torgvall."

Strength flooded Kern's body as the dark power sang. Wrapped in a calm voice or nay, it knew a dangerous threat. Kern swallowed hard. "I would prefer to find a different solution," he admitted.

Cailt laughed, though not necessarily in favor of Kern. "As do a few others who have come to speak with me, Wolf-Eye, arguing in your defense. As Jaryyd said, we shall see what happens, shall we?"

"Yea," Kern agreed. Unable to ask for anything more.
At least, on that subject.

He watched as the Grand War Host of several hundred
men shook itself out into a ragged line, being stretched between the two retreating banners, never having seen anything like it. The line grew thinner, and longer, over time,
until there was one warrior for every ten paces or so. Half a
league, at least, they stretched across the sward. Kern expected his warriors to be caught in the procession somewhere out on the red-banner wing. Looking for him?
Mayhap they were. But they'd keep. They'd keep.

Now, with a nod from Cailt, Loht blew one long blast to
start the hunt moving forward. At each end of the line, the
red and black banners waved, and moved ahead, pacing the
hunt.

"There is more life than you would think on the steppes,"
Cailt said, leading his large horse forward by its bridle. No
other charger had mounted yet, waiting for the host's leader.
"Some large game—elk and deer might cross—but mostly
small game, which is hard to hunt with a bow. Even traplines
aren't as useful within the tall grasses."

Kern could see that, stomping forward through the
sward. He had finally given over to eastern tradition and
had cloth wrapped about his legs. Not for any threat of
cold, though, but the sharp-edged grasses, which actually
cut at unprotected flesh. One shallow scratch, even two,
was hardly worth complaining about. But over hours, the
grass blades could leave a man's legs raw and bleeding.

"We move forward for a league, two, beating the brush
and driving all game ahead of us. Then we bend the wings
around and forward. Forming a large cup." He held his
hands before him, heels touching, then slowly bent his fingers forward. "By afternoon, the banners will be far ahead
of our position, then we wrap them in." He closed his fingers, forming a large circle with his hands. "Tighten it

down, wade in, and we'll have enough game trapped within our trap to feed the host for weeks. Nothing escapes."

Which was part of Kern's final concern. "Nothing," he repeated. He felt a flush on the back of his neck. "That is one thing I'd like to bring up with you, Cailt Stonefist."

"Your wolf."

Did nothing escape the attention of this man? Any chance remark or blurted comment took firm root within his mind, it seemed. And he drew conclusions faster, tied them together stronger, than any other chieftain Kern had ever met.

What if he had turned north, and brought the bloody spear to Cailt Stonefist instead of to Murrogh? What might have been accomplished then?

What if . . .

Kern shook his head, avoiding the questions piling up in the back of his mind. "The wolf is not mine." No more so than a warrior could be thought of as "his." Certainly not in the same way a blade or bedroll was owned. "It is . . . has been . . ."

"A totem." It sounded so simple, coming from Cailt. "I know. And I won't tell you that there are nay a few who believe we should take this chance to be rid of it. But my command has been very clear. If a large wolf is seen, it will be left alone unless it clearly is not marked as yours."

Would that stop Hogann, or Cul, from risking Cailt's wrath?

"On pain of death, Wolf-Eye." Cailt all but read Kern's mind. "I do not make idle threats."

That surprised Kern, Cailt going so far to protect what many considered a dangerous beast. Even Kern was never too certain about the animal, knowing better than to ever turn his back on it. A wolf was still a wolf, no matter how odd it may act at times.

And was a Ymirish, then, still a Ymirish? Was Kern still

Grimnir's tool, a son of Ymir, even if he stood on the other side of the field and raised his blade against the Vanir?

In the end, would he be able to deny the call of his own blood?

Hard questions that plagued him as he shifted down the line, looking for his warriors. He knew from many of the dark, sidelong glances he caught—and all the ones he didn't, but were marked by a flare of pain and pressure at the fore of his mind—that he was not the only one asking them. And should the answers not be to the liking of Cailt Chieftain, then what?

Kern looked back down the line, saw Cailt Stonefist now astride his horse and leading the center forward at a slow pace. Remembering what the war host's leader had let drop between them, of the fate that had fallen to the Ymirish, Torgvall.

Remembering as well, Cailt Stonefist did not make idle threats.

21

TWO DAYS AFTER the hunt found Kern crouched at the edge of a low mesa, leaning out over the fall, his gaze roaming across the steppes. A collection of small rocks in his hand, he tossed one, then another, out over the abyss. Marking time. The delay, then the distant clatter of each pebble skipping down along the face.

A sharp wind kicked gritty dust off the mesa's dry top, swirling it over and around him in a tiny cyclone. He squinted his eyes against the dust devil.

Pitched another stone.

Listened to the fall.

After rolling out his bedroll in the late afternoon, he had climbed the ridge to escape. Ducking the questioning glances. Needing one moment to slip out from beneath the heavy silences that had followed him for several days at meals and on the march. And to see. To look out over the Hoath Plateau's eastern lands and wonder where out on those desolate plains they would find Grimnir.

Or where Grimnir would finally find them.

The morrow, Kern decided. One more day.

The news might not be good, but he did have a view he could appreciate. Here the Hoath Plateau leveled out between the Eiglophian Mountains along its entire northern border, and the rise of the Black Mountains to the south and west. Having lived for so long in Conall Valley, Kern had always looked upon the Black Mountains and their Snowy River country as great, looming peaks. Now, caught between them and the Eiglophians, he knew the Blacks for the foothills they really were.

The Eiglophian Mountains were massive. A barrier separating Cimmeria from Vanaheim, and Asgard, and even parts of Hyperborea to the far, far east. Winds whipped down from those ranges, carrying a cold with them that could only come from such snowcapped peaks, or from the northern wastes that stretched beyond their rise through Asgard and Vanaheim. Cold enough for hailstones, the day before, but those clouds had moved on quickly.

The sky this day spread a brilliant blue field overhead, running into dark clouds many, many leagues to the west. The breeze was dry, but still crisp with the reminder that spring had not yet blended into summer. Not this far north. Not so high over the Valley or Murrogh Forest, either one.

But a good, clear day. And from here Kern could see over leagues of rolling hills and open grassland. A few narrow, blue ribbons stretched into the distance; streams and small creeks, crisscrossing the open land. Occasionally, he knew, another mesa might rise up out of the plateau. But for the most part, there should have been a great deal of open land out there where warriors could lose themselves. Even so many.

Three hundred warriors at least, all counted. And they were not done building. Men and women continued to trickle in from all directions. Hoathi and Maughan and warriors from half a dozen other villages Kern had never heard of, who had somehow found out about the Grand War Host being put together under the leadership of Cailt Stonefist. And the Galla, of course. Warriors from one tribe after another. A half dozen to ten at a time, they came down off the Black Mountains in answer to Tergin's signal fire.

They all came, with swords and spears and shields and often little else except the desire to stand against the Vanir invaders who had wrecked and ravaged their way across Cimmeria for too many years.

And by all reports, still not strong enough.

"Thinking about jumping, pup?"

Hydallan's voice startled Kern, who had neither seen anyone begin the climb from below nor heard an approach. Too lost in his own thoughts, yea, but still, seeing the entire pack spread out behind him, all sixteen, set him back a pace. Even Valerus, though the southerner was nay a good climber. And Wallach! With one hand missing, the arm turning black and septic, he'd nay reason to make such a climb.

"How did you find your way up here?" he asked.

Daol smiled. His gray eyes bright and alive, like a hunting falcon. "Ehmish and I scouted a good trail ahead of the host. An easy hike, with very little climbing." His voice sharpened. "If you'd been around, you'd have known."

"Busy," Kern said, returning his attention to the scene below, to the anthill activity of so many men and women as they fetched water, checked their weapons and their armor, and built up many, many cooking fires.

Food was hardly a problem anymore, with the success of Cailt's hunt, and few clansmen saw any reason to hold back with good meat to stake out over a fire. Kern still found it hard to believe the war host had stirred up so much game. Closing ranks across a wide stretch of the sward, the red and black banners finally bending around to close the circle, they had then tightened the noose to strangle the creatures within just as Cailt had planned it.

Finally, the grasslands had been unable to hide them all. Strange, to see a puma running side by side with a stag, and among a stampede of hares and quail, fox and pheasant and, yea, wolves too. Predators and prey were all among the hunted now, and had no time for their usual chases. Pacing, bounding back and forth, and occasionally making a break for an edge of the closing noose.

The puma made it, coming in low and fast, leaping past a startled Hoathi who picked up a set of bloody stripes for his slow blade.

The stag did not.

So much meat was not about to escape the war host's grasp, and half a dozen arrows brought it down in a tumble. Then it was out swords and to work as well. The slaughter was frenetic and bloody, and left behind tired arms and the warriors spattered in so much blood one might believe they had already come against Grimnir's hordes.

But nay. That was not the case, yet.

Kern studied the western horizon again. Felt the stares burning into his back and tamped down the threat of power that whispered to him, as if he'd need it to defend against his own.

They stood back of him, waiting him out. Not one of them said a word, or moved to join him. But neither were they going to retreat and leave him be, he knew. His only decision was to slip over the edge of the drop, and climb for the lower steppes. But he knew they'd be waiting for him there. Or back at camp. Or on the field of battle.

And he owed them better than that.

He stood, tossed his final few stones out over the drop, and left them to rattle and clatter away in a fast, violent fall.

"I've had some things to think over," Kern said.

His heels hung out over the drop. The gusting winds tugged his long, frost blond hair out to the right in ragged streamers. Whipped more dirt off the mesa and swirled it around him in another quick dust devil. He swallowed against the gritty taste and the tight knot in his throat. Finally, stepping away from the cliff, he walked over to the waiting pack.

Stopped soon enough to leave a wide gulf between them. Several steps that not anyone seemed willing to cross. They waited, as if expecting more from him.

Always, always expecting more.

"I've nay any need to explain myself," he said.

That struck at a many of them like a slap. Daol and Reave, who had stood by him since childhood. Desa. Aodh. Ehmish, whom Kern (and many of them) watched over like a son. Hydallan, who had acted as much a father to Kern as he'd ever known.

Wallach Graybeard, pale and sweating and feverish, with dark pits for eyes, having given more to the pack than anyone save Ashul's sacrifice in Gaud. Kern saw the old veteran recoil and felt the worse for it.

The man should have been back in Murrogh getting his arm shaved and cleansed and maybe—maybe!—saved. At least made comfortable for his end. Kept warm and preferably drunk. Not hauling himself atop a mesa after a full day's run, tying a tourniquet around his arm, higher and tighter every day, so he could buckle his cuff over the black stump without the unbearable pain.

"You haven't before," Brig Tall-Wood said. Seeming to agree.

Cul's man stood off to one side, right at a break in the group, as if caught between his own divide. On his left were the Taurin—Ossian, stroking his goat's beard, standing in front of Danon and dour Mogh—and Valerus and

Nahud'r and Gard Foehammer. The outsiders and rogues who had made themselves a part of the pack. On Brig's right were the Gaudic. Kern's friends and teachers, and the ones who had felt indebted to remain with him.

Were his warriors breaking apart? Showing fracture lines that had been there all along?

"Nay, you haven't before," Brig repeated. "But we're asking it now. *I'm* asking, Kern."

There were many ways for Kern to answer. Including walking off and leaving the pack behind, letting them find their way with Cul Chieftain or Cailt, or with a new leader from among them. He could also cut Brig out from the others and turn all the questions and the doubts against this man who had run with them for so long, and all that time holding a knife at Kern's back.

But what would either accomplish? Whether he'd ever wanted it or not, the pack was his responsibility. And that included Brig, for as long as the man continued to step up among them. He had saved Kern's life, more than once, and if Kern would throw that aside for what the man might have done, could have done, was thought to do . . . he'd have been no better than Cul. Judging the man before the action.

"What would you know, Brig Tall-Wood?"

"When you left us before the Frost Swamp. You did not think to come back. Yea?"

That cut to the heart of it.

"Nay. I did not. I was certain the Murrogh would kill me, no matter what was proven about Morag. And I'd have put it on Grimnir, as part of the northern invasion, and damned my own honor!" It had been that important. That crucial to turn the war host north.

"But Maev kept them from it. And Cul, then, for his own reasons. Then everything happened so quickly. A truce with Cailt Chieftain. You, and Daol, and Aodh, showing up as you did. Nothing happened the way I'd expected."

At least this last mystery had been explained easily enough. It had been Brig's idea to run after Kern, he knew, and not a moment after he'd ridden away on Valerus's horse. He'd spoken none of his suspicions, though now it was clear he'd seen through Kern's plans from the moment he laid them, and when he could not be turned from it, Daol and Aodh had run with him.

Putting themselves in place just in time to see Torgvall ride north from Clan Lacheish. Aodh had called for arrows, seeing only an enemy within reach. It had been his shaft to bring down the horse and capture the golden-eyed warrior.

A good thing Torgvall had fallen out of Cailt Stonefist's favor by running. It was all that kept Kern's men alive when the Lacheishi patrol surrounded them and took them prisoner.

And having Torgvall to question, and prove Kern's accusations against the Vanir, the Ymirish, and Grimnir, might have sealed the bargain between the clans. One decision leading to another and building on yet another. Like ripples, spreading out across the water. Or, how a single stone, dropped into a stream, can divert its path.

But to flood, or to feed new lands? That remained the question.

"Does it matter?" Ehmish asked. "How it happened?"

The young man chewed on his lower lip. Shuffled around as if he wanted to step forward, but wasn't going to be the first. "It happened, Kern. Look down there again." He gestured toward the mesa's edge. "That is *your* war host."

Nay! "It is Cailt Stonefist's," Kern said.

Hydallan kicked at a large rock sitting on the ground.

Sent it skipping and rolling toward the edge of the mesa, and over, crashing down the side. "Crom's golden orbs, you would be saying that, stupid pup. Was nay Cailt Stone-fist who came a-looking for the bloody spear. You shoved it down his throat. And was nay him who brought the clans together round Murrogh either."

"Or," Daol said, "the one who apparently convinced Ros-Crana to finally come out of the western lands. Was quite a tongue-lashing you must have left her with."

Reave smiled thinly. "I did nay hear you'd been in the baths together that long," he said, feigning admiration. Desagrena elbowed him in the gut, though it was like hitting a tree trunk for all the good it did.

Kern shook his head. "That's not it. Not at all."

Ossian glowered, tugging at the rings braided into his goat's beard. "Puts your hackles up, they don't fall all over themselves the way we do to listen? Running with us isn't quite the same, yea?" He shrugged. "Doesn't matter. Without you, there would be nay Grand War Host. It's yours as much as it's anyone's."

"And I don't want it!" Kern yelled.

That silenced everyone for a spell, and he breathed deep, tasting the dirt and the static charge on the strengthening breeze. Windstorm this night. And Grimnir . . .

"Grimnir's host has been gathering strength as well," Kern reminded them. "Even if Ros-Crana were to find us, and we don't know her host isn't already dead, strewn across the plateau, I think we are overwhelmed."

Old Finn spat to one side. "Know soon enough."

"We'll know on the morrow!" Kern told them.

The dark rage was there, ready to sweep him away, but not now, not now. He could nay bury it again, he knew. It was all he could do to keep it in check even during the most calm of moments. And this was not one of them.

"Taste the air," he said. "Check the sky." Many craned

their heads up, licked their lips. Read the weather in the way any Cimmerian learns from an early age if he does not want to get caught in a spring flood, a winter blizzard, or unprepared for a coming drought.

Hydallan did not bother. The elder tracker kept his thumb on such things by matter of habit.

"Dry winds from the north and west. Been blowing stronger all day. Can taste the lightning. Be a windstorm this night, but good weather, I'm a-guessing."

"Then explain to me how there have been black clouds piled up on the western horizon since the morn, and they've not swept over us. Or how the winds bear no hint of the rain they must be carrying." Heads swiveled. Hydallan frowned into the distance, caught unawares. Kern tasted their fear, metallic and warm, at the back of his throat. "Tell me how that can be explained by any reason other than the arrival of Grimnir and his sorcerers."

Now he had them. Now he let them see a part of what had driven him so far away.

Hydallan grabbed the peaked, rabbit fur hat from his head and wrung it between a pair of gnarled, leathery hands. "Can't," he finally admitted. "Must be there, sure enough. And you're right, pup. The morrow it is."

The others were quiet, studying the dark wall of clouds.

"We know Grimnir escaped Broken Leg Glen with a solid host left to him," Kern said softly, also staring off to the west. "He had raiders by the score rallying at Venarium, and that was after he'd already passed through and scooped up a good number. We've an idea what Lodur brought across the Pass of Noose. How many more Ymirish are there with that kind of strength? We've heard reports of large troops such as these hitting all across the Hoathi lands. Now, you can be sure, by Crom, they've flocked to Grimnir's banner."

"What if they have?" Gard asked. "Where did you ever think this was heading, Kern Wolf-Eye?"

That was just it. He wasn't certain anymore. Not after Cul's admission in the Murrogh camp. It had raised doubts. All of the doubts that Kern had kept buried for many months. Where things were heading now. What Kern could have done better, different, at Callaugh, at Conarch. Even as far back as Gaud, when Cul had claimed Burok Bear-slayer's legacy. Could he have stopped it then?

Could he have lived another life? Never to be tempted by his Ymirish heritage?

"It all might have happened so much differently."

"What?" Daol asked. "Kern, by Crom's long spear. Finally. What *is* it?"

Daol had caught a hint of Kern's uncertainty. Had been on top of it since that night in the woods, when the dark power had first sung through his blood. But that wasn't all there was, and at the moment was hardly even the most of it. So Kern fed him the easier of two very difficult truths.

He told them all about Cul's admission. And Maev's words.

"I do not believe it would have happened that way," he admitted. "I think Gaud was nay ready for me as anything but an outcast who walked among them. Winter-born. The blood of wolves. But now I wonder, and I question all that has come before. What if . . ." He scrubbed hands over his face. "Mayhap we might have saved so much spilled blood. And Wallach's hand." He swallowed hard. Looked to Ossian on one side, Aodh on the other. "Ashul's life," he said. Apologizing to both men: her kinsman and her lover.

Ossian snorted. "Ashul? She knew the risk. We all did. We *chose*." He folded his arms across his chest. "Ashul be dead at Taur, Kern, you nay comes along when you did! My father, he never goes to Gaud with Maev, with the others. And you would be less prepared when Grimnir slaughters his way through the valley? And he would have—this year, next year. You know this now."

"We can't know anything about what might have happened."

"We know enough," Aodh said. He brushed down his moustache. "We've each of had our own reasons for being here. And Ossian's right. Ashul knew. Even at the end, she knew the truth. That we stood by you, nay matter what else. Because you are one of—"

. . . them . . .

"—us."

Kern blinked. Every thought erased out of his mind, as if a hand had wiped them away, but one. Ashul, lying in the muck, her hair spread out in a dark fan and blood pooling in the gut wound. Trying so hard to say one last thing before she died.

Whu—One! One of . . .

"What did you say?"

Ossian spread his hands, as if the answer was so apparent he was surprised it needed repeating. Mogh and Danon also nodded. Mogh, dour-faced as ever, spoke for the Taurin. "One of *us*, Kern Wolf-Eye."

Daol and Reave nodded. And Ehmish. Wallach and Nahud'r and even Valerus. Soon it was nearly all of them. Only Gard hesitated, just the moment, but then he as well.

Kern noticed also they had all closed ranks, moving in toward each other. Taurin and Gaudic and Cruaidhi and Aquilonian. No fracture lines, except the ones Kern might have opened by remaining so distant, letting emotions and their questions fester. He was still held just outside of arm's reach, a gulf that no one had crossed, but then, he had always known that little bit of distance, hadn't he? As outcast, then as leader.

His wolves. They deserved so much better.

What they had was him.

"In desert," Nahud'r said, breaking the sudden silence, "one can be caught by storms so fierce, raging unchecked for so many, many leagues, the winds pick up all sand and move it from one place to other. And when great sands blow, they scour land and everything that fall into their path. Everything."

There were only a few nods, Kern saw, as the warriors all tried to picture one of the great sandstorms from Nahud'r's many tales. Hard to imagine. He checked the western horizon. Then again, mayhap not.

Nahud'r shrugged. "Like riding through sword grasses of your plains, only grasses cut also at hands and faces and eyes."

Another reason the dark-skinned Shemite wore a scarf wrapped about his face?

"How do you survive these storms?" Kern asked. The Shemite was a natural storyteller. Drawing one in, often despite oneself.

"Of three ways," the dark-skinned man promised. "Many ride as hard as can away from blowing sands. Racing ahead. Praying to Anu"—he raised both hands to touch his brow—"they find shelter, or that winds lose strength. Others, we dig hole in the sands. Cover selves with cloak, and again, pray to Anu"—again, the gesture of respect—"to let the sands blow by and not bury us alive."

He had them all now, Kern saw. The exotic place. The looming danger. Everyone waited. Everyone looked at each other.

Finally, it was Ossian who asked. "And the third way?"

The Shemite grinned. And it was nay pleasant. "They say if you cover eyes, and hands, and ride as hard as can *into* the storm, you ride out other side before death comes."

"That works?" Kern asked, doubtful.

A shrug. "No one I hear ever pray hard enough to later say."

A grim outlook. And one most Cimmerians could appreciate. "Tomorrow," Kern said, "we ride into the storm."

·Nahud'r raised his hands, touching them to chest, to chin, and to his brow before saluting Kern. "And tomorrow I pray," he said. Grinned. "Very hard."

Most of the pack grinned with him. Ready to challenge the gods. Kern nodded his thanks. "We should head down, then. Give Cailt Stonefist an idea of what lies ahead."

A great deal of blood and death. And nay any way to cheat it this time that Kern could see. Like Nahud'r's storms, there would be no simple tricks the morrow. No battlefield foolery would cloud the golden eyes of Grimnir. Especially if they believed Torgvall, and what Kern now felt was true as well. That he was a spy in the Cimmerian camp. An unwilling one, but a spy nonetheless.

Well, Kern had thwarted Grimnir's carefully laid plans before, by putting himself in front of the sword to stop the war between Clans Murrogh and Lacheish. If he could do so again, he would. The Great Beast was not infallible, nay matter what he might know . . .

Or *believed* he knew.

"Kern?" Daol asked. He frowned at Kern's slack expression. "Aren't we heading down?"

Crom's swinging sword! Kern did have a final trick, mayhap. One Grimnir had handed to him. But it might come at a terrible cost. One Kern wasn't certain he was willing to pay.

"What would you give?" he asked Daol. Stepped back and brought them all in with a glance. Asked them all. "What would be worth bringing down the Beast?"

Silence. And it was Reave who answered for them all. "Nay cost would be too large," he said. There were answering nods all around.

It would have to do. He could not explain any more to them than that. And he had to guess that whatever Grimnir's powers, they all had limits. Including any ability to see through Kern's eyes. Hear through his ears. Those had been Torgvall's words. Not *knows what I know*.

"Daol," Kern said. "Ossian. Brig. You three run ahead of us. Find Cailt Chieftain and let him know what we've seen. His own outriders will know the same by darkfall, but let's give him as much time as possible. Tell him—" Careful. "Grimnir must have his eye on us by now. He comes straight for us."

"He'll wants to hear it from you," Ossian said.

"Tell him," Kern said. "Tell him exactly that. And then tell him that we still volunteer to vanguard the war host."

"We does?" asked Ossian.

"Yea. Running out in front of the first line, on the northern approach, as his plans called for. I'll be right behind you. And he can give me the final orders then."

Brig frowned. "But why—"

"Just trust me," he said. Having a good idea what it would cost them all in the end. "Tell him exactly, and let the dice fall how they will, Brig Tall-Wood. Even you should understand that."

That Kern was gambling. Rolling the bones, and with nothing less than their lives wagered on it. The warrior seemed to pick up on it. He also, very obviously, did not understand. But he nodded. "Going to make it hard on us, taking the first line."

"Then it's hard," Kern said. "Anyone want to argue?" No one did, and Kern laughed. The first time in days. It felt good. "Never seen so many warriors eager to follow a man into death." He tried on a grim smile. It didn't feel completely out of place, either. "But at least I'll be in good company."

There were a few nods. Dark smiles from Ossian and Gard. Old Finn shrugged, and laughed. "Died this last winter, the lot of us. Just refuse to lie down yet."

Kern nodded, though not easily. The words were likely true for too many of the warriors here. But he wouldn't shame them again by not valuing their loyalty, their sacri-

fice. Hard enough it was, that he took for granted their trust
and devotion yet still failed to give the same back.

"Well, we're not quite ready yet. So let's move."

He watched the three race off, following his commands.
Gathered the rest of his wolves around him, and proceeded
at a slower pace, giving them time. Drawing from his
friends the strength he'd need to see this through, even
while knowing he'd likely betrayed them all.

He had shared with them so much.

And still, he had not shared everything.

22

THE CLOUD COVER slowly rolled forward over the plains like Aquilonian soldiers marching in a perfect line of battle. Kern kept a nervous eye on them. Their unnatural behavior. The way they drew a blanket over the plateau from the nearer Black Mountains north to the Eiglophians. There would be blue sky, deepening toward sapphire as the sun fell toward the Pictish wilderness far, far to the west, then, suddenly, there were piles of storm clouds: purplish-black, like swollen bruises, crashing through the heavens with terrible thunder and hammering the ground with strikes of brilliant, violet-clad lightning.

The building storm drove the winds before it, whipping them across the plains without reason. Gusts drove in from the north, then south. There might be a lull, then Kern and his warriors ducked forward as they ran directly into a powerful blow, the sharp winds hurling dust and grit and bits of grasses into their faces.

A wolf's howl rose somewhere behind them. Calling

them back. Encouraging them forward. No way for Kern to tell. Still his warriors held hands up to shield their eyes, blinked away the lightning's afterglare, and continued to press on.

Surging toward the first of the Vanir horde.

The raiders ran slightly in advance of the storm. Better than twenty men and women, some with war bows strung and arrows nocked, most with heavy blades waving overhead or beating them against their shields and breastplates as they called out berserker cries and charged crosswise along a low hill.

They'd caught Kern's pack in the wide lowlands that ran between the plain's few rises. Pinned them in place with staggered flights of arrows.

"Nay good." Wallach Graybeard slammed up against Kern's side, taking some protection from Kern's shield. Shouting above the winds. "Seeing them ahead of Grimnir's main host."

Kern nodded. The pressure in his head felt as if it might split his skull at any moment, but he could still reason. Just. And he saw as well that if Grimnir had already lost control of such large throngs, his war host had to be greater than anything seen above Conarch.

Desagrena piled in next to the two, then Garret and Mogh and Gard Foehammer. All of them carried shields, Garret's with two arrows already hammered into the facing, and added them against Kern's to form a temporary bulwark. A dangerous tactic, as it also gave the archers a larger target at which to aim.

Gard grunted as a shaft slipped past the outside edge of his shield and scored a thick, bloody stripe across his forearm.

"To me!" Kern yelled, taking the chance. "Shields in!"

There weren't many more. Ossian, Danon, Old Finn, and Nahud'r. Ehmish's buckler was not a great help, though he added it as well. Reave made up for it, carrying the full-body shield he'd salvaged from the doppelgänger in the Frost Swamp. Dragging his greatsword behind him for the moment.

It was enough to shield themselves and their own archers, who each crowded up right close behind another warrior. Hydallan and Daol, Brig and Aodh.

"Move," Kern yelled, pacing his warriors forward. He used a crack between the overlapping shields as a window by which to see. "Forward. Forward. Loose!"

The pack staggered to a halt, waiting as the paired archers leaped to either side. Bowstrings sang. Kern saw two Vanir bowmen tumble to the ground, and a third staggered with an arrow caught in the meat of his upper thigh.

Then they were moving forward again, Kern guiding them. "Loose!"

Only one Vanir this time. A swordsman.

Three, again, the next. Then two.

Daol crowded up close. His ear bleeding where another Vanir shaft had come close. Too close. "Kern! I keep looking behind. We may be too far forward. I can only see—"

"Nay bother me with that now, Daol!"

Kern didn't want to hear. Never turned to look himself, in fact. Let Grimnir believe what the Great Terror would believe. That was part of the last service his wolves might perform for Cimmeria.

"But if we don't—"

"Loose," Kern yelled, though it was early. Daol and Hydallan were late getting off the mark, though Brig and Aodh each found a victim among the charging raiders.

Cutting the raiders' numbers by nearly half. Thinning out their charge, so a few heartbeats later, when Kern called them to "Break!" the Vanir were hammered back with overwhelming strength, unable to match the ferocity of Kern's warriors.

Shields separated and warriors charged forward, bowl-ing into the Vanir line. Daol and Hydallan managed to put their last arrows into the chest of one onrushing berserker, spinning him to the ground. Kern took an overhead blow against his target, feeling the shock deep down in his bones. Then sidestepped and stabbed once . . . and again. He punched the tip of his short blade into a man's side, just behind the raider's cuirass.

A golden-haired raider with curls very unlike many Vanir. This one had Aesir blood. Not a common sight, but not unknown either. And he bled just as red as a warrior of Vanaheim. His face twisted in pain. He staggered and fell just as hard to the ground, where Kern could step in and stick his blade through the man's neck, just to be certain.

All around, the Men of the Wolves were handing out much the same punishment. Gard Foehammer thrust for-ward with his pike, skewered a flame-haired raider with long horns thrusting from his metal helm as wide as his shoulders. Nahud'r and Wallach rushed another, knocking him over, pinning him to the ground beneath Nahud'r's shield while Wallach used his pike-hand to slash out the invader's throat. Ossian and Finn, another. Desa, one of her own.

As hard and ferocious as that, the Vanir's front line was slaughtered. Four more raiders rushed up behind them, and were set upon three to their one.

Two men at the back turned and fled.

Reave charged after them, still dragging his greatsword one-handed. And Danon and Desa as well. Kern waved up Valerus, who had ridden at a safe distance behind, and fol-lowed with the rest of the wolves.

The slope of the hill was very easy, hardly more than a knoll, actually, but at least it was something. One benefit to Cailt's decision, pressing hard from their previous day's camp, was to get out of the flat sward and into a region with a little more character. It wasn't what Kern and his warriors were used to, with forests and thickets and ravines and ridgelines. It was better than nothing at all.

But the cloud cover was very nearly overhead, and it worried Kern. Already the late afternoon had taken on a twilight gray, with the shadow of those thick stormrunners falling over them in a chilling shroud. The thunder was no longer distant footfalls, but rolling, harsh peals, which echoed across the plains forever. Lightning flared—two strikes . . . nay three!—and they left an afterglow against Kern's eyes that nearly matched the violet flames leaping at the edge of his vision.

And every one of his warriors had halted at the crest, he noticed. Reave first. The others soon behind. No one hurried to be first down the far slope.

Kern himself was nearly at the top when Valerus reined up hard next to him, horse snorting and pawing hard at the earth.

"We've a strong line moving up on our left," the horseman called down. "Not as many as I'd like to see, though. I've been watching, and if—"

"Nay bother me with details," Kern shouted him down. Knowing there were *some* men moving up hard after them was something, though. Cailt had not left them hanging out as nothing more than wolfbait. Or so he wanted to believe.

Then he reached the top of the hill, shouldering up between Reave and Daol, and knew that it wasn't likely to matter.

Grimnir's army had arrived.

Half a thousand strong. More! They swarmed across the plains in large gatherings, any one of which was strong enough to overwhelm a small village. At least one troop Kern could see might have been able to challenge strongholds such as Murrogh, or Callaugh. Many, many warriors had scattered out in smaller packs, though, or ran crooked paths between the different mobs as if unable to decide which to join.

Men on horseback. Men riding larger beasts, which Kern knew from facing Grimnir before would be mammoths. Most afoot, with war dogs chasing between. There would be Ymirish among them. Warriors. And sorcerers.

There were also several creatures that could have been Grimnir. Large, hulking brutes, shambling forward with clubs or large axes or warhammers. One of these threw back its head and howled, a long mournful cry more at home on the side of tall, snowcapped mountains than the local plains. Yeti. Dragooned from the Black Mountains, or the Eiglophians.

And riding the savage winds high above, the creature Kern had already seen through Lodur's eyes in the skies above Lacheish. The wyvern. It shrieked and wheeled about and struggled as if fighting a leash.

Lightning beat down against the earth, stabbing into the invading army. As if the clouds walked on those jagged, bright legs, marching alongside them.

Kern swallowed hard, his throat dry and tight and tasting like old wool. His muscles trembled with pent-up energy. His blood sang with a call to power. Tempting him, with his enemy now so very, very close. Pushing so hard that Kern raised a hand to the side of his head and pressed back, to keep his skull from splitting.

Stormrunners chased overhead, and the winds whipped long hair out to one side, then the other. It tugged at the hem of Kern's cloak. He slipped the knot and let it fall to the ground behind him. Retrieved the bloody spear he still carried in his bedroll, wrapped in its own small blanket. He tucked the broken shaft into his wide leather belt at the small of his back, then tossed his bedroll atop the fallen cloak. Kept only an oilskin pouch of flatbread and dried meat, his leather flask, and his weapons. Stood there beneath the bruised and blackened sky in his chain-mail vest and kilt and leggings, stripped to fighting weight, as anyone who had not already done so did the same.

Off a ways, a large troop turned toward the hill on which Kern's men and women waited. No easy vanguard, this time. Fourscore Vanir warriors, at the least.

"This is it," Kern said. Loud enough for the others to hear, though barely.

He took one step forward. Then another. Reave paced alongside him on the left. Daol on the right. Matching Kern stride for stride. He picked up his knees a little farther. Put them down harder. Thrust his shield forward and kept his sword safely pointed out to his side and down as he pushed for the Vanir line, desperate to sell his life for as high a price as he could get.

Spread to either side, his pack ran with him.

In the dark shadows of Kern's mind, roaring in his ears, the fires of his Ymirish blood stirred all the harder as if recognizing his desperation and determination both. Kern stole from the energy. Let it fuel his muscles as he channeled his focus into the run, his grip on his sword, the sight of the enemy moving toward him in large numbers. Refusing to release the darkness, nay matter what happened.

Let it sing through his blood, his mind. He'd not answer its call.

Let the curse die with him.

Two hundred paces. A hundred.

The distance shrank, and already arrows were beginning to fall around them. Reave let one slip by his shield, taking it through his upper arm, and kept running. Another slapped into Mogh's upper leg, knocking his stride out from beneath him. He went down in a tangle of shield, sword, and limbs, and was left behind.

Two hammered into Kern's shield. One quick swipe of his blade across the facing, though, stripped them away.

Having left the hill's slope behind them, Kern sprinted forward at the head of his pack, Valerus pacing them at the far side with his horse reined in at a canter. Ahead, the forward host among Grimnir's army stormed for them, blades waving and screams of hatred on their lips.

One or two stumbled, then fell, as Daol's arrows, or Brig's, found victims among the tightly packed throng. Another pair fell right on their heels. Then four . . . five!

And from around a rise on the far, far left, a dozen Cimmerian chargers raced across the plains. Bareback riders, they clamped muscular legs tight against their horses' barrels, holding themselves tall above their mount as they loosed flight after flight of swift death. Behind them a challenging roar sounded as a thick swarm of warriors ran down onto the battleground. Not much more than threescore, perhaps four counting the chargers.

The warriors Valerus had mentioned to Kern, coming on hard. Turning the attention of the Vanir host away from such a small threat as Kern's wolves, striking deep into the Vanir flank. Swords hacking and slashing. Men killing and bleeding and dying.

The invaders turned. Arrows slashing in at the chargers now, knocking two men . . . three . . . from their mounts. Taking the horse right out from under a fourth. The chargers wheeled back and forth along the enemy line, wounded and harried, but keeping up their own volleys.

"Kern?" Valerus yelled, raising his lance in the air.

Kern waved him forward. "Go!"

Valerus kicked, and the Aquilonian warhorse reached into its strong reserves to leave the charging pack behind as it raced ahead for the dying cavalry stand. Like a thunderbolt of their own Valerus swept up behind the Cimmerian chargers, his iron-tipped lance raised in challenge, calling them to follow, to charge!

He was by them in a heartbeat, crashing through the

Vanir line and followed not three lengths back by the remaining chargers. Valerus skewered one warrior, then another, and finally broke his lance on a third. Then it was out with his heavy war sword, slashing along one side, then the other, as he pushed deeper into their middle. The Cimmerians had likewise given up their bows for blades. And they hacked their way through the center of the host, riding down at least a dozen men before they broke out another side with half the men they'd started with.

Four left. Valerus among them.

But what they had done was smash a once-strong enemy line into chaotic frenzy, with warriors uncertain which way to turn. Toward the sixty-or-so swordsmen, chewing through on the flank, at the remaining cavalry, or for the small pack of misfits who had rushed up during the confusion and now fell into the Vanir with blades crashing down against steel and skulls.

"Crom!" Kern shouted. He kicked a dead man off the end of his sword. Turned the desperate backhand slash of another against his shield. "Crom!"

He called on the Cimmerian god. Not for strength, or for skill. Crom had long ago done all he could—all he would—for the Cimmerians: strength and cunning, and the will to meet any challenge in life. But with the dark power coursing through him, drawing him closer and closer to an edge he would not be able to hold against, Kern could think of no better truth to cling to.

He would champion the Cimmerian maker, and defy Ymir, right up to the very end.

By Crom and the blood of his mother, he swore it!

LODUR BENT THE winds around him. Letting the strong gusts fill his cloak, pulling the white bearskin out behind him like a set of his own wings. Laughing into the sky.

With three other sorcerers who marched elsewhere on the great battlefield, all of them along the rearward lines, he helped hold the great storm in check. Matching his strength against it. Stumbling under the backlash as thunder beat down in protest, shaking the ground and throwing lesser men to their hands and knees.

He chose one of these weak Vanir who knew the insult of falling right before him, and violet-clad lightning struck down once more.

The energy struck the hapless man in the side of the head, coursed through his body until it bled into the ground. It ripped a low, charred furrow through his skin the entire way, cooking his brain and stopping his heartbeat.

He stepped over the corpse with barely a glance down at its ruined face. The scent of charred flesh was strong, burning at the back of Lodur's throat. But just as strong was the rush of fresh strength that warmed him, and bled back into the storm, which growled in contentment. A deep reserve of raging power that the sorcerers fed, warped, and drew from as they needed.

Lodur more than others, as it turned out. He had no choice, as the great beast in the sky pulled against his control, wanting its freedom to kill and to feed. Wanting—more than anything—to strike at the Ymirish who had enslaved it.

The wyvern. A hunter of the skies. Such a powerful creature to have under his control. Let Grimnir increase his hold over the beasts of the north and the mountain slopes. Mammoths and saber-tooths, and the yeti, which might be considered distant kin to the Ymirish, in fact, but to Lodur were still nothing more than simple, savage beasts.

Leave for him the greater challenges. And the greater glory once victory was theirs and the entirety of Cimmeria lay open for the northern hordes to sweep down and feed off of for years to come. As befitted sheep.

Sheep with teeth, however. Never any forgetting that. Especially when the forward vanguard of Cailt Stonefist struck from the north, just as Grimnir had foretold. This was why Lodur marched on the left wing. Why Grimnir was even now turning the magnificent hordes into an enveloping line which would surround, collapse against, and strangle the life from this "Grand War Host."

"A Great Hunt it shall be." Grimnir's laugh, when it came, was nothing pleasant to most ears. It promised pain and suffering and blood. Lodur had enjoyed it, certainly. "Cailt Stonefist will live to regret. Though not for long."

And leave for Grimnir this Cailt Chieftain as well. The Lacheishi's insult, while fresh in Lodur's mind, was far from troublesome now that his true enemy had arrived. No sorcerer, and few Ymirish, could miss it. That taste of Ymir's deep, pure ice, corrupted as it was by the leathery flavor of Cimmerian blood. Grimnir had marked the foul one as certainly as the descendant of Ymir himself had been marked after his long plunge down the side of the bluffs over Clan Conarch. Not physically, perhaps, as Grimnir's scars were seen, but their false brethren was known to the others now.

Kern was here.

And Lodur hunted *him*.

Ahead, he knew. Ahead, where the calls of battle and first blood had drawn the attention of every last Vanir like dogs after table scraps. From the sounds of it now, the confusion and cries of pain, this first skirmish was nothing to be remarked upon as a great victory. Not yet.

Grimnir's plan was taking time, though not too much longer. Some men had broken for the fighting without pause, of course, and the Ymirish let them go. There was no controlling them all, these raiders with their bloodlust and greed. Hard enough it was to rein in most of them, turn the hordes on Grimnir's command, and prepare to set them against the Cimmerians without mercy. But it was being done. A little while more, a shift of perhaps half a league to get everyone in place, and it would be accomplished.

Which was why, in the next moment, Lodur staggered, and nearly fell, when one of his sorcerer brethren screamed within his mind. Lodur felt his brother's pain and the betrayal of it when one of the four sparks hovering at the back of his mind suddenly flared in bright, white agony—and then was gone.

Grimnir's savage roar did not require Ymirish blood to hear. It carried over the plains. Rage, mixed with pain.

Then came the commands, amplified by the strength of the storm, like Ymir's own thunderous voice. "Turn! They come at our backs! Turn, and KILL!"

From the south? Lodur was not so far away from Grimnir, who held the center of their line, that he could not see the Great One as he stalked forward with a massive warhammer in one hand and a battle-axe in the other. Half again as tall as a large man, he raised weapons overhead and called the storm's fury down against Cailt Stonefist and the Cimmerian dogs.

But then Grimnir hesitated, with lightning striking all around him, burning the ground with glassy scars, still not completely certain.

He needed eyes on the battle. Lodur understood this, and so hurried forward with the men and women of his own war host surrounding him. It took some time, crossing the length of a long, low rise, but there saw it for himself.

Below and far ahead, a troop of Cimmerians had smashed into one of the larger Vanir mobs. The fighting was far enough along, had spread itself out over a wide area with dozens of warriors having at each other with blade and spear, axe and hammer, that it was hard to tell at a glance how many. But Lodur guessed at forty to sixty fighting men and women . . . a few horses . . .

And the wolves!

Yea, they were there. A thrill of warmth crawled up Lodur's spine, to set eyes on the battlefield and know Kern was, at least, within his reach.

But not Cailt Stonefist's Grand War Host. Not even close to all the strength of Cimmeria was here. *Tricked!* Lodur heard Grimnir's maddened bellow. And knew that it was the bulk of Stonefist's war host that had slammed in behind the horde's far flank. This was a diversion.

Well, if so, it was Lodur's to deal with, now that Kern had arrived. No way to tell which one was his false brother, not among the high emotions and thoughts of rage that littered the landscape like scattered gems to his senses. But Kern was here. Here, not to the south.

"We'll just have to find him among his mongrel warriors," Lodur said. Barely more than a whisper. "One, by one, by one."

He waved his men forward. Then tugged hard on the mental leash anchored at the back of his mind, and was rewarded with a hate-filled shriek from high overhead. "Feast," he commanded it, and sent the wyvern rushing forward on a sweep of leathery wings.

"Kill them all."

23

EHMISH HAD NEVER seen so much spilled blood and death at one place before this day. And that surprised him.

Battle had seemed to be his life for the past several months. If not fighting, the pack was always healing up from wounds or preparing for its next scrap. But in truth those were simply a very few, violent moments. It was actually during the long, hard runs *between* battles where the Men of the Wolves had lived their lives. Those were the times when lovers were taken, or mourned. Friendships begun. When the real sacrifices were made to set aside one's own health and life for the good of the pack or to walk the razor's edge of honor versus duty.

And when boys truly grew into men.

Even so, what he had seen on the field had not come close to preparing him for this. Ehmish had missed the battle above Conarch last winter, and stories did not compare. The shouts of rage and the screams of dying men, the crash of lightning and the ringing clash of steel against steel, these all echoed in Ehmish's ears until he barely understood anything out of the din of combat. Not even a yell to *ware!*

It was all he could do to set his stance, thrust forward with his broadsword, or turn a blow against the buckler strapped to his arm. A mindless haze, hypnotizing him into automatic, soulless response.

Not even one that could be broken by an earsplitting shriek of hatred and hunger.

A large weight hit him from behind, smashing him flat toward the ground. It was all Ehmish could do to get his sword out to one side, blade flat, to prevent himself from falling on the steel's sharp edge. He tasted blood and dirt in his mouth. Heard the pounding of many, many feet against the earth.

And felt the beat of leathery wings stirring the air over him as a set of wide, outstretched claws came within an arm's length of where he had stood not a heartbeat before. He wrenched his head to one side to follow the wyvern's stooping dive. Saw it snatch up another man farther along, then rise again with wide, leathery wings grabbing for air.

"Keep your head, boy. Or lose it."

Gard Foehammer rolled off Ehmish, saw a Vanir rushing up, and stabbed from the ground to run the raider through the gut.

Gard had lost his pike. Left it stuck earlier through the eye of a wooly mammoth, Ehmish remembered, digging into the brain. He had two long, shallow cuts across his chest, and a deep one against the side of his leg that had slashed away one of his leggings as well.

"Didn't . . . couldn't . . ."

"Battle blindness. You stop thinking, then you stop caring. Well, even if you don't care, Ehmish, consider the rest of us who do. Stay alive!"

It seemed a long way to come back, but Gard's harsh

words broke the spell and washed away the numbing haze he'd let crawl across his mind. Ehmish picked himself up from the ground. Saw that Gard and Garret Blackpatch had both come upon him and were holding off raiders on either side. And Mogh, on a third. The Taurin had cut away his leggings as well, and snapped off the arrow that had taken him in the thigh. Part of the shaft still poked out of a bloody wound.

His silver-chased blade was still a mite too heavy for him, though he was growing into it fast. Gard tripped a Vanir, who sprawled roughly at Ehmish's feet. One hard, overhand chop, and the man's head rolled free. Blood sprayed in a warm jet, soaking Ehmish's boots and kilt in gore and crimson.

Another moment to breathe. Another glance. They still fought along the northern fringe, more west than they had ever wanted to be. Driven there by the tides of battle, the four of them. Six! He found Ossian and Desagrena also nearby, fighting side by side against a Ymirish warrior.

"Others?" he asked.

He'd not seen Kern or anyone else since their last push to link up with Cailt Stonefist, the Lacheishi chieftain holding a solid but bending line to the south. Every push, though, had ended up with the Vanir rallying more men, shoving them farther north, farther west, as the wolves gave up ground for time.

How long ago had that been? Half a flask of water. Time for a stolen bite of meat from the small leather pouch tied to his belt.

"Kern?" he asked again. "Daol?"

"Nay." Mogh said. "Not any of 'em. Dead or scattered now."

Ehmish doubted Kern was dead. The man seemed indestructible, though he'd pushed the edge many times. He glanced around wildly, intent on finding their way back through the widespread fight.

Then was half-blinded when a strike of forked lightning hammered down into the earth only a stone's throw from him. Ehmish immediately dropped down, beneath any sword cuts he hoped. Blinking rapidly to clear his gaze.

Saw the blurry outline of a man approaching. A big man. A very, very big man.

Grimnir was his first thought. The size. The bestial face twisted in a snarl of animal rage. But Grimnir did not have a hide of snow-gray fur and would never have settled for a simple oak branch for a club. And he knew what this was. Valleymen had tangled with such creatures before, when hunger drove them down out of the mountains.

"Yeti!" Ehmish shouted, leaping forward. He raised his buckler high overhead, getting it between Gard Foehammer's back and the mountain creature.

Taking the hard blow against his target, he heard the *snap* of breaking bones. Felt himself being hurled back, to slam up against Gard and knock the larger man sprawling. At least his warning gave Garret a chance to get turned around, his shield ready as the yeti clubbed him aside as well.

Mogh had moved to help Ossian and Desa finish off the Ymirish warrior, the three of them rushing forward to tackle him to the ground and slice his throat in a wide, bloody gash. Now Mogh scrambled back, though far too late. "Ehmish!"

Dizzy with pain, Ehmish rolled to one side to avoid the giant club. It smashed into the ground right where his head had been. But he struck his broken arm against the ground doing so and nearly blacked out. Growling, snarling, he struggled against the smothering darkness and clawed his way back to life. Refusing to lie down and die, he'd at

least face his death like the man the pack had helped him
become.

Except that it wasn't him, growling and snarling.

His vision clearing, Ehmish saw a wolf crouched in
front of him. A large one, as big as . . . Frostpaw! Crom
take him now if Kern's dire wolf hadn't leaped in front of
Ehmish, driving the yeti back several steps. Being a mountain creature, the yeti knew the danger of such an animal. It
took a moment's pause, and Ehmish could not have blamed
it. The wolf weighed easily as much as he did, with ivory
fangs like a mouthful of tiny daggers.

It was enough. The first arrow whistled in, embedding
itself in the yeti's chest. It roared in pain and anger. A second and third, into its arm, and the creature lost the club.
Two more in the gut folded it over, and the dire wolf leaped
to get its powerful jaws around a thick-muscled throat,
dragging the mountain creature down to the ground, tearing its life from it.

Then the wolf leaped back, and paced from side to side
as if trapped.

Ehmish had not looked behind him. Had not considered
it while death stared him in the face and the wolf had
shown itself his sudden defender. But then he realized the
wolf would never have charged a battlefield of its own will.
The animal knew better. It would have come only if driven
onto it . . .

"All right, boy?"

People should really stop calling him "boy."

But the voice! He knew it. And at that moment she
could have called him anything and never been slapped
back for it.

Ehmish leaned back, cradling his broken arm to his
chest. Stared up at the woman standing next to Gard Foehammer, with the dozen archers that surrounded them and

half a hundred men behind them. She had pale skin and dark smudges under both eyes, and looked about ready to fall over herself and just about as beautiful as Ehmish had ever thought.

"Where's Kern Wolf-Eye?" she asked.

Ros-Crana and her western war host had finally arrived!

OLD FINN WAS the first of Kern's wolves to fall.

The battle, stretching between the last of the holdouts in the north and Cailt's hard-hitting attack from the south, had thinned itself out on this stretch of the field—About midway between the northern holdouts and southern offensive, where the storm seemed to lull, and the tempest winds battered them not quite so heavily. Here, the Vanir and what few Ymirish they'd come against had not been able to summon anywhere near their real strength.

It allowed Kern and Reave to lead a push against the raiders. Old Finn and Nahud'r were with them, Daol nearby; there were no more than that. Kern had lost his men to the tides of battle. All but these.

Even so, they knew how to fight as a pack where the raiders merely fought for themselves. Together the four drove a half dozen Vanir right back to the side of a gentle slope, where Daol had sneaked up through the grass and created for himself a hunter's blind. The archer's last three arrows dropped two of those raiders, then a Vanir war dog, which had struck his scent and charged him, jaws snapping.

Reave, having finally given up his weighty, full-body shield, came overhead with his greatsword and took the arm of another warrior. Blood sprayed in a warm geyser, splashing Kern across the face even as he rammed his short blade through the chest of the next man in line. Salty on his lips, stinging his eyes, he backed off a pace and let Hydallan step up to trade ringing blows with another.

He wiped his eyes clear with the heel of his hand, smearing the blood across his face like a bandit's mask. And had barely moved forward again when Finn's leg took a violent kick against the knee from Reave's victim, whom he had left, thrashing about on the ground, to help Hydallan.

Finn's leg caved. He dropped to one knee.

The last Vanir easily beat a hesitant sword aside.

Then shoved an arm's length of steel through Finn's chest.

Kern leaped forward, but too late, too late. He smashed his shield into the other man's arm, came overhead with his sword, and rained terrible, chopping blows across the raider's neck and shoulder, caving in through the man's chest and driving him away from Finn as if such a violent death might bring the old man back.

Wanting to hurt, and kill.

And *destroy*.

The power sang through Kern's blood, and darkness stirred. He felt a rush of power cleanse through him, driving away the fatigue of such a long and bloody battle. Called down the skies to aid him. And in the back of his mind, he heard Grimnir's roar of hatred.

That might have been the end of Kern's resistance if he hadn't kept raining blows against the dead man. He did it even as a forked tongue of lightning snaked its way down from the heavens, smashing into the body, as if the gods had decided to deliver the final blow.

And was thrown backward by the concussive blast and the smash of Crom's own thunder.

"Kern!" Hydallan and Daol were at him in an instant. And Nahud'r, who suddenly rejoined them.

Kern heard the heavy beat of his own heart pounding in his head and the roar of blood in his ears. He tasted blood in his mouth, and couldn't be certain it wasn't his. It felt as if he'd been beaten again, on the floor of Morag's tent.

Opening his eyes, he saw only vague outlines through the violet flares sheeting across his vision.

Daol, the closer of them all, reeled away in pain. "Crom's sweet curses," Hydallan swore.

Nahud'r slapped his hand down across Kern's eyes, burying him in sudden darkness. "Your friends, Kern. Fight it!"

"Pull it back," Kern muttered, realizing the power had slipped away from him. "Pull it in. Smother it." He gave himself a pair of deep breaths, then knocked Nahud'r's hand away and tried his sight again.

Normal. As normal as he could call it with violet sparks still jumping at the edges.

In control. If just.

Daol had his hands pressed against his temples, eyes squinted closed. Kern sat up swiftly, rising to his friend's side. "Pain?" he asked.

"Like my head is splitting in two. And my eyes are burning." Daol was obviously reaching for words to explain it. "Hard to say," he said.

"Nay. I've a very good idea. Try to look again."

He did. His eyes were red-rimmed and tearing, but he could see. He looked at Kern. And there was something like understanding on his face. "Ymirish," he said. Not as an accusation—Kern wasn't sure he could have taken that—but a simple fact. "Nearly happened that night with Cul, is that it?" He waited for Kern's nod. "I should have guessed."

"I should have told you." But then Kern remembered, looked beyond Daol. "Damn."

Old Finn lay stretched out on the ground. Sword still stuck through his chest. Eyes open. Aodh knelt on the ground next to him, as if looking for something he could do. Together, Reave and Nahud'r took down another raider, then returned quickly.

"Vanir." Reave stuck the end of his greatsword into the earth. Rested forward against the heavy crossbar. "Running hard our way."

Kern nodded. He walked over to Finn, pulled the sword from his chest, and hurled it aside. Daol also stepped near.

"My fault, Kern. I had the extra arrow. Shot the Crom-cursed dog with it instead. I saw Aodh and Nahud'r running up from behind. Knew you'd take the raiders down and thought . . . I thought . . ."

Laying a hand on his friend's arm, Kern shook his head. "You did what you thought best. Old Finn, so did he." He reached down and closed the man's eyes. Aodh found Finn's broadsword and laid it across the old man's frail body, folded his hands over the hilt. "He died well." There were few greater compliments to pay a fallen warrior.

"Kern." Reave said, glancing from the small group and back over his shoulder. "Vanir. Coming."

"Yea, Reave. I hear you."

He shuffled a few steps up the hill's slope. Just enough to see over some of the nearby fighting. Saw a pair of war dogs drag a clansman down. And a pack of Vanir running east, chasing after a limping horse and its slumped-over rider. Not Valerus. No saddle.

He also saw a Ymirish warrior in flight, chased by a half dozen men who had also broken through the Vanir lines form the north. Lightning struck to either side of them. Then took one man down when the arc of violet-white energy smashed down and into his back. But still the Ymirish had no chance.

They caught him. Dragged him down. Hacked him to pieces.

And yea. Kern saw them now. Twenty . . . thirty warriors streaming their way. Vanir. The long-horned helms made it easy to recognize them, even at a hundred paces or better. Even in the gloom beneath the storm. Then a break, and another fifty or better chasing behind them. Swords waving overhead. Howling their own desperate battle cries.

"Plan?" Reave asked. The large man sounded tired. After losing Desa when the press of fighting had broken them apart, he'd worked in a tireless frenzy to cut down any Vanir who got in their way. Not that it had helped.

Kern found his sword. His shield. He took up a wide-legged stance on the slope. He had nothing more. Grimnir was too far away. There were too many warriors between them and the Great Beast for six men to fight their way through. Especially with a second host running up after them.

But still he nodded. "Take as many with us as we can."

Reave smiled. He had blood staining his teeth and the spatter of more gore across one side of his face. "S'a good plan," he said. And moved to put himself to one side of Kern.

Then Nahud'r. Aodh. Hydallan started up the slope as well. But not Daol. He stared back along the way the Vanir charged at them. Hesitant. As if not sure of his eyes.

Of his ears.

"I'm not so sure," he began. Then slashed his sword overhead in victory. "Listen!"

Kern wasn't certain what he should be listening for. Over the clash of swords and the roar of the storm's wind and smashing thunder, he heard men shouting and dying, and the howls of distant battle cries.

Howls?

Hydallan had stopped as well. But rather than look back, he nodded past them all. "Kern."

Kern looked. So did the others. And saw the wolf—their wolf—bounding up the slope not a stone's throw away. Gaining the top of the hill, pacing a moment, then looking back down as if presiding over the entire battle. Even in the gray and waning light, Kern saw that the animal's fur was matted with sweat and blood. But not its own, it seemed. The wolf's golden eyes burned in the dim light, staring back down the slope at Kern. Then it threw back its head and howled.

To be answered after the next long heartbeat by several voices calling out of the north. Howling in response.

"Gut me if I'm nay a-hearing the boy in there," Hydallan said. Still not looking back.

"And Desa!" Reave yelled. Grabbed up his sword and held it at the ready.

And if they were indeed part of that mob chasing down the Vanir, they'd found at least half a hundred friends besides. "Let's go see," Kern said, mostly to himself. Not quite ready to lie down and die yet. Nay. Not quite.

There were only thirty or so Vanir between him and an answer. Hardly worth the thought. Behind him, Frostpaw howled again.

Kern could nay have said it better himself.

CHASING THE STORM eastward, pushing her warhost to the limit of their endurance, Ros-Crana hadn't been certain she could catch up in time.

When she saw the lightning, stabbing down from the swollen storm clouds in repeated strikes, as if the skies had suddenly gone to war with the land itself, she knew it for a fact. They were still several leagues shy of the advancing front.

"It's begun," she said to Longtooth. To Carrack and Dahr who also stood near.

"Yea. And we've only a guess as to where they might need us." He panted, the last day's run having taken a lot out on his years. "And when."

But Ros-Crana had read the trail sign as well as anyone. They had some idea of the size of Grimnir's massive war host, having spotted the different tracks all converging on one huge, easterly push. She set her hand on the hilt of her new sword. For such a light and well-balanced weapon, it had felt awfully heavy the last several leagues. But for now she drew fresh strength from its touch. Licked the burning sweat from her lips.

"*Where* is the place we arrive at. The *when* is as we arrive. They need us. That's enough."

Still, the old warrior's expertise was not to be brushed aside so easily. "I run for the northern edge of that lightning. Carrak, with me. Dahr, pull thirty men and follow with Sláine Longtooth. Circle 'round to their southern side. Or, if you think best, come at them from right behind."

"Meet somewhere in the middle?" Longtooth asked

As plans went, it had seemed good enough. And Ros-Crana had gathered her warriors, and *run*.

Now they ran again. Sword out and freshly blooded on the life of the luckless Vanir who had come over a hillock at the wrong time. The balance of her northwestern war host, arrived late but here. With Longtooth and Dahr not far behind. From what Gard Foehammer promised, this Cailt Stonefist needed their help. Needed every able warrior that could be thrown into battle, if they had hope of running Grimnir to earth and driving a blade through his heart of black ice.

Pausing just long enough for Gard to twist Ehmish's broken arm into line, then bind it tight with leather straps and a broken spear shaft, they set off at a good measure. The boy managed to keep up, though it obviously cost him dearly. And when Kern's companion wolf dashed ahead of them, racing a swerving path across the field, it was also Ehmish who first howled the wolf's call.

Nay. Not a wolf's call. Kern's call. Better than any shout, the high, long howl would reach across the plains and find the Wolf-Eye if he still lived.

Like avenging wraiths, her people swept across some of the heaviest fighting on this northern edge of the battle-field. If there were more than two . . . three dozen clans-men left alive—out of nearly a hundred, according to Ossian—she'd have been surprised. It was the bloody work of moments to set the Vanir fleeing and to be after them de-spite the infernal lightning that smashed down around them, or the death that occasionally fell out of the skies on leathery wings and with a violent, raging shriek.

The second time the wyvern stooped over her company, it came away with two warriors snatched up, one in each powerful claw.

Two Callaughnan, she saw. Two of her own who would never again see the mists of Callaugh Glen.

Anger seized her. Blossoming into a full-on rage when she saw the creature wheel about in the sky and simply drop the struggling bodies. Letting them flail, briefly, be-fore they smashed into the plains.

The wyvern glided up, spreading its wings to cup the air and hover as a flash of lightning suddenly snaked across it path, nearly taking the monster down. Then it screamed and dived again, coming in at an angle to her host.

Strength surged in her arm as she raised her sword over-head in a two-handed grip. The blue-iron weapon gleamed darkly in the fading light beneath the storm shroud.

"You want a fresh victim?" she yelled at the sky, veered away from the safety of the host. "More blood? Another life?"

The wyvern shrieked, adjusted its course, and came right at her as if answering her challenge. Ros-Crana ran along the edge of a low-lying hill. A perfect target.

"Take me!" she yelled. Leaping high into the air. Bring-ing her war sword around with every bit of strength she possessed, or could summon.

The blade sang, slashing through the air with a dark

gleam. Using her momentum, hacking down in an over-head strike, she cleaved the blade through one of the claw's heavily muscled talons, and the bone within, in the instant before the wyvern could snag her right out of the air. Blood sprayed and the creature jerked its claws back by reflex.

Ros-Crana had never known a moment of doubt, and had timed the wild attack near-perfect.

Near-perfect.

The bloody stump did brush against her as the great creature winged by overhead, and with the speed of its dive it was enough to knock her aside head over heels. The world spun sickeningly around her. Ground, then dark sky, then ground again.

She took a guess, and reached out at the last possible second. Her feet struck the earth, too hard and fast to catch her, but enough to let her curl down into a rolling somer-sault and absorb the worst of the fall. She felt pain blos-som against her left side, where the creature's claw had clipped her.

What she did not do was lose her blade.

Several warriors among her host had fallen off their run, dismayed at her sudden action and disbelieving that she survived. Ehmish stood there, slack-jawed and staring. Many waved their swords overhead, simply accepting. Though they, too, had slowed.

The wyvern raced away into the distance, then pulled up for the dark cover of the clouds. Shrieking in pain, now.

"What are we waiting for?" she asked. Limping for-ward, willing her bruises and any broken bones to quiet, for now. She raced up the length of her running line, mov-ing for the front. "After the Vanir, the Ymirish, and Grimnir!"

"Grimnir!" her warriors shouted back. And there were more howls. Not all of them from Kern's warriors.

Then ahead came a real wolf's call. A long, challenging

howl that could only have come from the throat of Kern's companion animal. It was answered by Ehmish, and by Desa, who shouted and pointed.

At half a dozen men who suddenly charged off a nearby hillside, running right down into the teeth of the fleeing Vanir.

And, of course, leading the way would be Kern Wolf-Eye. A handful against five times their number, Kern attacked!

"Stupid, selfish, beast of a man!" Ros-Crana hardly bothered to compare her recent walk with insanity to Kern's reckless charge. Hers had worked, after all. His was about to get him killed, and with help just arriving.

But then the first of the Vanir crashed into Kern's short line, and *Crom's gift!*—were actually thrown back.

If she hadn't seen it . . . Well, there would certainly be many such acts of strength and bravery this day.

Like a river flood crashing against a boulder, the Vanir shattered against Kern's position. Several went down, never to get back up. Two, she swore, were lifted bodily off their feet and *thrown* back into the onrushing horde, which stumbled and staggered forward, and was brought to a standstill yet again as the rest of the small force piled up behind or started to force their way around that short, sturdy line.

Blades were working their damage now, ringing against other swords, smashing against shields and, occasionally, into flesh. At least one among Kern's small group went down under the press of bodies. Then a second.

The remaining four formed a square, backs pressed against each other as the Vanir swarmed past them. Then Ros-Crana's warriors were buying them some relief as they finally struck into the back of the mobbed-up throng.

Blades rose and fell, and Ros-Crana's strong war sword sang through the air as it smashed one raider's blade in the side, breaking it, then took his head right after.

Waging forward, fighting between Gard Foehammer and Desagrena, Ros-Crana cut one more down from behind. And saw her companions do the same.

The Vanir broke in every direction then, with nay thought to holding together. One moment they were all fighting for their lives, and the next her war host stood nearby, planting and exhausted, covered in blood, with a few of them giving chase to some of the scattered raiders.

Kern limped forward, his leggings turning dark with soaked blood and a gash opened up over his left eye. He looked beat on and abused, but had that same challenging gleam in his eyes she recalled from Callaugh.

"What kept you?" was all he asked.

"It's a long run from Callaugh."

"It is at that. But good to have you here with us."

She watched as he turned to his fallen men. Saw that, yea, he did still carry the bloody spear. Of course he did. He'd tucked it into his belt at the small of his back, and seemed to have all but forgotten it. Sword on one hand, shield in the other, as he checked on his two fallen men.

Hydallan had a bad slash across his ribs. But he'd live through it. Aodh's sword arm looked as if it might be cut to down near the bone. Reave looped a strong leather cord in a tourniquet around that arm. Tightened it down.

Kern knelt by each one of them a moment. Spoke a few words. They nodded, then he rose to face her again.

"Sword blooded?" he asked.

But it was Ehmish who answered for her, shaking his head. "You would not believe it, Kern."

He shrugged. The man's voice was cold, but his golden eyes were furious with their own inner fire. "We've still Grimnir to deal with. I'm telling you now, we won't stop. No matter who falls by the way, or what the Terror finally throws against us. Your warriors will need to carry that weight."

Ros-Crana smiled thinly. She'd come too far now to be left behind at the end. And it was nothing less than she'd have expected from him. "We'll guard your back," she promised. "If nothing else, it will make for a good end."

"Worth a fireside tale," Nahud'r promised, slinging gore from the edge of his scimitar.

"Or a song," Kern said. "A song of victory or a song of death. Time to discover which.

"Now let's end this. Once and for all."

24

"SO WRONG," LODUR whispered.

The winds whipped about him, screaming a banshee's wail, snatching his words away and losing them in the covering storm before they barely reached his own ears. Long before they reached the Vanir, who rushed by in directions as Grimnir sent them. Warriors being used to shore up a line. Or to force an advance through which the Great One might push his remaining yeti, or his final troop of pikemen, or the last mammoth.

Near the end of everything, now.

"So very, very wrong," he said again.

Mayhap the Vanir could not hear him, but Grimnir did. Through the link he held with his Ymirish, if no other way. Pacing, holding the center of his own army and moving it forward step by step as if by his indomitable will alone, the Great One now turned and growled a warning. "Mind your tongue, or lose it."

And the Great Beast went back to stalking the Cimmerians' Grand War Host, still trying to break its spine. Still finding it a harder task than anyone had ever expected.

Lodur did not fear for his life. Not when Grimnir needed his two remaining sorcerers, now more than ever. He did not bother to make a point of it, however, just as he could not entirely shake the doubts that had chased him all the way back from the northern line where victory should have been assured and the corrupted one already dead. He could recall how *close* it had all felt. The ringing clash of steel against steel. The screams and shouts of men and women, warriors all, in agony and fury. Betrayal. Rage. Such sweet, sweet tastes that had sat on the back of his tongue as he relished the moment.

All snatched away in an instant, when Lodur had not been minding the larger battle but was busy searching for Kern.

It happened so quickly, he had barely escaped with his own life. And there hadn't been enough strength left on the field for him to draw upon, rallying against the turn of fate, as everything had already been turned back to strike hard at Cailt Stonefist and the bulk of the Cimmerians' Grand War Host.

Pulling back along the western retreat to join Grimnir's thrust, he'd thrown a host of warriors into the Cimmerian advance. When that failed, he'd struck at them from the skies with lightning and death on leathery wings. Doing what he could.

He'd finally returned and reported the failure, no matter how much it shamed him and put all of Grimnir's plans at risk.

Did Grimnir see that? How thin the line now stretched between failure and success?

Mayhap not. Walking among the killing grounds and stepping over the bodies of so many fallen clansmen, everything would seem to be moving in Grimnir's favor.

The stench of death was ripe in the air. The odor of bodies releasing themselves. Charred flesh and the acrid tang of lightning. Blood mixed with earth; clinging to his boots and the hem of his white cloak. All good signs.

There were bodies of the Hoathi. The square-jawed Murroghan. Lacheish with their shaved temples, and the topknots of Galla tribesmen.

But then Lodur kicked over one woman, and saw the craggy features of a Callaughnan. Even here! On the southern edge of battle!

At every turn, in fact, Grimnir's desires had been thwarted. The arrival of western clans at not one point on the battlefield, but two. That Clan Lacheish and Murrogh had not beaten each other half to death *before* moving to the plateau. And the Galla! Who could have foreseen they would come out of the mountains in such numbers to support the Hoathi, with whom they had always feuded.

With the mighty war host Grimnir raised, two of these three certainly would have been overcome. They'd have smashed so many of the larger clans no further resistance would have been possible. That would leave all of Cimmeria open to the Ymirish plans.

But all three . . .

Lodur skulked behind the battle lines, watched by Grimnir's remaining saber-tooth as the great snow cat might have watched for prey on the northern wastelands. He listened to the sky's pain as thunder ripped through the heavens. He summoned men from a rear guard and threw them forward himself, taking action against the doubts and fears that threatened to distract him here, now, on the eve of their ultimate victory.

Grimnir still held the center, pushing Cailt Stonefist back toward one of the plateau mesas step by merciless step. Lodur must never forget that. And the great chieftain was already half-blinded by one of his brethren's sorceries, mad with pain and making mistakes, costing lives. It would be enough. Together, the descendant of Ymir's First Born and his greatest, most reliable of sorcerers would shove Stonefist back against the mesa's sandstone cliffs, and there smash him beyond recovery. Not the arrival of fresh warriors or the paltry victory Kern Wolf-Eye had gained to the north could be enough to turn this side of the battle.

It would happen as foretold by the Great One.

It must!

He railed at the skies, giving voice to his own frustrations as he shouted down the thunder and worked to expel his doubts, once and finally.

Though there were certainly more Vanir bodies littering the plains than Cimmerian. But with such an advantage to begin with, not even the arrival of the westerners could make the difference.

Though the fire of another Ymirish sorcerer had also been quenched in blood; overrun by Cailt Stonefist and this Sláine Longtooth in a desperate bid to halt Grimnir's advance.

That had turned the situation desperate for the remaining two, yes. Keeping the storm under their control, holding that reserve of power should they still need it, required they expend greater personal strength or sacrifice more lives from the Vanir numbers. They would manage. They would.

Though even now, the wyvern Lodur had thought to have completely under his control was barely just. Screeching its madness as it circled among the clouds, refusing to hunt. It had eaten, and beyond that had little more desire to kill for the sake of killing. Lodur had forced it, for a time, but that Callaughnan woman and her cursed singing blade had hurt the creature enough for it to refuse another such push. Yet.

Mayhap he *should* release the wyvern. Send it winging

back to its mountain lair, where he could find it again as needs be. With the pressing need to keep the storm surging, to preserve their final advantage and ensure victory, he likely should have done so before. But to release so grand a prize for a single wound . . . it galled.

"No!"

Refusing to be beaten by such circumstance, Lodur drew down the lightning. Three violet-clad strikes walked over the earth, taking two lives at random from the Vanir hordes and sacrificing one of Lodur's warrior-brothers as well. Pressing the surge of power into his mind, he channeled it to Grimnir and back into the storm and let the flow of true power burn away a bit of his own strength as well.

Whatever he needed to keep control. Just a bit longer.

The Ymirish's death had brought Grimnir around in a raging fury. Golden eyes aflame and a snarl twisting his already-ruined face. Then the rush of strength coursed from the Ymirish to his master, and Grimnir had staggered to one side, eyes wide with fiendish delight, his mottled hide flushing dark with power. Holding his heavy weapons high overhead, he bellowed a great roar at the heavens that cracked the sky like Ymir's true voice. Reveling in the strength and his newfound plan.

"Again!" Grimnir ordered, forcing his will upon Lodur while the bond was strong. And the lightning walked.

Two Ymirish warriors fell to the needs of their master this time. The channel burst wide, and like a great beacon Grimnir now glowed within a nimbus of power. Not the storm shroud nor the failing sun, which fell closer and closer to the western horizon, could create a darkness capable of dimming his strength. And, summoning Lodur to his side, the two together rallied the rear guard and the core of the Grimnir host. Several hundred men and women. Vanir and Ymirish.

"FORWARD!" Grimnir ordered.

His merest whisper came with the strength of fifty men as he threw his best and strongest into the teeth of Cailt Stonefist and the war leaders of so many of Cimmeria's great clans.

Lodur smiled as well, having siphoned off enough power for his own. Strengthening his mental grip over the wyvern, healing his own fatigue, and for one last thing as well. To feel back along the bloodline link that connected all Ymirish and sense out Kern Wolf-Eye.

Who just then was close by and moving forward quickly.

Never realizing that he ran straight to his own death.

WHEN THE SKIES split open, Kern and Ros-Crana had been working side by side to break through a rearward patrol of Vanir.

A brawny lot, these raiders, carrying battle-axes and heavy war swords, commanded by a Ymirish warrior with a fanatic's gleam in his golden eyes. But with nearly three to their one, the Cimmerians were wolves on a great bear. They swarmed over the enemy, breaking their line into a dozen smaller battles. Blades rose and fell, rose and fell, and it was more Vanir blood than Cimmerian that stained the ground black.

Ros-Crana traded high, swinging slashes against the Ymirish's greatsword, her blade ringing against his in clear, pure tones. Kern came in low and from the side, looking for an opening that would let him loose the man's lifeblood out across the blood-soaked ground.

Then he felt the darkness surge within him in a too-familiar feeling. One he had recently experienced. He dodged back and tackled Ros-Crana. Bearing her back to the ground, out from under the greatsword's long reach, while the violent strike of lightning crashed down over the powerful warrior and hurled him aside as if he'd been nothing more than a child's rag doll.

It left the warrior in a broken pile, while somewhere ahead of them Grimnir's roar echoed over the plains in a rage of fury and pleasure both.

The stench of charred flesh and ozone mixed hideously, burning behind Kern's eyes. He tasted blood on his lips, and spat.

"Keep running!" Kern ordered, regaining his feat in a bound and pulling Ros-Crana along with him.

He saw Reave and Nahud'r breaking forward of the thinning Vanir lines. Daol. Desa, Ossian, Ehmish, and Gard. And Frostpaw! Trapped on the battlefield, the dire wolf was doing all it knew how to do. It ran with its pack. Every so often it looked aside and howled, as if wanting to warn Kern that he ran into danger, not away from it.

As if he didn't know that. There was nay sign of Garret Blackpatch or Mogh breaking through the last skirmish. "Let them come through safe," he whispered.

"How did you know?" Ros-Crana asked, shouting to be heard above the din of battle, the howl of the wolf and the winds. "The lightning?"

"Happened earlier," he said. Wanting to let it rest at that. Knowing he could not. "Felt similar. The air. Thought it might be coming for me again."

"Lightning rarely strikes again."

"Don't you believe that. Not this day."

The farther south they moved, the sharper some of the hills sloped and the more often they came across the occasional upthrust of rock. There were also more corpses, Vanir and clansmen both. Kern nearly stumbled at one point, feet burning as he raced across a killing ground of bodies and charred, smoldering grasses. Shadows whispered to him, pressed. Formed an image of Grimnir within his mind, bellowing at the sky with an aura of dark power cascading around him. And in his bright shadow walked another man, a Ymirish sorcerer with the winds whipping about him in a cyclone of power.

Grimnir had walked here!

"This way." Kern turned, following the echo of power. Pointing his short blade a bit more east than south, toward the tall shadow of a nearby mesa, he led the mixed company of wolves and Callaughnan slightly off their original line.

"How do you know?"

How to answer that? There was no way. Even if he'd been of a mind to, how would a dog describe its sense of scent, or an eagle its superior vision to a man nearly blinded. It was simply more of what one might already feel, or know. Instinct.

Sorcery.

Kern shoved aside that thought. Not hard to do as they were soon challenged by a half dozen Vanir standing guard over a field of recently slain kinsmen. The wounds on the bodies were horrible and fresh, with arms missing and chests caved in on so many of them. Still, the raiders had been checking them quickly with stabs into the chest, the throat, just to make certain.

Kern and Ros-Crana each ran over one, hardly slowing. Left the other four to those who followed. Racing at the head of a snarling wolf pack for the end of the world.

That is what it looked like. The end of the plains. Where the ground ahead, running even or maybe slightly downhill, simply dropped away. Then nothing, until the steep mesa cliffs, as if a void had simply opened in the plateau. The clash of men at arms and the shouts of the dying were loud now, and seemed to come from that void. Below their line of sight.

A steep drop-off only, as it turned out.

They leaped out over the fall, dropping close to a man's

length before hitting the actual slope. Running down into
some lowland depressions that stretched for a league, at
least, and finally butted right up against the mesa's sandstone cliffs. And here, across the entire plateau, men struggled and fought and died. Several hundred Vanir, with their
Ymirish masters whipping them on. At a guess, not nearly
so many Cimmerian warriors. Though it might be close.
Kern could tell them apart by the way the clansmen would
attack, press, then retreat as needs be, while Vanir raiders
simple came at them again and again, pressing the Cimmerians back at all costs.

Kern took this all in with a glance, lengthening his
stride as they raced down the hill, the line of warriors
spreading out on the attack.

Lightning flashed below, and he blinked away the afterimage. He'd felt the strike coming again, and the life it had
taken in a rush of strength. The dark power hammered inside his head for release. It had slipped out once too often
now. It was not going to be denied forever.

Just long enough, he hoped.

Coming down off the slopes, leading much-needed reinforcements, Kern heard the rousing cheer sent up by the
Cimmerian war host. There were few northerners in their
way, though these quickly formed a hasty line of defense.
One archer who had carefully hoarded his arrows began to
loose one shaft after the next.

Kern raised his shield and tried to ignore that one,
hastily searching for where they might be needed most.
About anywhere, it seemed.

Bearing spears, hung with different totems, dipped and
waved in distress all across the battlefield, including the
curling ram's horn of the Lacheish straight ahead. Vanir
horns sounded the attack, adding their mournful dirge to
Frostpaw's nearby howl and the wyvern's shriek as it

stooped and raked its claws through a knot of Cimmerian swordsmen.

Kern also counted several fists of bareback chargers, wheeling about over open ground, readying for another charge. Only one man among them in chain mail, the armor a dull gray next to the much darker leathers of his companions.

So, Valerus had also made it through!

"Kern!" Daol shouted in his ear, thrust a hand forward nearly straight in line with the Lacheishi standard.

The winds kicked up dust and grit, bits of grasses, throwing the debris in their faces. Kern's eyes watered, and his vision wavered, but there was still no missing what Daol's hunter's eyes had spotted first.

Grimnir!

The Great Beast was here. Holding the center of the battleground, bright with his own power as he laid about with battle-axe and warhammer, the giant-kin stood out like a god among mortals. Half again as large as any man, with thick muscles stretched under a mottled, gray hide the color of ancient, rotten snow, his golden eyes blazed with fresh fire and his bellowing roar stormed up at the heavens.

Kern slowed long enough to gauge the strength between their reinforcements and Grimnir's rear guard. His eyes watered again, tearing up. He felt the darkness stir within him as it did when he felt threatened. Which was when he saw Lodur, the Ymirish sorcerer. Kern hadn't seen the frost-bearded man since Taur. And he had grown thinner— nearly gaunt. But still, he *knew*. And what was more, Lodur was not surprised to see him, to *know him*, either.

He stood not far back from Grimnir, surrounded by a thin guard of Vanir. And between Kern and that line was a great deal of open (watery) space.

No Ymirish warriors.

Only a double handful of Vanir at best.

Then a spike of pain tore through Kern's mind, and he *felt* the presence moving in at his side hard and fast and strong.

He barely had time to tense for the impact, then it was on him! Knocking him into a barrel roll across the hard ground as claws dug into his back and a fanged maw came within a handbreadth of his throat.

One of Grimnir's great, white-furred cats. A northern saber-tooth.

Its breath stank of fresh meat, and Kern could guess what kind. Its claws were razor-sharp, like a handful of daggers raked across his leg, his chest.

In the end, about all that saved him was the light hand required by his short blade. He had held on to it while the saber-tooth pounced, and managed to get it between his neck and those snapping jaws. The animal bit down on the blade, and Kern swiped the sword aside, flaying open its cheek and ripping a bloody gash down the side of its face.

The animal leaped one way. Kern rolled free the other, wondering how he had missed it on the grassy plains.

But the illusion was already falling apart even as he rolled to his feet, coming up in a guarded crouch. Like bursting up from a still pond on a summer's day, the blurry landscape shifted around him, and suddenly he saw the Vanir warriors where they had crouched in hiding, cloaked beneath Lodur's dark sorcery same as the great cat had been. Wrapped in the storm's winds until the eye simply wanted to slide away to look elsewhere.

A trap! And his warriors, Ros-Crana's, were running right into it.

"Ware!" Kern shouted. "Vanir!" He had time for little else, searching for the cat before it struck out of ambush again.

But the wolf already had it in a death grip.

Having chased after Kern and the others this far, it had come over the ridge and down onto the flats. Certainly it knew the scent of the cats. It had fought them before and knew them as a threat to be dealt with at once. Frostpaw had powerful jaws clamped about the saber-tooth's neck, dragging it around to prevent it from whipping its sharp claws up, and wasn't about to release it until death.

With Kern's warning the illusion had apparently come undone for everyone. A few warriors were unlucky enough to have a Vanir at their elbow when the sorcery broke, and they were taken down quick and brutal. Throats slashed. Blades driven through backs.

The others managed to at least get a sword or shield up in time, most of them, as the field erupted in fresh, desperate fighting. Reave's greatsword slashed around in a wide arc, protecting Daol as well as Nahud'r, spoiling one ambush. Ehmish was set upon by two raiders, and with his broken arm would have been easy meat if Gard hadn't stepped in with a strong blade and a shield to help protect the younger man.

Desa and Ossian fell back under a rush, tried circling around the far side.

Garret had disappeared.

Ros-Crana and another of her men barreled right into a trio of raiders, and all went sprawling hard over the ground. A broadsword flashed up, then sliced down hard. Blood spurted in a crazy fountain.

Someone in that pile would not get up again.

Kern raced up as hard as he could from the back of the pack. His wolves and Ros-Crana's warriors threw themselves forward one struggling step at a time. Far from an open race, it was now a defiant struggle even to get near Lodur. Or Grimnir, who hacked and beat his way at anything the Cimmerians could throw at him.

The Great Beast had already taken a lance though his gut.

Since it was hardly slowing him, he did not bother to pull it out. A Murrogh charger raced in, his second lance thrusting forward. Grimnir batted it aside and used his battle-axe to split the horse's head open, dropping the animal.

A backhand slash with the heavy weapon cleaved the warrior in two right after.

The warhammer laid about with savage fury, breaking skulls and shattering bone.

With these, Grimnir clawed and battered his way through the thickest part of the fighting, right for a thick cluster of bearing spears, including Lacheish, as if ready to single-handedly wipe out the war host's leaders.

Exactly ready.

Kern struggled forward, laying about with his short sword, smashing his shield forward to take desperate blows off its face. Calling to his men, his wolves. Pushing them onward. The line surged, and halted. Spread wide and surged again. Kern couldn't have been more than a handful of heartbeats behind Ros-Crana now. Perhaps a good stone's throw behind Grimnir, in fact.

But in either case, it could be just late enough.

Nay! He had not come so far, halfway across Cimmeria and back again, over mountains and the Hoath Plateau, to be denied now. With his enemies before him, celebrating in the death and destruction they had wrought, his anger returned. Burning within him in a way he had not felt—truly felt—since that day at lakeside when he'd overcome it.

The dark power had stirred afterwards, yea, but not the mindless rage he'd suffered at Gaud, and in the presence of Cul Chieftain, and again at Gorram Village. A berserker's lust for battle and blood. And the singing call of his Ymirish heritage. The sorcery he wanted nothing to do with, though of course it was a part of him just as his Cimmerian blood and beliefs were. But which the stronger?

He did not know. Struggling forward. Blood rushing in his ears. His pulse hammering within his head as he *pushed* to make it.

Stealing time between heartbeats as everything slowed around him.

Ros-Crana, picking herself up from a tangle of limbs and blades. Bleeding, staggering, but ready with a dark, singing blade and every last measure of strength and skill she possessed.

Reave, stabbing his greatsword through a Vanir, but then swarmed by two others, pulled to the ground. Daol and Nahud'r pressing forward, but set upon by another wild berserker.

Lodur, the sorcerer, who stood just barely out of reach on the struggling field. He blazed with power of his own, fed from the storm. Tugging on the wyvern's leash as the creature turned in the sky, wheeling about for another diving charge.

And Grimnir! The Unnatural Terror who challenged the entire field with his thunderous roars. The Immortal Demon himself, descended of frost-giants and the bane of Cimmeria. He stormed forward with sparks striking from beneath his bare feet as their touch ruined the earth; weapons hacking, hammering, nearly within reach of a small knot of men that included Cailt Stonefist and Cul and Loht, Jaryyd, Hogann, and Sláine Longtooth.

Kern began to think about saving his friends, no matter what they had promised each other. Knowing he would not reach Grimnir in time.

Or wouldn't have, if two men hadn't dived in front of the beast.

One with a fast sword, slicing deep through Grimnir's side. Punching the blade's tip between two ribs.

The second, with a familiar style and a veteran's ease,

coming in behind the monster, trying to hamstring the brute while his pike-hand stabbed several times into Grimnir's side.

His men!

Brig Tall-Wood and Wallach Graybeard!

For a few long heartbeats, another half dozen steps, Kern thought Reave might extract himself from the tangle of bodies and blades. And Ros-Crana looked to be doing well now, laying about with her dark sword, driving one man back, then another, the fight taking everything she had left. But then she could not see the third warrior who slipped around at her blind side.

And his decisions were all taken from him.

Still ten paces to a dozen short, Kern raised his sword overhead and *heaved*, putting all he had behind the throw. Everything. His rage and strength. His focus. Every last measure of his regrets and his hopes. The pain of Ashul's passing, and Old Finn's. The raw emotion he'd shared on those two winters nights with Maev.

Letting slip the safeguards he had so carefully—so rigidly—kept in place these many weeks and months as the dark power coursed and raged and *flowed*.

Calling down the skies.

Guiding his hand, then his sword, with a phantom touch as it tumbled end over end over end.

The lightning ripped down and struck through his short sword just as it buried itself in Lodur's gut. A good arm's length of steel, it glowed violet-bright inside the harsh, glare of the long, lingering strike, which caught and held the sorcerer like an insect trapped in amber. A thunderclap broke hard against the plateau, and the force of it knocked aside Vanir and Cimmerians alike, hammering several warriors to the ground. Winds whipped up, gusting in a strong breeze to envelop Kern, pulling at his frost blond hair as the howling rose in an earsplitting banshee wail.

And Grimnir turned, his golden eyes alight with the same, sudden shock mirrored on Lodur's face as both witnessed the event and knew it for exactly what it was.

The dark birth of a new Ymirish sorcerer.

Darkness clouded over Kern's vision, reducing the land into deep shadow as he continued his blind run forward. Caught between heartbeats as warmth flooded through him. Not the false promise that rage had once bought him. True heat! Blossoming from deep inside as that tiny, cold spark deep at his core flared to life for the first time. A gift of his northern heritage.

And then another, as his mind opened to the storm.

Kern understood instinctively what Lodur and the others had done to create and keep the storm shroud pulled over the plateau. How they had fed it, and tapped into that reserve as needed. Connected through that coursing power, and their blood, Kern felt Lodur struggling inside the lightning, railing at the storm, his grip slipping, and knew he might wrest control from them now. He was more powerful at that moment, at his birth, than he would ever likely be again.

He felt the life force of his warriors surrounding him. Reave and Daol closest, but another five also struggling against the Vanir. They leaped through his mind like small, guttering torches in a dark night.

He also felt the wild spark at the back of his mind that was the dire wolf, Frostpaw. Knew that with a nod he could seize control of the beast and break it to his whim.

And three more ahead. Valerus. Wallach Graybeard. Brig. Wallach's torch was a mere whisper of the others. A dampened flame; its strength eaten away by the corruption now raging through his entire body. Kern could give him back his health, he knew. Rip the disease from him. Heal over his wounds. It would inflict all the pain normally required in months of healing, but what a simple cost to live again and an enticing taste to consider, as Kern would certainly share in the agony.

It repelled but tempted at the same time. His Cimmerian heritage, at war with the Ymirish. He only had to choose strength over weakness. His blood over his beliefs. And mayhap he would have.

If he believed that such unnatural power was ever to be trusted.

Kern took a struggling step as time reasserted itself. Then another.

He was running again. Or still. Vaulting the tangle of warriors where Reave wrestled for his life, then was free of the struggling field and running past Lodur. Kern felt the Ymirish pushing back against the lightning strike, caught in place by a web of his own foul sorceries as he pitted the same deep reserve of energy *against* as Kern had tapped *for*. The lightning crackled and burst about him. But slowly, from the blade shoved through his gut, he was dying.

Lodur might preserve his life by healing his wound. He might do so by casting away the storm's shattered balance.

He could not do both.

Certainly he could no longer maintain his hold on the wyvern, which shrieked with maddened fury and stooped one last time over the field.

And Kern could only do the one thing he'd sworn he'd do.

He cast his shield aside and ran forward, never looking back, as Grimnir roared his final challenge.

With blazing, feral eyes and a twisted snarl, the Great Beast laid about with his battle-axe and warhammer. As with the lance still shoved through his gut, Brig Tall-Wood and Wallach Graybeard had done little more than enrage him no matter how deep their cuts. His blood stained their weapons and splashed across the ground, yea. But his was a strength beyond anything faced before. Rooted in the blood he shared with all the Ymirish, and especially with his sorcerers, Kern knew.

Kern closed fast, heartbeats away, but still too far to do anything as Grimnir slashed his war axe at Brig Tall-Wood.

The warrior managed to dodge aside from the first blow, but stumbled and sprawled full length over the ground when he tried to slip around behind Grimnir. The beast's warhammer fell—

—and would certainly have crushed him if Wallach Graybeard hadn't leaped forward to push Brig violently aside, taking the smashing blow instead.

The sidelong blow picked Wallach up and hurled him several lengths, broken and already dying. Kern felt his man's pain. Felt the blood filling his chest. And could do nothing about it. What he owed he owed also to Ashul and Finn. To everyone who had died at Conarch, at Gaud, and along the entire trail. He could not save them all.

Including himself.

Kern moved with a feral grace, driving in low beneath Grimnir's next hammerblow, rolling and coming straight up into the giant-kin's shadow. He'd been here once before, on the bluffs overlooking Conarch. He remembered. A long, drawn-out duel where Kern had been overmatched at every turn. In strength. In skill. It had been all he could do, then, to stay alive.

But nay this time! Here was the assembled strength of Cimmeria. Chieftains and war leaders. He need only strike one blow for them. Just the one.

Almost without thinking, he reached behind and pulled the bloody spear from his belt. Put one hand at the broken end of the shaft. And drove it into Grimnir's chest with every last measure of strength he possessed.

All his hate. The pain. The warmth he'd only begun to experience.

He loosed the storm's power, drawing away even from that which held Lodur trapped. The lightning burst into a thousand tiny fragments.

He channeled it through himself. Added to it the strength it had fed him.

And more, he *refused* Ymir's dark call. He pushed it all away, letting the power course though him and from him, holding nothing back. Letting it burn from his system, scouring his blood of his Ymirish heritage, giving it all back and Crom take him if he'd leave a trace of it behind.

Everything. Pushed onto Grimnir with one single purpose in mind.

Severing the link.

Kern collapsed, unstrung and spent, at the feet of Grimnir. Unable to do much more than roll weakly aside, out from under the monster's dark shadow, as the Great Terror staggered back, stumbled, and dropped to one knee. Grimnir's final roar turned into a great, choking groan. It seemed the entire battlefield held its breath at that moment. And then the Cimmerians moaned as the fire-eyed demon climbed slowly back to his feet.

Hands clutched around the lance in his gut. Slowly pulling it free.

"You did what you could," Brig said, crouching next to Kern, blade out and ready to defend the fallen man. He laid a hand on Kern's shoulder. "Crom's blood, I thought you'd killed him."

"Not by myself," Kern said weakly. He tasted blood in his mouth. Felt as weak as a newborn. He held back the darkness by force of will, watching as Grimnir's wounds opened and began to bleed freely once more, seeing the gore that stuck to the lance's shaft, causing the northern warlord's hands to slip, and fresh blood seeping out around the bloody spear Kern had nearly fused into *the beast's* chest.

Great no more.

"He's mortal."

And whether the nearby warriors, the war leaders and chieftains, heard Kern, or saw it on Grimnir's face, they moved in against him with blades and hammers and axes. Weapons rose, and fell, battering down Cimmeria's greatest enemy. Knocking him to hands and knees. Inflicting a dozen lethal wounds and having at him for as long as their enemy continued to struggle.

Until Cailt Chieftain staggered up, raised his Cimmerian greatsword overhead, and brought it down across the back of Grimnir's neck once. Twice. And the head rolled free. Dropping to the ground. Lying there with a final snarl twisting his face.

And great, golden eyes staring across into Kern's.

Now. Finally. Kern could stop running.

EPILOGUE

THE SUN PEEKED through broken storm clouds, low on the horizon, ready to disappear somewhere far beyond the Hoath Plateau, Conall Valley, and the Broken Leg Lands. Its slanting rays warmed the sky with tints of gold and red. Cast those final moments of fair light across the emptying battlefield.

Kern watched the dying sun, sitting on a cold bench of crumbling sandstone at the foot of a rocky upthrust. The first, best place he could find once he'd recovered enough strength to take himself out of the way. And now he did not move. His mouth was dry, tasting of blood and dirt. His long, frost blond hair hung limp and heavy with sweat. Every muscle trembled with fatigue.

He sat with his legs splayed out, his shield and sword recovered but hanging heavy at his sides as if he no longer had the strength to lift them. He didn't. He could barely hold himself erect.

But he had seen it through. That much he could say.

He'd seen it finished.

Grimnir and his dark sorcerers had been the northern army's greatest advantage. The Vanir could never have matched the Grand War Host's strength otherwise, even counting their greater numbers. Now, with that leader fallen and those powers lost to them, the northerners broke and fled. A few Ymirish warriors attempted to rally the war host, but each one was soon overwhelmed by the clansmen's resurgent strength.

Cailt Stonefist collected two more heads with the same golden eyes Kern shared. Jaryyd Morag's-son led his men forward on a sweeping run, laying about with his warhammer, shattering several strong Vanir positions. And Cul raced alongside, protecting the man who was certain to become the new chieftain of Murrogh, his mighty blade collecting heads as well.

Of course, all three men saw Kern, still alive, lying near Grimnir. None of them offered a hand, though Cailt Stonefist traded a short stare with Kern, and nodded, if reluctantly. There was more than a little uncertainty showing on Cailt's stoic face. As if he still were not certain what he had witnessed.

Cul also looked but didn't seem to care one way or the other. As always, Kern was beneath his notice. Now more so than ever.

Of all the chieftains and war leaders, only Sláine Longtooth and Tergin of the Spider's Teeth tribe bothered to approach Kern at all. Each man crouched near him, held Kern's golden stare a moment, offered a grim smile, then left to continue their hunt of the reeling Vanir.

The slaughter, as might be expected, was terrible. Finally, the smarter and most able among the remaining Ymirish gathered to them the strongest arms they could find and fought their way free of the battlefield. They would be a problem still, but not this day.

For his part, Kern sat in the dust for a time. Listened to the storm break and the howl of the winds die out, while he stared at Grimnir's corpse, making certain he believed absolutely the northern warlord was dead and wondering how he himself had been spared when he'd pushed *everything* into that final blow. As above Conarch, pulling Grimnir over the cliff's edge with him, Kern had again offered up his own life in order to end the threat to Cimmeria. It had been rejected.

By Ymir? Or Crom?

As every Cimmerian knew, it was nay good questioning the gods. They never answered.

Struggling to his feet, Kern staggered over to where Brig Tall-Wood knelt with Reave and Daol and Nahud'r next to Wallach Graybeard. Someone had already closed the veteran's eyes.

Brig looked up and gave Kern a curt nod. "Still alive, Kern Wolf-Eye?"

"Still alive, Brig Tall-Wood."

There were so many men who would not be able to say that after this day. Kern stood there, staring down at another of his wolves. Wallach was beyond pain or any final words, so Kern gave the man the only tribute he could.

"He died well," he said. Everyone nodded, and he put a hand on Brig's shoulder. "One of us."

A moment of further silence was all Kern could afford. Dead on his feet, he walked over to recover his discarded shield. Found his sword lying in the dirt near where he'd struck down Lodur. No sign of the sorcerer, but Ros-Crana was there. Bent to one knee, leaning heavily against her blade, which she'd driven point first into the earth. Her skin was pale. Her face drawn and haggard. But she lived.

And Lodur?

"He pulled the blade free after the lightning shattered," Ros-Crana told him. "Cast it aside. I thought he might be recovering, Crom knows how. Tried to reach him. But that *creature* beat me to it." And she described the wyvern, maddened and terrible, diving down over the field to find its tormentor. "Grabbed him in its talons. Flew south for the Black Mountains."

There ended the last of Kern's immediate worries.

"What will you do now?" he asked her.

Ros-Crana looked up at Kern. Her grip tightened on her sword's hilt, and she seemed to wrestle with what to say to this man. Or waited for him to say something first. Finally, she shrugged. "I guess I'll go home. I've done most of what I came here to do. Except to say this. You were right. Before." She nodded. "My brother thought so as well."

Though it seemed such a small thing to have come so far, over such a hard road, to do, Kern knew her words were no small admission. And mention of her brother the highest praise.

Ros-Crana stood then and called for her seconds. And with them, she set off to count up her dead and salvage what she could, what she needed, from the battlefield.

Which left Kern to seeing to his own men. He sent Reave and Daol to go back for Hydallan and Aodh, and Old Finn's body. Had Brig and Nahud'r scour the nearby battlefield to see how many more of Kern's wolves they might find. He then removed himself from underfoot. Found his seat at the base of the small upthrust. And collapsed.

Never in his entire life had he thought to be so tired. So completely drained of strength. He checked his flask for a swallow of water, but found nothing more than few dribbles. Tossing it aside, he listened to the receding din of battle. Knew when the last Vanir had been driven from the flatlands, and the chase had moved to the plateau.

He watched the storm shroud break up into a patchwork of dark clouds and wondered if it would rain.

He waited while the battle ran down into a final, limping halt, and the last of the day faded.

Ehmish and Gard lived. That was the first news brought back to him, by the men themselves. The young man was battered and bloodied, but alive. And he walked on his own two feet, as a man should, when the two limped up together.

Gard Foehammer offered Kern a cloudy stare. "Saw Sláine Longtooth," the tall Cruaidhi said. "Offered me the fox's tail again."

Kern managed a weak nod. "You could start over, among your own kin."

"Done that once before, and see where it got me. Two lives is enough for any man. I'm fine where I am, Kern Wolf-Eye. And someone has to look out for the boy."

Ossian and Danon lived as well. And Garret Black-patch, though he had a sword thrust through his leg and would nay walk on his own for some time. Some of the Callaughnan helped him along, then left without a word.

Desagrena stomped up on her own, searching Kern's face carefully.

"He alive?" she asked. As if the question mattered nay one bit to her.

Kern nodded.

"Yea. Thickheaded ox. He would be."

She set about with Ossian, salvaging any gear they could from the battlefield. Good weapons and small trea-sures and other trade items. Foodstuffs and heavy cloaks whenever they could find them. The night would be cold, and possibly wet as well. And the wolves had dropped most of their own supplies out on the plateau. Someone would have to retrieve them.

Valerus volunteered, riding up with two Murroghan chargers flanking him. "Lost you on the field," he said. He glanced between his new companions. All that was left from his first charge? Or new recruits? "We just kept riding. Figured you to catch up eventually. Being on foot and all."

Which accounted for nearly everyone, once Aodh and Hydallan were helped back to the building camp. Then Brig finally found Mogh, buried under a pile of dead bodies back on the upper plateau. Alive, though barely. Broken ribs, a knife still stuck in his shoulder, and a cracked skull at a guess. Nothing likely to improve the man's sour mood.

By then the flatlands had been all but emptied of the Vanir hordes. A few wounded raiders to put to the sword as they were found. The winds had died down to a normal breeze, and hardly anyone glanced at the sky anymore.

Most clansmen not out on the plateau began to think about the night and cleared large areas among the dead. They dumped the bodies of Vanir into large piles. Laid every clansman out respectfully, kinsman or nay. Started fires. Scrounged for food. And some began composing songs to the dead, and songs of victory. They would pause in their work, and chant a line or a verse to try it out. Most had to do with the legendary strength of Cailt Stonefist, whose strong blade struck the head from Grimnir's shoulder. Murroghan warriors who saw their next chieftain swinging a mighty hammer on the battlefield. Even the Gorram, who saw the final lightning fall and knew they had triumphed over the hard road that started at their mountainside village.

Off to one side, tucked against the rocky upthrust, the Men of the Wolves were forgotten now.

Though not by all.

She found Kern still in place, slouched forward as if lying back might very well be the end of him, watching the sun as it first slipped beneath the breaking cloud cover, then sank toward the horizon. He did not hear her. He hardly bothered to turn his head anymore. By then, his muscles had grown so stiff, he wondered if he hadn't actually died and his mind had simply not caught up with it yet.

He noticed Maev not at all until she walked past his line of sight, blocking the sun for the moment.

"Made it back," she said. Eclipsing the dying light. "Again."

She wore the same white wrapping of combed wool. Carried a blanket of shaggy, brown fur in her arms. Raven dark hair, parted down the middle of her head and ragged cut below the shoulders. She wore a stone disk, hollowed in the middle, on a piece of cord about her neck. A symbol of her pregnancy.

Kern stared through her a moment. It was getting so very hard to think. He rocked his head to one side, staring up at her.

"Not everyone," he said. "Not this time." Wallach Graybeard and Old Finn, at the least, would never run with the pack again. Aodh and Mogh and Garret were still questionable.

Maev moved out of his view and around him. Draped the fur over his shoulders, his upper arms, and pulled him back into a slouch. He had no strength left to resist, even if he'd wanted to. And he didn't.

"You did what you could, Kern." Her tone was hardly warm. Resigned? Or mayhap only tired as well. "You always have."

"Was it enough?" His voice was cracked, and weak, but grew stronger with every word. "Cailt Stonefist leads a force in one direction, keeping the Vanir of a mind to retreat. Jaryyd of Murrogh splits off in another. Already, it seems, the common cause is being forgotten and dropped by the way."

He felt her nod. "It's the way of the clans, Kern Wolf-Eye. I should nay have to tell you that."

Nay. She should not. He'd lived it his life, outsider or outcast. And it had been the rock he clung to when the

power swept over him, nearly washing away everything he
had made of himself. "So close," he whispered. "The difference of a knife's edge."

"Will you tell me about it?" she asked.

"I am nay storyteller. Ask Nahud'r, if you want a fireside tale."

"I'm asking if you'll be coming back with us to Murrogh? Mayhap to Gaud?"

The sun struck the horizon, slipping fast now. Kern
watched it go, eaten away a slice at a time. "That is for the
morrow, Maev, Burok's daughter." And who knew what
that might bring. A return of the feud between Lacheish
and Murrogh, Galla and Hoath?

Cul Chieftain and Kern?

"You believe tomorrow will change anything? Truly?"

"I believe . . ." Kern hesitated. Then, "I believe many
things I mayhap doubted before. I believe a miracle may
occur, and the sun will rise in the east."

She laughed, brittle and sharp. "The sun rises in the east
every day."

"And each one is a new start," Kern said, as if agreeing.
"Many things will be the same. There will be Vanir to hunt.
Ymirish to worry after. Chieftains feuding. But one
thing . . . Mayhap one thing will change."

Maev shook her head. "I'm sure I don't know what you
mean." She rocked back, pulling Kern with her. Resting
him into her lap. Adjusting the blanket to better spread
across his shoulders, she brushed her touch against his
bared arm.

And recoiled.

"You . . . You are . . ." She reached down with both
hands, spread them across his shoulders.

"You are . . . *warm.*"

He nodded, once, as the sun slipped below the horizon.

Kern relished to its dying gasp that last shred of warming light. "One thing that can change," he said. "At times, that is all we can expect. Or need."

And somewhere back on the plateau, in the gathering dusk, a wolf howled.

In the land of Cimmeria, in the time when
Conan was King, a lone warrior battles
his own legacy—and a new legend is born.

AGE OF CONAN:
LEGENDS OF KERN

Don't miss the other adventures in this series

Volume 1:
BLOOD OF WOLVES
0-441-01292-2

Volume 2:
CIMMERIAN RAGE
0-441-01295-7

Conan graphic novels also available from
Dark Horse

Available wherever books are sold or at
penguin.com

Coming September 2005 from Ace

Rakkety Tam
by Brian Jacques
0-441-01318-X

Rakkety Tam MacBurl, the mercenary warrior from the borderlands, and the brave squirrel Wild Doogy Plum embark on a quest in this latest *New York Times* bestseller in the *Redwall* series.

Path Not Taken
by Simon R. Green
0-441-01319-8

John Taylor has just discovered that his long-gone mother created the Nightside, the dark heart of London. To save his birthplace, he will have to travel back to a distant—and probably deadly—past.

Also new in paperback this month:

War Surf
by M.M. Buckner
0-441-01320-1

Robots
edited by Jack Dann and Gardner Dozois
0-441-01321-X

Available wherever books are sold or at
penguin.com